Praise for Robert Silverberg

"WHERE SILVERBERG GOES TODAY, SCIENCE FICTION WILL FOLLOW TOMORROW."
—Isaac Asimov

"A MASTER OF HIS CRAFT AND IMAGINATION."
—*Los Angeles Times*

"SILVERBERG IS OUR BEST . . . TIME AND AGAIN HE HAS EXPANDED THE PARAMETERS OF SCIENCE FICTION." —*The Magazine of Fantasy & Science Fiction*

"ONE OF SF'S EMINENCES." —Brian Aldiss, *The Trillion-Year Spree*

"NO CONTEMPORARY WRITER HAS SHOWN A GREATER MASTERY OVER THE THEMES AND MOTIFS OF SCIENCE FICTION, AND FEW CAN MATCH SILVERBERG'S COMMAND OF LITERARY TECHNIQUE." —*Science Fiction Writers*, ed. E. F. Bleiler

KING~ DOMS
of the
WALL

Robert Silverberg

SPECTRA™

BANTAM BOOKS

New York   Toronto
London   Sydney   Auckland

KINGDOMS OF THE WALL
A Bantam Spectra Book / March 1993
Bantam paperback edition/February 1994

ISBN 0-553-56544-3

Published simultaneously in the United States and Canada

Bantam Books are published by Bantam Books, a division of Bantam
Doubleday Dell Publishing Group, Inc. Its trademark, consisting of the
words "Bantam Books" and the portrayal of a rooster, is Registered in U.S.
Patent and Trademark Office and in other countries. Marca Registrada.
Bantam Books, 1540 Broadway, New York, New York 10036.

PRINTED IN THE UNITED STATES OF AMERICA
RAD   0 9 8 7 6 5 4 3 2 1

FOR

URSULA K. LE GUIN

And yet all the time, below the fear and the irritation, one was aware of a curious lightness and freedom . . . one was happy all the same; one had crossed the boundary into country really strange; surely one had gone deep this time.

—GRAHAM GREENE

Journey Without Maps

1

THIS IS THE BOOK of Poilar Crookleg, I who have
been to the roof of the World at the top of the Wall
and have felt the terrible fire of revelation there. I have
seen the strange and bewildering gods that dwell there, I
have grappled with them and returned rich with the knowledge of the mysteries of life and of death. These are the
things I experienced, this is what I learned, this is what I
must teach you for the sake of your souls. Listen and
remember.

If you are of my village, then you know who I am. But I
want the story I am about to relate to be heard and understood far beyond our own village, and so I will tell you that
my father was Gabrian son of Drok, my House is the House
of the Wall, and my clan within that House is Wallclan. So I
come from a noble line.

I never knew my father when I was growing up, because he set forth on the Pilgrimage when I was only a small
boy and never returned. So there was only a hole in my
spirit where others have fathers to guide them. All that he
left me with to carry me through childhood and boyhood
was the memory of a tall man with bright eyes and strong

arms, sweeping me up and tossing me high overhead and laughing in a deep, rich voice as he caught me. It may not be a trustworthy memory. It may have been some other man entirely who lifted me and tossed me like that; or maybe it never happened at all. But for many years that was all I had of my father: bright eyes, strong arms, a ringing peal of laughter.

My father's father had gone to the Wall also in his time. That is the tradition of my family. We are folk of restless soul, Pilgrims by nature. We always have been. The Pilgrimage is the high custom of our people, of course, the great defining event of one's life: either you become a Pilgrim or you do not, and either way it leaves its mark upon you forever. And we are of the Pilgrim sort. We claim descent from the First Climber; we take it for granted that we will be Pilgrims ourselves when we come of age, and will go up into the fearsome heights where one's body and one's soul are placed at dread risk of transformation by the forces that dwell there.

Like my father, my father's father failed to return from his god-quest in the realms above.

As for me, I never gave the Pilgrimage a thought when I was young. I looked upon the Pilgrimage then as something that concerned older folk, people in the second half of their second ten of years. It was always certain to me that when my time came I would be a candidate for the Pilgrimage, that I would be chosen, that I would undertake it successfully. Taking the Pilgrimage for granted in that way allowed me not to think about it at all. That way I was able to make it unreal.

I suppose I could pretend to you that I was a child of destiny, marked from my earliest years for supreme achievement, and that holy lightnings crackled about my brow and people made sacred signs when they passed me in the street. But in fact I was an ordinary sort of boy, except for my crooked leg. No lightnings crackled about me. No gleam of sanctity blazed on my face. Something like that came later, yes, much later, after I had had my star-dream; but when I was young I was no one unusual, a boy among boys. When I was growing up I wasn't at all the sort to go about thinking heavy thoughts about the Pilgrimage, or the Wall and its Kingdoms, or the gods who lived at its Summit, or any other such profundities. Traiben, my dearest friend, was the one who was haunted by high questions of ultimate destinies and utmost purposes, of ends and means, of essences and appearances, not I. It was Traiben, Traiben the Wise, Traiben the Thinker, who thought deeply about such things and eventually led me to think about them too.

But until that time came the only things that mattered to me were the usual things of boyhood, hunting and swimming and running and fighting and laughing and girls. I was good at all those things except running, because of my crooked leg, which no shapechanging has ever been able to heal. But I was strong and healthy otherwise, and I never permitted the leg to interfere with my life in any way whatever. I have always lived as though both my legs were as straight and swift as yours. When you have a flaw of the body such as I have there is no other course, not without giving way to feelings of sorrow for yourself, and such feelings poison the soul. So if there was a race, I ran in it. If my playmates went clambering across the rooftops, I clambered right along with them. Whenever someone mocked me for my limp—and there were plenty who did, shouting "Crookleg! Crookleg!" at me as though it were a fine joke—I would beat him until his face was bloody, no matter how big or strong he might be. In time, to show my defiance of their foolish scorn, I came to take Crookleg as my surname, like a badge of honor worn with pride.

If this world were a well-ordered place it would have been Traiben who had had the crooked leg and not me.

Perhaps I ought not to say so cruel a thing about one whom I claim to love. But what I mean is that in this world there are thinkers and doers; doers must have agility and strength of body, and thinkers need agility and strength of mind. I had agility and bodily strength aplenty, but my leg was a handicap all the same. As for Traiben, the thinker, there was no strength in his frail body anyway, so why shouldn't the gods have given him this limp of mine as well, instead of me? One more physical drawback, among so many, would not have made his life any worse, and I would have been better fitted to be the person I was meant to be. But the gods are never so precise in parceling out our gifts.

We were an odd pair: he so small and flimsy and fragile, with no more strength to him than a gossamer, and me so sturdy and unwearying. Traiben looked as though you could break him with a blow, and you could. Whereas I have made it clear throughout all my days that if there is any breaking to be done, I will be the breaker rather than the broken. What drew us together, then? Though we belonged to the same House and the same clan within that House, that in itself would not necessarily have led to friendship between us. No, I think the thing that linked us so tightly, different though we were in so many respects, was the fact that each of us had something about him that set him apart from the others of our clan. In my case it was my leg. In Traiben's, it was his mind, which burned with such fierce brilliance that it was like a sun within his skull.

Traiben it was who first set me on the path that leads to the summit of the Wall, when he and I were twelve years old.

THE NAME OF MY village is Jespodar, which the Scribes and Scholars say is a word in the old Gotarza language that once was spoken here, meaning, "Those Who Cling to the Wall." I suppose we do. Our village, which is really not a village at all but a vast conglomeration of villages all tangled together, containing many thousands of people, is said to lie closer to the perimeter of the Wall than any other—right up against its flank, as a matter of fact. It is possible to take a road that runs out of the center of Jespodar that will put you on the Wall itself. If you were to make the great journey around the base of the Wall, you would come to scores of other villages—hundreds, maybe—along its perimeter; but none, so the Scholars tell us, actually abuts the flank of the Wall the way Jespodar does. Or so we are taught in Jespodar, at any rate.

The day of which I want to tell you, that day when my friend Traiben first lit the fire of Pilgrimage in my twelve-year-old mind, was the day of the departure of that year's Pilgrims. You know what great pomp and splendor that involves. The ceremony of the Procession and Departure has not changed since ancient times. The clans of every House that make up our village gather; the sacred things of the tribe are brought forth, the batons and scrolls and talismans; the Book of the Wall is recited, every last verse of it, which requires weeks and weeks of unceasing effort; and finally the forty successful candidates emerge from the Pilgrim Lodge to show themselves before the village and take their leave. It is a profound moment, for we will never see most of them again—everyone understands that—and those who do return will come back transformed beyond all knowing of them. That has ever been the way.

To me in that innocent time it was all just a grand festival, nothing more. For many days, now, people from the outlying districts of the village had been arriving at our House, which lay closer to the Wall than any other in Jespodar: we were the House of the Wall, the House of Houses. Thousands had come, thousands of thousands, so that the whole unthinkable swarm of festival-goers was crammed elbow to elbow all the time, packed so close together that often we found ourselves changing shape involuntarily, just from the heat and congestion of it all, and we had to struggle to get back to the forms that we preferred.

Wherever you looked, our Housegrounds overflowed with mobs of people. They were everywhere and they got into everything: they trampled our lovely powdervines, they crushed and flattened our handsome daggerfern bushes, they stripped the gambellos of all their ripe, heavy blue fruits. It had happened that way every year for more dozens of years than anyone can remember: we expected it and were resigned to it. The longhouses and the round-houses were filled, the meadows were filled, the sacred groves were filled. Some people even slept in trees. "Have you ever *seen* so many people?" we all kept asking each other, though of course we had, only the year before. But it was the thing to say.

We even had a few of the King's men in town to see the ceremony. They were swaggering thick-bodied men who wore robes of red and green, and they went striding through the crowds as if there was no one in their way. People stepped aside when they passed. I asked my mother's brother Urillin, who had raised me in my father's absence, who they were, and he said, "They are the King's men, boy. They sometimes come here for the Festival, to enjoy themselves at our expense." And he muttered a bitter curse, which surprised me, because Urillin was a mild and quiet man.

I stared at them the way I might have stared at men with two heads, or six arms. I had never seen King's men before; and, in fact, I have never seen them since. Everyone knows that there is a King somewhere on the other side of Kosa Saag who lives in a grand palace in a great city and holds dominion over many villages, ours among them. The King owns the magic that makes everything work, and so I suppose we are dependent on him. But he is so very far away and his decrees have so little direct bearing on our everyday life that he might just as well live on some other planet. We dutifully pay our tribute but otherwise we have no dealings with him or the government he heads. He is only a phantom to us. I scarcely thought about him from one end of the year to the other. But the sight of these men of his service, who had come such a great distance to attend our Festival, reminded me how huge the world is, and how little I knew about any of it except our own village lying in the shadow of the Wall; and so the King's men awakened awe in me as they went strutting by.

The days passed in rising frenzy and excitement. The moment of the Procession and Departure was approaching.

The chosen Pilgrims, naturally, were kept out of sight: no one had seen them for months and certainly nobody was allowed to see them now, at this time of times. They remained hidden away in Pilgrim Lodge, the twenty men in one room and the twenty women in the other, while food was shoveled to them through slots in the doors.

But the rest of us enjoyed constant revelry. All day and all night there was dancing and singing and drunkenness. Of course there was plenty of work to do too. Then as now, each House had its special responsibility. The House of Carpenters set up the viewing-stands, the House of Musicians played songs of jubilation from dawn to the moon-hours, the House of Holies stood in the plaza and chanted prayers at the top of its lungs, the House of Singers began to recite the innumerable verses of the Book of the Wall outside Pilgrim Lodge in continuous relays without break, and the House of Vintners put up its booths and opened casks as fast as we could drain them, which was very fast indeed. The House of Clowns went among us in yellow robes miming and making faces and gaily pummeling people; the House of Weavers brought forth the heavy golden carpets that must line the road to the Wall at this time; the House of Sweepers toiled to clean away the hideous mess that the multitudes of other festival-goers were creating. The only ones who had no duties were youngsters like Traiben and me. But we understood that the adults did their work gladly, for this was meant to be a time of universal celebration in the village.

We who belonged to the House of the Wall, naturally, had the task of coordinating all the activities of the other Houses. That is a frightful burden, but for us it is also a source of great pride. Meribail, my father's father's brother's son, was the head of our House then, and I think he went without sleep a dozen nights running as the day of the Procession drew near.

And then it was Departure-day itself: as always, the twelfth day of Elgamoir. The morning was steamy-warm, with steady rainfall. Every leaf of every tree glistened like a knifeblade. The ground was soft as sponge beneath our feet.

No one could ever say that smothering warmth and pelting rain are any novelties to us in our lowland home. Then as now, we lived all the year round in the kind of heat that stews one's flesh, and we loved it. But even so this was unusual warmth, unusual rain. The air was like a bog: that morning we felt as though we were breathing water. We were all of us decked out in our fine Procession clothes too, the blue leather leggings and scarlet ribbons and droopy-topped yellow caps that people wear at such times, children and elders alike. But we were wet to the skin, what with the constant rain and our own dripping sweat. I remember how hard I had to fight to hold my shape, so great was the heat, so sticky was the air. My arms kept melting and writhing, my shoulders would swing around at strange angles to my torso, and I would have to clench my teeth and force everything back into place. Traiben beside me was fluttering also from form to form, although however much he changed he somehow was always the same flimsy, hollow-chested, big-eyed Traiben with the pipestem legs and the scrawny neck.

As the hour of the Procession arrived there came a miracle. Just as the Singers reached the last words of the final verse of the Book of the Wall—the verse that is known as the Summit—the rain abruptly relented, the thick gray soupy mists thinned and vanished, the heavy shield of the sky became transparent. A cool swift wind began to blow from the north. Everything became wonderfully clear and radiant. The bright hot light of blue-white Ekmelios appeared and shone down dazzlingly upon us like a fiery jewel in the forehead of the sky. It was a double-sun day, even: that day we were able also to see the enormous remote sphere of red Marilemma, the sun that gives no warmth. We could see everything. *Everything.*

"Kosa Saag!" we all cried in one voice, gesturing with tremendous excitement. "Kosa Saag!"

Yes. The Wall was coming into view in all its immensity. It had, of course, been hidden by the murkiness of the morning air, but now it appeared above us, climbing and climbing and climbing. It pierced the sky and disappeared into the immeasurable heights. People fell trembling to their knees and began to weep and pray, stricken as they were by fear and humility at the sight of that gigantic mountain suddenly revealing itself.

Certainly Kosa Saag is always a mighty sight, even when the usual low-hanging clouds hide most of it from view and just the squat reddish base can be seen. But that morning it exceeded itself in awesomeness. It had never seemed so huge to me before. That day I imagined that I could see all the way to the home of the gods. Its endless slope went up and up, a colossal pink thing of unimaginable height and length and breadth lying upon the land like some enormous slumbering beast. I stared in wonder at its great intricate bulk, its pocked and pitted surface, its million spires and pinnacles, its uncountable caverns and crevices, its multitude of subsidiary peaks, its myriad turrets and parapets, its hundreds of spiny ridges and incomprehensible twisting trails leading to unknown lofty realms. And it seemed to me, even then, that in that moment of revelation I could feel the power of the mighty forces that dwell there beating down on me, the invisible fires that emanate from every stone face of the mountain, every rock, every grain of soil—the forces that seize so many of those who venture into those heights, transforming the weak and the unwary into things that can no longer be reckoned as human.

Because our clan within the House of the Wall was Wallclan, from which the heads of our House are always elected, Traiben and I had a privileged position for the

Procession. We were seated in the main viewing stand just opposite the stone roundhouse of the Returned Ones, which is just adjacent to Pilgrim Lodge, from which the chosen Forty would soon emerge. So we were at the very center of things. That was truly dizzying, to know that such a great multitude was arrayed around the central point that was us, spreading outward and outward to the borders of the village and far beyond, all the teeming thousands and thousands of people of all the clans of every House of our village, the highborn and the lowly, the wise ones and the fools, the strong and the weak, packed elbow to elbow in the grassy streets under the shadow of the great mountain that is Kosa Saag.

THEN CAME THE WORDS that changed my life. Traiben turned to me while we were waiting and said in an odd and somehow belligerent way, in a voice that had an edge on it, "Tell me, Poilar, do you think that you're likely to be chosen for the Pilgrimage?"

I gave him a strange look. As I have said, that was something I had never bothered to think about at all. I took it for granted, a given of my life. In every generation going back to time's first dawn someone of my family has been selected. I had no brothers or sisters; therefore I would be the one to go in my time. My limp would be no obstacle. Of course I would be chosen. Of course.

Hotly I said, "The blood of the First Climber runs in my veins. My father was a Pilgrim and so was his father before him. And I will be too, when my time comes. Do you think that I won't?"

"Of course you will," said Traiben, staring at me very intently. His eyes were like huge dark saucers with slits of light at their centers. "You'll go up there the way so many others have before you, and you'll climb and climb and climb, and suffer and suffer and suffer. And more likely than not you'll die somewhere up there, the way most of them do, or come back a babbling madman. Well, what's the good of it, then? What's the point? What value is there going to be in all your hard work, Poilar? If all you do is go up there and die. Or come back crazy."

Even for Traiben, this was going a little far. It sounded like blasphemy to me.

"How can you ask such a thing? The Pilgrimage is a holy task."

"So it is."

"Then what are you saying, Traiben?"

"That it's nothing at all just to be a Pilgrim. All it is is a lot of walking, that's all. On and on and on, up and up and up. You move one foot and then the other and before long you're higher up the mountain than you were before. Any stupid animal can do that. It's only a matter of endurance. Do you understand me, Poilar?"

"Yes. No. No. I don't understand you at all, Traiben."

A little smile appeared on his face. "I'm saying that being picked for the Pilgrimage is no big thing in and of itself. It's a nice honor, yes. But in the long run honors don't mean a great deal."

"If you say so."

"And neither does simply gritting your teeth and making the climb, if you're doing it without any real sense of why you're putting yourself through such an ordeal."

"What does matter, then? Surviving until you get to the Summit, I suppose."

"That's part of it."

"Part of it?" I said. I blinked at him. "It's the whole idea, Traiben. That's why we go. Climbing all the way up to the Summit is the entire point of making the Pilgrimage."

"Yes. Exactly. But once you reach the Summit, what then? What then, Poilar? That's the essential question. Do you understand?"

How difficult Traiben could be, how bothersome!

"Well," I said, "then you go before the gods, if you can find them, and you perform the proper rites, and then you have to turn around and make your way down."

"You make it all sound very trivial."

I looked at him and said nothing.

He said very quietly, "What do you think the actual purpose of the Pilgrimage is, Poilar?"

"Why—" I hesitated. "Everybody knows that. To present ourselves before the gods who live atop Kosa Saag. To find them and ask their blessing. To maintain the good fortune of the village by paying homage to the holy ones."

"Yes," he said. "And what else?"

"What else? What else can there be? We climb up, we pay homage, we come down. Isn't that enough?"

"The First Climber," said Traiben. "Your great ancestor. What did He achieve?"

I hardly had to think. The words came rolling out automatically, straight from the catechism. "He offered himself to the gods as an apprentice, and they taught Him how to use fire and how to make the tools that we needed for hunting and building, and how to raise crops, and how we could clothe ourselves in the skins of animals, and many other valuable things. And then He descended from the mountain and taught these things to the people below, who had been living in savagery and ignorance."

"Yes. Therefore we revere His memory. And you and I, Poilar—we can do just as He Who Climbed did. Climb the Wall, find the gods, learn from them the things we need to know. That's the real reason why we go: to learn. To learn, Poilar."

"But we already know everything that anybody needs to know."

He spat. "Stupid! Stupid! Do you really believe that? We're still savages, Poilar! We're still ignorant! We live like beasts in these villages. Like beasts. We hunt and we raise our crops and we tend our gardens. We eat, we drink, we sleep. We eat, we drink, we sleep. Life goes on and on and nothing ever changes. Is that all that you think there is to being alive?"

I stared. He was utterly bewildering.

He said, "Let me tell you something. I intend to be a Pilgrim too."

I laughed right in his face. "You, Traiben?"

"Me. Yes. Nothing can stop me. Why do you laugh, Poilar? You think they'll never choose anyone as weak as I am? No. No, they will. They'll choose you despite your crooked leg and they'll choose me even though I'm not strong. I'll make it happen. I swear it by He Who Climbed. And by Kreshe and all the sacred ones of Heaven!" His eyes began to blaze, bright with that hot eerie Traiben-brightness of his that made him so mystifying and even frightening to all who encountered him. There was a Power about Traiben. If he had been born a Witch instead of into the House of the Wall, he would have been a santha-nilla with great magic at his command, of that I'm sure. "There's work for us to do up there, Poilar. There are important things that need to be learned and brought back. That's why the Pilgrimages began—so that we could sit at the feet of the gods and learn the things they know, the way the First Climber did. But for a long time now nothing useful's been brought down from the mountain. We make no progress. We live as we've always lived, and when you stay in the same place, you start to slide backward, after a time. The Pilgrimages still go forth, yes, but either the Pilgrims don't return or they come back crazy. And they bring us nothing useful, so we stay forever in the same place. What a waste, Poilar! We have to change all that. We'll go up there together, you and I, side by side, rising through Kingdom after Kingdom just as the First Climber did. We'll meet the gods, just as He did. We will have their blessing. We'll see all the wonders and learn all the mysteries. And together we will return, with new knowledge that will change the world. What kind of knowledge that is, I can't begin to say. But I know it's there. I know it without any question. We have to find it. And so we have to make it happen that we become Pilgrims, you and I. Are you following me? *We have to make it happen.*"

And he stretched his hand toward me and encircled the thick part of my arm with his fingers, three above and three below, digging his fingertips into my flesh so that I had to gasp with the pain of it: and this was little Traiben, who had no more strength than a fish! Something leaped from him to me in that moment, something of the strange fire that burned within him, something of the fever of his soul. And I felt it burning within me too, an utterly new thing, the passionate yearning to find my gods on that mountain, and stand before them, and say to them, "I am Poilar of Jespodar, and I am here to serve you. But you must serve me too. I wish you to teach me all that you know."

He held me like that for a long moment, so that I thought he would never let go. Then I brushed at his hand, gently, as one might brush at a glitterfly hovering around one's head that is too lovely to hurt, and he released me. But I heard him breathing hard beside me, in hot excitement. It was a troublesome thing for me, this frenzy of Traiben's that had come over him so passionately and that he had passed over into my spirit.

"Look," I said, desperate to step back from the intensity of the moment, for passion of that kind was something new to me and it was making me tremble, "the Procession is going to start."

INDEED EVERYONE WAS UTTERING little hsshing noises to silence his neighbor, for the grand march was beginning. The Sweepers in their purple loincloths went dancing by, whisking dangerous spirits out of the roadway with their little brooms, and then, in silence, came the heart of the Procession out of the heavy morning mists that lay at the lower end of town. My father's father's brother's son Meribail led the way, all bedecked in a shining and magnificent cloak of scarlet gambardo feathers woven tightly together. Beside him on the one side was Thispar Double-Lifer, the oldest man of the village, who had lived seven full tens of years. Traiben's father's father's father, he was. On the other side of Meribail was another of our old ones, the double-lifer Gamilalar, who had lately celebrated the beginning of his seventh ten. Following these three in the Procession came the heads of all the Houses, walking grandly two by two.

But my mind wasn't on the Procession. It was full of Traiben's words, which had set me aflame with new and consuming ambitions. He had put an urgent need into me that had never been there before.

And so I made my vow. I would climb the Wall to its utmost point. I would attain the Summit. I would stare into the eyes of the gods, from whom all wisdom flows, and I would absorb all that they could give me. Then I would return to our lowland home, which only a few had ever succeeded in doing, and most of those no longer in their right minds. And I would teach to others everything that I had mastered on high.

So be it. From that moment on my life's goal was graven in stone.

And it was Traiben's goal too. How strange! That frail awkward boy had dreams of being a Pilgrim? It seemed almost comical. They would never choose him, never, *never*. And yet I understood that when Traiben desired a thing, Traiben was capable of attaining it.

Together we would achieve the Pilgrimage, Traiben and I. We were twelve years old, and our lives were irrevocably set from that moment forth.

2

THE EVENTS OF THAT day's Procession passed before me as though I were watching them in a dream. The heads of all the Houses went past me, stiff with their own importance. Then came the Musicians, filling the air with the sounds of their thunbors and gallimonds and bindanays, and after them the Jugglers, prancing and leaping and turning handsprings and changing shape with careless frenzy as they tossed their sharp-bladed sepinongs high and deftly plucked them from the air. The sacred things were brought forth next, carried on cushions of bronzy green by solemn-faced Holies; and then, walking by themselves to no rhythm or beat whatever, came five or six Returned Ones, moving in worlds of their own, honoring the Procession by their presence but not a part of it any real way. After they had passed Pilgrim Lodge they drifted off into the throng and would not be seen again that day, or, for all anyone knew, that year.

The dancing was next. Each House's dancing-clan appeared in turn, richly arrayed, doing the special dance of that House. The Weavers did the hawk dance, the Scribes did the shambler dance, the Butchers did the bear dance, the Vintners did the rock-ape dance. The Witches danced the conjuring dance, the Carpenters danced the hammer dance. And so on and so on through the wind-sprite dance of the Jugglers, the waterfall dance of the Growers, the fire dance of the Healers, the sky-wolf dance of the Judges. And finally, masked and robed in the most splendid way of all, came the dancers of the House of the Wall, enacting the slow and majestic steps of the Wall dance.

There was more, much more: you know the pomp and splendor of the Pilgrim Procession as well as I. The hours floated by in dazzlement.

And Traiben's words continued to burn in my soul's heart.

For the first time in my life I had some glimmering of who I was.

Do you know who you are? "I am Mosca," you say, "I am Helkitan," "I am Simbol Leathermaker," or whatever your name may be. But your name is not you. "I am Poilar Crookleg," I would tell people, and yet I had no real idea who or what Poilar Crookleg might be. Now I began to see. Traiben had turned a key in my mind and I started to understand myself a little. Who was Poilar? Poilar is He-who-will-be-a-Pilgrim. Well, yes, but I knew that already. What kind of Pilgrim will Poilar be? One who understands the purpose of the Pilgrimage. Yes. Yes. Because I was born into the House of the Wall, I might have looked forward to a lifetime of performing rites and ceremonies, but that had never seemed to be a thing I was going to do. So I remained unformed and undirected. My future life had no shape. But now I knew—I knew, I really *knew*, not simply assumed— that I had been born to be a Pilgrim. Very well. For the first time I understood what that meant.

"Look," Traiben said. "The doors of the Lodge are starting to open."

So they were, the two great wickerwork doors embellished with heavy bronze bands that are opened only on this one day of the year. They swung back slowly, protesting on their thick stone hinges, and the chosen Pilgrims came forth, the men issuing from the left-hand chamber, the women from the right one. Out into the sunlight they came, pale and blinking, because they had not been seen in the open since the day the chosen ones' names had been announced, half a year ago. Blood streaked their cheeks and hands and forearms and clothing: they had just performed the Sacrifice of the Bond that is the last thing they do before leaving the Lodge. They were lean and hard from all the training they had undergone. Their faces, mainly, were somber and drawn, as though they were marching not to glory but to their deaths. Most of the new Pilgrims looked that way every year, I had already noticed. Why, I wondered, was that? They had striven so hard to be chosen; and after much travail they had gained what they sought: why then look so downcast?

But a few, at least, seemed transfigured by the honor that had come to them. Their eyes were turned rapturously toward Kosa Saag and their faces were shining with an inner light. It was wonderful to see those few.

"Look at Galli's brother," I whispered to Traiben. "Do you see how happy he is? That's the way I'm going to be when my time comes."

"And so will I."

"And look, look, there's Thrance!" He was our great hero then, an athlete of legendary skill, flawless of shape and tall as a tree, a godlike figure of wondrous beauty and strength. Everyone around us stirred in excitement as Thrance emerged from Pilgrim Lodge. "He'll run straight up to the Summit, I'll bet, without ever stopping to catch his breath. He won't wait for the others—he'll just take off and keep going."

"He probably will," said Traiben. "Poor Thrance."

"Poor Thrance? Why do you say a strange thing like that? Thrance is someone to be envied, and you know it!"

Traiben shook his head. "Envy Thrance? Oh, no, Poilar.

I envy him his broad back and long legs, and nothing else. Don't you see? This moment right now is the finest moment of his life. Everything can only get worse from here on for him."

"Because he's been chosen to be a Pilgrim?"

"Because he'll run ahead of the others," said Traiben, and turned away, wrapping himself in a cloak of silence.

Thrance went trotting past us down Procession Street, a jubilant figure, head upraised toward the mountain.

We were almost at the end of the Procession now.

The last of this year's Pilgrims had passed by, and had taken the turn past the huge scarlet-leaved szambar tree in the plaza, the place where all roads meet, the spindle marking the point from which everything in our village radiates. They swung sharply around the tree and went to the right: that would put them on the road toward Kosa Saag. Behind them came the final group of marchers, the saddest ones of all—the great horde of defeated candidates, whose humiliating task it was to carry the equipment and baggage of the winners as far as the village boundary.

How sorry I felt for them! How my heart ached for their shame!

There were hundreds and hundreds of them, marching five abreast past me for what seemed like forever. These, I knew, were merely the ones that had survived the long ordeal of training and selection; for many die during that time. Even after those deaths there were still, I suppose, eighty or ninety defeated ones for each of the chosen Forty. It has always been like that. Many come forward, but few succeed. In my year, which was a large one though not unusually so, there were four thousand two hundred and fifty-six candidates: each of us had less than one chance out of a hundred to be chosen.

Yet these defeated ones marched as proudly as though they had been winners—heads erect, eyes staring toward the mountain. It was like that every year, and I had never been able to understand why. Well, it is an honor, after all, to have been a candidate, even an unsuccessful one. But I would not have wanted to be among their number.

They went by, and suddenly Procession Street was empty.

"There should be Sweepers at the end as well as at the beginning," said Traiben. "To clear away the spirits that come flocking in after the people have passed."

I shrugged. Sometimes I had no patience with Traiben's strangeness. My attention was focused on the road to Kosa Saag, off to my left on the northwest side of town. The Pilgrims were in the flat part of the road now and therefore out of sight, with their pitiful train of baggage-bearers still in view behind them. Then the baggage-bearers vanished into the dip of the road and a moment later the first of the Pilgrims reappeared, visible again on the steeper part of the road where it rises just west of the center of the village and ascends into the foothills of the Wall. The double light of brilliant white Ekmelios and blood-red Marilemma cloaked them in an eye-dazzling aura as they made their way up the golden-carpeted road.

Watching them, I felt the most powerful sort of agitation, almost to the point of sickness. I trembled; my throat went dry; my face became stiff as a mask. I had seen this moment of the Pilgrims' departure every year of my life, but this time it was different. I imagined myself among them, going up and up and up the Wall. The village dwindled to a dot behind me. I could feel the air growing cooler and thinner as I climbed. I put my head back and stared toward the remote unknown Summit and my brain whirled with wonders.

Traiben was gripping my arm again. This time I didn't brush him away.

Together we counted out the names of the mileposts as the Pilgrims ascended:

"Roshten . . . . Ashten . . . . Glay . . . . Hespen . . . . Sennt. . . ."

Ordinarily the Sennt milepost was as far up the Wall-road as one could see from the lowlands. But as I have said, that day had become one of great clarity, and we were able to make out one more winding of the road, to the milepost known as Denbail. Traiben and I whispered its name together as the Pilgrims reached it. That was where the golden ceremonial carpet came to its end and the stone-paved road lay bare. Here the defeated ones had to hand over the equipment, for they were allowed to go no farther on the upward route. We stared, straining our eyes, as the Forty took their packs and gear from those who had borne them up till now. Then the defeated ones swung around and began their descent; and the Forty resumed their climb, continuing on up the road until within moments they were lost to our view in the mists and twists of the upward path.

3

THAT NIGHT WAS THE first night that what I call my star-dream came to me.

It was a night of many moons, when spangled light danced on the wall of our house. Some find it hard to sleep in all that brilliance, but I was tired from the day's events, and I slept the sleep of the utterly exhausted. In the depths of the night I found myself dreaming of the worlds beyond the World.

In my dream I climbed Kosa Saag with no more effort than if I were climbing to the top of someone's barn. Up and up I went, through each of the Kingdoms of the Wall, and it took no time at all. Traiben was with me, somewhere just behind, and other friends too, but I paid no heed to them and went on and on with tremendous ease and swiftness until I had attained the Summit. And there I stood beneath the worlds of Heaven, which are the stars. I saw those far worlds swarming in the sky like blazing fiery spirits. In some lofty place I danced beneath their cold light. I felt their force and strangeness. I sang with the gods and tasted the wisdom that they have to teach. My great ancestor the First Climber, He Who Climbed, the holiest of men, appeared and stood before me, and I became one with His spirit. And when I came down from the Wall my face was shining and I held out my hands to those who greeted me and they knelt before me and wept with joy.

That was my dream. It would come to me many times again in the years ahead, as I lay sleeping under the shadow light of the spirit sky. And those who lay with me as I dreamed it would tell me afterward that I turned and tossed and murmured in my sleep, and reached upward with my hands as though trying to grasp Heaven itself.

A curious dream, yes. But the most curious thing about it, that first time, was that everyone else in the village seemed to have had it also.

"I dreamed you climbed the Wall last night and danced at the Summit," said my mother's brother Urillin when I came from my sleeping-place in the morning. And he laughed, as though to tell me that it was foolish to put much stock in dreams. But within the space of a single hour three other people told me that they had dreamed the same thing; and Traiben too said that he had; and a little while afterward as I walked through the streets, thick with the litter of yesterday's festival, I saw everyone staring at me with big eyes and pointing and whispering, as if to say, "He is the one who danced at the Summit. The mark of the gods is on him, can you see?" And it became more certain to me than ever, not that I had ever had any doubt, that I was destined to be a Pilgrim and accomplish great things.

From that day on scarcely an hour of my life passed without my giving thought to the time when I would make my ascent to the Summit. Each year on the twelfth day of Elgamoir I watched the new Forty emerge from the Pilgrim Lodge and make their way up the side of Kosa Saag until that terrible and wonderful moment when they could no longer be seen, and the only thought in my mind was that another year had gone by, and I was one year closer to the time when I would take that road myself.

BUT I WOULD NOT have you believe that the climb I would someday make was the only thing on my mind in those years, however dedicated I might have been in my soul to the great adventure that lay ahead. I thought of the Pilgrimage often; I dreamed of it frequently, and of the mysteries that waited for me atop the Wall; but I still had to get on with the business of growing up.

I had my first mating, for one thing, when I turned thirteen. Her name was Lilim, and as is usual she was a woman of my mother's family, about twenty-five years old. Her face was round and rosy, her breasts were full and comforting. The lines of age were evident on her face but she seemed very beautiful to me. My mother must have told her that I was ready. At a gathering of our family she came over to me and sang the little song that a woman sings when she is choosing a man, and though I was very startled at first, and even a little frightened, I recovered quickly and sang the song that a man is supposed to make in reply.

So Lilim taught me the Changes and led me down the river of delight, and I will always think kind thoughts of her. She showed me how to bring my full maleness forth, and I reveled in the size and stiffness of it. Then in wonder I touched her body as the hot, swollen female parts emerged. She drew me to her then, and led me into that place of moisture and smoothness of which I had only dreamed up till that moment, and it was even more wonderful than I had imagined it to be. For the time that our bodies were entwined—it was only minutes, but it felt like forever—it seemed to me that I had become someone other than myself. But that is what making the Changes means: we step away from the boundaries of our daily selves and enter the new, shared self that is you-and-the-other together.

When it was over and we had returned to our familiar

neuter forms we lay in each other's arms and talked, and she asked me if I meant to be a Pilgrim, and I said yes, yes, I did. "So that is what the dream meant," she said, and I knew which dream she was speaking of. She herself was a failed candidate, she told me, but her lover Gortain had been chosen for the Forty in their year. He had gone up the Wall and, like most Pilgrims, had never been heard of again. "If you see him there when you go up," Lilim said to me, "carry my love to him, for I have never forgotten him."

I promised her that I would, and said I would bring Gortain's love back to her when I returned, if I found him on the Wall. And she laughed at that, amused by my cockiness. But she laughed gently, because this was my first mating.

I had many other matings after that, more than most boys my age, more than was reasonable to expect. The act lost its novelty for me but never its wonder or power. When I went up into Changes I felt that I was going among the gods, that I was becoming like a god myself. And I hated to return from the place where Changes took me; but of course there is no staying there once the high moment is past.

I remember the names of all but a few of my partners: Sambaral, Bys, Galli, Saiget, Mesheloun, and another Sambaral were among the first ones. I would have mated with Thissa too, of the House of Witches, whose strange elusive beauty appealed to me greatly, but she was shy and coy and I had to wait another two years for that.

It was easy for me to speak with girls and easy indeed to fall into matings with them. Behind my back it was whispered, I know, that they were attracted to me on account of my bad leg, girls oftentimes being perversely drawn to flaws of that sort. Perhaps that was so in a few cases, but I think there were other reasons besides. Poor Traiben's luck with girls was not so good, and now and again I would take pity on him and send one of mine to do a mating with him: I sent Galli that way, I recall, and one of the Sambarals. There may have been others.

When I was almost fifteen and the time of my candidacy was drawing near, I fell seriously in love with a girl of the House of Holies whose name was Turimel. I bought a love-charm from an old Witch named Kres, so that I might have her, and later I learned that quite by coincidence Turimel had bought a charm from Kres also, in order she might have me; and therefore our coming together must have been foreordained, not that much good came out of it for either of us.

Turimel was dark and beautiful, with shimmering hair that tumbled in long cascades, and when we made the Changes together she carried me on such a journey that I would altogether lose my mind, forget even my name, forget everything but Turimel. In the moment when her breasts came forth it was like the revealing of Kosa Saag through the clouds; and when I entered the sweet hot female cleft that the Changes opened to me, I felt that I was walking among the gods.

But there was a doom on our love from its first moment, since those who are born to the House of Holies are forbidden to undertake the Pilgrimage. They must remain below, guarding the sacred things, while others perform the task of climbing to the gods who live at the Summit. Nor is there any way that one of the Holies can resign her birthright and enter some other House. So if I were to choose to seal myself to Turimel, I would certainly lose her when I set out on my Pilgrimage. Or if I wanted to remain by her side I would be compelled to renounce the Pilgrimage myself; and that seemed just as dire.

"I'll have to give her up," I said to Traiben one gloomy morning. "From here the road leads only to a sealing, if I stay with her. And I can't seal with a Holy."

"You can't seal with anyone, Poilar. Don't you understand that?"

"I don't follow your meaning."

"You are meant for the Pilgrimage. Everyone knows that. The mark of the gods is on you."

"Yes," I said. "Of course." I liked to hear Traiben say such things, because in fact despite my dream and my family heritage I had begun to feel not at all sure that I would be chosen, and each day then I had to fight my way through a thickening forest of doubt. That was only on account of my age, for I had reached the time when a young man doubts anything and everything, especially concerning himself.

"Very well. But if you seal yourself to someone and she isn't chosen, what becomes of your sealing?"

"Ah," I said. "I see. But if she and I are sealed, won't that influence the Masters to pick her also?"

"There's no reason why it should. They don't take sealings into account at all."

"Ah," I said again.

I thought of Lilim, whose Gortain had gone off to the Wall and never returned.

"If you want to get sealed," Traiben said, "then by all means get yourself sealed. But you have to resign yourself to the likelihood of losing her when you go up the Wall. If you seal with Turimel, that's a certainty: you already realize that. Choose a girl of some other House and the situation's almost as bad. There's no better than one chance out of a hundred that she'll also be selected for the Forty. That's essentially no chance at all, do you see? And in any case, would you want to leave a fatherless child behind, as was done to you? Better not even to think about sealing, Poilar. Think about the Wall. Think only about the Wall."

As ever, I was unable to pick a hole in Traiben's reasoning. And so I resigned myself to remaining forever unsealed. But it hurt me; it hurt me terribly.

Turimel and I spent one last night together, a night when all the moons were overhead, two in their full silver brilliance and three as shining crescents, and the air was clear as the King's crystal goblets. We lay closely entwined on a soft mossy bed on the north saddle of Messenger Slope, and softly I told her that I was bound for the Pilgrimage and would accept no possibility of failure, and for an instant I saw pain pass across her face; but then she put it away and smiled gently and nodded, with tears glistening in her eyes. I think she had known the truth all along, but had hoped it was not so. Then we made all the Changes one by one until we had spent the last of our passion. It was a sad and wonderful night and I was sorry to see it end. At dawn a gentle rain began to fall, and hand in hand we walked naked back to town under pearly morning-light. Three days later she announced her sealing to some young man of the House of Singers, whom she must already have been holding in reserve, knowing that sooner or later I would forsake her for Kosa Saag.

After Turimel there was this one and that one and the other one, but my soul had hardened from its wound and I never spoke of sealing with any of them, and I never stayed with any of them long enough for them to hatch the idea themselves. Very likely they all knew I was bound for the Wall anyway. In every year-group there are certain ones whose Wallward destiny is known to all. Thrance was one such, the year when I was twelve. And I was another. People said they could see the mark of the Wall on me. It was the star-dream that had shown it to them, the dream which the whole village dreamed the same night. I searched for the mark in my mother's reflecting-glass, but I could never find it. I knew it was there, though. I had no doubt.

THE BEGINNING OF MY sixteenth year arrived. On the tenth of Orgulet a messenger of the House of the Wall brought me the traditional sheet of elegantly lettered parchment, ordering me to report, along with all the other members of my year-group, to the assembly-place known as the Field of Pilgrims. At last my candidacy was at hand.

I remember the day well. How could I not? Four thousand two hundred fifty-six of us: not the biggest year-group that had ever been, but not the smallest, either. Ekmelios was so hot that day that the sky sizzled. We formed forty-two lines of one hundred on the velvety red grass of the Field of Pilgrims, and those who were left over made up a line of just fifty-six. I was in the short line: I took that as a somber omen. But Traiben, standing not far away in another line, winked and grinned at me as if to tell me that everything was going to be all right.

Now came the terrifying hour of First Winnowing, which I dreaded more than death itself.

Of all my four years as a candidate, nothing was worse than First Winnowing. I trembled like a leaf in the wind as the Masters of the House of the Wall moved silently among us, pausing here and there in the rows to tap candidates on the shoulder and thus to tell them that they were dismissed from the competition.

Winnowing can fall on anyone, like a lightning-bolt, and there is no more appeal from it than there is from lightning. The Masters alone know the reasons why they decide to end a candidacy, and they are under no obligation to reveal them.

That was why I feared this moment so much. Because I was young and ignorant I thought of First Winnowing as a process controlled by sheer whim and impulse, or even by private grudge, and therefore one that took no account of the merit that I was certain I possessed. Had I done something years ago to annoy or offend a Master, which had stuck in his memory like a cinder in the eye? Why, then, he would tap my shoulder and all would be over for me with that tap: no Pilgrimage for Poilar, no ascent of the Wall, no view of the mysteries of the Summit. Not even the omen of my star-dream would matter, if someone wanted to tap me out. Nor would my descent from the First Climber help me. There are very few members of the House of the Wall who *don't* claim descent from Him; and even if half of them are lying, that still leaves a great multitude in whose veins His blood flows. So Climber-blood is not an automatic ticket to the Pilgrimage. Was I standing with one shoulder higher than another, and was that bothersome? Tap. Was the glint of my gaze or the set of my jaw too arrogant? Would the fact that one of my legs was lame count against me, despite all I had done to compensate for that accident of birth? Tap. Tap. Was some Master's knee aching that morning, making him irascible? Tap. And out goes Poilar.

As I say, I was young and ignorant then. I had no understanding of the real purpose of Winnowing.

And so I stood as stiff as a tree, trying not to tremble, as the Masters moved among us. Tap! and Moklinn was gone, the tall graceful boy who was the finest athlete the village had seen since the great days of Thrance. Tap! and the simpleton girl Ellitt was dismissed. Tap! and there went Baligan, the younger son of the head of the House of Singers. Tap! Tap! Tap!

What was the criterion? Casting Ellitt aside I could understand, for her mind was like a child's, and she would perish quickly on the Wall. But why tap splendid Moklinn? Why tap Baligan, whose soul was as pure as a mountain stream? So it went, the tap falling upon some obvious choices for culling and on some of the finest young people of the village. I watched the tapped ones drift away, looking stunned. And I waited in a chill of fright as the Master who was tapping in our line made his unhurried way down the rank toward me. He was Bertoll, my mother's oldest brother. All the Masters were men of my own family: it could not be helped, I was a member of Wallclan. And so they all knew of my obsession with the Wall. Unwisely, rashly, boyishly, I had told everyone again and again that I meant to see the Summit. They had merely smiled. Had I angered them with my boastfulness? Had they decided to teach me a lesson?

I died a thousand deaths in those few minutes. I wished a million million times that I had been born into any other House, that I had been a Carpenter, a Musician, even a Sweeper, so that none of the Masters would have known what was in my soul. Now Bertoll was going to tap me, purely to cut me down for my brashness. I knew he would. I was certain of it. And I vowed then and there that if he did I would kill him and then myself, before the moons rose that evening.

I stood still as stone, eyes rigid, staring forward.

Bertoll passed me by without even looking at me, and went on down the row.

Tears of relief ran down my cheeks. All my fearful sweaty imaginings had been for nought. But then I thought: What of Traiben? I had been so concerned with my own fate that I hadn't bothered to think about him. I swung around and glanced behind me, down the line next to mine, just in time to see that line's Master go past little scrawny Traiben as though he hadn't been there at all and reach out to tap a great sturdy boy behind him.

"It makes no sense," I said to him when the Winnowing was over. A hundred and eighty had been tapped; the rest of us were free to continue our candidacies. "My leg is crooked, and I irritate people because I seem so sure of myself. You can't run a hundred paces without getting dizzy and you scare people because you're so shrewd. Yet they let you and me pass, and tap someone like Moklinn, who's better fitted for climbing the Wall than any three of us. Or Baligan, the kindest, most thoughtful person I know. What standards do they use?"

"That is a mystery," said Traiben. "But one thing I know: Winnowings are meant not to punish but to reward."

I stared at him, baffled. "What does that mean?"

"That some of us are deemed too good to be sent to the mountain."

"I still don't understand."

Traiben sighed, that terrible patient sigh of his. "Look," he said. "We send forth our Forty every year knowing that most of them are going to die on the Wall, and that those few who eventually do come back are going to be changed the way Returned Ones always are, and will simply skulk around meditating and praying forever afterward, having as little to do with the rest of us as possible. It's a gamble that we always lose. We send them up there to learn something useful from the gods, and for one reason or another they don't succeed. Nobody who makes the Pilgrimage is ever again going to play an important role in the life of the village. Hardly anyone has since the First Climber Himself. Agreed?"

"Of course." We had been through all this before.

He said, "If we give our forty finest to the mountain each year, what will become of the village? Who'll lead us? Who'll inspire us with new ideas? We'll lose our most talented people, year after year. We'll breed their abilities out of the race until we're nothing but a tribe of dullards and weaklings. And therefore certain candidates have to be held back. They have to be saved to meet the future needs of the village."

I thought I saw where he was heading now, and I didn't like it.

"Undertaking the Pilgrimage is the most important deed any of us can do," I said. "The Pilgrims are our greatest heroes. Even if they don't manage to learn the things that you think they're supposed to be learning up there. By sending them up the Wall, we pay our debt to the gods, as He Who Climbed taught us that we must, and so we insure their continued blessing." You can see that I was quoting catechism again.

"Exactly," Traiben said. "Pilgrims are heroes, no doubt of that. But they are sacrifices, also."

I stared. I had never seen it that way.

He said, "And so the Masters choose people like you, who are strong and determined, or people like me, who are clever and resourceful. That's what heroes are like. But you and I are troublesome in other ways. We may be heroes, yes, but we're too odd and too prickly to make good leaders down here, you and I. Can you imagine yourself as the head of the House? Or me? And so we can be sacrificed. We can be spared for the Pilgrimage. Whereas Baligan obviously will head his House some day. And Moklinn has a perfect body: it mustn't be wasted on the Wall."

"Thrance had a perfect body too," I said. "But he was chosen."

"And has failed to return, isn't that so? Thrance was selfish and proud. Perhaps the Masters thought the village was well rid of him."

"I see," I said, though I wasn't quite sure that I did.

I was shaken by what Traiben had said. In just a few minutes he had once again turned my world upside down. I had been so very pleased that I had managed to last through the First Winnowing. I wondered now: Was my surviving the Winnowing really something to be proud of, or was it merely the sign of how willing the village was to dispense with me?

But just as quickly I recovered my equilibrium. Becoming head of my House had never been part of my plan. To make the Pilgrimage was. I had passed the first of my many tests: that was all that really mattered.

AND SO MY CANDIDACY began.

The early days of it saw a surprisingly gradual onset of the demanding discipline of the selection process. We were divided into forty groups of about a hundred each—Traiben and I landed in different groups—and from then on we moved as a group from one House to the next for our instruction and our examinations. But at first everything was deceptively easy.

We were asked at the beginning to write short essays on why we wanted to be Pilgrims. I remember mine almost to the word:

"1. Because I believe that undertaking the Pilgrimage is the finest thing anyone could possibly do. It is our duty to go to the gods above and worship them and learn from them the things they have to teach us. Of all the traditions of our people, it is the holiest and noblest, and I have always wanted to be obedient to our great traditions.

"2. Because my father was a Pilgrim in his time and I think and hope that he may still be dwelling in one of the Kingdoms of Kosa Saag. I have not seen him since I was a small child and it is my great dream to encounter him once again when I climb the Wall.

"3. Because I have spent my whole life looking up at Kosa Saag and marveling at its greatness, and now I want to test my strength against the mountain and see if I am equal to what it will ask of me."

It was a good essay. At least, it got me through the Second Winnowing. Ninety of us were dismissed at that Winnowing. Whether it was for writing poor essays or for some other reason, I have no idea; but I suspect the essays really were of no great significance in the process. It was the task of the Masters to find some reason or other for discarding all but forty of us in the course of the four years, and they could use almost any pretext at all—or none—for dropping us from the roster.

Then there was religious instruction. We read the Book of the First Climber, though of course we had read it a thousand times already, and we discussed the story of His life, His conflict with the elders and His being cast out of the village and His decision to climb the Wall, which at that time was not permitted, and the things that He learned during His Pilgrimage on its heights. And also we were drilled in the names and visages of the gods and all their special attributes, as if we could expect to meet them along the mountain path and must therefore be sure to recognize them and greet them with the proper greeting. So we sat in the little hut of instruction as though we were small children while someone from the House of Holies held up one sacred portrait after another, and we shouted out the names: "Kreshe! Thig! Sandu Sando! Selemoy!" It felt strange to be back in school, since, as is true of almost everyone else, my formal education had ended with my first ten of years. But for all we knew we *would* meet Thig and Selemoy and Sandu Sando on the slopes of the Wall; and so we listened to the old stories all over again—how Kreshe had made the World and set it afloat on the Great Sea and how Thig the Shaper had reached into the still molten rock of the new-made World and pulled the Wall out of it, stretching it high in order to make a place for us to live that would be close to the stars, and how after the sin of our First Fathers we had been hurled down from the Summit into the lowlands by Sandu Sando the Avenger and forbidden to return until we were worthy, and all the rest of the tales of our childhood.

In those first days we had to go to other classes where we were taught the nature of the Wall. The most remarkable thing about these classes was how little seemed to be known about Kosa Saag, for all the thousands of years that we had been sending our Pilgrims up its face.

Our teachers, of course, had never been very far up the Wall themselves: just the usual excursions to the permitted holiday zones just above the village, and no farther. There was nothing very surprising about that, I suppose. Our teachers had never been Pilgrims. Only the Returned Ones had any first-hand knowledge of the extraordinary place where we were going to go, but you wouldn't really expect Returned Ones to do anything so obvious and straightforward and useful as to come into our classrooms and give us lectures on what they had experienced. That is not their way. I had hoped that they would make an exception to their rule of lofty and mystical withdrawal from all daily matters for the sake of helping us understand what was in store for us, but they did not do it. The Returned Ones shared nothing with us, nothing at all. And so our teachers, who were just the usual babbling drudges from the House of Scholars, served us up a foggy third-hand mix of rumor, legend, and guesswork which was just about as close to useless as anything could be.

They taught us that the Wall is a place where the power of the gods is so great that change comes freely and amazingly to those who live their lives upon it, and all is magic and mystery and strangeness beyond our comprehension. And they warned us of the danger of encountering change-fire as we climbed. The very stones of the Wall, they said, give off a secret heat that will kindle into raging conflagration the flame of transformation that always burns quietly and gently within us, and turn climbers into monsters if they are willing to let it happen.

Everything was fluid up there, they said. Nothing was fixed, nothing was as we understood things to be. It was all because of that strange fire that lay within the rocks, which no one could see but which was easy enough to feel. "The Wall is said to be a place where reality bends," our teachers told us solemnly. How were we supposed to interpret that? They couldn't say. "On the Wall," they declared, "the sky sometimes is below and the ground is above." Well, yes, and what were we to make of that? They spoke of monsters, demons, and demigods who waited for us above the cloud-line in the innumerable Kingdoms of the Wall. They warned us of lakes of fire and trees of metal. They talked of dead people who walked with their feet turned back to front and their eyes staring like hot coals out of the backs of their heads. They let us read the Secret Book of Maylat Gakkerel, which was supposed to be the three-thousand-year-old testimony of the only Returned One who had ever said anything at all about what he had encountered while climbing Kosa Saag, other than the First Climber Himself. But unlike the Book of the First Climber, which is stark and simple in its narrative of His visit to the abode of the gods and its account of the things they taught Him while He was there, the Secret Book of Maylat Gakkerel was all ornate parable and poetry, a welter of fanciful detail written in a cryptic style so remote from any kind of modern speech that it had to be embedded in footnotes and commentary a dozen times as long as the Secret Book itself. Very few of us could get through more than a dozen pages of it. All I remember was a kind of feverish haze of murky description that made no sense, a magical fairy-tale of heights that

turned into abysses, of raindrops that became knives, of
rocks that danced and sang, of demons who furiously
hurled their limbs one by one at climbing Pilgrims until
there was nothing left of them but bouncing skulls, of wise
men who offered counsel along the way but spoke all their
words in backwards language. The whole of the Secret Book
might just as well have been written in backwards language
for all the help it gave me.

I decided that the classes were simply part of the
Winnowing. They were intended to terrify us by making us
see that nobody who lived in the lowland villages really had
the slightest knowledge of what awaited those who journeyed on the Wall. The things we were learning struck me
as being mere fables that could be of no possible practical
use, and therefore after a few weeks I stopped paying attention to them. Others, believing that their lives would de-
pend on how well they mastered this mass of foolishness,
took copious notes and in a little while, as the contradic-
tions and mysteries piled up, they began to go around with
dazed, bewildered expressions on their faces.

About a dozen members of my group resigned their
candidacies during this period. Most of the dedicated note-
takers were among them. I was convinced that they had
filled their minds with so much nonsense about the Wall
that they became too frightened to continue.

We had other classes that were far more valuable: I
mean our classes in survival, where we were taught the
techniques of mountain-climbing, and of coping with the
special conditions that were believed to exist in the higher
reaches of the Wall, and tricks of hunting and foraging
that would come in handy once we had exhausted the
food we had carried up from the village in our packs. Here
too the instructors were forced to rely on a lot of myth
and supposition, on account of the taboo against the
Returned Ones' revealing their experiences on the Wall.
But there is no taboo against climbing the lower reaches of
the Wall, at least as far as the Hithiat milepost, and so we

were allowed to get some small taste of what might be waiting for us.

I had been as high as Hithiat already, of course. Everyone has: we all sneak up the Wall when we are young. Most of us stay up there only a few hours, but the boldest will risk remaining overnight. That was what I had done when I was fourteen. Galli went with me then. She and I had just become lovers, and we enjoyed daring each other to do all sorts of outrageous things: we slipped into the place where the sacred things were kept and handled some of them, we stole a bottle of dream-wine from the Wallclan treasury, we went swimming in the Pool of the Housemothers one moonless night. And then I said, "I want to climb the Wall. Do you?"

She laughed. "Kreshe! You think I'm afraid of that?"

Galli was big and hearty, as strong as any man, with a loud deep voice and a laugh that could be heard three Houses away. We set out early one morning, getting past the gate-guards with the usual line about going to make a sacrifice at Roshten Shrine, and then of course as we approached Roshten we darted into the thick jungle behind it and went scrambling up the back way on the forest road that parallels the main one. It was a clear day and by the time we reached the Glay milepost we were astounded at how much of the village we could see below us, and when we got to Hespen we stopped a long while at the parapet, struck silent by wonder. Everything lay spread out below us in miniature. It was like a toy model of the village. I felt as if I could reach out with my hand and gather it all up in a single swoop. We could see the House of the Wall right below us with the scarlet szambar tree at its center, looking no bigger than a matchstick, and the House of Holies next to it, and Singers on the other side, and then any number of other Houses, Healers and Carpenters and Musicians and Clowns and Butchers, spreading away and away and away to east and west like little dark circles in the green of the forest, until finally the Houses came to their end and there was only green, with perhaps the barest hint on the horizon of the foreign villages that lie beyond the boundaries of our own.

We went on that day, Galli and I, to Hithiat milepost, where the road got very rough and we began to lose our nerve. Here the face of the Wall was soft and pitted, and pebbles kept tumbling down from above us with little slithering sounds. Sometimes larger rocks fell; a few huge boulders too, which hit uncomfortably close to us and went bounding away. The boulders made us very uneasy. It was getting dark, besides. And everyone knew that it was crazy to go beyond Hithiat. I was aware that Galli feared hardly anything, and she knew that I was like that too, and so it occurred to me that one of us might try to bluff the other into going beyond Hithiat, and that if we began to talk about it we probably would actually do it, since neither of us had the courage to confess any sort of fear or weakness to the other. But that was not what happened. We had that much common sense, at least. Instead we went off the gravelly road into a flat mossy place, where we watched Ekmelios set and then ate the little bit of meat and cheese and wine that we had carried with us. After that we took off our clothes and sang the Change-songs to each other and brought ourselves out of neuter, and I lay down on top of Galli's great firm resilient body as though it were a bed; and she embraced me and took me inside her, and we ran through some very wonderful Changes indeed.

"Do you feel the change-fires?" she asked me.

"No. Do you?"

"I don't think they're very strong, this close to the village. But it frightens me, to think that we could be turned into monsters on the Wall."

"Even when we go higher up, we won't be transformed unless we want to be," I said. "The change-fires don't take control of you against your will. The only ones who are transformed are those who don't have the strength to remain themselves."

"How do you know that?" Galli asked. "I never heard anything about that."

"I know," I said solemnly. But the truth was I was only guessing.

Darkness came. We were too frightened to sleep. So we sat side by side waiting for dawn and wondering about the screeching sounds that drifted down to us from the pinnacles we could not see, for everyone knows the dire tales of the Wall-hawks that are bigger than a man and carry Pilgrims off in their beaks. But the Wall-hawks, if that was what they were, let us be, and at dawn we returned to the village. Nobody minded that we had been gone. Galli's father was a drunkard, and as for mine, of course, he had vanished on the Wall long before. The gentle Urillin, my mother's brother who had had charge of me since I was a boy, never could stand to punish me for anything. So nothing was said about our absence. And that was the great adventure that Galli and I had in the highlands.

But the training classes that took us up the Wall now were much harder work than my outing with Galli. Instead of following the main road or one of the back roads we had to hack our way through the foothill forests, scrambling over colossal rocks and the gnarled roots of trees, and sometimes go straight up bare cliff faces, using all our skill with our ropes and our sucker-pads to keep from falling and being smashed. And there was no meat and cheese and no wine and certainly no making the Changes when we came out finally at Hithiat milestone. We undertook at least one climb a week, and it was brutal, exhausting stuff. We came back bruised and bloody. I worried about Traiben, since he was in another group and I couldn't be close at hand to help him through. But he managed. Sometimes I met him after hours and gave him special coaching, showing him ways of carrying himself through the difficult places, of wedging his feet into cracks or looking for horns of rock to grab while shifting his position. The climbs were not only strenuous, they were dangerous too: on our fifth climb a boy named Steill, from the House of Leather-makers, became lost in the woods and we searched for him half the night before we found him at last, lying broken in the moonlight at the bottom of a deep ravine with his brains spilling out of his head. He must have walked off the edge at dusk without knowing what he was doing, though someone whispered that a shambler had come upon him and pushed him over the edge. We all trembled at that: for the shambler is said to be as big as a roundhouse, but makes no sound in the forest and leaves no footprint. Be that as it may, Steill was dead, the first of our number to die in candidacy. But not the last.

4

AGAIN IT WAS THE twelfth of Elgamoir, and another
Forty set out on their journey up the Wall. I watched
them go with new respect, for I was in the second year
of my training now and I knew what they had gone through
in order to reach this point.

That year also two new Returned Ones arrived in the
village. That was always a memorable moment, since it
happened so infrequently. One was called Kaitu, and he had
been on the mountain nine years. The other was a woman
named Bril, who had gone up six years before. I saw them
when they came stumbling down into the plaza together,
dirty and ragged, with that look of glory in their eyes that
all the Returned Ones have. Children ran up to them to
touch them for luck. Old women sobbed in the street.
Someone from Holies was summoned, and led them to the
roundhouse where Returned Ones live. Later I heard tell
that Bril had reached halfway up the Wall, and that Kaitu
had succeeded in going nearly to the Summit, but I wondered how much substance there was to any of that. I had
listened to them babbling in the street, and I was beginning

to understand the truth about Returned Ones: most of them, perhaps all, lose their minds on their journeys, and they come back empty and incapable of thought. That they come back at all is a miracle. But it is folly to expect them to be able to say anything sensible about where they have been or what they have seen, and that is why each new group of Pilgrims goes forth with so little firm knowledge of what lies in wait for them.

None of that mattered to me. I was committed to my path, come what may. I intended to succeed where the others all had failed.

But I confess I did try, despite everything, to question the man Kaitu about what he had seen and done. This was three days after his return, and he had not yet taken up permanent living in the roundhouse, but still could be seen wandering around in the streets. I found him there, near the wineshop of Batu Mait, and took him by the elbow and led him inside for a couple of bowls of young golden wine. He seemed pleased at that. He laughed, he winked, he nudged my elbow. And when he had finished his second bowl I leaned close to him and whispered, keeping my voice low so that old Batu Mait would not become aware of the sin I was committing, "Tell me, Kaitu. What did you see up there? What was it like?"

Kaitu caught me by the wrist in a splayhanded grip, three fingers above and three below the way Traiben sometimes did, and shook my arm so hard that I spilled my wine. "Gods!" he cried. "Trees! Air! Fire!"

"Yes, I know, but—"

"Fire! Air! Trees! Gods!" And then, in a soft cozening voice, "Buy me more wine and I'll tell you the rest." His eyes were shining crazily.

I bought him more wine. But nothing else he said was of any more use than what I had heard before.

Afterward I told Traiben what I had done. He chided me for it. "The Returned Ones are sacred," he said. "They should be allowed to go their own way unmolested."

"Yes, I know. But I wanted to find out what it was like for him on the Wall."

"You'll have to wait and see, then."

WE WERE GROWING OLDER, entering the final few years of our second ten, coming toward the midpoint of our lives, the twentieth year, when Pilgrimages commence. We were old enough to be sealed now, old enough to be making children instead of simply mating for pleasure. But for me the Pilgrimage was everything. The Pilgrimage, and the mysteries of the Kingdoms of the Wall.

The tenth of Orgulet came round again, and another Winnowing was held. There were only eighteen hundred of us left now—still a substantial multitude, but less than half of those who had begun the quest. We stood in lines of twelve dozen in the Field of Pilgrims and the Masters passed among us, tapping as they had done before. This time I had no fear. I had done well in every test, I had mastered every skill: it would be insanity to dismiss me from the Pilgrimage. Indeed, the Master passed me by, and Traiben as well. But two hundred of us were tapped that day, and no reason given.

I felt sad for them. They had shown neither cowardice nor weakness of body nor wavering of purpose; and yet they had been tapped, all the same. They had suffered in the foothills as I had suffered, clambering up ropes and clawing bare rock, and yet they had been tapped. Well, I felt sad for them but not *very* sad. Two hundred more were gone, and I was two hundred places closer to selection for the Forty.

The third year of our training was the worst: it was like swimming in a sea of fire. All the impurities were being burned out of us. We became gaunt and scarred and tough, and every muscle of our bodies ached all the time.

We would rise at dawn and climb the hideous greenstone hills on the eastern edge of the Wall between Ashten and Glay, cutting ourselves in a thousand places as we dragged ourselves across the crumbling ridges. We caught small animals with our hands and ate them raw. We dug for roots and gnawed them, dirt and all. We threw rocks at birds to bring them down, and got nothing to eat that day if we failed to hit our marks. We crawled in mud and shivered in stinging rain. We fought duels with gnarled cudgels, so that we might learn how to defend ourselves against the beasts and phantoms that were said to inhabit the mountain. When we became too filthy to stand our own stink we bathed in rivers so icy they burned the skin, and lay awake all night on miserable outcroppings of jagged stone, pretending they were beds of soft leaves.

Many of us died. We fell from exposed outcroppings; we were caught in turbulent streams and were swept away; we chose the wrong berries to eat in the wilderness, and perished in agony, bellies bloated, vomiting black bile. I witnessed at least five or six of the deaths myself. Two were boys I had known all my life.

Others could no longer bear the strain, and withdrew from the training. Every day our teachers told us, "There is no shame in withdrawing," and anyone who believed that gladly accepted the chance. By the beginning of our fourth year there were only four hundred left. This time the tenth of Orgulet saw no new Winnowing: it would have been too cruel to dismiss any of us at this point. We were doing our own Winnowing now, our numbers reduced daily by weariness or illness or fear or simple bad luck.

Once again my self-confidence wavered. I went through a difficult time when I was certain that I was going to fail. My doubts grew so strong that finally I went to the shop of Thissa the Witch and bought myself a charm for success. Thissa was a candidate for selection herself, and everyone thought she stood a good chance. My hope was that she would have some private desire to see me chosen as one of the men of her Forty, and so would give me a good spell.

But Thissa was cool to me at first. She moved about her shop in a busy way, moving things from one counter to another as though she had no time for me. "I am busy with a curse now that has to be ready by nightfall," she said. And she looked away.

I was persistent, though. "Please, Thissa. Please. Otherwise the Masters may tap me at the next Winnowing."

I stroked her hand and nuzzled against her shoulder. She was wearing a thin light robe, bordered all around with mystic signs worked in golden thread, that showed the outlines of her shoulders and hips. I told her how much I admired her slender supple body, how beautiful her amber eyes were. We had done a few matings by this time, Thissa and I, though she was always distant and reluctant with me, and there had been a strangeness about her embrace, a kind of tingling feeling that she gave off, that had left me puzzled and uneasy, rather than properly satisfied, each time. But despite all that she was beautiful in her delicate way, and I told her so.

She told me to spare her the flattery, as she had told me all too many times before; but nevertheless she seemed to soften a little. And in the end I prevailed after much coaxing, and she cast the spell for me, which involved mixing her urine with mine and sprinkling it outside Pilgrim Lodge while saying certain special words. I knew it was a good spell. And indeed it was. Nor would she take any money from me for it.

After that my mood turned optimistic again. Everything was going the right way for me. I had never felt happier or more vigorous in my life. My crooked leg meant nothing in these trials: it was no handicap at all, for I had strength instead of grace, and agility instead of speed, and confidence enough for three. Traiben too was still among us, and I was no longer surprised at that, for he had toughened amazingly in these years and no one could call him a weakling now, though it still seemed to me that he was frail and easily wearied. The flame that burned within him saw him onward. We both of us knew that we would survive and prevail until the end.

But as always Traiben had his strange moments. One day he said to me quite abruptly, "Tell me, Poilar, do you think life has any real purpose?"

As always when he asked questions of that sort some lines of the catechism leaped readily to my mind. "Our purpose is to go to the gods at the Summit and pay our homage to them, as the First Climber taught us to do," I said. "And learn useful things from them, as He did, and bring them back to enrich our nation."

"But what *point* is there in doing that?"

The catechism offered me no clues about that. Puzzled, I said, "Why, so we can lead better lives!"

"And what point is there in *that*?"

He was starting to anger me now. I shoved him with my open hand. "Stop this," I said. "You sound like a child who keeps on asking, 'Why,' 'Why,' when things are explained to him. What point indeed? We want to lead better lives because that's better than leading worse ones."

"Yes. Yes, of course."

"Why do you waste your breath with meaningless issues like these, Traiben?"

He was silent for a time. Then he said, "Nothing has any meaning, Poilar. Not if you look at it closely. We say, 'This is good,' or 'This is bad,' or 'The gods will thus and so,' but how do we know? Why is one thing good and another thing bad? Because we say so? Because the gods say so? How do we know that they do? Nobody whom I know has ever heard them speak."

"Enough, Traiben!"

But when these moods possessed him there was no stopping him. He would endlessly pursue some strange line of inquiry that would never have occurred to anyone else, until he reached a conclusion that seemed to bear no relation to any question he had been asking.

He said now, "Even though nothing has any meaning, I believe we should seek for meaning all the same. Do you agree?"

I sighed. "Yes, Traiben."

"And so we must climb the Wall, because we think that the gods will it, and because we hope to gain knowledge from them that will better our lives."

"Yes. Of course. You belabor the obvious."

His eyes were aglow. "But now I've come to see that there's a third reason for going up. Which is to attempt to discover what kind of creatures the gods may be. How they are different from us, and where their superiority lies."

"And what good will that do?"

"So that we can become gods ourselves."

"You want to be a god, Traiben?"

"Why not? Are you content to be what you are?"

"Yes. Very much so," I said.

"And what are you, then? What are *we*?"

"We are the creatures whom the gods created to do their will. The sacred books tell us so. We were meant to be mortals and they were meant to be gods. That's good enough for me. Why isn't it good enough for you?"

"It isn't because it isn't. The day I say, 'This is good enough for me,' is the day I begin to die, Poilar. I want to know what I am. After that I want to know what I'm capable of becoming. And then I want to become it. I want to keep reaching higher all the time."

I thought of my star-dream, and how as I lay in its throes I would toss and turn and reach my hands toward Heaven. And I thought that I understood something of what Traiben was saying; for, after all, did I not burn with a hunger to climb that mountain to its loftiest point, and stand before the holy beings who inhabited its crest, and give myself up to their will so that I might become something greater than I had been?

But then I shook my head. He had gone too far. "No, Traiben. I think it's wild nonsense to talk about mortals becoming gods. And in any case I don't want to be one myself."

"You'd rather stay a mortal?"

"Yes. I'm a mortal because the gods mean me to be a mortal."

"You ought to give more thought to these matters," Traiben said. "Your mind marches in a circle. And your feet will too, if you're not careful."

I shook my head. "Sometimes I think you may be crazy, Traiben."

"Sometimes I wish you were crazier," he said.

THE NUMBER OF REMAINING candidates dropped and dropped. We were down to a hundred, ninety, eighty, seventy. It was a strange time for those of us who remained. We were all fiercely pledged to the Pilgrimage: anyone who might weaken and drop out had already done so, and anyone clumsy or careless enough to be killed or injured in the course of the training was long gone from our midst. We who had lasted this long meant to stay the course. A powerful kind of comradeship had developed among us. But there were still too many of us; and so we eyed our dearly loved comrades with unashamed ferocity, privately thinking, *May the gods blight you tomorrow, may your soul drain out of your body like a trickle of cold water, may you fall from the cliff and shatter both your legs, may your courage desert you entirely. Anything, so long as you cease to stand in my way.* And then we would smile, because everyone knew that everyone else was thinking the same things about him that he was thinking about them.

Seventy was a critical number: it brought on the Final Winnowing, the Silent Winnowing, when the actual Forty would be chosen. So once again we stood in the field, just a handful of us where more than four thousand had been three years earlier, and the Masters moved among us. The curious thing about this last Winnowing was that there was no tap: thirty were to be eliminated, but they would not be told. That is why this was called the Silent Winnowing. We were to be left in the dark another six months, not knowing whether we had been dismissed or not, but still undergoing all the trials and hardships of the training.

"Why do you think it's done this way?" I asked Traiben.

And he said, "Because there's always the chance that some of the chosen Forty will die during the final months of the training, and then they can be replaced from among the Thirty. But the replacements, if they should be needed, won't ever know that they were replacements: everyone who goes up on the Wall must think that he was one of the elect."

"So you and I might be among the Thirty ourselves, then?"

"We are of the Forty," said Traiben calmly. "Our task now is simply to survive until the Closing of the Doors."

Indeed he was right. The day of reckoning came, the tenth of Slit, which is exactly half a year prior to the day of the start of the new year's Pilgrimage. And at dawn of that day the Masters came to us where we slept and woke some of us, including Traiben and me, and took us to Pilgrim Lodge, and thereby we knew that we had been chosen. I felt none of the ecstatic joy that my boyhood self would have expected, only a mild flicker of satisfaction. I had worked too long and too hard for this to be capable of reacting with any great emotion now. One phase of my life had ended, the next was beginning, that was all. Once those great wicker-work doors had closed behind us, we would not go out into the sunlight again nor see any living person other than ourselves until the tenth of Elgamoir, when we would begin our ascent.

I was not surprised to see that Kilarion the Builder had been chosen. He was the biggest of us by far, and the strongest: a little slow-witted except when it came to his own trade, but a good man to have with you in a difficult spot. The selection of Jaif the Singer pleased me also, for he was calm-natured, steadfast, and reliable. But why had the

Masters given us sly, slippery little Kath, of the House of
Advocates? Kath was good at talking, yes, but what use
would a glib tongue be on the slopes of the Wall? Or
someone as hot-blooded and impulsive as Stapp of Judges,
in such a dangerous environment? Naxa the Scribe too: why
had they picked him? He was clever, nearly as clever as
Traiben, but he was pedantic and obnoxious and there was
no one who liked him. And then there were a few others—
Thuiman of the Metalworkers, Dorn of the House of
Clowns, Narril the Butcher—who were decent enough
sorts but of no particular distinction or merit, and they
would not have been among my first choices if I had been a
Master. And Muurmut of the Vintners, a tall, stubborn,
red-faced man, tough-willed and full of strong opinions
but often wrong-headed and rash—would he be any asset
to a group such as ours? But Traiben's words of years before
still burned in my mind. We Pilgrims were not necessarily
the finest that the village had to offer. Some of us might
have been sent to the Wall simply to get rid of us. I might be
one of those myself, for all I knew.

During our time in Pilgrim Lodge we twenty men
were kept apart, as always, from the twenty women in the
adjoining chamber. That was hard, going so long without
mating: since my fourteenth year I hadn't known more
than a few days of abstinence, and here we were condemned
to half a year of it. But the years of training had so annealed
my soul that I was able to handle even that.

At first we had no idea who our female counterparts in
the other chamber might be. But then Kath found a
speaking-hole that linked one chamber to the other, high
up on the wall in the dark storeroom in the rear of the
lodge, and by standing three men high, Kilarion with Jaif
on his shoulders and Kath on Jaif's, we were able to make
contact with the women on the other side. Thus I learned
that my robust old friend Galli was among the Forty, and
delicate narrow-eyed Thissa, she whose skill was for witchcraft, and the remote and moody woman called Hendy,

who fascinated me because in childhood she had been stolen away to our neighbor village of Tipkeyn and had not returned to us until her fourteenth year. And the sweet Tenilda of the Musicians, and Stum of the Carpenters, and Min the Scribe, all of them old friends of mine, and some others, like Grycindil the Weaver and Marsiel the Grower, who I did not know at all.

We waited out our time. It was like being in prison. We did some things of which it would not be proper for me to speak, for only those who are about to be Pilgrims may know of them. But most of the time we were idle. That is the nature of the time in Pilgrim Lodge. Mainly it is a time of waiting. We had exercise rungs in Pilgrim Lodge, and used them constantly. To amuse ourselves in the long dull hours we speculated on the nature of the meals that came through the slots in the doors twice a day, but it was always the same, gruel and beans and grilled meat. There was never any wine with it, nor gaith-leaves to chew.

We sang. We paced like caged beasts. We grew restless and listless. "It's the final test," Traiben explained. "If any of us snaps during this period of confinement, someone from the Thirty will be brought in to replace him. It's the last chance to see whether we are worthy of making the climb."

"But anyone brought in now would have to know that he's a replacement," I objected. "So he'd be a second-class Pilgrim, wouldn't he?"

"I think it rarely happens that anyone is brought in," said Traiben.

And in fact we held our own, and even went from strength to strength, as the final weeks of our time in Pilgrim Lodge ticked away. Impatient as I was to begin my Pilgrimage, I remember attaining at the same time a kind of cool serenity that carried me easily through the last days, and if you ask me how one can be impatient and serene at the same time I can give you no real answer, except to say that perhaps only one who is a member of the Forty is capable of such a thing. I even lost track of the days, toward the end. So did we all, all but Naxa, who was marking out the time in some private Scribe-like way of his, and who announced at last, "This is the ninth day of Elgamoir."

"The eighth, I make it to be," said Traiben mildly.

"Well, then, so even the brilliant Traiben can be wrong once in a while," said Naxa in triumph. "For I tell you by the beard of Kreshe that this is the ninth, and tomorrow we will be on Kosa Saag."

Traiben looked disgruntled, and muttered something to himself. But that night when the slots in the doors opened and our dinner-trays were pushed through, we saw bowls of steaming hammon and great slabs of roasted kreyl and tall pitchers of the foaming golden wine of celebration, and we knew that Naxa's count of days had been right and Traiben for once was in error, for this was the feast of Departure that they had brought us and in the morning our Pilgrimage would at last commence.

5

THE FINAL RITE OF our stay in Pilgrim Lodge took place at dawn: the Sacrifice of the Bond. We were all awake and waiting when the slots opened for the last time and a beautiful young grezbor came wriggling through, a sleek pink-hoofed one with dazzling white wool, not your ordinary farm grezbor but one of the prized pure-bred ones of the temples. After it, on a golden tray, came the silver knife of the Bond.

We knew what we were supposed to do. But in the face of the actual fact we looked uneasily at each other. The grezbor seemed to think it was all a game, and went trotting around from one of us to another, nuzzling against our knees, accepting our caresses. Then Narril picked up the knife and said, "Well, considering that it's a skill of my House—"

"No," said Muurmut brusquely. "Not a Butcher, not for this. We need some style here."

And he took the knife from Narril before Narril realized what was happening, and held it aloft, and waved it solemnly toward this side of the room and that one.

"Bring me the animal," he said in a deep, dramatic tone.

I gave him a contemptuous look. Muurmut seemed both foolishly pompous and grandly impressive, but rather more pompous than grand. Still, the Sacrifice had to be carried out, and he had taken possession of the rite, and that was all there was to it. Kilarion and Stum grabbed the poor beast and brought it to Muurmut, who stood very tall in the center of the room. Muurmut turned the knife so that it glinted in the light of the window overhead and said in a rich formal voice, "We offer up the life of this creature now as a bond between us, that we should all love one another as we set forth in our high endeavor." Then he spoke the words of the slaughtering-prayer as any Butcher might have done and made a swift cut with the knife. A line of crimson blossomed from the throat of the grezbor. It was a good clean killing: I give Muurmut credit for that much. I saw Traiben look away; and I heard a quick little gasp of dismay from Hendy.

Then Muurmut held the body forward and we came toward it one by one, and dipped our fingers in the blood and smeared it on our cheeks and forearms as the tradition required, and we swore to love one another in the ordeal ahead. Why must we do this? I wondered. Did they fear we would become enemies on the mountain, without the oath? But we rubbed the blood on each other as though it was really needed. And in time I would come to see that indeed it had been.

"Look," Jaif said. "The doors—"

Yes. They were swinging open now.

I felt nothing, nothing at all, as I came forth from Pilgrim Lodge that morning and stepped forward into the Procession. I had spent too much of my life waiting for this moment; the moment itself had become incomprehensible.

Of course there was plenty of *sensation*. I remember the blast of hot moist air as I came through the doorway, and the fierce light of Ekmelios jabbing me in the eyes, and the sharp bitter smell of thousands of damp sweaty bodies. I heard the singing and the chanting and the music. I saw the faces of people I knew in the viewing-stand just opposite the roundhouse of the Returned Ones, where Traiben and I had been sitting eight years before on that day when we first vowed that we would achieve the Pilgrimage. But though a million individual details struck my senses and engraved themselves permanently upon my memory, none of it had any meaning. I had been locked up; now I was coming out into town; and I was about to go for a walk.

A walk, yes.

Because I was of the House of the Wall, I was the first one out of the Lodge and I was the one who would lead the group of Pilgrims in the Procession: naturally Wall always goes first, Singers second, then Advocates, Musicians, Scribes, and so on in the prescribed order that was set down thousands of years ago. Traiben, because he was of the Wall also, walked just behind me: he had felt too shy at the last to want to be first. Beside me on the right was the only woman of my House who had been chosen, Chaliza of Moonclan. I had never liked her much and we didn't look at each other now.

Procession Street in front of me was empty. Everyone else had passed through already, the heads of the Houses and the double-lifers and the Returned Ones and the jugglers and musicians and all the rest. I put one foot in front of the other and set out down the street toward the center of town, toward the plaza with the bright-leaved szambar tree, toward the road to Kosa Saag.

My mind was empty. My spirit was numb. I felt nothing, nothing at all.

THE HEADS OF ALL the Houses were waiting in the plaza, ringing the szambar tree. As tradition required, I went to each one in turn, touching the tips of my hands to theirs and getting little smudges of blood on them: first Meribail, the head of my own House, and then Sten of Singers, Galtin of Advocates, and so on in the proper order. Our kinsmen were there to pay their farewells, also. I embraced my mother, who seemed to be very far away. She spoke vaguely of the day when she had stood by the same scarlet-leaved tree to say goodbye to my father as he was about to set out on the Pilgrimage from which he did not return. Beside her was my mother's brother, he who had raised me like a father, and all he had to say to me now was, "Remember, Poilar, the Wall is a world. The Wall is a universe." Well, yes, so it is, Urillin; but I would have preferred some warmer words than those, or at least something more useful.

When we had finished the circuit of the szambar tree and had spoken with all those who waited there to see us off, we were far around to the other side of the plaza, looking toward the mountain road. The golden carpets had been laid, stretching on and on and on like a river of molten metal. The sight of them broke through my trance at last: a shiver went down my middlebone and I thought for a moment I would start to weep. I looked toward Chaliza. Her face was wet with the shining streaks of tear-trails. I smiled at her and nodded toward the mountain.

"Here we go," I said.

And so we went upward into the land of dreams, into the place of secrets, the mountain of the gods.

Step and step and step and step. You take one, and another, and another and another, and that is how you climb. From all sides we heard cheers of encouragement, shouts of praise, the clangor of jubilant music. The shouts came even from behind us, where the candidates who had not stayed the course humbly walked, as the tradition requires, carrying our baggage. I glanced back once and was amazed to see how many of them there were. Thousands, yes. Eyes gleaming with our reflected glory. Why were they not bitter and envious? Thousands of them, whose candidacies had failed: and we alone, we few, had won the prize that all had sought.

Everyone knows the lower reaches of the road. The

ancient white paving-stones are smooth and wide and the palisade lining the road is bright with yellow banners. Taking care to walk only on the golden carpet of honor, we passed through the heart of the town and down into the place where the road descends a little before it turns sharply upward again; and then we were at Roshten Gate, where the guards stood saluting us, and one by one we touched our hands to the Roshten milepost to mark our departure from the village and the real beginning of our ascent. I still led the way, although we no longer held strict formation and Kilarion and Jaif and some of the others came up to walk beside me. Already the air seemed fresher and cooler, though we had hardly begun to climb.

Kosa Saag filled the entire sky in front of us.

You hardly perceive that it is a mountain, once you are on it. It becomes the world. You have no sense of its height. It is simply a wall, *the* Wall, a wall that stands between you and the unknown regions of the world on the other side. And after a time you cease to think of it as something vertical. It unfolds before you as a long winding road, going on and on and on and generally not rising as steeply before you as you might expect, and you take it one step at a time without thinking of all that lies ahead of you, for you know that if you allow yourself to think of anything more than the next step, and maybe the one after that, you will lose your mind.

We went quickly through the mileposts we all knew: Ashten, Glay, Hespen, Sennt. Certainly every one of us had been up this far at some time or other at holiday times when the Wall is open for the sacred ceremonies in honor of He Who Climbed, and probably we had all come sneaking up here on our own now and then as Galli and I had done. At each milepost marker there was a little prayer to say, since each is sacred to some particular god. But we paused as briefly as we could to get these said, and moved along. As we went up I looked over at Galli, and she grinned at me as if to tell me that she too remembered the time we had come this way together as children, and had made the Changes on the bed of moss back of Hithiat. Thinking of that day now, I remembered the feel of Galli's breasts in my hands and the wriggling of her tongue in my mouth and I wondered if she would want to play a few Changes with me that night when we camped. For it was half a year since I had had a mating, and in my mood just then I could have done Changes with all twenty of the women of our Pilgrimage without pausing to catch my breath.

But we had more climbing to do, first.

It was all easy and familiar. The Wall road below Hithiat is kept in good repair and the grade is gentle, as mountain roads go; and as I have said we had all been up here many times. We moved along at a good steady clip, joking and laughing, pausing now and then at the lookout points to see the village becoming ever tinier below us. If the laughter was occasionally louder than the jokes seemed to merit, well, so be it: we were excited and eager, and the mountain air, already fresher than the muggy air of the village, exhilarated us. I remember one of the women— Grycindil the Weaver, I think it was, or perhaps it was Stum the Carpenter—coming up alongside me and saying gleefully, "Suppose they lied to us, and the road is this easy all the way to the top! Suppose we're at the Summit by tomorrow afternoon, Poilar! How fine that would be!"

I had been wondering the same thing myself: Is this all there is to it? Will it be no harder than this, right to the Summit?

"Yes, how fine that would be," I said to her. And we laughed in that over-hearty manner that we had fallen into to hide our fears. But I knew in my heart that the road would grow more difficult before very long, and that very likely within a few days we would discover that there was no more road at all, only the steep harsh face of the Wall that we would have to scale in utmost hardship. And she, I think, knew it also.

•   •   •

AT DENBAIL MILEPOST CAME the business of receiving our gear from our carriers. We stood just beyond the edge of the ceremonial carpet and the defeated candidates who had borne our things this far reached forward—for they were forbidden to set foot on the uncarpeted paving-stones of the upper road—and handed our packs across to us. Mine was being carried by a woman of the Jugglers named Streltsa with whom I had mated once or twice in an earlier year. She stood well back from the carpet's edge and leaned far over to pass it to me, and as I reached for it she laughed and drew it back, so that I had to strain awkwardly toward her to get it. My bad leg failed me and I began to topple, though I righted myself before I fell. While I was still off balance she caught me with her left hand and pulled me toward her and bit me on the side of the neck, hard enough to draw blood.

"For luck!" she cried. Her eyes were wild. She had drugged herself with gaith.

I spat at her. She had forced me to step back onto the carpet, which was anything but lucky. But Streltsa only laughed again and made a kiss at me in mid-air. I snatched my pack from her and she air-kissed me again. Then she reached down into her bodice and pulled something out and tossed it to me. By reflex I snatched it with a quick grab before it fell.

It was a little carved idol made of white bone: Sandu Sando the Avenger. His eyes were bright green jewels and he was in full Change, with his penis rising erect out of his thighs like a tiny hatchet. I glared at Streltsa and started to hurl it over the side of the parapet, but then I heard her little cry of shock and fear and I stopped myself before I had thrown it. I saw her trembling. She was gesturing to me: *take it, keep it.* I nodded, suddenly afraid amidst my anger. Streltsa turned and ran back down the path. Then the anger returned and I would have run after her and flung her down the mountain if I had not been able to gain control of myself in time.

Thissa the Witch had seen the whole thing. She dabbed at the blood on my neck.

"She loves you," Thissa whispered. "She knows she will never see you again."

"She will," I said. "And when I come back, I'll tie her down naked in the plaza and put her through the Changes with her own filthy little idol."

Color rose in Thissa's delicate cheeks. She shook her head in horror and made a quick Witch-sign at me, and took the Avenger from my nerveless hands and tucked him deep into my pack.

"Take care not to lose it," she said. "It will protect us all. There are many evils ahead of us." And she kissed me to calm me, for I was shivering with fury and with fright.

It was not a good way to have begun the journey.

Our bearers now were gone, and only we of the Forty remained. The uncarpeted road here was far rougher than it had been just outside town—the paving-stones had been laid down an immensely long time ago and they were cracked and tilted at crazy angles—and I knew from my climb long ago with Galli that it would get rougher yet, very soon. The packs were crushingly heavy: we carried in them enough food to last for weeks and as much camping equipment as we could manage to haul, aware that there would be no way to obtain any as we climbed. Beyond Denbail too, the road doubles back into a fold of the Wall and curves around to a side from which the village is no longer visible, which gave us all a powerful sense of having broken the last tie with our home and gone floating off into the empty sky. But it was at Hithiat milepost that the real strangeness began.

We reached it in late afternoon and by common unspoken decision halted to consider the thing that was next to be done.

It was time to choose a leader. We all knew that. They had told us in the training sessions that we were to elect a leader as soon as we were beyond Hithiat, because without one we would be a serpent with many heads, each yearning to go in the direction it preferred and no two agreeing.

There was an uneasy moment, just as there had been at the time of the Sacrifice of the Bond, when no one was quite sure of how to go about doing what was necessary to do. I remembered how Muurmut had seized the moment and made himself its master, and I was not going to let him do that again here.

"Well," I said. "My House is the House of the Wall. This is the place of my House. I've waited all my life to reach this place. Stay with me and I'll take you to the Summit."

"Are you nominating yourself, Crookleg?" Muurmut asked, so I knew right away there would be trouble with him.

I nodded.

"Seconded," said Traiben.

"You're of his House," said Muurmut. "You can't second him."

"Seconded, then," said Jaif the Singer.

"Seconded," said Galli, who was of the Vintners, Muurmut's own House.

Everyone was silent a moment.

Then Stapp of Judges said, "If Poilar can nominate himself, so can I." He looked around. "Who seconds me?" Someone snickered. "Who seconds me?" Stapp said again, and his face began to go puffy and hot with anger.

"Why don't you second yourself too, Stapp?" Kath said.

"Why don't you be quiet?"

"Who are you telling to be—"

"You," Stapp said. Kath raised his arm, not necessarily in a menacing way, and an instant later Stapp came jumping forward, ready to fight. Galli caught him by the middle and pulled him back to his place in the circle.

"The Bond," Thissa whispered. "Remember the Bond!" She looked pained by the threat of violence among us.

"Does anyone second Stapp?" I asked.

But no one did. Stapp turned away and stared at the Wall above us. I waited.

Thuiman of the Metalworkers said, "Muurmut."

"You nominate Muurmut?"

"Yes."

I had expected that. "Seconds?"

Seppil the Carpenter and Talbol the Leathermaker seconded him. I had expected that too. They were very thick, those three.

"Muurmut is nominated," I said. You will notice how I had already taken charge, here in the time before the choosing. I meant nothing evil by it. It is my way, to lead; someone has to, even when no leader has been appointed. "Are there any other nominations?" There were none. "Then we vote," I said. "Those who are for Poilar, walk to this side. Those who are for Muurmut, over there."

Muurmut gave me a sour look and said, "Shouldn't we set forth our qualifications before the voting, Poilar?"

"I suppose we should. What are yours, Muurmut?"

"Two straight legs, for one thing."

It was cheap of him, and I would have struck him down then and there except that I knew I could turn this to better advantage by holding my temper. So I simply smiled, not a warm smile. But Seppil the Carpenter guffawed as though he had never heard anyone say anything funnier. Talbol the Leathermaker, who was not the sort to stoop to such stuff, managed a sickly little grunt as his best show of solidarity with Muurmut.

"Yes, very pretty legs," I said, for Muurmut's legs were thick and hairy. "If a leader must think with his legs, then yours are surely superior to mine."

"A leader must climb with his legs."

"Mine have taken me this far," I said. "What else do you have to recommend your candidacy?"

"I know how to command," said Muurmut. "I give orders which others are willing to follow, because they are the correct orders."

"Yes. You say, 'Put the grapes in this tub,' and you say, 'Crush them in such-and-such a fashion,' and you say, 'Now put the juice in the casks and let it turn into wine.' Those are very fine orders, so far as they go. But how do they fit you to command a Pilgrimage? The way you mock my leg, which is as it is through no fault of mine, doesn't indicate much understanding of someone you have sworn in blood to love, does it, Muurmut? And if a leader is deficient in understanding, what kind of leader is he?"

Muurmut was glaring at me as though he would gladly have heaved me from the mountain.

"Perhaps I shouldn't have said what I did about the leg. But how will it be for you in the dangerous places, Poilar? When you're climbing, will you also be able to think clearly about the things a leader must think about, when every step you take is hampered by your infirmity? When the change-fires begin to assail us, will you be strong enough to defend us against them?"

"I have no infirmity," I said. "All I have is a crooked leg." I would with great pleasure have kicked him with it too, but I restrained myself. "As for the change-fires, we don't as yet know whether they're real or myth. But if they're real, why, then, each of us must do his own defending, and those who are too weak to resist their temptations will fall by the wayside and turn into monsters, and the rest of us will go onward toward the gods. That is the Way, as I understand it. Do you have any other qualifications to put forth on behalf of your election, Muurmut?"

"We should hear yours, I think."

Quietly I said, glancing from one to another of my fellow Pilgrims, "The gods have chosen me to bring you to the Summit. You all know that. In a single night every one of you dreamed the dream that I dreamed, in which I was designated. You know that I can lead, and that I can think clearly, and that I am strong enough to climb. I will bring you to the Summit if only you follow me. Those are my qualifications. Enough of this talk: I call for the vote."

"Seconded," said Jaif.

"Seconded again," said Thissa softly.

And so we voted. Muurmut and Seppil and Talbol stood to one side, and all the others moved across the circle to me, three or four of them very quickly, then another few after a little hesitation, and then, in a general rush, everyone who was left. Even Thuiman, who had nominated Muurmut, deserted him. So it was done. Muurmut made no effort to disguise his fury. I thought for a moment he would attack me in his rage, and I was ready for him. I would hook my crooked leg behind his good one and throw him to the ground, and seize him by the feet and spin him around and press his face into the stony ground until he submitted to me.

But none of that was necessary. He had better sense than to lift his hand against me in front of the others, and in any case he could see the one-sidedness of the vote. So he came over grudgingly to offer me his hand afterward with the rest. His smile was false and his mien was sullen, though, and I knew that he would let no opportunity pass to displace me, if he could.

"Very well," I said. "I thank you for your support, all of you. And now we must talk of what lies ahead." I looked around. "Who among us has been beyond Hithiat?" I asked.

I heard nervous laughter. We had all come this far during our training, and most of us had gone up the Wall on our own once or twice out of sheer mischief, perhaps as high as Denbail, even to Hithiat. But no one goes beyond Hithiat if he has any sense. Still, I thought it was a useful thing to ask, though I expected no reply.

To my surprise Kilarion put up his hand and said, "I have. I've been to Varhad to see the ghosts."

All eyes turned to him. The big man smiled, enjoying the attention his boast had earned him. Then someone laughed again, and others took it up, and Kilarion's face darkened like the sky before a storm. The moment was suddenly very tense.

"Go on," I said. "We're all waiting to hear."

"I went to Varhad. I saw the ghosts and did the Changes with one. Anyone doesn't believe me, he can fight me," Kilarion said, drawing himself up even taller. And he clenched his fists and stared from side to side.

"No one doubts you, Kilarion," I said. "But tell us when it was that all this happened."

"When I was a boy, with my father. Every boy in my clan comes up here with his father when he turns twelve. Axeclan is my clan." He was still glowering. "You think I'm lying, do you? Wait and see what's in store for you up ahead."

"That's what we want you to tell us," I said. "You know and we don't."

"Well," he said, suddenly ill at ease and uncertain of himself. "There are ghosts. And white rocks. And the trees are—well, they're ugly." He paused. He was groping for words. "It's a bad place. Everything moves around. There's a smell in the air."

"What kind of smell?" I asked. "What do you mean, everything moves around?"

"A bad smell. And things—move. I don't know. They just move."

Poor thickbrained Kilarion! I looked over at Traiben and saw him fighting to smother laughter. I shot him an angry glance. Patiently I asked Kilarion again what Varhad was like, and he replied just as fuzzily as before. "A bad place," he muttered. "A very bad place." And that was all we got from him. So whatever he might have learned up there would be of no use to us. The little that he told us was enough to make us decide to make camp at the level of Hithiat on our first evening, though, and wait until morning before going on into the unknown reaches of the Wall above us.

Thus it was that I found myself back at that mossy field where Galli and I had enjoyed each other long ago. But there were no Changes played that night, despite all the pent-up desire that had accumulated in us in our half a year in Pilgrim Lodge. Sometimes desire can build to a point where there is no easy way to express it, and that was how it was for all of us that first night. We had been apart so long that it seemed too great a thing to break the abstinence so soon. And so the twenty men camped to one side of the field, and the twenty women on the other. We might just as well have been in our separate halves of Pilgrim Lodge.

I think none of us slept well that night. From higher on the mountain came sharp hooting cries that trailed off into terrible screeches, and sometimes the ground rumbled beneath us as if Kosa Saag meant to hurl us with a single casual shrug into the distant valley. A mist as cold as death slipped down from somewhere and wrapped itself over us as we lay. I wondered if it was the change-fire, rising up out of the ground to tempt me into taking on some strange new form. But I looked down at myself and I was still who I had been, so I knew that we had nothing to fear yet from that direction. And I slipped into a light doze.

In the middle of the night, though, I awakened and suddenly felt the thirst of the damned take hold of me, and I rose and walked to the little stream that ran through the middle of our moss-patch. When I knelt to drink, I saw my face reflected in the water by moonlight all twisted and distorted, which frightened me, and I saw something else too, a glitter in the stream-bed, as of red eyes looking up at me. It seemed to me they were the eyes of Streltsa who had bitten me at Denbail milepost, and they were weeping blood. Quickly I jumped back and whispered a whole string of prayers to every god I could remember, one after another.

Then I looked across through the mists and I saw the strange woman Hendy up and walking about amidst the sleeping women. For a moment desire stirred in my loins, and I thought how good it would be to go to her and sing the song of mating to her and pull her down in the moss with me. But Hendy was a stranger to me, nor had anyone I knew ever spoken of mating with her either, and this hardly seemed a fit time to approach her for such a thing. I had already been bitten once this day. We stared at each other in the mist, and Hendy's face was like stone. After a time I turned away and went back to my bedroll, and lay face up on it without moving. The mist opened and the stars appeared. I trembled beneath their light and put my hands over my manhood to protect it. Though the stars are gods, not all of them are benevolent ones. They say that the light of some stars does good magic, but the light of other stars is poison, and I had no idea which stars might be above me that night. I longed for morning to come. It was a thousand years in coming.

6

ABOVE HITHIAT LIE THE ghost-realms, where—so
we had been taught—certain Houses of our village
had dwelled long ago, until they angered the gods in
some fashion and were forced to abandon their homes.
During our training our teachers had told us a little of what
had happened then, how the part of the mountain where
these ancient folk lived had become less and less hospitable
each year and the people who lived there had had to relin-
quish their settlements little by little as conditions wors-
ened, moving steadily to lower zones until no one dwelled
on the mountain at all any longer and our race was entirely
confined to life in its lowland valley. But we were not
prepared for the deathly look of the place, or the strangeness of it—any of us but Kilarion, and I think even he had
forgotten how frightful a place it was.

The road here was broken and dangerous. At least it
was a road, though; later on we would have no such luxury.
But the paving-stones were split and broken and lifted at
angles so that in some areas it would have been better to
have none at all, and more than once we crossed a region

where swift streams had cut deep gullies away under the path so that the paving-stones were balanced over emptiness and seemed ready to crack beneath our feet and drop us into an abyss. We fastened prongs to ropes and threw them across to the far side to anchor them in the earth, and crossed with care, clinging to the ropes. Some of us were shivering with fright at every step. But the fragile roadway somehow held together.

The air was changing too. We had expected it to get cooler as we went higher, but in this zone it was oddly hot and moist and dank, more so than on the hottest lowland day. No rain fell, but billowing bursts of wet steam issued noisily from vents in the flank of the mountain. The steam had a sour, sulphurous smell that utterly pervaded the atmosphere, just as Kilarion had warned. Everything was rotten and mildewed here. Pale spores floated in the air. Things grew on things. Dense beards of white mossy fungus coated the whole landscape. We went lurching through it, for there was no avoiding it, and it tangled itself around our legs and hands and made us choke and sneeze. The trees were wrapped in thick sheets of this stuff that trembled in the wind so that the trees themselves seemed to be shaking. They looked like the ghosts of trees. The rocks too were fouled with this deathly moss. Their surfaces quivered like live things, or like dead things that could not hold still. I thought I understood now what Kilarion had meant when he said, "Everything moves around."

The Wall itself seemed to be rotting. When you touched it with your fingertip it crumbled, that was how soft the stone was. There were caves everywhere, some of them very deep—dark mysterious holes leading into the heart of the great mountain. We looked into them but of course could see nothing and did not choose to investigate.

There was a constant fall of little pebbles, and sometimes larger things, that had rubbed loose from the higher regions. Now and again we would hear a great rattling and thudding from above and chunks of rock bigger than our heads would come bounding down. Some fell very close indeed to us. The crumbling went on all the time, a steady loss of substance, so that I began to imagine that Kosa Saag must have been ten times as big a million years ago as it was now, and that in another million years it would have crumbled away into something no bigger than a stick.

An hour or so above Hithiat we encountered the first ghosts.

We were no longer walking along a narrow strip on the edge of the mountain but now were on a flat, broad outcropping that was almost like a plateau, though a slight sense of strain told us that we were continuing to climb with every step. Finally we came to Varhad milestone, the last of the series. It was weathered and worn, no more than a splinter of black rock with a few barely legible letters visible on its moss-encrusted surface.

At this level the air was thicker and more moist than ever and its smell was abominable. In the rocky, foggy meadows on our left-hand side we discovered the ruins of the abandoned settlements. The ancient inhabitants of this region had lived in narrow tapering huts made of long slabs of pink stone set into the ground on an inward lean and covered above with thatching. The thatching had long since rotted away, all but a few bleached strands, and the jagged stone slabs were festooned with shrouds of the white fungus. There were groups of these tottering houses, ten or fifteen in each little group, clustered every few hundred paces apart. They were frightening to behold: decayed, dismal, forlorn. The ruined houses looked like funeral monuments. Truly we had entered a village of the dead.

"This is where the ghosts are," Kilarion told us.

But we saw no ghosts anywhere about, and Kilarion grew red-faced and insistent when Naxa the Scribe and Kath the Advocate jeered at him as a tale-teller. His shape began to flutter as his rage mounted; his face became round and meaty and his neck shrank into his shoulders. The dispute got hotter and hotter until suddenly Kilarion gathered little Kath up under his arm like a bundle of dirty clothes and rushed with him toward the brink of the cliff, as though intending to hurl him over. Kath squalled like a beast being dragged to slaughter. We all shouted in alarm but none of us was in a position to stop him except Galli. As Kilarion went lurching past her Galli caught him by his free arm and swung him around with all her considerable strength, so that he lost his grip on Kath and went slamming into one of the ruined huts that stood nearby. He hit it so hard that the cluster of stone slabs fell apart and went toppling over.

Half a dozen strange pallid creatures had been hiding in the hut. They sprang up now, terrified, and began to caper about in wild circles, flapping their arms like birds. I suppose they were hoping to be able to fly away from us. But all they had were arms, not wings.

"Those are the ghosts!" someone screamed. "The ghosts! The ghosts!"

I had never seen such horrid sights. They had the shape of men, but were very long and thin, more like walking skeletons than live people, and they were covered from head to foot with strands of the white fungus that infested this entire zone. It had woven itself into their hair, it ran along their limbs like a garment, bunches of it jutted from their mouths and ears and nostrils. With every movement they made they released clouds of spores, which caused us to back away in fright, fearing that we would breathe them in and be contaminated by the terrible stuff that sprouted from them.

But these folk evidently wanted no more to do with us than we with them. It took them some few moments to overcome their terror, and then they turned and scampered up into some hillocks beyond their huts, leaving a thinning residue of spores in the air behind them. We covered our faces with our hands, scarcely daring to draw a breath.

"You see?" Kilarion said, after a time, when it seemed safe to put down our hands and move along. "Did I lie to you? This place is full of ghosts. They are the spirits of the old villagers that this white mossy stuff has conjured up."

"And you say you made the Changes with one of them?" Kath asked in a stinging tone. He had recovered now from his fright, and red blotches of anger glowed in his cheeks. "Were you so lustful when you were a boy, Kilarion, that you would do the Changes with something like that?"

"She was only partly a ghost," said Kilarion, looking aggrieved. "She was young and very beautiful, and there was just a little of the white stuff on her."

"A beautiful ghost!" Kath said scathingly, and we all laughed.

Kilarion grew red again. He glared at Kath and I got myself ready to interfere in case he was having any thoughts of making a second try at throwing Kath over the edge of the cliff. But Tenilda the Musician said something soft to him that soothed him and he growled and turned aside.

I could see that Kilarion, like Muurmut, might be a problem. He was slow of thought but easy to anger, a bad combination, and enormously strong besides. We would have to handle him with some care.

The ghosts we had frightened were watching us from a distance, peeping out from behind the mossy hillocks. But they ducked down shyly whenever they saw us looking at them. We continued on.

THERE WERE OTHER CLUSTERS of ruined huts ahead. All of them were tightly wrapped in the shroud-fungus. Everything here was. A more dismal landscape would be hard to imagine: white, silky, bleak. The trees, small and crooked and practically leafless, were almost entirely swathed. Patches of old dead fungus lay everywhere underfoot, forming a sort of white crust that crunched as we stepped on it. Even the Wall, which here lay far to our left, had a whitish glint as though the fungus had taken possession of great sections of it also.

Now and again we would see more ghosts flitting

about on the hillsides. The elongated wraithlike beings were too timid ever to come near us, but ran back and forth on the slopes, trailing long streamers of their fungus-shrouds behind them.

To Traiben I said, "What are these ghosts, do you think? Pilgrims, are they? Who never went any further up the mountain, but became infested with this white fungus and had to remain down here where it lives?"

He shrugged. "That could be. But I suspect otherwise. What I think is that this region never was abandoned by the ancient settlers, despite the things our teachers told us."

"You mean what we're encountering are the descendants of the very people who built these huts long ago?"

"So I believe, yes. This was probably good farming land once. Then the shroud-stuff came and ruined it. But instead of fleeing, these people stayed. There must be a low level of change-fire here, that has worked a transformation on them of a sort, and now the fungus is a part of them. Perhaps it helps to keep them alive. There doesn't seem much to eat in this zone."

With a shudder I said, "And will it become a part of us the same way?"

"Very likely not, or there'd be no Returned Ones. Every Pilgrim who goes up the Wall and comes down again must pass through this district. But they don't bear the infestation." He gave me a somber grin. "Still, I think we would do well to wrap wet cloths over our faces to keep the spores away. And we should make our camp for the night in some happier place."

"Yes," I said. "That seems wise to me too."

We hurried on through this blighted land of ghosts with our heads down and our faces covered.

Ghosts followed us all the way, keeping well back from us. Some of them seemed more bold than the others, dancing up to us and whirling so that their shrouds swept out airily behind them, but we threw rocks at them to prevent them from coming close. After what we had seen and what Traiben had said, we all dreaded the fungus. It was all around us, impossible to avoid. I wondered if I had already taken it into my lungs. Perhaps it was hatching right now in some moist dark cavern of my body, seizing possession of my interior and soon to issue forth from my mouth and my nostrils. The thought sickened me and I went to the side of the road and violently heaved up everything that was in my stomach, praying that I might be heaving up any spores that were within me also.

Kilarion was proven a truth-teller once more before we left the ghost-land; for we even saw a ghost as beautiful as the one he had claimed he had made the Changes with, that time when he came up here with his father when he was a boy.

She appeared on a rocky ledge just above us and stood singing and crooning at us in an eerie, quavering voice. Like all her kind she was slender and very long-limbed, but just a faint coating of fungus covered her breasts and loins, and none was visible around her face. What little she had on her body gave her a sleek, satiny sheen and made her look soft to the touch, altogether appealing. Her eyes were golden and had a slight slant to them, and her features had a strange purity. A beautiful creature indeed, this ghost. She said something to us in soft, furry tones that we could not understand, and beckoned as if inviting us to come up and dance with her.

I saw Kilarion trembling. The muscles of his huge body bunched and heaved and cords stood out along his throat. He looked to her and there was a desperate expression in his eyes.

Perhaps this was the very ghost he had embraced here long ago. No doubt she still had some magic over his soul even now.

I kicked sharply at his leg to get his attention and pointed up ahead when he gave me an angry glance.

"Keep moving, Kilarion," I said.

"Who are you to tell me what to do?"

"Do you want to spend the rest of your life living in this place?"

He muttered something under his breath. But he understood what I was saying, and walked on, eyes averted.

After a time I looked back. The ghost-witch, for surely a witch of some kind was what she was, was still beckoning sinuously to us. But now, with the light coming from behind her, I was able to see the faint pale cloud of spores rising about her lovely head. She went on gesturing to us until we could no longer see her.

We marched grimly through that land of hot dank mists and quivering fungus shrouds and evil sulphurous stinks for hour after hour as the day waned. There seemed to be no end to it. But at last, toward nightfall, we emerged into a region where the air was clear and sweet and the rocks were free of fungus and the trees once more had leaves, and we gave thanks to Kreshe the Savior for our escape.

7

NOW WE WERE ABOVE the highest milestone whose name anyone still knew, entering territory that was completely unknown to any of us.

There was a sort of path here, but it was narrow and vague and erratic, and it seemed best, in the gathering darkness, not to try to go on this late in the day. So we made camp for our second night on the Wall. My mind was full of thoughts of the land of ghosts, of its sinister spores, its beckoning witches.

But then I put such thoughts aside. One does not get up the Wall by thinking of what is behind one, any more than by fretting about what lies ahead. You must live in the moment as you climb, or you will fail utterly.

We had camped in a kind of little earthen pocket in a sheer, steep gorge right on the lip of the Wall, which Kilarion had found by scrambling on ahead of the rest of us. The bare rock face of Kosa Saag rose almost vertically in a series of sharp parapets just in back of us, disappearing into the dimness overhead. We saw hairy gnomish faces peering down from out of those parapets, bright-eyed rock-apes of some sort, who jeered at us and tossed hand-fuls of pebbles at us. We ignored them.

On the other side of us lay a vastness of open air, with the lights of some distant village, not our own, sparkling like glitterflies far out in the black valley below. A little stony rim no higher than our knees provided a kind of natural barrier just at the edge of our campsite; beyond it was a straight drop into a pit of immeasurable darkness. There was a swift stream running across the corner of the gorge. A few strange trees grew beside it. They had spiral trunks, twisted like a screw, and stiff, angular upturned leaves; and from their boughs dangled a great many heavy fruits, a reddish blue in color. They were long and full like breasts that held milk, and were marked even by small protrusions like nipples at their lower ends. Little tufts of grass grew there also, purplish, with a knifeblade sharpness to them; otherwise the gorge was barren.

Thuiman, Kilarion, and Galli found some bits of dry wood along the canyon wall and built a sputtering fire. The rest of us unpacked our bedrolls and laid out our places for the night. We were all famished, for no one had wanted to pause for a midday meal in the land of ghosts. So we brought out cheese and dried meat, and some jugs of wine. I saw Marsiel of the House of Growers eyeing the breast-fruits on a tree overhanging our campsite with some inter-est and called out to her, "What do you think? Are they safe to eat?"

"Who knows? I've never seen anything like them."

She pulled one off, hefted it, squeezed it, finally slit its glossy skin with the nail of her forefinger. A reddish juice oozed from the break. She shrugged. Tossing it from one hand to the other, she looked around at the rest of us.

"Does anybody here want to taste it?"

We all stared, not knowing what to do.

They had warned us in our training that we would be able to carry with us only enough food to last us for the first few weeks of the climb, and then after that we would have to live on whatever we might find. And the things we found were not likely to be familiar to us. Well, we were resigned to the necessity of eating unknown things sooner or later. But how could we tell what was edible and what was poisonous?

Traiben said, "Give it here, Marsiel. I'll try a bite."

"No," I said at once. "Wait. Don't do it, Traiben."

"Somebody has to," he said. "Do you want to?"

"Well—"

"Then I will."

"Are you afraid, Poilar?" Muurmut called. "Why? What are you afraid of? It's only a piece of fruit!" And he laughed. But I noticed that he made no offer to take it from Traiben and try it himself.

It was a dilemma. Of course I had no wish to see my closest friend eat poison and fall down dead before my eyes. But I was afraid to bite into the fruit myself. So were we all; we wanted to live. That was only normal caution. But Traiben was right: *someone* had to taste it. If I was unwilling to do it, then he would. There is a line between caution and downright fear, and I had crossed it just then. I could not remember ever having been so cowardly in anything before.

Sick with shame, I watched as Traiben pulled the fruit apart where Marsiel had broken its skin. He scooped out a small mound of orange pulp and swallowed it without hesitation.

"Sweet," he said. "Good. Very good."

He took a second mouthful, and a third, and nodded to show his pleasure.

"Let me have some," Kilarion said.

"And me," said Thuiman.

"No, wait, all of you!" I shouted. "How can you know so soon that the fruit is safe? Suppose it has a poison in it that takes an hour to act, or two? We have to see what happens to Traiben. If he's still well in the morning, then we can all have some."

There was some grumbling. But generally everyone agreed that what I had said was wise.

I went over to Traiben afterward and said quietly, "That was crazy, what you did. What if you had curled up and died right on the spot?"

"Then I'd be dead. But I'm not, am I? And now we can be pretty sure that that fruit is good to eat. Which will be useful to know if we encounter a lot of it higher up."

"But you could have *died*," I said.

He gave me one of his patient all-enduring looks, as though I were some cranky child who needed to be seen through an attack of the colic.

"And if Chaliza had tasted the fruit in my place and she had died, or Thissa, or Jaif? Would that have been any better?"

"For you it would."

"For me, yes. But we are a group, Poilar. We are a Forty. And we all have to take turns tasting strange things when we find them, whatever the risks, or we'll surely starve in the upper reaches of the Wall. Do you understand why I did what I did? I have had my turn now. I've done my duty and I think that I'll survive it, and perhaps it'll be a long while before I need to risk myself again, for which I'm profoundly glad. But if I had refused the risk, how could I have expected others to take it for me? We need to think of the survival of the Forty, Poilar, and not only our own."

I felt doubly shamed now. I cringed within for the dishonor of it.

"How stupid of me not to see it," I said. "We are all one. We owe our lives each to the other."

"Yes."

"I wish now I had taken the fruit from you."

He grinned. "I don't. You still have your turn as taster ahead of you. I've survived mine."

He seemed smug about that. Which made me angry, after all my concern for him. But he had risked himself to taste the fruit and I had not. He has a right to his smugness, I told myself.

IT WAS NIGHT NOW. A chill came into the air and we thickened our skins against it, and sat huddling close together around the dying fire until there was nothing left but embers. One by one we began to go off to our bedrolls.

"Is that a Wall-hawk?" Tenilda asked suddenly.

We were standing near the rim of the gorge just then. She pointed into the abyss. I followed the line of her arm and saw a creature hovering out there in mid-air, a good-sized bird of some sort. It moved closer as I looked, coming so near that I could almost reach out and touch it. It seemed to be studying us.

The bird was a repellent-looking thing with a round shaggy body about the size of a child's, from which two powerful sets of golden talons jutted. Its bright yellow beak had the shape of a hooked knife, and its eyes were red and huge. Curving wings of skin, longer than a man's arms, held it aloft, beating fiercely. I saw claw-tipped spikes like little bony fingers protruding from their outer edges. I smelled the musky, acrid odor of its thick black fur and I could feel the cool wind coming from its wings. It did not dart about, but held itself in the same place in the air; save for those strenuous wingbeats it was utterly motionless, so that one might almost think it was dangling from a cord that descended from the sky.

I had seen Wall-hawks now and then swooping high over the valley, but never one at such close range. I had no doubt, though, that a Wall-hawk was what this ugly creature was. It did not seem big enough to be able to carry off a grown man, as the village fables said; but it looked dangerous all the same, devilish, malevolent. I stood as if frozen, staring at it in weird fascination. And it stared back with evident curiosity. Perhaps it had only come on a scouting mission, not to attack.

"Step aside, Poilar," said a voice behind me.

It was Kilarion. He had picked up a rock the size of his head and was making ready to throw it at the hovering bird. I heard him humming the death-song.

"No," I said. "Don't!"

He ignored me. Shouldering past me to the rim, he swung himself about in a half-circle, pivoting off his left knee, and hurled the rock upward and outward with all his tremendous strength. I would not have believed it was possible to throw so big a rock so far and so hard. It rose on a short arc and caught the Wall-hawk in its belly with a sharp thud. The bird let out a piercing shriek loud enough to have been heard down in the village and fell from sight, plummeting as if dead, a sudden swift descent; but as I leaned over the rim and peered down I thought I saw it make a recovery in the darkness below and go flapping out into the night. I was uncertain of that; but it seemed to me I heard its far-off angry screeching.

"Killed it!" Kilarion said, proudly preening himself and doing a little dance of self-congratulation.

"I'm not so sure," I said gloomily. "It'll be back. With others of its kind. You should have left it alone."

"It's an evil bird. A filthy, loathsome bird."

"Even so," I said. "There was no need for that. Who knows what trouble it will bring?"

Kilarion said something mocking and walked away, very pleased with himself. But I remained uneasy over what he had done, and I called aside Jaif and Galli and Kath and one or two others and suggested that we stand guard through the night, two of us at a time until morning came. It was a good idea. Galli and Kath stood first watch and I lay down to sleep, telling them to call me when my time of duty had come; but hardly had I closed my eyes, or so it seemed, but I felt Galli roughly tugging me awake, and I looked up to see the night astir with fiery red eyes wheeling above us like demons.

There were five or six hawks overhead, perhaps—or ten, or twenty, more likely; who had time to count? The air was thick with them. I saw their eyes; I felt their beating wings; I stared in dismay at their sharp, ravening beaks and talons. We were all up and defending ourselves with cudgels and stones now as they swept and swirled among us, furiously clawing us and biting us and screeching. They were like wild fiends. Kilarion carried one bird on each shoulder—they had singled him out, it seemed, as the one who had thrown the rock—and they struck at him with their talons again and again, flapping their great wings furiously, while he struggled to seize them by their ankles and pull them free of him. I went to his aid, cudgeling a hawk loose. It flew straight up when I hit it, squawking madly and swinging about to come at me, but I held it off with fierce swings of my stick. Kilarion meanwhile had ripped the other bird free of his flesh: I saw him smash it to the ground and bring his heel down on its chest. From far away on the other side of the stream I heard one of our women screaming. And I saw, by glinting moonlight, Traiben with a pile of stones stacked in front of him, snatching them up one by one and calmly hurling them with great accuracy toward any hawk that came near him. I had a glimpse of Hendy standing by herself, her head thrown back and her eyes gleaming strangely as she slowly swung a cudgel from side to side in a wide arc about her, though there were no hawks in her vicinity. Kath, meanwhile, had rekindled our fire, and was handing blazing torches out to several of us, who thrust them upward at the attackers.

Then it ended, as suddenly as it had begun. One of the hawks gave the command to retreat—it was unmistakable, a clear harsh honking cry that reverberated off the side of the Wall like the sound of a gallimond played in its highest register—and all of them took off at once in a great clatter of bare thrashing wings, screaming to the stars as they went. One snatched up a chain of sausages that we had left unfinished by the fireside at suppertime, and flew away with it. We saw the whole host of them for a moment outlined against the moonlit sky, and then they were gone, all but the one Kilarion had trampled, which lay dead near Marsiel's bedroll. She kicked it aside with a little cry of disgust, and Thuiman scooped it up on the end of a stick and tossed it over the rim of the gorge. In the silence, the sound of our rough breathing was loud as thunder. We were all stunned by the suddenness and fury of the attack, though it had been so brief: the Wall had given us only the merest hint of the torments it could offer, as if to put us on notice of the sufferings ahead.

"Is anyone hurt?" I asked.

Nearly all of us were, to some degree or other. Fesild of the Vintners was the worst. She had taken a long cut across her cheek that ran close to her eye, and another, very deep, on her left shoulder. Her face was all blood and her left arm was jerking as though it wanted to leap free of her body. Kreod, one of the three Healers among us, went to deal with her. Kilarion had been badly cut too, but he laughed his wounds off. Talbol had a slash the length of his arm, Gazin the Juggler a bright red set of crossmarks on his back, Grycindil a torn hand, and so on. The binding of wounds went on almost until morning. I myself had been bruised more than a little by wings but I had shed no blood.

Traiben counted us, and reported after a time that we were all accounted for. None of us had been carried off by the hawks: our only loss in that regard had been the chain of sausages. So the tales of how Wall-hawks would snatch unwary Pilgrims from the trail and devour them in their eyries were only fanciful myths, as I had always suspected. The hawks were simply not big enough to do such a thing. But they were troublesome birds all the same, and I knew we would have more grief from them higher up.

As the red light of rising Marilemma came into the sky, Kilarion squatted down beside me where I sat kneading my bruises and said in a quiet voice quite different from his usual one, "It was stupid of me to throw that rock, wasn't it, Poilar?"

"Yes. It was. I remember telling you something of that sort when you did it."

"But I saw the hawk hanging in the air and I hated it. I wanted to kill it, because it was so ugly."

"If you want to kill every ugly thing you see, Kilarion, it's a wonder you've allowed yourself to live so long. Or have you never seen yourself in a mirror?"

"Don't mock me," he said. His voice was still soft. "I told you, I think it was a stupid thing to do. I should have listened to you."

"Yes. You should."

"You always seem to be able to see what will happen before it happens. You knew that if I hit the hawk with the rock, it would come back with others of its kind and attack us."

"I suspected it might, yes."

"And earlier you made me keep moving, when I might have stopped and done the Changes with that ghost. You were right that time too: the ghost would have taken me. I would have become a ghost myself, if I had gone with her. But I was too stupid to see that for myself." He was staring bleakly at the ground, pushing pebbles around with his finger. I had never seen him so dejected. This was a different Kilarion: reflective, brooding.

I smiled and said, "Don't be so hard on yourself, Kilarion. Just try to think things through a little before you act, all right? You keep out of a lot of trouble if you get into the habit of doing that."

But still he stared down and pushed pebbles. Sadly he said, "You know, when we were picked, I was sure that I would be the leader of our Forty. I'm the strongest. I have great endurance and I know how to build things. But I'm not clever enough to lead, am I? The leadership has to go to someone like you. Traiben's even cleverer than you—he's cleverer than anyone—but he's not a leader. Neither is Muurmut, though he thinks he is. But you are, Poilar. From now on I'll follow whatever you tell me to do. And if you see me about to do something dumb, just say very quietly in my ear, *Wall-hawks, Kilarion.* Or *ghosts.* To remind me. Will you do that for me, Poilar?"

"If that's what you want, of course."

He looked up at me. His eyes seemed almost worshipful. It was embarrassing. I grinned and slapped him on the thigh and told him what an asset he was to us all. But secretly I was relieved. A stupid man who admits that he's stupid is far less of a danger to his comrades than one who doesn't. Perhaps Kilarion would be less of a problem than I had feared a little earlier. At the very least I would hold some ascendance over him for a while, until his stupidity came bursting through once again.

WE WASHED OURSELVES IN the cold little stream and had a morning meal of cold puffbread and moonmilk. It was necessary to help some of those who had been worst injured by the hawks. Since Traiben had not died during the night, nor so much as complained of feeling unwell, we ate some of the breast-fruits too—they were cool and sweet and tender—and stowed as many of them as we thought we could carry in our packs. Then we made ready to leave the gorge.

Getting out was harder than going in had been: the little ravine turned very narrow at its upper end and after another hundred paces unexpectedly terminated in a naked shield of rock that rose absolutely vertically as far as we could see. Kilarion, who had not gone all the way to this point when he had found the gorge for us the night before, was livid with chagrin. It was plain to him now that there was no road up; and he hopped about, stamping the ground and spitting in fury, like one who has been stung by a swarm of palibozos. "Wait," he said. "You all wait here." And off he ran back toward the entrance to our gorge, dropping his pack as he went.

We saw him minutes later, looking down and beckoning from one of the narrow parapets from which the rock-apes had jeered at us at twilight. He had found a path. We swung about and went the way he had gone, and he met us at the trailhead, which was an uninviting tumble of boulders that looked as though it led downward, not up. What impulse had led him to try it? It could not have been less promising. But it was the right way to go; and Kilarion glowed with satisfaction as he showed us how to circle a jagged little chimney-formation that marked the real start of the trail. He looked to me for approval, as if to say, See? See? I'm good for something after all! I nodded to him. He had his merit, yes.

The rock-apes reappeared in mid-morning, scampering along a row of finely eroded pink parapets not far above our line of march. They would hold to some needle-like outcropping of rock with one hand and swing far out to chatter derisively at us or pelt us with stones, or even their own bright yellow dung. One such missile struck Kilarion on his shoulder, which was already sore from the talons of the Wall-hawks. He made an angry rumbling sound and snatched up a jagged rock, and made as if to hurl it at his assailant. Then he must have thought better of it; for he paused in mid-throw, and glanced toward me with a foolish grin, as though asking me for permission.

I smiled and nodded and he threw, but the stone missed. The ape laughed wildly and showered him with bits of gravel. Kilarion hissed and cursed and threw another rock, as ineffectually as before. After a time the apes lost interest in us and we saw no more of them that morning.

There was nothing like a road any more, or any sort of regular path. We had to find our own trail as we climbed. Sometimes we had to haul ourselves up over rugged cliffs that were like staircases for giants, made up of blocks of stone twice the height of a man which had to be managed with rope and grappling-hooks. Sometimes we moved across a sharp rubble of broken rock where an entire ledge had collapsed into talus. I saw Traiben gasping and struggling as we made our way up this treacherous rocky fan,

and once he fell, and I paused beside him and held him up
until he had caught his breath, and walked with my arm
around his shoulders until he was able to go on again by
himself.

But for the most part the mountain at this elevation
was easier to ascend than we had expected, since what had
looked from below like a vertical wall of stone turned out in
fact to be a series of broad rocky slabs, each sloping upward,
to be sure, but not as steeply as we had thought from a
distance. In aggregate the angle was a sharp one; taken one
by one each slab could be crossed by mere steady plodding.

Not that I want you to think that any of it was easy.
Where there was a track we could follow without using
ropes, it was of crumbled rock, soft and gravelly the way
much of Kosa Saag's surface is, so that we constantly slipped
and slid and risked twisted ankles. We labored under heavy
packs and the sun was very strong. The hot blaze of white
Ekmelios dazzled our eyes and burned our faces and necks
and turned the rock slabs we were crossing into blinding
mirrors. We baked in the heat, instead of stewing and
simmering in it as one does when one lives in the lowlands.
We were used to that other kind of heat, close as a damp
blanket about us all the time, and we missed it sorely. There
was no warm thick haze up here to screen us from the fury
of the white sun, no gentle moist mists. The sultry humid
world of our village was very far away now.

Not only was the air much more clear at this level, it
seemed less nourishing too: dry, thin, piercing, disagreeable
stuff. We had to breathe twice as deeply as we were accustomed to in order to fill our chests, which made our heads
ache and our throats and nostrils feel chafed and raw. Our
bodies made adjustments to the thinner air as we climbed: I
could feel little alterations going on within me, breathing-
passages expanding, lungs belling out, blood traveling more
swiftly in my vessels. After a time I knew that I was adapting
successfully, or successfully enough, at least, to this new
environment. But I had never realized before what a rich,

intoxicating substance our lowland air was. It was like strong wine, compared with this harsh mountain air.

On the other hand, the water in this high country was far purer and more pleasing than village water. It had a magical clarity and sparkle, and it was always cold and fresh. But there was very little of it. Streams and springs were few and far between on these slopes. Whenever we found one we dropped our packs and knelt and drank greedily, and then we would fill our storage jars, for who knew how long it would be before the next fresh water?

We were cut off now from all view of our home territory. Below us everything was buried under thick white fog. It was as if a great swath of white fur lay upon our familiar valley. Now and again it would break a little, giving us a glimpse of greenness, but there was nothing there that we could recognize. So there was no longer any down for us, only up, up, up, up.

Kosa Saag was our entire world: our universe. We had begun to discover that the great mountain that we called the Wall was actually not one mountain but many, a sea of mountains, each one rising on the backs of those around it the way high waves rise in the midst of stormy waters. We had no idea where the summit was. Sometimes it seemed that we had already attained the highest peak, for we saw clear sky above it, but we were always wrong, because when we got to the top of that one we would find that there were new summits rising beyond it. One peak led to another, and another, and another. When we looked up we saw only an infinite perplexing complexity of pink rock: spires, parapets, shields, gorges. It seemed to go on all the way to Heaven. There was no summit. There was only the endless mountain above us, forever sloping away out of sight above us while we crossed its interminable lower reaches like a file of patient ants.

8

FROM THE START OF our climb we had been ascending the outer rim of the Wall, making our way through
the gulleys and pathways and outcroppings that jutted
from its great face. So it was easy for me to choose each
day's route: it stretched before us like a narrow continuing
highway winding along the face of the Wall and there was
no question about the best way to go, for there was only
one. But we were unable now to proceed any further in that
fashion, because we had arrived at a place where an impassable overhanging barrier of unscalable rock rose straight up
in front of us to a height that was beyond the limit of our
vision. We studied it a long while and there was not one of
us who saw any way that we could master it. No route
seemed to lead around to the side of it and to climb it was
unthinkable.

So we followed the only route that was possible to take,
which sent us turning eastward, into an interior valley of
Kosa Saag. There we camped for a little while in a sort of
forest, cool and shadowy, on this inner arm of the Wall. I
say "a sort of forest" because the plants that grew in that

place, though they were as tall as trees, were not anything at all like any tree of the lowland we had ever seen. They had no woody structure, but were more like giant blades of grass, or, rather, like bunches of grass stuck together, for each trunk seemed to be made up of a dozen or more thin, narrow shafts sprouting from a single base. Sticking out all along their sharp-angled sides, in place of leaves, were scores of wedge-shaped shoots that looked like hatchet-heads.

When you touched one of these trees, it made your hand tingle. If you held on very long after the tingling started, your skin began to burn.

There were small green birds of an unfamiliar kind in these trees, perching by twos and threes on the edges of the hatchetheads. Their bodies were round and plump, with tiny comical scarlet legs barely visible beneath their bellies, and their wings were short and so weak that it was all they could do to flutter from one hatchethead to another. It would be hard to conceive of birds that were more unlike the terrible Wall-hawks. And yet these clownish little birds were not to be taken so lightly, for their eyes were very fierce, strange white orbs that burned like miniature suns in their foreheads. There was bitter hatred in those eyes, and deep menace. Indeed, when Gazin the Juggler stood beneath one of those trees and called out laughingly to the birds above him, because their roundness and fatness amused him so, they responded with a downpouring of sticky spittle that brought howls of pain from him, and sent him rushing across the forest floor to plunge into the stream that ran through its middle.

The water of that stream was red as blood, very curious to behold. I feared for Gazin. But he sprang up out of it unharmed by that strange-colored water, rubbing at his arms and chest where the bird-spittle had struck him. There were welts and blisters all over him. We kept away from those trees thereafter.

Because I felt uneasy in this alien place, I asked Thissa

of the Witch House to cast a spell for our safety before we settled in for the night. Camping on the Wall's edge, we had spent our nights in narrow, secluded places, easily defended; but in this relatively flat terrain we were at the mercy of any wandering denizen of the Wall's interior districts.

She said, "I want something of Gazin's, for he was the first one injured here."

Gazin gave her one of his juggling-balls. Thissa drew something magical on it with the tip of her finger and buried it in a soft place in the ground beside the stream, and lay down to press her cheek against it. Then, still lying that way, she recited the spell for the safety of travelers. That is a long and very costly spell, which draws much energy from the Witch who utters it, because it is earth-magic and she must send some piece of her soul into the soul of the spirit of the place where it is recited. As she spoke it I saw her amber eyes lose their brightness and her slender body go slack with fatigue. But she gave unstintingly of herself to ensure our safety here.

I knew the spell would be a good one. I had had faith in Thissa's powers ever since that dark time in the third year of my training as a candidate, when I had begun to fear I would not be chosen for the Pilgrimage, and had gone to Thissa in her charm-seller's shop to ask her to cast a spell for my success. Surely the charm that she gave me then must have played a powerful role in my being selected. It was comforting to know that we had a Witch of her capability among us.

We pitched our bedrolls in an open place, far from the hatchethead trees and their unpleasant little birds. Stum and Narril were posted as the first guards in case Wallhawks or rock-apes or other troublemakers should arrive in the night, and I appointed Min the Scribe and Aminteer the Weaver as the second shift on watch.

The stars were unusually bright in the clear cool air that prevailed here, and had a hard sheen. Someone began calling off their names: there is Ysod, that one is Selinune, that is Myaul. From Naxa the Scribe came a chilly little laugh. "Stars of ill omen," he said. "Ysod is the star that crushes other stars and devours them. Myaul ate her own worlds. The light of Selinune is light that screams."

"Save your wisdom for some other time, Naxa," came a woman's voice, perhaps Fesild's or Grycindil's. "Don't frighten us with your filthy tales while we're trying to fall asleep."

"And there is Hyle among them," continued Naxa, unperturbed. It was in Naxa's nature never to let up, when there was knowledge he wanted to share with you. Scribes are worse even than Scholars when it comes to giving lectures; for everyone understands that the Scholar is learned, but the Scribe, who has picked up his knowledge while copying the texts of Scholars, is eager to impress you with what he has absorbed. "Hyle is the worst demon-star of them all," Naxa said. "Why, I could tell you stories of Hyle—"

"Good night, Naxa."

"The gods were walking among the stars," Naxa said, "and they came to Hyle, and Kreshe put out his hand—"

"I'll put out my hand and break your head," a new voice said. Kilarion's, it was. "Shut up and let us sleep, will you?"

This time Naxa relented. There was no more talk of demon-stars out of him that night.

I drifted off to sleep soon afterward. But in a little while I felt someone getting in beside me.

"Hold me, Poilar. I'm freezing. I can't stop shivering."

It was Thissa. The traveler-spell had drained her more deeply perhaps than she had expected and her entire body was trembling. I took her in my arms and almost at once, because I had gone so long without a mating, I began to slip into the Changes. In mating there is comfort; in mating there is unity and harmony, the transcending of self into something higher and deeper, and in a time of dark fear or of great stress we turn naturally to one another and enter the sexual state. It happened without my willing it, without my even wanting it. I felt the familiar stirring at the base of my belly, the shifting of the flesh as my hard maleness emerged from its dormancy.

Thissa felt it too. Softly she said, "Please, not now— I'm so tired, Poilar."

I understood. She had not come to me for Changes. She had a strange self-sufficiency, that woman: many Witches do. I forced myself back toward the neuter state, but it was difficult for me. My control kept breaking; my body slid again and again toward readiness. But I could tell that Thissa was in the state without breasts just now and I knew that if I touched her between the thighs I would find no aperture waiting for me. She was utterly neuter and intended to stay that way. I had no choice but to respect that. I struggled for control, and attained it, finally. We lay together calmly. Her head was against my chest, her legs were entwined with mine. She sobbed from weariness, but it was a soft, easy sobbing.

She said, after a time, "Someone here will die to-morrow."

"What? Are you sure?"

"I saw it in the fire."

I was silent a moment. "Do you know who it will be?"

"No. Of course not."

"Or how?"

"No," she said. "The fire was too low, and I was too weary to conjure it up again."

"We've only begun our climb. It's too soon for deaths."

"Death comes whenever it pleases. This will be only the first of many."

I was silent again for a long time. Then I said, "Will it be me, do you think?"

"No. Not you."

"You're sure of that, are you?"

"There's too much life in you, Poilar."

"Ah."

"But it will be one of the men."

"Jaif? Dorn? Talbol?"

She put her hand over my lips. "I told you, I wasn't able to see. Not clearly. One of the men. Let's sleep now, Poilar. Just hold me. Hold me. I'm so cold."

I held her. After a time I felt the tension leave her body as she drifted off into sleep. But I remained wide awake myself, thinking of the death that was marching toward us even at this moment. Perhaps the gods had chosen Muurmut: I would shed no tears for him. But what if it was Traiben, despite all his hunger to see things and understand them? I would not be able to bear the death of Traiben. Then I thought of this one, and that one, and still another. I lay like that for hours, or so it seemed. Overhead the stars grew even brighter and harder. I feared them: poison-stars, demon-stars, death-stars. Ysod, Myaul, Selinune, Hyle. I felt myself shriveling beneath their furious light.

Then Thissa was awake again.

"Go ahead," she said, in a soft voice different from the one she had used before. "You can if you want to."

She had become fully female. Her slim body, which had been nothing but cool smooth skin and fragile bones, was fuller, more womanly now. I felt soft round breasts against my chest. My hand slipped downward and there was an aperture, and it was warm and moist and throbbing.

Why this act of kindness? Thissa was altogether exhausted, and I knew from years gone by that she was not fond of mating even at the best of times. Had she lied to me, and was I the one who would die tomorrow, and this her way of sending me off to my death with a warm tender memory fresh in my mind? That was a somber thought, almost somber enough to discourage me from the mating. Almost. But my desires were stronger than my fear. She opened to me and our bodies joined; and though I could feel that disconcerting strangeness which her body emanated, as I had on earlier occasions when we had been lovers—an odd troubling tingling sensation which came from her in moments like this, somewhat like the throbbing sensation which certain strange fishes give off when you graze against them in the river—she brought me quickly to pleasure, quickly, quickly.

Afterward she said, "You are not the one who will die, Poilar. I'm certain of that."

Had she read my mind?

No, not even the House of Witches can do that, I told myself. Except for those Witches who are also santha-nillas, and santha-nillas are very few and far between.

I lay awake a little while longer, staring up at Hyle and Selinune. Then one of the moons—I think it was Tibios— came into the sky and its brightness dulled the terrible glare of the stars, for which I was grateful. I closed my eyes and fell into a troubled sleep, and then, I suppose, into a much deeper one: when I awoke we were long into morning and everyone else was up and about. Thissa smiled shyly at me from the other side of the stream. I realized they had not wanted to wake me; and I felt more and more certain that I was the one who had been singled out for death this day, and that all of them knew it, and that was why I had been allowed to sleep. But of course that was not so.

THE DEATH—OUR FIRST death on Kosa Saag—came with great suddenness when it came. That was about mid-morning, when we were well up above our campsite of the night before, crossing a narrow plateau that was bordered on one side by what looked like a lake of pitch and on the other by a steep shoulder of the Wall. The day was very warm. Ekmelios blazed right into our faces and there was no hiding from him. In places the ground was cracked open and narrow little columns of yellow and green light, something like marshlight, were rising from it. The air in these places had a dark, oily smell. Some of these small lights had broken free of the ground and were wandering about by themselves, easy as ghosts. We kept well away from them.

As we passed through a grove of small waxy-looking trees with thick crowns of glossy white leaves a band of rock-apes abruptly appeared as if they had risen straight out of the earth, screaming and chattering, and started tormenting us with pebbles, rocks, gobbets of mud, anything that their gnarled little hands could lift and throw.

These apes of the Wall were like cruel caricatures of men, miniature figures no more than knee-high to us, and gnarled and hairy and hideous. Their arms and legs were short and crooked, their noses were flat and huge, their eyes were immense, their feet turned outward and upward like huge hands. Yellow fangs jutted from their mouths. Reddish fur covered their squat little bodies and they had great tufts of it, like beards, around their necks. No wonder they hated us and bedeviled us so: for we were what they would have wanted to be, if the gods had not chosen to make them ugly.

At a distance they were nothing more than nuisances. But here, no more than twenty or thirty paces from us, they were dangerous. Their missiles fell upon us in thick clouds. There was not one of us who was not hit and bruised. The safety-spell that Thissa had cast for us in the forest had no power out here. We shouted at them in our fiercest way, and Narril and Thuiman pulled ropes from their packs and began to crack them like whips to frighten them off. That worked for a time; but then the apes saw how little harm the ropes could do and they returned, noisier and more bothersome than ever.

A great soft clod of greasy mud caught Stapp of the House of Judges in the face. It stunned him for a moment: I saw him coughing and gagging as he peeled it away from his eyes and lips and nostrils. Hardly was he able to breathe again but they hit him with a second one, even softer and looser, which splattered all over his face and chest.

That seemed to drive him berserk. Stapp was ever a man of quick temper. I saw him snorting and spitting mud. Then he yelled wildly and pulled out his cudgel and rushed madly forward, laying about him to right and left. Taken aback by his frantic onslaught, the rock-apes retreated a little way. Stapp pursued them, swinging his cudgel with lunatic zeal, as they edged back toward the pitchy lake. I called to him to come back, that he was moving too far away from us, but there was never any getting Stapp to listen to reason when his anger was upon him.

Then Kilarion started to run toward him. I thought at first that he too wanted to join the fray, that in his simple fashion he envied Stapp his fun; but no, this time Kilarion meant only to rescue him from his own folly. I heard him calling out to Stapp, "Get back, get back, the beasts will kill you." Kilarion ripped one of the little waxy-looking trees from the ground as he ran and swung it like a broom, sweeping the apes out of his path as though they were bits of trash. One after another they went soaring through the air as they were struck, and dropped in dazed heaps many paces away.

But for Stapp, Kilarion's help came too late. One moment he stood by the edge of the lake, cudgeling apes in hot fury; and in the next, an ape had leaped upon his shoulders from the side and drawn its sharp talons across Stapp's throat, so that a gout of dark blood came leaping out; and another moment more and he was falling backward, backward, twisting as he fell. He landed face downward on the black pitchy surface of the lake and sank slowly into it while his blood bubbled up about him.

"Stapp!" Kilarion screamed, kicking apes aside so fiercely that one of them perished with every kick. He held the little tree that he carried out toward the fallen Stapp. "Grab the tree, Stapp! Grab it!"

Stapp did not move. His life's blood had gone surging out of him in no more than an instant or two and he lay dead in the thick tar. Kilarion, at the lake's border, slowly pounded the crown of the tree against the ground in dull rage and bellowed in anger and frustration.

It wasn't easy to take Stapp from the lake. The pitch

held him in a gluey grasp, and we did not dare set foot in it, so we had to pull him out with grappling-hooks. Malti the Healer and Min the Scribe put together some words out of their memories to say for him, drawing the text from the Book of Death, and Jaif sang the dirge while Tenilda played the dirge-tune on her pipe. As for the special words that one must say when a member of the House of Judges dies, we couldn't remember them well, for there were no other Judges among us, but we did our best to say something. Then we buried him under a high cairn of boulders and moved on.

"Well," Kath said, "he was too hot-headed to have been a good Judge anyway."

When I looked back, several of the little yellow and green marsh-lights were dancing atop Stapp's cairn.

NOW WE MOVED OUTWARD toward the front edge of the Wall again, for on that side there was a kind of natural ramp which promised to take us upward, whereas inland the mountain's core rose in a single gleaming breathtaking thrust that struck our hearts with terror. For many days we wound our way along this outer ramp. It rose steeply but not unmanageably in some places, held level in others, and in some actually began to descend, giving us the disheartening thought that all we had accomplished in these days of struggle had been to discover a path leading down the far side of Kosa Saag that would take us to some unfriendly village of that unknown territory. But then we began to climb again, still keeping to the outer face of the Wall.

Strange winged creatures rode the air-currents high up in the great abyss that lay just beside our line of march. Not Wall-hawks, no: these had feathered wings. They seemed to be of colossal size, bigger than Wall-hawks: as big as roundhouses, for all we could tell. But we weren't sure. They were too far above us to judge. In the open space above us there was no way to establish scale. We saw them outlined against the brightness of the sky as they sailed on the lofty winds. Abruptly one would plummet like a falling stone, catching itself in mid-fall, rising again as if scanning for prey, finally darting inward to pick some hapless creature off the face of the Wall in one of the zones of the upper levels. It was a frightening thing to see, though they never came down as far as the level where we were marching now. Would we encounter them higher up? Would they swoop on us as we saw them swooping on other prey now? That was a dismaying thought, that there would be no safe harbor up there, that the Wall would test us and test us and test us, and would break us if it could. We might do better to turn again and head toward the interior of the Wall, I thought, toward some sheltered plateau where those deadly birds would not venture. But we had to go where it was possible to go, and for the time being the interior folds and gorges of the Wall were inaccessible to us and we were compelled to follow these outer trails.

As we ascended I could see more and more of the World. It was far bigger than I had ever imagined, rolling outward to the horizon for league upon league beyond all counting. Wherever there was a break in the white clouds below I was able to make out a host of rivers and hills and meadows, and more rivers and hills and meadows beyond those, and long green stretches of forest with dark smudges within them that I supposed were villages, so far away that very likely no one from any of the villages that cluster at the base of the Wall has ever been to them. Perhaps I was looking at the city where the King lives, for all I knew. I tried to imagine him in his palace, writing decrees that would go forth to provinces that were so far away that the new decrees would be obsolete and meaningless by the time word reached them that such-and-such a law had gone into effect.

At the very edge of the World I saw the sharp gray line of the horizon where the sky came down and touched the forest. What a strange place that must be, I thought, where your feet were on the ground and your head was in the sky!

Was it possible to get there some day and find out what it was like? I stood in wonder, trying to comprehend how long it might take, traveling on foot, to reach that place where the sky met the land.

"You would never reach it," said Traiben, "not even if you marched for a thousand thousand lifetimes."

"And why is that, can you tell me? It looks far, yes, but not as far as all that."

Traiben laughed. "You would march forever."

"Explain yourself," I said, starting to grow irritated with him now.

"The World has no end," said Traiben. "You can walk around it forever and ever and the horizon will always lie ahead of you as you walk toward it."

"No. How can that be? When you walk somewhere, sooner or later you get where you're going."

"Think, Poilar. Think. Imagine yourself walking around a huge round ball. A ball has no end."

"But the World does," I said, with a surly edge to my voice. Traiben could be maddening when he insisted on making you think. Thinking was play for him, but it was work for most of the rest of us.

"The World is like a ball. See, see, where it curves away from us in the distance?"

I stared. "I don't see."

"Look harder."

"You are a great pain sometimes, Traiben."

"No doubt that I am."

"And any fool can tell you that the World is flat."

"Any fool can, yes," he said. "Certainly that is true. But all the same, saying so doesn't make it flat."

I looked toward the horizon. Perhaps the land did curve away a little out there. A little, perhaps. But what Traiben was saying was blasphemy, and it made me uncomfortable. The World is the Boat of Kreshe, floating on the surface of the Great Sea. Boats are longer than they are wide, and not round anywhere. A ball will float on water also, yes. But the World is not a ball. Still, I had to admit to myself that I could see a slight curvature far off near the horizon.

A trick of my vision, I told myself. The floor of the World is as flat as a carpet and it continues in that flatness until one comes to the edge, where the land drops off into the Great Sea. Traiben is too intelligent for his own good, I told myself: sometimes he sees things that are not there and builds strange theories about them, and then he treats you with condescension because you will not agree with him that things are the way he tells you that they are.

I shrugged and we began to talk of other matters. Otherwise I might have been tempted after a time to throw him over the side of the Wall, which is no way to treat your closest friend.

9

WE WONDERED, AS WE climbed, why we saw no
sign of the myriad others who must have come this
way before us over the centuries: no campsites, no
discarded trash, no lost tools, no burial cairns. After all, our
village had sent its Forty up the mountain every year for
more years than anyone could reckon, and as I understand
it we are not the only village at the base of the Wall that
keeps the custom of Pilgrimage. It seemed to us also that
there had been very few choices of route facing us during
our ascent: that everyone who had come in earlier years
from our village, at least, must of necessity have taken the
same path we had, more or less. So where were their
traces?

But that was a sign of how innocent of the realities of
the Wall we still were. Even now, having been on Kosa Saag
for so long many weeks and—so we thought—having come to
an appreciation of its vastness, we had no serious understanding of its true size. We continued to think of it in
terms of the little road that runs up its flank out of our
village, which at that level is the only route that a sensible

person would follow in going upward: the familiar mile-stones, Roshten, Ashten, Glay, Hespen, Sennt, and so forth. We imagined that the path we were taking now was the only logical extension of that road, and that everyone who had come before us must have done as we had done. But what we were not taking into account was that our village road is to the Wall as a raindrop is to a mighty river. Beyond Hithiat milestone the village road goes on to Varhad of the ghosts, yes, but there were other ways to ascend beyond Hithiat that we had not bothered to consider, and each of those ways forks outward into a dozen other ways, each of which would lead you back and forth in its own fashion across the face of the Wall and through the twisted and crumpled maze of interior routes, so that it is probably the case that no two parties of Pilgrims have ever taken the same way up Kosa Saag after the first few days of their climb. I should have kept in mind my mother's brother Urillin's parting words to me, that the Wall is a world, the Wall is a universe. But I did not arrive at an understanding of that until much later.

It was not to be long now, though, before we would find some sign of those who had undertaken the ascent of Kosa Saag before us.

We had slipped into a steady rhythm of climbing. Rise at dawn, bathe and eat, walk until midday. A meal; some singing; a time to relax; and then on the trail again until nightfall neared and it seemed wise to find a place to camp. We knew that we were gradually gaining elevation as we went, but this part of the climb seemed almost static, so gentle was the advance. It lulled us into a false sense of ease. Even Muurmut, who throughout the climb had been quick to dissent with any decision of mine that troubled him, was quiet. Most days the weather was fair, cooler than we were accustomed to but not at all unpleasant. Some days there was rain, occasionally even cold sleet; but we endured it.

Occasionally at night we heard the roaring of demons or monsters from the desolate hills above us. It was fearsome stuff, but we told ourselves that their roaring might be the worst part of them and they might well flee at our approach. Even the awareness that we now had exhausted all the food we had carried with us from the village did not trouble us. We foraged for our provender along the way, each of us taking a turn at sampling the strange berries and roots we found as Traiben had done that early time in the grove of the breast-fruit trees. Once in a while someone became ill for a few hours that way, and so we learned which things not to eat; but in general we ate well. The hunting was good and there was fresh meat to roast every evening.

Some couples formed but didn't last. I mated with sweet pretty Tenilda the Musician a few times, with Stum, and once with Min, who did whatever her friend Stum did, and with Marsiel the Grower. I would have mated with Thissa again also, but she was ever shy and uneasy, and I knew better than to approach her. But I looked longingly after her. And then there was the dark, quiet woman called Hendy, she who had been stolen and kept in the village of Tipkeyn from her tenth year to her fourteenth and so was like a stranger to us all. I desired her greatly and I knew I was not the only one. I spoke with her a few times, but it was like speaking with water, like speaking with the wind. Hendy went her own way, saying little to anyone, making her own camp at a distance from ours, and though I was tempted now and then to venture over to her in the darkness and see if she would receive me, I had a good idea of what the reception was likely to be.

Galli, who long ago had been my lover and now was my friend, saw what I was doing. "You should leave both those women alone, Poilar," she said to me one afternoon as we trudged along an unchallenging trail.

"Which women?" I said.

"Thissa. Hendy."

"Ah. You've been watching me?"

"With half an eye. I need no more than that. Sleep with Stum, if you like. Sleep with Tenilda. Not those two."

"Those two are the only ones who truly interest me, Galli."

She laughed. "Even I interested you once."

"Once," I said. "Yes."

"But I'm too fat for you now? You prefer your women more slender, I think."

She sounded amiable and playful, but she was serious behind the sportiveness.

"I thought you were beautiful when we were young. I think so now. I'll spend tonight with you, if you like, Galli. You are ever a dear companion."

"A companion, yes. I take your meaning." She shrugged. She was not easily wounded in these matters. "As you wish. But if you want a mate, stay away from those two. No good will come of your bothering them. Thissa's frail and too easily harmed, and she's a Witch beside. Hendy is so very strange. Choose Stum, Poilar. She's a good woman. Strong, like me."

"Too simple, though. And too much the friend of Min. I think you take my meaning. Friendship between women is a good thing but it makes a man uneasy when his mind is on the Changes and her mind is with her friend."

"Then Tenilda. Beauty and intelligence there, and a good heart besides."

"Please," I said. "Enough of your help, Galli!"

I did indeed spend that night with her, for in truth I had never lost my fondness for her, even if the strong desire had long since abated. It was like spending the night with a favorite cousin, or even a sister. Galli and I lay together and laughed and told stories of old times and finally we made the Changes, in an easy, halfhearted way, and she fell quickly asleep beside me, snoring. Her great warm bulk nearby was comforting. But her words kept me awake. Thissa frail and too easily harmed, Hendy so very strange. Was that what attracted me to them? Was Galli right that I should put them from my mind?

·   ·   ·

JUST AS WE WERE beginning to think once again that the climb would be as simple as this all the way to the Summit, we came to a place where all trails seemed to end and there was no way to proceed. This had happened to us before, and we had found some means of getting around the obstacle. But this time it seemed as though we were blocked wherever we turned.

We had been following a northerly track around the eastern face of the Wall. The wind, coming briskly out of the north, was strong in our faces, and the air was clear and fresh as young wine, and far below we could see the dull silver line of what must have been some gigantic river, seemingly no thicker than a hair to us as it wound its way through a distant blue valley. We moved with a swift step, singing joyously as we marched. In late afternoon we found our path swinging sharply toward the west, and then abruptly came the great surprise, for we discovered ourselves looking into a gigantic rift that sliced deep into the heart of Kosa Saag. It was many leagues wide—how many, I could not say—from south to north, and seemed to plunge on westward to the limits of our vision, as though the Wall were actually two pieces from here on up, cut in half by this immense sundering that we now confronted.

We halted, astonished by the splendor and magnitude of what we beheld. Wherever we looked we saw new peaks, a host of them, pink stone strongly ribbed with black, an army of peaks of great size and majesty high above us on both sides of the rift. Lightning flashed atop those peaks. Feathery strands of cloud, like veils of the sky, blew straight southward from their tips, quivering as if whipped by a terrible gale.

I had never seen such beauty. There was a wondrous music in it that filled my soul so full that I had to struggle for breath. What a grand sight it was! It was so grand that it terrified me. It seemed as if the sky were breaking open up there, and strange light was shining through a window that opened out of the future. I felt sure that it must be the light of other days I saw, time running backward, events from beyond the end of the world shining toward the beginning. There were gods walking around up there. I heard their rumbling footsteps. I wondered if the First Climber had come this way in His pioneering ascent, whether He had looked upon this sight which now so dazzled me. He must have, I thought. He must. And had been inspired by the grandeur of it to continue His upward journey to the abode of the gods. As was I. As was I.

I stood staring, lost in awe.

Naxa came up alongside me and said, "It is the land of the Doubles that we see. Or rather, we see its light, for there is no way we can see the land of the Doubles itself."

"The Doubles?"

"Our other selves, perfect and invulnerable. They live in the Double World, which hangs downward in the sky and touches the upper reaches of the Wall. It is all written in the Book of the Double World."

"That's not a book that I know," I said. "You must tell me more about it some day."

"Yes," Naxa said, and smiled his annoying little smile; and I knew I would never hear a thing about the Double World from him again. But I would learn of it somehow from another source, I vowed.

I couldn't take my eyes from those lofty peaks. None of us could. Wherever we looked, great stony spires whirled toward Heaven. A hundred craggy pyramids of tumbled rock jutted into the sky on all sides of us. Some seemed kindled into pink flame by the light of setting Ekmelios. Some, which must have been capped by snow, blazed such a fierce white that we could hardly bear to look at them for long. Bright rainbows leaped from gorge to gorge. Below us, looping saddles of rock descended dizzily into a dark chasm that seemed to have no floor. We saw the tops of gigantic black trees, far below, trees which must have been fifty times a tall man's height.

As we stood lost in all this magnificence, Dorn the

Clown came to my side and said quietly to me, "Poilar, our path ends a hundred paces in front of us."

"This is no moment for joking, Dorn."

"And I offer you no jokes. The path drops off into utter nothingness. I've just been to see. There's no way forward from here at all."

It was the truth. Our little cliffside trail ran a short way into the rift, narrowing as it went, and simply disappeared not very far ahead. I followed it to its end and finally found myself standing in a place scarcely wider than my own feet, clinging to the mountain's rough skin and peering awestruck into windy emptiness. There was nothing whatever in front of me but the open air of the great rift. To one side of me was the Wall, to the other was the air. Only one direction remained, and that was behind me, the path by which we had just come. We were trapped in this stony pocket. We had wasted many days: weeks, even. It seemed to me we had no choice but to retrace our way, returning along the gentle, deceptive grade we had been following until we discovered some line of approach that would allow us to resume the ascent.

"No," said Kilarion. "We'll go up the Wall."

"What?" I said. "Straight up?"

Everyone was laughing at poor stolid Kilarion.

"Straight up," he said. "It can be done. I know that it can. There's a place a little way behind us where the face is cracked and knobby. That'll provide us with handholds. The gods have already given us sucker-pads. Between the one and the other, we'll be able to make it."

I turned and looked back. What I saw was a bare sheet of vertical stone that rose so high it made my neck ache to look up at it. In the afternoon shadows I made out what might have been a few spurs of rock protruding from it, far above.

"No one can climb that, Kilarion."

"I can. You can. We all can. It's not as high as it looks. I'll go up and show you. And then we'll all go up. Otherwise we might have to turn back as far as the place where Stapp died before we find another way through. I'd rather walk up the side of this mountain than see Stapp's grave again."

Kilarion had shown us already that he was good at finding trails, that in fact he had some natural gift for divining the ways to conquer Kosa Saag. Perhaps he was right again. But it was getting too late in the day to make this attempt, even assuming it could be done at all. I said, "We'll go back until we find a place to camp, and stay there for the night. In the morning you and I will try this wall, Kilarion."

"I know we can make it."

"You know that *you* can make it. I want to see if the rest of us can."

And so we doubled back through the deepening shadows to locate a campsite. In our exhilaration that day none of us had noticed the way the trail was pinching in; retracing it now, I thought for a time we would have to go all the way back to last night's campsite to find a place wide enough to be safe for sleeping, and that would mean many hours of risky hiking in the dark. But we did not have to do that. Another campsite that we hadn't troubled to take note of when we were coming the other way lay only an hour back from trail's end, next to a tiny trickle of fresh water. The site was small but adequate, and we huddled in there as best we could, listening to the wind whistling above us.

In the morning Kilarion and I set out together to attempt the climb.

We both carried our full packs. The test would have been meaningless otherwise. Kilarion chose the place where we would ascend, walking back and forth along the trail for nearly an hour before deciding on it.

"Here," he said at last.

I looked up. The Wall here seemed smooth and utterly vertical.

"There's water oozing here," said Kilarion. "See? There will be cracks in the rock." We unpacked our climbing-ropes and hitched them about our waists. Then we turned away from each other to transform our left hands for the climb. Like most men I am uneasy about performing any sort of shapechanging in front of a stranger of my own sex, and it seemed that Kilarion was the same way. When we faced each other again we had brought forth our sucker-pads. I saw Kilarion's eye dart questioningly toward my lame leg, as though he was wondering why I had not changed that too while I was at it. But he didn't say it. I gave him a flinty glance by way of telling him that there was nothing I could do about that leg, and that in any case it was no handicap to me. And I reached around behind me into the pack, where I kept the little idol of Sandu Sando that Streltsa had forced upon me on the day of Departure, and rubbed it twice for luck along its holy place.

"Ready?" he said.

He slammed his climbing-hook into the rock, pulled himself upward on it, and began to walk up the sheer stony face.

When the slack in the rope that linked us was almost gone, I followed him. I had climbed many a rock wall in my training years, though never one like this; but I told myself that it only was a question of addressing each moment of the climb in its turn, rather than thinking about the totality of what needed to be done. Kilarion moved swiftly and deftly above me, cutting back and forth along the rock to find the best handholds. As he had guessed, the stone was riven with cracks, and there were spurs and even some narrow ledges on it too which had been invisible from below. I grabbed for the spurs; I wedged my hand or sometimes my whole arm into the cracks; I used my climbing-hook and my sucker-pads to pull me past the smooth sections. And I rose quickly and efficiently, readily keeping pace with Kilarion as he went upward.

The essence of climbing a rock like this is remembering to let your legs do the work. The arms are agile and versatile but they soon grow weary if they are called upon to carry much of your weight. That was why Kilarion had looked dubiously at my twisted foot. Since he was going first, it would be up to me to hold us both in place if he were to fall; and he must have been wondering how much strength that bad foot of mine might actually have.

I would show him. I had lived with that foot, and the lame leg to which it belonged, for two tens of years. It had taken me this far up Kosa Saag. It would take me up this rock face too, and all the way up the rest of the mountain.

Cunningly I wedged my toes into crevices as I reached for the handholds above. I kept myself well supported until I was ready to scramble to the next level. The bad leg was no poorer at this game than the other one: I had to insert it at a different angle, that was all.

The first minutes were easy ones. Then things grew a little more difficult, and I found that I had to lunge at some of the handholds, leaping up to them and leaving myself unsupported for a moment as I made the reach. Once a handhold crumbled like rotten wood at the touch of my hand and broke away; but I was braced by my feet when that happened.

My breath was loud in my ears; my heart pounded. Perhaps I felt afraid, a little. But Kilarion moved inexorably onward above me and I would not let him think that I couldn't keep up. As I had been trained to do, I plotted my course several moves in advance, constantly working out sequences, calculating, I will go *here* after I have reached *there*, and then I will go *here*.

There was one troublesome moment when I made the stupid mistake of glancing back over my shoulder to see how high I had risen. I found myself looking down into a gorge that seemed as deep as the Wall was high. My stomach lurched and my heart contracted as though it had been squeezed and my left leg began to twitch violently, jabbing rhythmically into the air.

Kilarion felt my jouncing motions rising up the rope to him.

"Are you dancing, Poilar?" he asked.

That was all it took, that one lighthearted question. I laughed and the terror drained out of me. I turned my concentration back to the rock.

You *must* concentrate in the most intense way. You must see nothing but the tiny crevices and glittering little crystal outcrops just in front of your nose. I went up, up, up. Now I was spreadeagled to my limits, inching along a pair of parallel ridges that were set precisely two Poilar-leg lengths apart to form a kind of chimney. Now I hung suspended from a horn of crystal no longer than my inner thumb. Now my cheek was flat against the rock and my feet groped for purchase in empty air. My arms ached and my tongue felt oddly swollen.

Then, suddenly, there was a hand dangling in my face and I heard Kilarion's ringing laughter as he reached for my wrist, caught it, and pulled me up across a rough rocky cornice onto a place where I could roll over and lie flat.

"You see?" he said. "There was nothing to it!"

We were on top. The climb had taken forever, or else only a moment: I was not sure which. The only certain thing was that we had accomplished it. There had been times along the way, I realized now, when I had been sure we would perish. But now, as I lay laughing and gasping on a horizontal surface, it seemed to me that Kilarion was right, that there really had been nothing to the climb at all.

After a time I stood up. We had reached a broad plateau, so deep and wide that I thought at first that we had reached the Summit itself, the very top of Kosa Saag, for everything seemed flat in all directions. Then my eyes focused on the distance and I saw how wrong I was: for I could see now, so far away to the southwest that it was almost at the limits of my vision, the next stage of the Wall rising above the floor of the plateau.

It was a numbing sight. What I saw out there was a great shining mass of pale red stone, shrouded at the base by a swirl of misty morning air and disappearing overhead in thick clouds. It tapered upward to infinity in a series of diminishing stages. It was like one mountain rising upon another. The whole Wall must be like that, I realized: not a mountain but a mountain range, immense at the base, narrowing gradually as you went higher. No wonder we couldn't see the Wall's upper reaches from our valley: they lay hidden from our view within the natural fortress formed by the lower levels. I came now to understand that in truth we had only begun our ascent. By reaching this plateau we had simply completed the first phase of the first phase. We had merely traversed the outer rim of the foot-hills of the tremendous thing that is Kosa Saag. My heart sank as I began to comprehend that our climb thus far had been only a prologue. Ahead of us still lay this vast mocking pink staircase outlined against a dark, ominously violet sky.

I turned away from it. We could deal with that awesome immensity later. Sufficient unto the day is the travail thereof, says the First Climber; and He is right in that, as He is in all other things.

"Well?" Kilarion asked. "Do you think the others can get themselves up here?"

I glanced back over the edge of the rock face we had just ascended. The trail at the base of the vertical cliff was incredibly far below us; at this distance it seemed no wider than a thread. It was hard to believe that Kilarion and I had scrambled up such a height of inhospitable stone. But we had. We had. And except for a couple of troublesome moments it had been a simple steady haul, or so it seemed to me in retrospect. The climb could have been worse, I told myself. It could have been very much worse.

"Of course," I said. "There's not one of them who couldn't manage it."

"Good!" Kilarion clapped me on the back and grinned. "Now we go down and tell them, eh? Unless you want to wait here, and I go down and tell them. Eh?"

"You wait here, if you like," I said. "They'll need to hear it from me."

"We both go down, then."

"All right. We both go down."

WE DESCENDED BOLDLY, EVEN rashly, quickly swinging ourselves from ledge to ledge with our ropes, hardly pausing to secure our holds before we were off again. The mountain air does that to you, that and the exhilaration of knowing that you have conquered fear and attained your goal. I suppose in our exuberance we might well have levered ourselves right off the face of the cliff into the abyss beyond the trail-ledge. But we did not; and quickly we were down again and trotting back to camp with the news of what we had achieved.

Muurmut said at once, "That way is impossible. I saw it myself last night. It goes straight up. Nobody could climb it."

"Kilarion and I have just climbed it."

"You say that you have, anyway."

I looked at him, wanting to kill. "You think that I'm lying?"

Kilarion said impatiently, "Don't be a fool, Muurmut. Of course we climbed it. Why would we lie about that? Climbing it isn't as hard as it looks."

Muurmut shrugged. "Maybe yes, maybe no. I say that it's impossible and that if we try it we'll die. You're stronger than any two of us, Kilarion. And you, Poilar, you can climb anything with your tongue alone. But will Thissa be able to climb it? Or Hendy? Or that darling little Traiben of yours?"

Clever of him to pick the three who mattered most to me. But I said sharply, "We'll all be able to climb it."

"I say no. I say it's too dangerous."

I hated him for inspiring doubt in us when what we needed now was sublime self-confidence. "What are you suggesting, then, Muurmut? That we sprout wings and fly ourselves to the top?"

"I'm suggesting that we retrace our steps until we find a safer way."

"There is no safer way. This is our only choice. Short of simply creeping back to the village like cowards, that is, and I don't choose to do that."

He gave me a scowling look. "If we all die on this rock-climb of yours, Poilar, how will that get us to the Summit?"

This was opposition purely for the sake of opposition, and we both knew it. There were no paths to follow but this one. I wanted to strike him and break him; but I kept calm and said indifferently, "As you wish, Muurmut. Stay right here and live forever. The rest of us will continue the climb and take our chances on dying."

"Will they?" he asked.

"Let them decide," I said.

So we had what amounted to a second election. I asked who would come with Kilarion and me up the face of the rock, and immediately Traiben and Galli and Stum and Jaif and about half a dozen others raised their hands—the usual dependable ones. I could see doubt on the faces of Muurmut's henchmen Seppil and Talbol, and on Naxa's face also, and on a few of the women's. More than a few, in fact, and some of the other men. For a moment I thought the vote would run against me, which would end my leadership of the climb. Some of the waverers, the most timid ones, edged toward Muurmut as though they intended to remain behind with him. But then Thissa put her hand up high and that seemed to be a turning point. By twos and threes the rest hastened to vote for the climb. In the end Seppil and Talbol were the only ones remaining in Muurmut's camp, and they looked at him in confusion.

"Shall we say farewell to the three of you now?" I asked.

Muurmut spat. "We climb under protest. You risk our lives needlessly, Poilar."

"Then I risk my own as well," I said. "For the second time this day." I turned away from him and went to Thissa, whose decision had swung the vote. "Thank you," I said.

The quickest flicker of a smile crossed her face. "You are welcome, Poilar."

"What a pain Muurmut is. I'd like to throw him over the edge."

She stepped back, gaping at me in shock. I could see that she had taken me seriously.

"No," I said. "No, I don't mean that literally."

"If you killed him it would be the end of everything for us."

"I won't kill him unless he forces me to," I said. "But I wouldn't weep for very long if he happened to have some terrible accident."

"Poilar!" She seemed sick with horror.

Perhaps Galli was right. Thissa was terribly frail.

FOR THE GENERAL ASCENT we divided ourselves into ten groups, all of them groups of four except for one, which consisted only of Kilarion, Thissa, and Grycindil, because Stapp's death at the lake of pitch had left us with an unequal number. My own group was Traiben, Kreod, and Galli. Mainly we roped ourselves with the men going first and last and the women in between, for most men are stronger than most women and we knew it would be best to have a man below to hold the group if anyone fell. But in my group I took care to have Traiben climb just below me and Galli to have the important bottom spot, for Traiben was weak and Galli was as strong as any man among us but Kilarion. I let Muurmut go up with his friends Seppil and Talbol and Thuiman, even though they were all strong men and would better have been used to bolster some of the women. But I thought, if any of them should fall, let them all fall together, and good riddance.

Once again Kilarion led the way. He was very much more cautious in the climb now with Thissa and Grycindil than he had been with me, and I understood that on our earlier climb he had been deliberately challenging me to keep up the pace. When his group had gone far enough up the cliff so that Grycindil had begun her climb, I started up alongside them, keeping a little to the left to avoid any pebbles that might be scraped loose from climbers above me. Ghibbilau the Grower took the next group up, with Tenilda and Hendy and Gazin. After them went Naxa, Ment the Sweeper, Min, and Stum, and then Bress the Carpenter, Hilth of the Builders, Ijo the Scholar, Scardil the Butcher. And so we all went, group after group. Now and then I heard brittle nervous laughter from below me; but I knew better this time than to look back and see how they were doing.

Midway up, Traiben found himself in difficulties.

"I can't reach the next hold, Poilar!"

"Twist your hips. Angle your body upward."

"I've done it. I still can't reach."

Cautiously I glanced toward him, focusing my vision so that I saw Traiben and only Traiben, nothing below him. He was awkwardly wedged into a barely manageable foothold a few paces to the side of the route I had been taking, and he was straining desperately to get a grip on a jagged knob of red rock that was well beyond his grasp.

"I'll go a little higher," I told him. "When the rope goes taut, it'll pull you closer to it."

I forced myself upward. Lines of fire were running across my chest and back now from the effort of this second climb of the morning. But I pulled myself as far as I could go without making Traiben's weight an impossible burden on me that would rip me loose and send me plunging past him. Galli, far down the rock, saw what I was doing and called up to me that she had a good grip, that she would anchor me while I pulled. But I doubted that even she could hold us all if I fell, bringing Traiben down with me.

"I can't reach it," Traiben muttered. He spoke as if every word cost him a great price.

"Change!" Thissa called, from somewhere far above us. I looked up and saw her peering down at us over the cornice of the plateau. She was feverishly making witchery-signs at us, thrusting both thumbs of each hand at us like little horns. "Can you? Make your arm longer, Traiben! Make it stretch!"

Of course. Make it stretch. Why else were we given shape-changing by the gods?

"Do it," I said.

But controlling your Changes is not such a simple thing when you are in terror of your life. I watched as Traiben, trembling below me, struggled to adjust the proportions of his frame, shifting his shoulders about, loosening the bones of his back and arms to achieve the greater reach. I would have gone to him to stretch him myself, if I could. But I had to hold us in our place. His fumbling went on and on, until my own arms began to tire and I wondered how long I could stay where I was. Then I heard an odd little giggle come from him and when I glanced at him again I saw him weirdly distorted, with his left arm far longer than the right and his whole body bent into a tortured curve. But he had hold of the knob he needed. He hauled himself up; the slack returned to the rope; I pressed myself against the rock until I was limp, and let my lungs fill gladly with air.

After that the rest was almost easy. For the second time that morning I came to the top of that wall of rock. I pulled Traiben over the cornice, and Kreod, and then came Galli on her own, looking as unwearied as if she had been out for a stroll.

One by one the other groups followed, until we were reunited on the plateau. I saw everyone blinking and looking about in wonder, astounded by the size of this great flat place that Kilarion had brought us to.

"Where do we go now?" Fesild asked. "Where's the Wall?"

"There," I said, and pointed to that remote rosy bulk in the southwest, dimly visible behind its screen of wispy white clouds and congested haze.

The others began to gasp. I think they had mistaken

the pink gleam of it on the horizon for the sky; but now the comprehension was breaking upon them, as earlier it had broken upon me, that we were looking at last upon the true Wall—the Wall of the many Kingdoms of which the fables told, the Wall within the Wall, the immense hidden core of the mountain sheltered here in these interior folds and gorges, that great thing which still remained for us to conquer.

"So far away?" she murmured, for the plateau was vast and anyone's soul would quail at the distance we had to travel across it in order to resume our climb. The magnitude of the climb that awaited us afterward took another moment to register itself upon her soul. Then she said, very softly: "And so high!"

We all were silent in the face of that colossal sun-shafted thing that lay before us. Such pride as we felt in having scaled the rock face below us shriveled to dust in the contemplation of what still must be done.

10

I COULD NOT TELL you how long we spent in crossing
that broad plateau. Many weeks, it must have been: but
each day melted into the next and we kept no count. It
was a rough, barren, scrubby place, sunbaked and stark and
not nearly so flat as it had appeared from its edge, with dips
and ridges and valleys and chasms to bedevil us every day.
Even where it was level, the land was rocky and difficult to
traverse. The vegetation was coarse and, for the most part,
useless to us: woody, stringy, thorny, all but leafless, offering little but bitter roots and dry tasteless fruit. The only
animals we saw were small gray furry creatures, ugly and
scrawny and lopsided, which scuttered before us as we
marched. They were too quick for us to catch nor would
they come near the traps we set, but it was just as well: we
would not have had much nourishment from them, I think,
nor any pleasure. The occasional shallow streams we found
were sparsely inhabited also, though by patient hours of
fishing we came up with netfuls of bony silvery wrigglers
out of which we made meals of a sort.

From the second day of the crossing, or maybe it was

the third, I felt myself beginning to hate the plateau. I had never felt such hatred in my life as the hatred I felt for that plateau. It was a wasteland that gave us no upwardness, and the upwardness was all I desired. Yet it had to be crossed. So in its way it was part of the upwardness, a necessity of the route; but I hated it all the same. There was no grandeur here. The great peaks of the rift were behind us, hidden from our view by tricks of the land; and the great peak that was Kosa Saag, the peak of peaks, lay impossibly far in front of us across the plateau; and so I hated it, because it must be crossed.

We marched from dawn to dusk, day upon day upon day, and the mountain seemed to remain at the same distance all the time. I said as much one afternoon when I had grown very weary.

"The same distance? No, worse, it moves backward as we approach," said Naxa dourly. "We'll never reach it even if we march for a thousand years."

And voices came from behind us, grumbling and muttering to much the same purpose. Muurmut's, of course, was prominent among them.

"What do you say, Poilar?" Naxa asked me. His voice was like an auger, drilling into my soul. "Should we give up the climb and build ourselves a village here? For surely we gain nothing by going forward and I doubt very much that we could ever find our way back."

I made no reply. Already I regretted having spoken in the first place, and it would be folly to let myself be drawn into a debate on whether we should abandon our Pilgrimage.

Grycindil the Weaver, who had grown very sharp-tongued on the plateau, turned to Naxa and said, "Be quiet, will you? Who needs your gloom, you foolish Scribe?"

"I need my gloom!" Naxa cried. "It keeps me warm by night. And I think you need something from me, Grycindil, to keep *you* warm." He nudged her arm and pushed his face close to hers, grinning evilly. "What about it, Weaver-girl? Shall you and I weave a few Changes tonight?"

"Fool," answered Grycindil. And she poured out such a stream of abuse that I thought the air would burn.

"You are both of you fools," said Galli, but in a good-humored way. "In this thin air you should save your breath for some better use."

Kath, who was walking beside me, said in a low voice, "Do you know, Poilar, I wouldn't mind drowning Naxa at the next stream, if only so that I would never have to hear that whining voice of his again."

"A good idea. If only we could."

"But I confess it troubles me also that the mountain grows no closer."

"It grows closer with every step we take," I replied sharply. I was getting angry now. Perhaps I had doubts of my own that were causing a soreness in my soul. Naxa was only a nuisance but Muurmut had the capacity to make real trouble, and I knew that very shortly he would, if this kind of talk continued. I had to cut it off. "It only *seems* to stay at the same distance, is what I told Naxa. And we're in no hurry, are we, Kath? If we spend all the rest of our lives on this Pilgrimage, what harm is there in that?"

He looked at me for a long moment, as though that was a new thought to him. Then he nodded, and we went onward without speaking again. The grumblers behind us ceased their chatter, after a time.

BUT THERE HAD BEEN poison in Naxa's words, and all that day it seeped deeper into my soul. That night when we camped I sank into such a dark brooding and despondency that I scarcely knew myself. All I could think was, This plateau has no end, this plateau has no end, we will spend all the years of our lives attempting to cross it. And I thought, Naxa is right. Better to turn back, and build a new village for ourselves somewhere on the lower slopes, than to expend ourselves in this interminable and futile quest.

The urge to make an end to this Pilgrimage came on me in wave after wave. Naxa was right. Muurmut was right. All the faint-hearted ones were right. Why struggle like this, in hope of finding gods who might not even exist? We had thrown away our lives in this foolish Pilgrimage. Our only choices now were the disgrace of an early return to the village and the death that waited for us in this wilderness.

Such thinking was terrible blasphemy. At another time I would have fought it away. But this night it was too much for me; it overwhelmed me; I could not help but yield to its power and temptation; and in yielding I felt my soul beginning to freeze, I felt my spirit becoming encased in ice.

This was all strange to me, this embracing of defeat and despair. It was the dreariness of the plateau that did it to me, that and Naxa's insidious poisonous words. While the others sprawled about the campfire that night singing village songs and laughing at the antics of Gazin the Juggler and Dorn and Tull, our two lively Clowns, I went off by myself and sat bleakly in the saddle of a gray rock encrusted with dry moss, and stared empty-eyed at the miserable distances that still confronted us. Two moons were aloft, the cheerless Karibos and Theinibos, and by the harsh light that comes from their pockmarked faces I saw only sorrow and grief in this withered eroded landscape. I think it was the worst hour of my life, the hour that I sat there watching spiny-backed night-beasts scampering across that desolate waste; and by the end of it I was ready to strike camp and slink back down the side of the Wall that very evening. For me the Pilgrimage was at an end then and there. It had lost all meaning. It had ceased utterly to make sense. What was the good of it? What was the good of anything? There was nothing to gain in this place but pain, and then more pain; and the gods, in their eyrie far above, were looking down at our struggles and laughing.

The enterprise to which we had shaped our lives

seemed pointless to me in that dark moment. I found myself wishing that I had lost my footing on Kilarion's cliff and gone plunging to a swift doom, rather than having lived to come to this place of interminable toil.

Then suddenly Traiben stood before me.

"Poilar?"

"Let me be, Traiben."

"Why do you sit here like this?"

"To enjoy the lovely moonlight," I said bitterly.

"And what are you thinking as you sit here in the lovely moonlight, Poilar?"

"Nothing. I'm thinking nothing at all."

"Tell me," Traiben said.

"Nothing. Nothing. Nothing."

"I know what you're thinking, Poilar."

"Then you tell me," I said, though I feared that he truly did, and if that was so I was far from eager to hear it from him.

He bent down a little way, so that his great saucer eyes were on a line with mine, and I saw something in those eyes—a force, a ferocity, a fury—that I had never seen there before. Surely there was a Power in him.

"You're thinking of the village," he said.

"No. I never think of the village."

"Of the village, yes. Of our House. Of Turimel the Holy. You're lying on a couch with Turimel in our House and you and she are making the Changes together."

"At this moment Turimel is happily lying with Jecopon the Singer, to whom she was sealed five years ago. I never think of Turimel." I turned away from that fierce unwavering gaze of his. "Why are you bothering me like this, Traiben?"

He caught me by the chin and pulled my head around.

"Look at me!"

"Traiben—"

"Do you want to go home, Poilar? Is that it?"

"This plateau makes me sick."

"Yes. It makes all of us sick. Do you want to go home?"

"No. Of course not. What are you saying?"

"We made a vow, you and I, when we were twelve."

"Yes, I know," I said, with no strength at all in my voice. "How could I forget." I adopted a high mimicking tone. "We will climb to the Summit, and meet the gods, and see all the wonders and learn all the mysteries. And then return to the village. That was what we swore."

"Yes, and I for one mean to keep my oath," said Traiben, still glaring at me as though I were the sworn enemy of his House.

"As do I."

"Do you? Do you?"

He took me by the shoulders and shook me so hard that I thought my shape would begin to shift.

I let him shake me. I said nothing, I did nothing.

"Poilar, Poilar, Poilar, what's wrong with you tonight? Tell me. Tell me!"

"The plateau. The moonlight. The distances."

"And so you want to turn back. Oh, how happy Muurmut will be, when he finds out that the great leader Poilar is broken like this! The Summit means nothing to you any more. The gods. Our vow. The only thing you desire is to give up and go back."

"Oh, not so," I said, without much conviction. "Not so at all."

He shook his head. "What I say is true, but you won't admit it even to me."

"Have you become a Witch, Traiben, that you can read my mind so easily?"

"I could always read you, Poilar. There's no need to pretend with me. You want to turn back. Is that not true?"

His eyes were blazing. To my amazement I realized that I was afraid of him, just then.

I could make no answer.

He said, after a long while, speaking now in a cold and quiet tone, "Well, let me tell you only this, Poilar: I mean to keep my oath whatever you may do. If I'm the only one of us who wants to go on, then so be it. I'll go on. And when you get back to the village, a year or two from now, or three or four, and they ask you where Traiben is, you can say that he has gone to the Summit, that he's up there right now, discussing philosophy with the gods." He stood back and held out his hand, fingers outstretched in the farewell sign. "I'll miss you, Poilar. I'll never have another friend like you."

Angrily I slapped the hand down to his side.

It seemed to me that he was patronizing me. I couldn't stand that, not from him. "This is foolishness, Traiben. You know that I'll be at the Summit with you, when you get there."

I snapped the words out at him. I meant them to be full of conviction. But the conviction wasn't there, and Traiben knew that as well as I.

"Ah, but will you?" he asked. "Will you, Poilar?"

And he walked away and left me there not knowing whether I was lying to myself or not.

I SAT ALONE IN bewilderment for another hour or more; and then, when everyone else had gone to sleep except those who were on watch, I returned to the camp and slipped into my bedroll. That night I had the star-dream again, the one that I had been having since I was a boy, but it had never been as intense as this before, not even on that first night when the entire village had dreamed it with me. I stood alone, poised on a black jagged mountaintop where icy winds blew. All about me was the god-light, the devil-light, the light that comes out of the end of time and goes streaming toward the beginning. I flexed my legs, I bent and leaped and went soaring toward Heaven, toward the radiant country where the gods abide. And the stars, alive and vibrating and warmer than any fire could ever be, opened to me and embraced me and took me among themselves, and I felt rivers of god-wisdom rushing into my soul.

All the doubt that had infected me in this dismal place was burned out of me in that moment of starfire. The ecstasy of the Pilgrimage possessed me fully once more, and when I awakened, what seemed like moments later, morning had come and the light of both suns was hammering joyously, white over scarlet, against the slopes of the distant Wall. I would have climbed it in a bound, if it had been closer. I knew I would never waver in my faith again. Nor did I, except for a little while just before our Pilgrimage's end; though whether I came down from the Wall with the same faith in which I ascended it is something for you to measure and judge when you have heard all my story.

But my vision of the night healed me of my dark uncertainties. And I could see in the eyes of all the others that morning that once again those around me had shared my dream, even Muurmut, who hated me and would gladly have overthrown me. They looked at me just then as though I were no mortal being, but someone who was at home among the gods of Heaven.

Even so, there was no end to the grumbling. When we resumed our march a few hours later, I found myself walking in a group with Galli and Gazin and Ghibbilau the Grower and Naxa the Scribe; and we had not gone a hundred paces before Naxa began speaking as he had the night before, the same doleful stuff about how the Wall seemed to be getting farther away from us every day, instead of closer. "What I am reminded of," he said, "is the tale of Kesper the Scholar, who angered the gods by declaring that he intended to become as wise as they are. So they caused it to happen that for each book Kesper read, he would forget two others. It is the same with us, I think: for each step we take, the mountain moves two paces back, and so—"

Without pausing an instant for thought, I turned on him and knocked him sprawling in the dust.

He crouched there, trembling, amazed, looking up at me like a wounded beast. A little trickle of blood dribbled across his face where my blow had split his skin.

I pointed past him, back toward the rim of the great rift.

"Go," I said. "Now. That way."

"Poilar?"

"We don't need whiners and complainers among us. They have no value." I prodded him with the tip of my cudgel. "Get out of my sight, Naxa. Get going right now. Down the Wall, back to the village. The downhill route ought to be easier for you than the way up was."

He stared at me.

"Go on. Go!" I raised my cudgel.

"But I'll die, Poilar. I'll lose my way and die. You know I will. You're deliberately sending me to my death."

"Others have found their way down alone, isn't that so? You can too. And you'll enjoy being back home in the nice warm village. You'll live in the roundhouse with the other Returned Ones. You'll wander around town and do whatever you please, anything at all no matter how outrageous, and no one will dare say a word against you." I glanced around. "Are there any others here who want to go back with Naxa? He says that he's afraid of going down the Wall alone. You can keep him company on the way."

They were all staring at me with frozen faces. No one said a word.

"Anyone at all? Speak up, now! This is your chance. The return party sets out right now." They were silent. "Nobody? All right. So be it. He goes alone, then. Get moving, Naxa. We're wasting time here."

"For the love of Kreshe, Poilar!"

I shook my cudgel at him. Naxa scrambled back beyond its reach, just a few steps away from me, and paused there as if still not believing I was serious. I started toward him and he moved away from me again. I watched him as he went slinking off toward the east, pausing now and again to look back over his shoulder at me. After a time he disappeared behind a rise in the ground and I could see him no longer.

"All right," I said. "Let's go."

"Well done," Muurmut said. "How brave you are, Poilar, striking down the terrifying Scribe. And what a wise leader, to cast a chosen Pilgrim out of the Pilgrimage."

"I thank you for your praise," I said to him, and turned away.

I put Naxa out of my mind. We marched on.

Many hours later we stopped to rest and have our meager midday meal. I was sitting on a rock gnawing a bit of ancient dried meat when Thissa and Grycindil and Hendy came to me and stood before me, shifting uncertainly about as though they had something they needed to say but feared to tell me.

"Well?" I asked finally, since they did not seem to want to begin.

Very softly, trembling a little, Thissa said, "Poilar, we've come to ask you to pardon Naxa."

I laughed. "Naxa's gone. Naxa's forgotten. He doesn't exist any more. Don't talk to me about Naxa."

But Thissa said, "That was not a good thing you did, driving him away from us. I think it will anger the gods. I feel the air hot with their displeasure."

"If the gods are annoyed with me, then let them tell me so, and I'll do penance," I said to her. "Naxa was a drain on our spirits. We're better off without him. Ask Kath. Ask Jaif. Ask anyone. No one liked him. No one wanted him."

Hendy stepped forward then and said, in that cool strange voice of hers that I had so rarely heard, "Poilar, I know what it is to be cast out from one's own kind, to be alone the way Naxa is alone now. I feel his pain. I ask you to forgive him."

That startled me and troubled me a little, that Hendy should be pleading Naxa's cause; for I still desired Hendy, who had kept so aloof from everyone throughout our Pilgrimage, and it was odd and somehow disagreeable that she would speak out for Naxa when she had shown such indifference to me and to everyone else. It roused a kind of jealousy in me that she should do that. But there was something touching about it also, the two outcasts drawn together this way, Hendy and Naxa.

I said to her, more gently than I had replied to Thissa, "Even if I wanted to, there's nothing I can do. Naxa's a whole morning's march behind us now. Wherever he may be, we can't take the time to go back and look for him. He's on his own. He'll have to manage by himself, and there's no help for that."

"Oh, he's not all that far away," said Grycindil, laughing.

"What?"

She grinned mischievously. "He's been slinking along behind us all morning, trying not to let you notice him. Hendy and I saw him a little while ago. He's hiding right in there, behind those hills."

"*What?*" I cried again. Enraged, I grabbed up my cudgel. "Where is he? Where?"

But Grycindil put her hand to the cudgel and kept me from going after him. Which was wise, because if I had had Naxa before me at that moment it would have been the end of his life.

She said, "Naxa's a fool. You heard me tell him so yesterday. But even fools have a right to live. If you drive him away, he'll surely die in this wasteland. And he is one of us, Poilar. Do you want the death of a Pilgrim on your soul? For surely the gods will hold his death to your account when we reach the Summit."

"Who knows how the minds of the gods work?" I asked her. I was still shaking with rage. "If Naxa has any sense, he'll keep away from me. I don't ever want to see his face again. Tell him that for me."

"Have a little mercy, Poilar," Grycindil said.

"Let me be."

"Poilar, we beg you—" said Hendy softly.

That weakened me a little. Yet I turned my back on her.

"Let me be," I said again.

"I'll put a spell on him," Thissa said, "to keep him from uttering foolishness from now on."

"No. No. No. No. I want no more of him."

The fury that Naxa had aroused in me was slow to leave me. But in the end they swayed me, Thissa by her visionary force, and Hendy by her compassion for the outcast, and Grycindil by her willingness to forgive a man who had grossly offended her only the day before. I gave my word and off they went to fetch him, and soon afterward Naxa came trailing into camp, hanging his head with shame and fear. There was no complaining out of him from that time onward.

11

THE PLATEAU DID NOT grow more lovable, nor was
there any pleasure to be had in traversing it. But I set a
quick pace and everyone followed, and we moved
onward across its tiresome wastes toward our goal.

For the most part time was suspended for me in that
time, and I experienced none of the impatience or despair
that had brought me earlier to so dark a place. I wanted
only to be going upward again; I would let nothing get in
the way of that. Sometimes I felt a twinge of renewed
restlessness, and then I took to scanning the horizon for
signs that we were actually making progress: looking to see
if certain prominent hillocks or ridges or sinkholes that lay
before us were changing their position in relation to the
great distant mountain mass that was the next level of the
Wall, for example, as we marched. And of course they were.
We were advancing steadily, however it might seem to us
that we were not. The plateau was bigger even than we had
thought it was, but beyond question we were getting across
it. The mountain that rested upon it loomed over us, now.
No longer was it just a pale red glow on the horizon.

And there were signs now of new things ahead.

Thissa felt them first. "This place is inhabited," she said suddenly, in a steep dry place of many stony buttresses, higher than any of the surrounding land.

"Where? By whom?"

"I don't know. I feel presences." She hesitated a moment. Then she pointed toward a place far down below us, fairly close, so it seemed, to the base of the mountain. A river of black water flowed in from the east there and mingled in a raw rocky chasm with a swift river of white water coming in from the west to become a single turbulent waterway. "There," she said. "Right over there, by the two rivers."

"What sort of presences?" I asked. "Dangerous ones?"

"I can't tell. Perhaps."

"We should go around them," Jaif said. "We'd do well not to get mixed up with anyone here."

But it was too late. Our arrival had not gone undetected. We had entered all unknowing into the first of the Kingdoms of the Wall, and those who inhabited it were already aware that we were moving across their territory. It would not be long before they caused us grief.

THERE WERE FLYING DEMONS in the sky that night. None of us had ever seen such creatures before. Gazin the Juggler said that they were wind-sprites, which I had always thought of as mere things of myth and fable. But the Wall is a place where all myth and fable is made real. Still, I know that Gazin was mistaken. These were no sprites, but demons.

We were camped in a windswept declivity surrounded by vile bushes that had red thorns, bright and gleaming with a sinister phosphorescence. It was a dismal, dreadful place, but there was a spring of fresh cool water at its center, and we had no alternative but to camp where the water was.

For much of the evening we saw great birds circling above us, dim black shapes coursing slowly through the dark sky. We took them to be birds, at any rate. But then moons began to appear above the horizon, first gleaming Sentibos and little Malibos soon afterward, and by their sharp cold light we discovered that the flying creatures were not birds at all, but rather some kind of baleful winged beast.

They had bodies not very different in kind from ours, but very frail and small, like a child's, soft and flabby, with flimsy arms and dwarfish legs. Such beings would have seemed feeble and pitiful if they had been confined to life at ground level. But those sad little bodies hung suspended from huge hairy wings of enormous spread and great power that carried them in a kind of tireless gliding way unhurriedly through the air. It was then that Gazin the Juggler told us that these creatures were wind-sprites, and of course the wind-sprite dance is the special property of the Juggler House, so he might reasonably have known how they were supposed to look.

Gazin must have been wrong, though. He was simply trying to assert his own importance, as Jugglers will do; but he had never seen a wind-sprite, for such creatures were known only in ancient times. I had always understood the wind-sprites of the old tales to be delicate and elfin things, and these were hardly that. Though their bodies were so little, they were as shaggy as beasts, covered with thick rank grayish-blue fur which gave them a foul, malevolent look. The deliberate motion of their great wings was ominous and disagreeable. When they swooped down over us close enough for us to have a clear view of their faces, we saw that they were astonishingly ugly, with flat black noses and nostrils that were gaping holes and eyes like green fire, and tall ears tipped with tufts of thick hair. They had four great yellow teeth, two above and two below, that jutted far beyond their lips and went across each other like curving daggers. The feeble hands ended in savage talons. Could there have been any creature less sprite-like and more hideous?

They circled above us for hours, far into the night, never once attempting to land. One passed almost within reach of me, and I smelled the sour smell of its wings and heard it hissing to itself in a low malevolent voice.

As these wind-sprites, or demons, or whatever they were, soared over us again and again, they screamed at us—harsh, raucous cries. After a time it seemed to me that the rhythm of their shrieks was much like speech: that they were saying something to us—shrieking it at us, rather—using words, actual words, but in a language I could not understand. It was like a language one might hear in a dream, although in dreams one can sometimes understand unknown languages, and I could not make a syllable's worth of sense of what these flying monstrosities were trying to tell us. But their tone was malign. It had the sound of a spell. Worse: the sound of a curse.

I saw Thissa huddling against a rock, shivering and weeping. Now and then she would make a Witch-sign as one of the sprites passed close to her. Naxa went to her and slipped his arm around her as though to comfort her. I heard him speaking softly to her, and she nodded, and then he put his head back and shouted something to the creatures overhead. But I had no idea what he might be saying to them.

Most of us went sleepless that night, sitting up beside the fire with our cudgels in our hands, ready to defend ourselves if the need arose. The need did not arise, though; and as dawn came the demons vanished as if frightened of the light.

Throughout all that day we marched at an unusual speed, almost as though by going without sleep we had gained some new energy: but in fact I think it was only a mark of our fatigue that we pushed ourselves onward so unreasonably, heedless of the toll it was taking on us, or perhaps we simply moved fast to get ourselves away from the country of the flying demons. If that was our hope, it was an idle one, because they were back above us as soon as darkness fell, circling and circling and circling, shrieking their curses at us once again.

And once again I heard Naxa shouting back to them, seemingly using the words of their own harsh tongue. I went to him and said, "Are you able to understand their language?"

It was the first time Naxa and I had been near each other since I had allowed him to return to the Pilgrimage. He eyed me fearfully, as though he thought I would strike him with my cudgel. Then he threw a nervous glance toward Thissa, who was nearby, perhaps meaning to summon her to his aid if I chose to attack him. But Thissa was staring off into some realm of mystery and whispering to herself.

"Are you?" I asked.

He moistened his lips. "A little," he said, looking down at the ground. He was terrified of me.

"What language is it that they speak, then?"

"The name of it is Gotarza. A very ancient language, one that was spoken in our land many cycles ago. I studied it when I was a boy. We Scribes keep knowledge of such things." Naxa hesitated. "And what they are saying, I think, is *Come and be melted, come and be melted.* Or perhaps it's *You will be melted.* I can't be sure. My knowledge of Gotarza is very uncertain."

"Melted?" I said.

"That's the one word I have no doubt of. Like a waxen figure, is what they mean. It's a word of change. Think of the way a waxen figure will soften and run and change its form when a Witch heats it to cast her spell."

"And they want us to melt?" I asked.

Naxa nodded.

"This makes no sense to me."

"Nor to me, really. I've been telling them to go away, that we will never do as they wish us to. Perhaps they can't understand me. I tell you, Poilar, my command of their language is extremely weak. But Thissa agrees with me that they're beckoning us onward to something strange."

"Do Witches study the ancient language also, then?"

"No," said Naxa. "But Thissa speaks the language of the mind. She reads the demons' meaning without using words. And that's why she's so frightened. Thissa understands all languages—the language of the rocks, the language of the trees, the language of the demons of the air. She is a santha-nilla, Poilar. There's powerful magic in her. Didn't you know that?"

I looked at him, taken aback. I had not known, no, though I was aware that Thissa's powers were strong. But that strong? No more than a handful of santha-nillas are born in any generation. I had lain in Thissa's arms and made the Changes with her more than once, and yet I had never realized that she was a Witch of the most powerful kind. I wondered now if the troublesome tingling that came from her when she made the Changes, that odd and disturbing emanation, was a sign of her special gift, which I had been too ignorant to understand. But evidently Naxa had not been so obtuse.

"The village allowed a santha-nilla to go on the Pilgrimage?" I asked. "That's hard to believe. There are so few of them, Naxa. I would think that they'd want to prevent her from going, to save her for the needs of the village."

"They didn't know," Naxa said. "No one down there did. She hid it from them. Because she felt that the needs of the village would best be served by having her go on the Pilgrimage, I suppose. But I thought you had certainly found it out. Inasmuch as you and she—" He let his voice trail off and shook his head. "You must cherish her, Poilar. And protect her."

"Yes," I said.

"The sky-demons frighten her very much. All this talk of melting—"

"No harm will come to her," I said. "No harm will

come to any of us, I promise you. No one's going to be melted. I won't allow it to happen." Though of course I had no idea what it was that I was pledging myself to prevent. Melted? Melted? It made no sense to me at all. But I would wait and see.

THERE WASN'T LONG TO WAIT. We were almost to the far side of the plateau, now. The Wall once again rose before us, straight up to the heavens. We had nearly reached the place just in front of it where the black river and the white one flowed together; and as we came down out of a group of low smooth hills round as breasts into the meeting-place of the waters, we saw a congregation of grotesque beings waiting for us there—hundreds, even thousands of them, massed together, milling about. Some were on our side of the water, some were standing right in it, and the rest—the preponderance of them——were fanned out all across the gently rising land on the farther bank, a chaotic multitude that extended well out into the hazy distance.

They were misshapen beyond belief. Nightmare figures, they were. No two of them were alike. There was nothing the mind could imagine that I did not see beside those riverbanks. Some were short and squat like gnomes, and others were tall as giants, but drawn out very thin, so you could snap them with an angry glance. There was one with a single great eye that filled most of his face, and one beside him with a row of little glittering eyes like black beads that ran all around his head, and another that had no eyes at all or nostrils either, only a gleaming half dome from mouth to forehead.

I saw ears as long as arms, and lips like platters, and hands that dangled to the ground. One had no legs, but four arms on which he spun like a wheel. Another had two fleshy wings sprouting from his cheeks and hanging down alongside him like curtains. One had hands like gigantic shovels thrust out before him; one had a male member long as a log jutting forth as though he was in perpetual Change;

one had tails fore and aft that lashed like furious whips. There was one that was twisted and gnarled like a tree ten thousand years old; another had no features at all, but was perfectly smooth and blank; and another appeared to be without bones, and moved like a writhing coil of rope.

I saw more, much more. Little shuffling ones, and gaunt angular ones, and great spherical ones. Creatures covered with bristling spines, with rough pebbly bark, with scales like a glittering fish. Ones with grassy skin, and ones with hairy hides, and ones that were transparent, so you could see their organs beating and throbbing and the middlebone running like a white mast through their torsos.

A torrent of questions rose in me. Why were all these creatures here, in this bleak forlorn place? Where had they come from? How was it that they had such variety of form, each one different from the next, each one uglier than the next?

Traiben was beside me. I said to him in awe, "The gods must have had spoiled fish to eat, the day they created these monsters! Can there be anything more ghastly in all the world? What reason could there possibly have been for bringing such things into existence?"

"The same," he said, "that there was for creating you and me."

"I don't follow you."

"These are people, I think," said Traiben. "Or were, at any rate. People much like any of us, beneath their deformities."

That was a dismaying idea. "No!" I cried. "Impossible! How can these be any kin of ours?"

"Look closely," he said. "Try to see the form that underlies the form."

I made an effort to do as he urged me: to screen out the superficial manifestations of strangeness, and to look beneath the bizarre chaotic exteriors, seeking not for the things that made these beings so strange but for the aspects of bodily design that they might have in common with one another, and with us. And I saw, as my bedazzled eyes roved down the baffling ranks of them, that the basic structure of their bodies was not very different from ours: that the great majority of them tended to have two arms, two legs, a head, a central torso. Those which had hands had six fingers on each, in the main, just as we do. Those which had eyes generally had two. And so forth. There were wild deviations from the norm wherever I looked, but there was a distinct norm, and that was a shape much like ours.

"Well?" Traiben said.

"They are a little like us in some respects," I admitted uneasily. "But it's a coincidence and nothing more. Some bodily forms are universal, that's all—an obvious shape for beings of a certain shape to have. But such similarities don't prove any—"

"What do you make of that one?" Traiben asked, pointing. "Or that? And that? There is change-fire at work here, Poilar."

"Change-fire?" And I shivered out of fear. For as he said the word I imagined I felt invisible waves of dreadful diabolical force sweeping up out of the parched earth and beginning to turn my body into something as monstrous as any of the creatures before me.

"The power of this place has transformed them into these things you see," said Traiben. "But once they looked like you and me."

I looked. What he was showing me, here and there in this nightmare horde, were a few that in a dim light could almost have passed for one of us. Their forms were different from ours in only two or three trivial respects. I said as much to Traiben, and he nodded.

"Yes," he said. "The transformations haven't been as great in them as in the others."

"Are you saying that all these creatures began by looking as we do, and then were reshaped into these forms?"

"Indeed. These things we see before us must be the Melted Ones that Naxa told us of."

Of course! How else could such shapes have come into being? It was as if they all had been put into a crucible and heated until they were soft, and then drawn out while still pliable, and modeled randomly into a myriad weird and fanciful designs. If that was so, I thought, then the ones that looked somewhat like us might be ones who had incompletely melted, ones in whom the process had not been taken through to its fullest degree.

And I felt new terror. Bodily transformation is no unusual thing among us, as I scarcely need tell you. It is our birthright, our natural condition, for us to be able to alter our forms in certain small ways as the need requires. But this was shapechanging beyond all reason or possibility. No Changes that we do create transformations anywhere near as grotesque as could be seen here at this meeting-place of the two rivers, and of course we take pains to return ourselves to our basic forms when the occasion for Changes is ended. Here was an entire population of people who had gone through the most extreme Changes imaginable, and must have stayed that way, locked perpetually into this terrible strangeness. But why? Why? And how? It was in our training days that we first had heard, and only half believed, those dire tales of change-fire, the force that rises from the depths of the mountain, and the strangenesses that it creates. We believed it now. The ghosts we had seen early in the climb must have felt change-fire's power. But what stood before us now went far beyond that, and struck bewilderment into me, both because I feared we ourselves were at risk, and because I could not imagine what purposes of the gods there could be that were served by allowing such monstrosities to be brought into being. That was beyond my understanding.

But I knew now what Thissa feared.

To Traiben I said, "Are we at risk of being altered the way these people were?"

"It could be. I have no understanding of how change-fire works, whether it strikes you against your will, or you must yield yourself up to it. We need to move carefully here."

"Yes. And so we will."

BY NOW ALL THIRTY-NINE of us had descended to the river-valley, and we stood in little groups, staring in shock at the scene before us. The closest of the monsters were ranged along the water's edge in a tight pack right in front of us, separated from us by an open stretch of sandy ground no more than twenty or thirty paces deep. Here they had taken up a stance as though they were the front line of a defending army and were staring back at us, pointing and gaping and calling out to us in harsh thick-tongued voices. Even if I had had any comprehension of their language, it would have been impossible to make out anything clearly in such a great hubbub.

"They're speaking Gotarza," Naxa said. "The same language the demons used. That much I can tell."

"But can you understand what they're saying?"

"A little. Just a little."

I asked him to translate for me, but he simply shook his head impatiently and cocked his head forward, frowning, murmuring to himself. I waited. The Melted Ones seemed to grow more unruly: they were grimacing, glaring, shaking their fists at us if they had anything that was like a fist. It looked certain that they would attack us. Kilarion, just behind me, said into my ear, "We should put our strongest people in front, Poilar. And get ready to fight."

"We wouldn't have a chance against this many," I told him.

"Poilar's right," said Kath. "We've got to bluff them. Walk straight forward as though we own this land, and make them give way before us."

That sounded best to me. Retreating would be pointless. The Wall lay before us; we had to move ahead. I started to give the signal to advance.

Naxa, just then, turned to me and said, "I think I've

made some sense out of what they're yelling now. The Nine Great Ones are waiting for us, is what they say."

"And who might they be?"

"How would I know? But they're telling us that the Nine Great Ones are waiting for us somewhere on the other side of the river. The rulers of this Kingdom, is my guess. Or its gods, maybe. We're supposed to go across to them. We have to ask their permission to cross their territory—that's what I think they're telling us."

"And how are we going to know which ones they are? What do these Nine Great Ones look like? Are they giving you any clue?"

Naxa shrugged. "I don't really know. They aren't being very clear, and now they're all shouting at once. I can barely pick out individual words, let alone figure out very much of what they might mean."

"All right," I said. I stared into the chaos on the far side of the river. "Let's go across and look for the Nine Great Ones, then. And try to find out what they want with us."

Once more I gave the signal, and we went forward. The Melted Ones grew even more agitated as the distance between their front rank and ours dwindled. It seemed as if they meant to hold their ground, or even to move in around us. But when we were nearly close enough to be touching them with the tips of our cudgels they began to back away, keeping just out of reach but maintaining their massed formation and effectively restraining us from any rapid march through their number.

In that way we approached the river. As we strode forward they continued grudgingly to retreat. The water swirled up around our thighs and hips, but went no higher; and though we staggered and stumbled on the rocky bed as the force of the swift flow struck us, we made it across to the far side without serious accident.

They seemed taken aback that we had crossed. Now that we had, they gave ground more rapidly, allowing us a foothold on the riverbank and watching us uneasily from a distance, where they drew together in a tight, dense phalanx. They muttered and glowered at us. I had a sense that any attempt on our part to proceed further into their domain without the blessing of the Nine Great Ones, whoever or whatever they might be, would be met by fierce resistance. But of them I saw no apparent sign: only these multitudes of deformed and bizarre creatures, none seemingly having any more authority than any of the others.

Since twilight was now coming on, I gave the order to make camp. We would decide in the morning what to do next.

12

IN THE GATHERING DARKNESS we watched the Melted Ones roaming about, foraging over the dusty ground for their dinner. They appeared to eat whatever struck their fancy—twigs, dirt, even their own excrement—and we stared at them in revulsion, scarcely able to believe that they were anything other than brute beasts. But greater horror came with nightfall. The sky-demons returned, swooping up out of the blackness at the base of the Wall, and circled swiftly overhead, their powerful wings beating in steady unhurried pulses, their green eyes blazing like angry disks of strange fire above us.

They had come to feed, but not on us.

It was a dreadful sight. The Melted Ones stood smiling vacantly as if lost in dreams, heads upturned, arms—those which had such things as arms—spread wide. And the demons, shrieking ferociously as they came, flew down upon them to drink their blood. Frozen, we watched the flying creatures fasten upon their victims, descending on the Melted Ones and grasping them with their talons, enfolding them in their great shaggy wings, sinking their curving yellow teeth into their throats. The ones that they chose made no attempt to flee or to defend themselves. They gave themselves to their devourers unhesitatingly, almost ecstatically.

The monstrous meal went on and on. For minutes at a time the feeding demons would cling to their prey, busy at their work. Then the wings would open and throb, the winged creatures would spring into the air, and the Melted Ones—emptied and pale, red trickles of blood running from their ravaged throats down onto their chests—would stand statue-like, still upright for a moment or two, before toppling to the ground. When one fell it lay without moving. But the demon who had drunk its life, after circling the sky in a burst of wild energy, came quickly enough down to feed again, and again and again.

Though we were numb with shock and disgust we remained on guard, ready with our cudgels. But the demons never ventured into our little camp. They had enough ready provender waiting for them just across the way.

I turned to Traiben after a time and saw him looking upward, more fascinated, so it seemed, than appalled. His lips were moving. I heard him counting under his breath: "Seven . . . eight . . . nine. One . . . two . . . three. . . ."

"What are you doing, Traiben?"

"How many demons do you make it out to be, Poilar?"

"About a dozen, I suppose. But why should that matter in the slight—"

"Count them."

"Why?"

"Count them, Poilar."

I humored him. But it was difficult to get a good count; the demons were in constant motion, alighting, feeding, leaping aloft again. At any time there might be four or five of them sucking blood and four or five more wheeling through the night sky, but one would descend and another would arise while I was making my tally, and I had a hard time keeping them sorted out. Irritably I said, "Something like nine or ten, is what I get."

"Nine, I would say."

"Nine, then. How many there are hardly seems of any importance."

"What if these are the Nine Great Ones, Poilar?" said Traiben quietly.

"What?" I blinked at him uncomprehendingly. Traiben's notion had taken me utterly by surprise.

"Suppose that these are the kings of the Melted Ones," he went on. "Perhaps created by whatever force it is that has brought the Melted Ones themselves into being. And reigning over them by strength of will, or perhaps by some kind of magic. Breeding them, even, to serve as sources of food."

I fought back a shudder. More carefully, this time, I counted again, following the wheeling winged forms as they moved in the darkness. Nine, so it seemed. Nine. Yes. Who moved as they pleased among these miserable creatures, feeding on them at will. The Nine Great Ones? These repellent blood-drinkers? Yes. Yes. Surely Traiben was right. These demon-birds, or whatever they were, were the masters of this Kingdom.

"And we're supposed to ask permission of *them* to pass through this place?"

Traiben shrugged. "There are nine of them," he said. "Who else can they be, if not the Nine Great Ones who rule here?"

I SLEPT VERY LITTLE that night. The sky-demons remained with us far past midnight, feasting insatiably, and I sat up, clutching my cudgel, afraid that they would attack us when they tired of the blood of the Melted Ones. But they went only to their own. At last they disappeared, flapping off to the west, and then the moons themselves vanished from sight, dropping behind the looming bulk of the Wall, so that we were plunged into darkness. It was then that I slept, but briefly and poorly, dreaming that hairy wings were fastened about my body and glistening fangs were reaching toward my throat.

My sleep, such as it was, was broken by a cry of anguish. I came awake at once and heard the sound of Thissa's wailing.

"Thissa? What is it, Thissa?"

"Death!" she called hoarsely. "I smell death!"

I went to her side. "Where? Who?"

"Death, Poilar." She was shivering. Words in an unknown language came tumbling out of her. Unknowable santha-nilla words, I suppose: magic-talk, the voice that rises out of the well of mysteries. I held her and she fell asleep in my arms, murmuring, "Death. . . . Death. . . ."

There was nothing I could do in the darkness. I sat holding her until Ekmelios crossed the horizon and the plateau was lit by brilliant morning light.

Dozens of Melted Ones, drained white, lay motionless across the way, scattered about on the ground like broken boughs after a wind has rampaged through the forest. They appeared to be dead; very likely they were. The rest, the whole immense horde, sat huddled close together, watching us sullenly. No demons were in evidence. I was without any idea of what to do next. The Melted Ones had allowed us to come this far but evidently they would let us go no farther unless we acknowledged them in some unfathomable way, and if we tried to move forward without the blessing of the Nine Great Ones they would surely resist our advance, so I supposed, and throw us back by sheer force of numbers. I saw no way to reach the Wall other than through the Kingdom of the Melted Ones. But how could I parley with those blood-drinking birds? We were stymied. It was the first great test of my leadership and I felt myself faced with failure.

Then, while I hesitated, Grycindil came running to me, crying that Min and Stum were missing.

A group of the women, said Grycindil, had gone down

to the river at daybreak to bathe. Min and Stum had not been among them, which Grycindil thought was odd, for of us all Min was the most fastidious about such things; and Stum, who was her friend, always went wherever Min went. When they were done bathing the women filled a flask with cold water and went looking for them, thinking that they were still asleep, and planning to splash them for a prank. But no one could find them, Grycindil said. She and Marsiel and Tenilda and Tull had searched through the entire camp.

"Perhaps they've gone off for a morning walk by themselves," I said, and the foolishness of my words made them die in my throat even as I spoke them.

I called everyone around me and told them of the disappearance. There was great consternation. I went to Thissa, who still sat stunned and trembling, and asked her to cast a searching-spell.

"Yes," she said. "Yes, I will."

She gathered little sticks and said the words and threw the sticks again and again. But each time she shook her head and snatched the sticks up and said it was no good, that there was too much noise and confusion all about her. Even when she drew Witch-lines on the ground and knelt to whisper god-names to them, and dropped the sticks within those lines, she could learn nothing that was of any use to us. The strain on her was terrible: her eyes became very bright and large, her face grew rigid.

"Are they still alive?" I asked her. "Can you tell us that much?"

"Please," she said. "Let me rest. All this is beyond my understanding, Poilar." And she began to weep and shake like one who has been taken ill. I told Kreod the Healer to comfort her.

We divided ourselves into six search parties and went off in different directions, with Kilarion leading one group back across the river to look for them to our rear. Seppil and Dorn and Thuiman and I went forward, toward the masses of Melted Ones, and I stared into the teeming multitude of them, trying to catch some glimpse of Min and Stum among them. But I saw nothing. Nor did any of the other search parties. We didn't learn a thing. There were muddy tracks all over, but who could say what they meant?

Everyone was looking at me. I was supposed to tell them how we were going to deal with this. But I was far from having any solution.

I looked to Traiben, to Jaif, to Naxa, to Kath. They had no help to offer me.

Then I became aware of a stirring behind me in the ranks of the Melted Ones. I saw Talbol gaping and pointing, and Muurmut grunted sharply like one who has been struck. I turned and stared, as amazed as they were by the terrible apparition that was approaching us.

A Melted One who might almost have been Min—whose face and form were oddly like hers, although much deformed and distorted in the manner of their kind—had emerged out of that hideous multitude and was making her way unsteadily toward us. My first thought was that the creatures who had captured Min had made a crude copy of her after their own fashion. But then she came closer, and I recognized Min's familiar lively eyes and the tattered green shawl of her House that she always wore, and I realized that this was no copy of Min, but Min herself, a Min who had undergone a strange transformation: a melted Min, in fact.

She moved in a dazed, tottering way. Tenilda and Tull ran to her, reaching her just as she was about to fall, and carried her into our camp.

"Min?" I said, kneeling over her. She had a deathly pallor and the alterations in her appearance were frightful. It was as if she had been softened and reworked all down the left side of her face and upper body, but not on the right. Her ear, her nose, her lips, her cheekbones, all bore the mark of the change. She had had fine delicate features but now, on one side, they looked blurred, coarse, as though they had flowed and run. The texture of her skin on the changed side was different too, glossy and unnaturally sleek. I bent close to her. "Can you hear me, Min? Can you tell us what has happened to you?"

She seemed no more than half conscious. Something like a convulsion swept through her for a moment. She rose a little. Her eyes rolled in her head; she grimaced and her lips turned back to bare her teeth in a frightening way. Then she fell back and grew calm again, though her breath was coming in harsh gusts.

Change-fire, I thought. She has felt the touch of change-fire on her body, and it has done this thing to her.

"The Pit—" she murmured. "The Source—Stum—"

Her voice trailed off.

"Min? What are you saying, Min?"

Someone tugged at me. It was Jekka the Healer. He said, "Step aside, Poilar. Can't you see she's in no condition to talk right now?"

I gave way, and Jekka bent above her and touched her the way a Healer touches one who is ill. Deftly he redirected the flow of the life-forces through the channels of her body, guiding air and warmth and light into beneficial paths. After a time some color came into Min's cheeks and her breathing grew normal. She put her hand to her face, her shoulder, her arm, exploring the things that had been done to her. Then she made a little despondent sound and I saw her shape flicker quickly, as though she were trying to return herself to her proper form. A quick shuddering eddy of Change passed over her but when it ended her body remained distorted as before.

Quietly Jekka said, "Save your strength, Min. There'll be time later to put you back the way you were."

She nodded. I heard someone softly sobbing behind me. Min was a terrible thing to behold.

She sat up and looked about like one who is awakening from a dreadful dream. No one spoke. After a time she said, very quietly, "I've been among the Melted Ones."

"Yes," I said. "Yes, we know."

"They stole us in the darkest part of the night, Stum and me, so quickly we had no time to cry out. Hands over our mouths—they lifted us—carried us—"

"Rest now," Jekka said to her. "There's time to talk about it later."

"No. No, I have to tell it. You need to know this."

Nor would she be denied. Shaken and weak though she was, she forced the story out of herself.

She and Stum, she said, had settled down for the night at the edge of the camp, perhaps in an unwise location, where they were more vulnerable to marauders than the rest of us. But how a party of Melted Ones had been able to steal unnoticed into our camp, Min could not say: perhaps those on watch, whoever they had been at that time, had fallen briefly asleep, or perhaps a spell had been cast, or possibly the whole thing had happened so swiftly that even the most vigilant of sentries might not have noticed. In any event, however they had managed it, the Melted Ones had seized Stum and Min with great efficiency and had taken them quickly off into the darkness for a considerable distance in what Min believed had been the direction of the Wall: though she had been unable to see anything at that moonless hour, she was certain that her captors had been moving on a steady uphill grade.

"We entered a kind of cave," she said. "I think it must have been right at the base of the Wall. Everything was very dark all around, but the moment we were inside I could see a strange sort of light, a green glow that seemed to be coming right out of the ground. There was a sort of antechamber, and then an opening in the floor of the cave, which was the mouth of a long steep passageway that slanted sharply downward to form a deep shaft. The light was rising from the bottom of the shaft. The Melted Ones let us look right over the edge. It is the Source, they kept saying. It is the Source. They speak the old language, the Gotarza. We Scribes understand a little of that."

"Yes. Yes, I know," I said.

"I couldn't tell you what's down there at the bottom. Something bright, something warm. Whatever it is, it's the thing that melts the Melted Ones." Min's hand went to her transformed cheek, perhaps without her realizing it. A deep shudder ran through her and it was a moment before she was able to speak again. "They wanted to change us," she said finally. "And send us back to you as ambassadors of a sort, in order to show you what a wonderful thing it is to be melted. They pushed us forward—toward the rim of the Pit—"

"Kreshe!" someone murmured, and we all made the sacred signs that ward off evil.

Min said, "I felt the heat of it. Just on one side, the side of me that they were holding toward the glow. And I knew that I was beginning to change, but it was no kind of change I had ever felt before. I heard Stum cursing and struggling next to me, but I couldn't see her, because they had me turned facing away from her. She was closer to the Source than I was. They were chanting and singing and dancing around like savages. Like animals." Min faltered. She closed her eyes a moment and drew several slow, heavy breaths. Jekka put his hands to her wrists and held her, calming her. Then she said, "I kicked someone, very hard. His body was soft and it gave against my foot like jelly, and there was a scream of horrible pain. I kicked again and then I got my hand loose and poked my finger into someone's eye, and my other hand was loose, and a moment later there was confusion all over the place. Stum and I both were able to break free. They came running after us, but I was too fast for them. They caught up with Stum, though. I managed to get to the mouth of the cave, but when I looked back I saw her still deep inside, practically at the edge of the Pit, fighting with half a dozen of them. She was yelling to me to get out, to save myself. I started to go back for her. But then they swarmed all over her and I knew that there wasn't a chance—I couldn't see her any more, there were so many of them—like a mound of insects, the whole heap of them piling on top of her, and all of them moving forward, pulling her closer and closer to the Pit—"

"Kreshe!" I muttered, and made holy signs again.

"I knew it was hopeless to try to rescue her. There was no way I could do anything for her and they'd only get me again too if I went back in. So I turned and ran. They didn't try to stop me. I came outside—it was still dark—and tried to find my way back to camp. I must have wandered in circles for a long while, but finally the sun came up and then I knew which way to head. There were Melted Ones everywhere around, but when they saw me they simply nodded and let me go by, as though I were one of them." The harsh glitter of sudden fear entered Min's eyes. She touched her altered cheek again, prodding it fiercely with her fingers as though the flesh were stiff as wood. "I'm *not* one of them, am I? Am I very ugly? Is it disgusting to look at me? Tell me—Poilar—Jekka—"

"One side of your face looks a little different," I said gently. "It isn't so bad. It won't be hard to fix it—isn't that so, Jekka?"

"I think we should be able to induce a complete counter-Change, yes," he said, in that ponderous way that Healers sometimes use. But it seemed to me that there was very little confidence in his tone.

WE RESOLVED TO GO into that cave and see what had become of Stum. By brilliant white noonlight Thissa cast a spell of wind and water that carried her into some other world, and when at last she rose from her trance she pointed a little way to the west and north and said, "There is the path we must take."

Would Stum be still alive when we found her? Thissa offered us nothing about that. But few of us thought so, and I for one hoped she was not. By now the power of that hot glowing thing which Min had called the Source must surely have transformed Stum into something that was very little like the good sturdy Carpenter we had known. Better by far that she had perished at their hands, or found some way of doing away with herself. Yet if there was any chance at all that Stum lived, it would be a sin to leave her behind, however altered she might be; and even if she were dead, honor required us to make an attempt at retrieving her body and giving it a proper burial.

So we broke camp and set out toward the cave of the Source along the route that Thissa had shown us.

Despite my fears the Melted Ones offered no opposition. Our bold decision to march on once again into their midst appeared to stun them, as it had before when we were on the other side of the river. They fell back once more like mere phantoms of air as we advanced, glaring at us in suspicion and hatred but retreating steadily with every step we took. Kath and a few of the others wondered out loud if we were marching into a trap. This is too easy, they said. And of course Muurmut let his doubts be heard also. But I ignored them all. Sometimes a time comes when you must simply go onward.

The soil here was dry and hard, gray and lifeless, with a disagreeable powdery crust. There was a distinct upward trend to the land: as I have said, we were nearing the end of the plateau at last, after all these weeks of flatness, and the next vertical level of the Wall, which once had been nothing but a rosy glow on the horizon, now was so close that it seemed we could reach forward and touch it. It soared above us in the sky, rising to some immense disheartening height, its lofty upper reaches lost in the clouds. But we could not allow ourselves to think about that now.

"There," Thissa said, pointing. "Over there. We go that way." And Min, who for all her weariness had insisted on walking at the front of our line of march, nodded and said, "That's the cave they took us to, right there. I'm certain of it."

I saw a dark round opening in the side of the Wall, a little less than twice the height of a man above the ground. A narrow pebble-strewn path led upward to it. It was like the sort of hole that you see sometimes in the trunk of a great tree, where a swarm of stinging palibozos will make its nest. Crowds of Melted Ones had followed us here; they spread out now to both sides and watched uneasily to see what we would do.

"Six of us go inside," I said. "Who volunteers?"

Min was the first. "No," I said. "Not you."

"I must," she said, with great force.

Kilarion stepped forward also, holding his cudgel high. Galli followed, and Ghibbilau, and Narril the Butcher, with six or seven others after them. Traiben was among them, but I shook my head at him.

"You mustn't go in," I told him. "If anything bad happens to us in there, your cleverness will be needed to guide the others afterward."

"If anything bad happens in there you may wish you had use of my cleverness then," he said, and shot me such a poisonous look that I relented. So it was Kilarion and Galli and Traiben and Ghibbilau and Min and Narril and I who entered the cave.

The place was wider and deeper than I had expected, a great roomy cavity with a high irregular ceiling. There was a small semicircular chamber at the opening, and a larger one beyond. An eerie green glow suffused everything, as though a fire fed by some strange wood were burning in back; but we smelled no smoke and saw no sign of flames. The light was rising through an opening in the floor of the rear chamber. It was clear and steady, not flickering as bonfire-light would be.

"The Pit," Min said. "Which leads to the Source."

Warily we went deeper in. Min would have moved more hastily. I wouldn't let her, catching her by the hand when she made as though to go plunging forward. A few of the Melted Ones came in with us; but they hung back, staying well out of our way. There was no immediate sign of Stum. I posted Narril, Galli, and Ghibbilau as guards between the two chambers, and went on inward with Min and Kilarion and Traiben.

"Look there," Traiben said. "Behold the Nine Great Ones of this miserable race!"

At the back of the cave, where the green light was strongest, the upper part of the cavern wall was furrowed and groined by a group of sharply outlined natural arches that sprouted just above the hole in the floor. Each one formed a kind of craggy perch; and from each a sleeping bird-like creature of great size was hanging head downward deep in dreams, with its huge shaggy wings wrapped close about its body. So far gone in their slumbers were they that our intrusion disturbed them not at all. A dozen or more of the Melted Ones knelt in pious postures below them, gazing up worshipfully at the dangling sleepers.

"The air-demons!" Min whispered. "The blood-drinkers!"

"Yes," said Traiben. "But the demons are at rest, now."

How peaceful they seemed, basking in the warmth from below! But I could see the dreadful wide-nostriled faces and the great curving yellow teeth, and what held them so tightly to their stone perches were the hooked talons that had gripped the victims whose throats they meant to rip. So this was how they spent their days, hanging in placid sleep above the Source that sustained them, before emerging at dusk to feed upon the blood of their faithful followers.

"Stum?" Min called. "Stum, where are you?"

No answer came. Min took a step forward, and another, until she was almost at the rim of the Pit. Holding one hand over the maimed side of her face as though to protect it from the force from below that had changed it, she looked over the edge of the abyss.

Then she uttered a sudden sharp cry and a moan; and I thought she was going to cast herself in. Quickly I seized her by the wrist and pulled her back. Kilarion took her from me and gathered her against his broad chest and held her fast. I went to the edge and peered down.

I saw a long sloping narrow-walled passageway, descending farther than I could measure. There was something that might have been a stone altar down at the bottom of it, with something dark and squat, like an idol, seated upon it. Pulsating waves of brilliant light radiated from it, crashing against the walls of the shaft and blurring my sight with its tremendous dizzying force. And I knew that the tales of change-fire we had heard during our training were true, that this must be one of the places where it radiates from the bowels of the mountain, that terrible force that we are shielded against in our snug village at the bottom of the Wall, because we live so far from its source. I felt the powerful warmth of that light licking against my cheek; I could feel the shapechanging power within my body instantly awakening and unlimbering itself, and fear ran through my soul. We were at risk here, I knew; and would be, I suspected, all the rest of the way to the Summit.

I saw one other thing before I pulled back from that dread abyss: something lying sprawled at the foot of the altar, something shapeless and puddled and terrible which might once have been alive.

"Poilar, what do you see down there?" Kilarion asked.

"You don't want to know."

"Is it Stum? Is she dead?"

"Yes," I said. "At the bottom. They must have thrown her in. Come on: let's get out of this place."

At that Min let out a piercing wail of such power and fury that the startled Kilarion let go of her. I thought that what she intended to do was to hurl herself into the Pit after Stum, and I braced myself to block her; but no, no, she went around to the other side, snatching Traiben's cudgel from his hands and running up a little ridge in the cave wall to a place where she would have access to the sleeping Great Ones. With a swift vehement swing she knocked the nearest one from its perch. It dropped with a thump and lay on the stone floor, feebly fluttering. Swinging again, Min smashed it a crushing blow across the middle of its back and kicked its broken body behind her toward the abyss. Kilarion, with a cry of glee, picked it up by one scaly taloned leg and flung it over the side.

Min, meanwhile, had knocked a second of the demons down, and a third. They flopped about helplessly, barely awake and understanding nothing, as she killed them. The Melted Ones who had been kneeling below the sleepers seemed stunned into paralysis by Min's wild onslaught. They drew together, trembling and whimpering. Kilarion now was enthusiastically cudgeling alongside Min, and I caught the fever too, wrenching one of the Great Ones down with my bare hand and breaking its wings with a single cudgel-blow before tossing it into the Pit. Ghibbilau and Galli came in at the noise, with Narril right after them, and they joined us as we slew. Only Traiben stood aside, looking on in amazement.

Six, seven, eight, nine—the last of the evil birds went over; and for good measure Kilarion encircled half a dozen of the bleating, blathering Melted Ones in his great arms and shoved them down also. Then we all rushed forward, out of that dismal cave, into the sweet holy light of day.

13

O N A BARREN STONY outcropping swept by harsh
winds, half a day's march above the plateau, we held a
memorial service in honor of Stum. We were sad-
dened greatly to think that she would never come to behold
the gods of the Summit. Stum had been an earnest, sturdy,
buoyant woman unafraid of all obstacles: she deserved
better fortune than she had had.

I asked Min and Malti to say the words of the Book of
Death for her as they had for Stapp, but Min was lost in
grief for her friend and could not do it, so Grycindil spoke
in her place. Once again Jaif sang and Tenilda played; and
then we built a cairn for Stum and made our farewells to
her, and set about continuing our journey toward the upper
regions of the Wall. For life is brief and the world holds
many perils, but the Pilgrimage must go ever onward.

It was a blessed mercy to be climbing again after such a
long while in the flatlands; and we rejoiced to be leaving the
doleful plateau and the dire Kingdom of the Melted Ones
behind. There was a fresh spring in our step and we moved
up the face of Kosa Saag with quick, steady strides.

From far away this part of the Wall had seemed to be an impassable steep curtain of stone, ascending in a single straight leap to the gates of Heaven. But that was just a trick of the eye. Once we were on it we found that it was not in fact as vertical as it appeared when viewed across the great expanse of the plateau, but rose in a more gradual way, climbing by curves and sweeps and swoops. There was many a foothold for the climber and frequent stretches where the slope was easy indeed. So in that respect this inner spire of the Wall was much like the outer face where we had begun our climb. And we moved swiftly, exceedingly swiftly, in those early days after leaving the plateau.

To cheer ourselves after the loss of Stum we told ourselves that the ascent would be an easy one from here on, that we would soon find ourselves in the home of the gods. It was the sort of thing Stum would have said.

But we were deceiving ourselves. The difficulties of the plateau might be behind us now, but new difficulties were already making themselves apparent.

How can I begin to tell you of all the hardships we experienced in this zone of Kosa Saag?

The air, for one thing, grew amazingly chill before we had climbed very far, and there were occasional white patches of unmelted snow on the ground, a truly strange thing for children of the torrid lowlands such as we were. Sometimes when we looked up we saw dark crusted clumps of old ice clinging to high spurs of the mountain that were hidden from the light of the sun. They seemed to have been there for centuries. The cold snowy crusts burned us when we touched them out of curiosity. They stung our fingers; they chapped and cracked our skin.

By our fifth day above the plateau we were huddling together at night for warmth, shivering and miserable. Well, our instructors had warned us that we must expect the air in these high altitudes to be colder. "I should think it would be warmer, rather," said Kilarion, pointing to bright

Ekmelios blazing in the sky above us. "After all, we're getting closer to the sun with every step we take."

We all laughed at Kilarion's simplicity. But no one, not even Traiben, could make a proper answer to him on that.

Our skins thickened once again to shield us from the worst of the bite and our hearts pumped faster to make our blood surge warmly within us. We were adapting to the cold, as we had earlier to the thinning of the air. But I wondered privately what sort of chill we would meet in the truly high regions of the Wall, if this was what we were encountering here.

Not only was the weather colder up here but the season was turning against us. We had had dry, bright weather for most of our climb thus far. But now came a time of frequent icy rain and occasional snow. One night there was a fearful storm when black howling winds raked the mountain, so fierce that I thought we would be hurled back down onto the plateau. Sharp sleet rode on the winds, sleet that nipped our faces and hands like fire, sweeping in upon us until we cried out to the gods to spare us. We found crevices and crannies and little caverns and tried to hide ourselves from the storm's fury, nestling together by twos and threes to give warmth to one another.

That night cost us a life. When I emerged at dawn, stiff and sore and more than half frozen, the first thing that took my eye was the rigid, staring face of Aminteer the Weaver, white as bone, jutting like a trail-marker above a white field of snow. He was buried to his neck. I shouted for help and we dug him out, but it was no use. Aminteer had chosen an unlucky place to pass the night, a pocket where the wind could pile the flakes high very quickly, and the sleet had trapped him as he slept. Perhaps he had died without knowing what was happening to him.

So there were three of us lost already, and we were scarcely beyond the first of the Kingdoms. I understood now why so few Pilgrims ever return from this journey. The mountain is very high and the hazards are beyond counting. That anyone ever reached the Summit was beginning to seem miraculous to me.

The snow and sleet abated and the cold lessened somewhat, but now we had rain, a steady maddening downpour that threatened to go on forever. We waited two days in a dank cave for it to end. During that time Jekka and Thissa and, I think, Malti, made an attempt to heal Min's ruined face with Changes and spells. I saw them huddled together in a far corner, murmuring and clasping hands and chanting, and lighting aromatic tapers and giving her potions and holy images to hold. But it was a failure. There was no way they could persuade her flesh to flow back to its original form and if anything I think they made matters a little worse. When they had done with her Min moved back into the deepest shadows of the cave and huddled there with her cloak pulled up over that side of her face. I heard her sobbing. I would have gone to her, but she waved me away. Later Galli tried to comfort her, and she too was refused. But afterward Marsiel and a few of the other women were able to talk with her, though she still remained withdrawn and somber and kept herself apart from the rest of us.

The next day, although the rain was still falling, we decided to go on.

It would have been better if we had stayed where we were. Soon after we took the trail we heard a deep rumbling sound from above. "Thunder," said Kath. But thunder was not what it was. A moment later Ijo the Scholar put his hand to his forehead and drew it away bloody. "Strange sort of rain," he muttered. I felt a stinging blow myself. Others cried out. A scattering mist of light pebbles was falling upon us. And then came the heavy thump of a solid boulder bigger around than my outspread hand could cover, which landed almost at my feet.

"Take cover!" Traiben cried. "Landslide!"

A moment later it was as if the whole mountain were falling upon us. The world shook beneath our feet. But Kreshe the Savior provided for us in that dark time of danger. An overhanging brow of stone was jutting from the breast of the Wall not far in front of us, and we ran frantically toward it while rocks great and small volleyed down all around us.

We got to the shelter just before the main burden of the rockfall hit, pressing ourselves in against it so wildly and chaotically that we began to laugh despite the gravity of the moment. But it was not a happy laughter. There we stood, jammed tight against one another, stunned and fearing for our lives, while a tremendous hail of tumbling rock came crashing down. The sound it made as it bounced along the flank of the Wall was like the hammering of giants on the mountain's side. The rain, no doubt, had loosened some slope far overhead. From our safe place we watched, astounded, as the great boulders slammed into the path we had just been on and went bouncing over the edge of the cliff.

It went on for minute after minute. We thought it would never stop. Tenilda and Ais began to beat time to imaginary drums as if they heard a secret music in the endless crashing. Jaif began to chant to their rhythm, a Song of the Falling Mountain. But then came one great earthshaking thud more terrible than anything that had gone before, and a second almost as frightful, and a third, and we all fell silent and stared at one another, thinking that this was the end of us. After that third crash, though, there were no more. An awesome hush descended. At last the thunderous booming had ceased, and we heard only the lesser sound of falling pebbles once more against the hissing of the rain. And then, only the rain.

Cautiously we peered out. A tremendous rocky mound, three times the height of a tall man, covered the place where we had been only a few moments before. It could easily have served as a cairn for us all. The trail we had been following was utterly shattered and buried behind us.

Through the providence of the gods none of us had

been killed or even injured. And gradually we began to shake off the impact that so much noise and fury had had upon us. But we had let our packs and bedrolls drop as we ran for safety, and much of what we had left exposed on the trail lay buried now beneath tons of stone. There was no hope of uncovering it. We had lost a great deal in the way of equipment and would have to share and make do with double service from now on. But we paused anyway to give thanks to Kreshe for our preservation before continuing onward.

Then I said, as we made ready to go, "Where is Min?"

My glance went up and down, up and down, and I saw no sign of her anywhere. I walked to the edge of the rockpile and kicked at it despairingly, thinking that she must have failed to reach the shelter in time, that she lay entombed now under that great mass here.

Then Hendy came forward and said, "I saw her turning back, just before the rocks fell."

"Back? Back where?"

"To the land of the Melted Ones. She was running. Down the path we had just come. I called to her but she kept going, and then there was the rockslide."

"It was because of her face," offered Marsiel. "She told me yesterday that she didn't think she could bear to let anyone look at her. It was after the Healers tried to repair her and failed—she said she was thinking of running away, that she didn't see how she could stay with us any more. And also on account of Stum—she was so very miserable about Stum. She was talking about going back to the place where Stum had died."

"And no one let me know of this?" I asked.

"I didn't think she really meant it," said Marsiel, very abashed. "I thought it was something that would pass. If I had understood—if I had only understood—"

I looked about, angry and confused. What sort of leader was I, to be losing my Pilgrims right and left like this, and the climb only begun?

The same thing must have occurred to Muurmut. He drew himself up tall and said, "Everyone stay here. I'll bring her back."

"Wait," I said. "I don't want you going anywhere—"

But I was too slow. Muurmut was already scrambling up the side of the great heap of rocks. He moved with astonishing agility for a man his size, and enormous determination. There was no sense ordering him back; he was already far up the mound, clambering swiftly. The ill-matched rocks slid and slipped beneath him, and for a moment it looked as if the whole mound would give way and topple him into the gulf just beyond. But he raced forward even as the rocks underfoot were moving past him, and somehow held his footing, passing over the crest of the huge cairn and disappearing on the far side.

I was furious. These empty-headed heroics were idiocy. Even if he found Min, how was he going to bring her back? Only someone of immense strength could negotiate that immense pile of jagged rock. Muurmut might make it alone, but not if he were carrying Min.

I had no choice, though, but to wait in this spot until Muurmut returned. If I had given the order to move on without him, I would have laid myself open to a charge of trying to rid myself of my rival, and in a crude and cowardly way besides.

He was gone more than an hour. Much as I would have rejoiced to have him perish on the slopes in his folly, I found myself instead praying for his safe passage, so that he would come back shortly and we might move along without further delay. But there was no sign of him for a long while.

Then we heard scrabbling sounds, and Muurmut appeared atop the rocks, red-faced, dirt-stained, sweating. In silence we watched as he lowered himself to the place where we stood and took a long drink of water from a flask that Grycindil handed him.

"Well?" I said, finally.

"She's gone."

"Dead?"

"No, that's not what I mean. But gone. I went back to the place where the trail winds round and round, and looked down over the edge. And I could see her far below, heading down the hill. Running. She was no bigger than a doll from where I was. I called to her, and I think that she heard me; and she may have called something back, but her voice was blown away on the wind. And she was running all the while. Heading for the plateau as fast as she could, as if that was the finest place in all the world. Heading for the Melted Ones."

"The *other* Melted Ones," Hendy said. "They are her people, now."

I shivered. But I knew that what Hendy had said was true. Min was lost to us. If Muurmut had succeeded in catching up with her, he could only have brought her back by force; and she would not long have remained.

And so we had the first of our deserters to the Kingdoms: the first of what we would learn to call the Transformed Ones, those who gave themselves up to the will of the mountain and surrendered themselves utterly to the power of change-fire. I muttered a prayer for Min, wherever she might be, whatever she was destined to become.

Muurmut beckoned for another water-flask. He must have put himself under tremendous strain in that futile chase. He drank deep; and then he looked around at everyone, grinning, puffing up his chest, preening. He was obviously immensely pleased with himself for having carried out that solitary trek rearward, and expected everyone else to be also.

I felt that I had to deflate him.

I looked at him and said, "I don't want anyone to go off on a solo expedition like that ever again."

"What?" Muurmut cried, and he gave me a look of pure hatred.

"What Min did is a sad and pitiful thing, Muurmut.

The hearts of all of us go out to her. But it was absolutely wrong for you to go running after her. There was no way you could have succeeded in catching up with her or bringing her back. And we've wasted valuable time here while we were waiting for you. We need to move forward—forward—forward all the time—"

His face grew sour and glowering. "I know what's right and what's wrong at least as well as you do, Poilar. I couldn't have lived with my conscience if I hadn't made the attempt. You look after your own, and let me be." And he spat against the side of the rockpile and walked off angrily with Grycindil's arm through his.

I heard more than a little muttering, here and there about me. For the first time some were taking Muurmut's side. They saw his pursuit of Min as bold and heroic. Indeed that was what it had been; but it had been folly, all the same. The problem was that I was the only one who seemed to understand that.

WE WENT HIGHER, AND the rain ceased, and the weather turned warmer again, though not nearly so warm as it had been in the lower reaches of the Wall. Once again we were forced by the shape of the cliff to turn toward an interior valley, and when we entered it we found it to be a hidden world of lush meadows and hills, as green and lovely as the plateau had been grim and dry.

This secret place within the vastness of the Wall gave us much pleasure, even though it slowed our ascent. It was like a great bowl, curving gently upward at the sides, but mainly all on one level. All about us rose lofty canyon walls of bright red stone banded with outcroppings of glossy black. One of them held the route that would allow us to continue Summitward; but we had no idea which one it was, or how to get ourselves up upon it. For days we made our way through this land of streams and thick grass with little sense of the proper direction.

I felt vulnerable to a rebellion. I doubted that anyone

else had a better idea of the right way to go than I did; but I had no idea at all, and I was the leader, and a leader must lead. Others look to him for strength and wisdom. Woe betide him if he doesn't provide those things.

Muurmut, during this time, kept silent. He might have said, "Poilar is leading us nowhere," or, "Poilar complained when I wasted an hour in search of Min, and here he is wasting days for us in this land of streams," or, "If Poilar doesn't know where he's going, perhaps there's someone else who does." He said nothing of this sort, though, at least not in my earshot. But I knew that he was thinking it. I could see it in his eyes, in the cocky set of his mouth, in his swaggering walk.

I wouldn't give him the satisfaction of a voice in councils. I consulted with Traiben often, of course, and with Kath, with Jaif, even with Naxa and Kilarion. They had some quality or another, whether it was Traiben's cleverness or Naxa's fund of information or Kath's cunning or Kilarion's intuitive skill on the trail or Jaif's sturdy good will, which led me to think they would be useful in helping me find the way. The one I never consulted was Muurmut. Perhaps it was petty of me; but he had obstructed me from the start, had sniped and grumbled and postured and hindered, and I wasn't about to take him into my confidence now.

I saw him staring at me from afar. He looked tense and angry all the time. No doubt his mouth brimmed with sarcasms and slurs. But he kept his silence.

None of those whom I consulted was able to suggest the way to find the upward path, any more than I. And so we wandered aimlessly, occasionally coming across our own earlier trail in some meadow, or a campsite we had used three days before. We were all like children here—or perhaps I should say like dreamers trying to find their way through an unknown world. They had sent us onto the Wall knowing nothing of the realities that lay ahead for us—all their teachings in those years of our training had been guesswork and fable and foolishness—and if we were in difficulties now, that was only to have been expected.

Then Grycindil came to me in late afternoon while we were making our camp for the night on mossy beds beside a clear sweet stream after a long day of pointless wandering. Darkness was just beginning to come on and a couple of the moons were edging into the sky. She said, "Poilar, Muurmut is having a very difficult time of it."

Grycindil and Muurmut had begun sleeping together after we had left the plateau. That seemed odd to me, because Grycindil, though a little quick-tempered, had always seemed to me a level-headed and good-hearted woman, and why she should want to entangle herself with an arrogant braggart and blowhard like Muurmut was beyond my understanding. But there is no accounting for reasons, where the Changes are involved. And perhaps there were qualities about Muurmut that I was simply incapable of perceiving.

I said, "We are all having a difficult time of it, Grycindil."

"It's different for him. He wants to be leader, and you stand in his way."

"I know that. It's nothing new."

"He has ideas about the right trail to take."

"Does he?" I said. "Let him speak up, then."

"No. You said harsh things of him after he went to find Min. He was furious with you for that. He was awake all night, saying, 'How could we not have tried to bring her back? How could we simply let her run away, and keep on going as if nothing had happened? And then for Poilar to tell me that I was wrong to do it—' The bitterness won't leave him now, Poilar. He sulks day and night. Sometimes I hear him crying, actually crying, a dry choking sort of crying, full of frustration and anger. He was in serious trouble two or three times while he was off looking for Min, do you know that? He was almost killed on the trail. Part of the path gave way beneath his feet and dropped into the abyss, and nearly took him down also. So for you to criticize him, then, when he came back—no, Poilar, he's not going to volunteer any ideas now. He's afraid you'll make him look foolish again."

"It was very brave of him to go after Min. But it was wrong, all the same."

"It wasn't, Poilar."

I shrugged. "It wasn't? Well, then, I was wrong, I suppose. Whichever you prefer to think. Listen, Grycindil, I'm sorry that Muurmut is suffering on my account. But it's all his own doing."

"Can't you ease things for him a little?"

"How? By making him leader in my place?"

"You could consult him once in a while, at least."

I gave her a close look. She was utterly sincere; and I beheld something in her eyes, a warmth, a love for Muurmut, even, that startled me. Again I considered the possibility that I might have underrated Muurmut. Even braggarts may actually have some virtues.

But I had no faith in Muurmut's judgment, because it seemed to me always that his thinking was corrupted by love of self, that he was forever trying to impress others with the strength, courage, shrewdness, and capability of Muurmut. A true leader has no interest in doing that.

So I said to Grycindil, "Let me think about it," meaning to do nothing. And she knew that I meant to do nothing; but the conversation had gone as far as it could, and she knew that also. So she turned away from me, murmuring to herself.

But scarcely any time later Hendy came to me, while I was looking about for a comfortable place to set my bedroll down for the night.

"Can we talk?" she asked. I was a little surprised at that, coming from Hendy, who had been so remote and aloof for so long; but she had seemed to be emerging a little from her shell lately. And her slender shoulders were set now in a posture of curious determination, very much at odds with the timid, hesitant bearing she usually displayed.

"Concerning what?" I asked her.

"Muurmut."

"Muurmut! Kreshe, woman! Selemoy and Thig! Are you all in league against me for Muurmut's sake? Tell me, are you making the Changes with him too?"

It was a crude thing to say. And my tone was so rough and loud that she backed away, but only a pace or two. Her eyes held steady on mine. "Too? Am I making Changes with so many people, then? Muurmut and which others, do you think?"

"That's not what I meant," I said, reddening, wishing I could call back my words. "But Grycindil just came to me to speak in Muurmut's favor. Well, at least I can see her reasons for that. But now when you show up also—"

She said quietly, "Muurmut is no lover of mine. And what Grycindil does with Muurmut is her own affair. I came to you because the trouble here can only get worse, and it will hurt us all."

"Trouble?"

"Between you and Muurmut. Oh, no, no, Poilar, please don't try to look so innocent. The two of you have been butting heads since Hithiat milepost and everyone is aware of it."

"He thought he was fit to be leader. I knew that I was. We've been butting heads because he disagrees with me."

"The same could be said the other way around."

"Do you believe Muurmut's better qualified than I to lead us?"

"No," she said. "He's rash and stubborn and he can be very foolish. But you underestimate him, Poilar. He has ideas to offer us. Some of them may be good ideas. And because you refuse to listen to them, you cause pain for him. If this goes on, he'll force us all to share that pain."

"What do you mean?"

"I mean a battle for the leadership."

"He won't try it," I said. "And if he does, only those few hangers-on of his will follow him."

"Are you willing to risk it?" Hendy asked. "A struggle for power up here, when we've come so far?"

Her dark eyes were shining mysteriously. A soft perfume was rising from her throat and shoulders, and I knew the fragrance must be that of her own skin. This show of strength was bringing a sudden beauty to life in her, and it was having a powerful effect on me.

I said, "Do you have any suggestions, then?"

"A reconciliation between you and him."

"There can't be a reconciliation when there was never friendship in the first place."

"Well, then, peace, at least. A handshake. You were very cruel to him, that time he climbed the rocks to look for Min. You could tell him that you regret that now."

"You swear to me that you haven't hatched this together with Grycindil?"

Her nostrils quivered in anger. "I've told you already that I haven't."

"She thinks the same way you do about this."

"Many of us do."

I considered that. I remembered the grumbling I had heard. A leader leads only by consent of the led. That consent might be withdrawn at any time.

"All right," I said, after a time. "I'll give him a handshake, if you think it'll do any good. What else do you suggest, Hendy?"

"That you invite Muurmut to share his ideas with us about the direction we should take."

"Grycindil said that also."

"As well she might have."

She stared me straight in the eyes for a long moment. Then she turned and walked away.

·   ·   ·

AROUND THE CAMPFIRE THAT night Jaif sang the Song of the High Peaks, and Ais and Tenilda made astonishingly lovely music by clicking sticks together, and Naxa told a long, involved, and oddly perverse comic fable that he said he had learned from a manuscript five thousand years old, which dealt with the mating of gods and rock-apes. Though we had achieved nothing useful in our day's travel, we were strangely cheerful that evening.

When Naxa was done I walked over to the place where Muurmut sat on the far side of the fire with Talbol and Seppil and said to him, "May we talk?"

"I don't know. May we?"

"Go easy, Muurmut. This has been too pleasant an evening to have it spoiled now."

"You came to me, Crookleg. There was nothing I wanted to say to you."

I could gladly have thrown him into the stream for that "Crookleg." But I held myself in check and said, with a quick glance at Grycindil—who was watching us from a distance—"I owe you an apology, Muurmut."

His expression was one of mingled amazement and wariness. "An apology? For what?"

"For some of the things I said to you when you came back after looking for Min."

He was all suspicion now.

"What are you getting at, Poilar?"

I took a deep breath. And told him that I never would have given him permission to go in search of Min the way he had if he had asked me, but that I had been wrong to accuse him of disobedience, because he had simply jumped up and run off impulsively, without taking the time to ask me whether he could. If there is no refusal of permission, I said, there is no disobedience.

He listened to these dry legalisms with a skeptical expression on his face, and made no reply.

"Furthermore," I said, "I told you then that it had been wrong for you to go after her. In fact I now realize that you did the right thing. If there was any chance at all that Min could have been found and brought back to us, what you did was worth trying."

Plainly Muurmut had expected none of this from me. I was amazed myself that I was able to say it. He continued to stare at me, as if weighing my words to find some secret mockery in them. But there was none, and he seemed to be struggling to believe that. Seppil and Talbol looked at each other in complete bewilderment. I saw Grycindil coming toward us, smiling.

"Well—" Muurmut began, and then he stopped, not knowing what to say.

I said, "I spoke too harshly to you that day. I regret that now. And so I wanted to tell you that I've come to think it was right of you to go in search of Min. And very brave to attempt it alone."

"Well," he said again, almost tongue-tied with perplexity. "Well, then, Poilar—"

He had never seen me in this mode before. No one ever had. And he wasn't at all sure what to make of it. Part of him must still have thought that I was setting him up for some new kind of humiliation.

I stared at him levelly. This was very difficult for me, but I was determined to see it through.

"Well, Muurmut? Are you going to accept my apology or aren't you?"

"If it's sincere, yes, I accept. Why shouldn't I? But I confess I don't understand why you're bothering."

"Because we've used up much too much energy in hatred," I said, "and now we have none to spare." There was little warmth in my tone, none in my eyes. It was hard, all right, forcing myself to crawl to him like this. But I held my hand out toward him. "Can we make an end to all this bickering?"

"Are you resigning your leadership to me, then?" he asked coolly.

Again I came close to dunking him. But I clenched my

jaw and replied, as evenly as I could, "Our fellow Pilgrims chose me leader by their vote. If they want to remove me by their vote, so be it. But resigning's not in my spirit. I ask you to accept me ungrudgingly as the leader of this Pilgrimage, Muurmut, as you should. And I'll promise you in return to put aside the coldness I've felt toward you, and draw you into my circle of advisers."

"You want us to be *friends?*" he asked, in disbelief.

"Allies, rather. Fellow Pilgrims, working together for the good of all."

"Well—"

Grycindil, who was at his side now, nudged him sharply with her foot. He glared at her; but then he rose, unlimbering himself until he stood high above me, for he was a very big man. My hand was still out. He took it, though his expression was a strange, strained one.

"Allies, then," he said. "Fellow Pilgrims. Yes. Yes. All right, Poilar. Fellow Pilgrims, working together."

It wasn't the most tender of reconciliations. But it did the job. Tomorrow, I resolved, I would quietly call Muurmut aside and ask him if he had any thoughts on how to leave this valley of streams.

As I walked back to my side of the fire Grycindil came by me and whispered a word of thanks. I nodded and kept going. None of this had been pleasant for me. I had done it the way one lets the cautery be put to a bloody wound: because one must.

14

EVERY MOON WAS IN the sky that night. In all that brightness anyone might have had trouble sleeping; but it was not the brightness that kept me awake. That little talk with Muurmut had left me utterly sleepless, my mind boiling over with turbulent thoughts. I lay tossing for what felt like hours, wondering if I had destroyed myself as a leader by my willingness to make the conciliatory gesture that I had offered Muurmut, which some might see as cowardice, or, at best, unsteadiness of purpose.

No, I kept telling myself. A leader can only gain by showing generosity of spirit. And it was wiser to neutralize and disarm Muurmut with kindness than to allow his rage to fester any longer in his heart.

But none of these fine philosophical thoughts helped me to get to sleep. I lay like a clamped fist, unable to let go. Finally I could lie there no longer. My eyes were aching and my face felt feverish. I slipped out of my bedroll and went down to the stream to splash water in my face.

The others, scattered here and there around the fire, were all asleep, all but Kilarion and Malti, who were on sentry shift. They looked half asleep themselves. As I went past them they nodded drowsily toward me. I envied them their drowsiness.

I looked across the stream and saw Hendy camped by herself, as she usually did. I had spoken to her more than once about the risks of keeping herself apart from the rest, but she did as she pleased all the same and finally I had ceased to trouble her about it.

She was awake and alert, sitting up in her bedroll with her chin propped on her hand, watching me. Her eyes were sparkling by the light of the many moons. I remembered how beautiful Hendy had looked, suddenly, while she had been urging a reconciliation with Muurmut upon me a few hours before, and how sweet the fragrance of her shoulders had been. I stared at her and waited, hoping against all hope that she would beckon to me. But of course she merely returned my gaze without responding. Then I remembered how in my anger I had asked her if she were making the Changes with Muurmut, simply because she had come to me to plead on his behalf; and I felt shame run through me like a bolt of lightning from head to toe.

I had to make amends for that bit of coarseness. Though I had had no invitation from her, I waded across the stream to her side of it. Halfway across I stumbled on a slippery rock and fell headlong, and for a moment I crouched there in the chilly flow, cursing my clumsiness, but laughing also. At such times laughter is best. But this had not been an amusing night for me and it seemed to be getting worse as it went along.

I picked myself up and went to her, and stood above her, dripping. She looked up at me and a flutter of some quick emotion—fear? Or something more complex?— showed on her face for a moment.

I said, "Well, I spoke with Muurmut as you asked."

"Yes. I know."

"I offered him an apology. He wasn't particularly graceful about accepting it. I may not have been all that graceful in the way I offered it. But we made peace, after a fashion."

"Good."

"And tomorrow I'll invite him into councils."

"Yes. Good."

She said no more than that. I stood there, waiting for something else. I felt more like a boy of thirteen than I did like the man of twenty years that I was, with half my life already behind me.

"May I sit next to you?" I asked finally.

Perhaps she smiled, a little. "If you want to. You're all wet. Are you cold?"

"Not really."

"I saw you fall as you were crossing the stream."

"Yes," I said. "I was looking at you instead of at the stream bed. That's a stupid way to cross a stream, I suppose. But I was more interested just then in looking at you."

She said nothing. Her eyes were unreadable.

I knelt beside her and said, "You know that I didn't mean it, don't you, when I asked you before if you were making the Changes with Muurmut?"

"I understood what you were saying, yes."

"It was because I was surprised that you were taking the trouble to speak up for Muurmut, when you had hardly ever involved yourself in disputes of any sort before. And you came to me right after Grycindil, who *is* making the Changes with him. So I felt outnumbered. And in my anger—"

"I told you that I understood what you were saying. There's no need to keep explaining it and explaining it. You'll only muddle things up again." Hendy put her hand on my wrist. It tightened on me with surprising strength. "I can't bear to see you shivering like this. Come in here with me." And she held the flap of her bedroll open.

"Do you mean that?" I asked. "I'll get everything all wet."

"Oh, you *are* stupid, aren't you?"

For the second time in five minutes I laughed at my own foolishness, and scrambled in beside her. She moved to the right-hand side of the bedroll to make room for me; there was open space between us. For the moment I made no move toward closing it. I sensed a war going on in Hendy between her innate mistrust of other people and the desire finally to let herself go, to open herself to another person and allow herself to be embraced. Thissa too had been like that. But Thissa was a santha-nilla, cut off from all those around her by the powers of her witchcraft: she could never be anything more than a visitor in the lives of others. Hendy, I suspected, was struggling to put an end to the aloofness that imprisoned her; and the struggle must not have been a simple one for her. But she had decided that now was the moment for ending it. I was amazed and grateful that she would choose me for that. She could have whatever she wanted of me, whether it be an hour's quiet talk or a gentle embrace or even the Changes itself. I told myself that I would be as patient and as gentle as I knew how to be. I had done all the clumsy things I meant to do for this night.

She said, lying back and speaking upward into the darkness, "You aren't really stupid, Poilar. You were trying to be kind, I know."

That is not the sort of thing to which one can reply. So I lay there quietly beside her.

"And you knew all along that there was nothing between Muurmut and me, that there never could be."

"Yes. That much I knew. Truly."

"I would never choose someone like Muurmut for a lover. He reminds me too much of the men of Tipkeyn who stole me from our village when I was a girl." She paused for a little while. Then she said, "I've haven't ever chosen *anyone* for a lover, Poilar."

I looked at her in astonishment. "You've never made the Changes, not ever?"

"That was not what I said," she replied, and I felt

foolish all over again. "But I've never *chosen* anyone. To choose means to express one's own free will."

I pondered that for a moment. Then my face grew hot with confusion.

"You mean that when you were living in Tipkeyn—without your consent—they attempted to—"

"Yes. Don't ask me about it. Please."

I couldn't stop myself. "But how could they?" I said. "It's impossible to force the Changes. How can it be done, if the woman doesn't initiate them in herself?" I faltered and fell silent. What did I know about such things? There were evils in the world beyond my dreaming, and unquestionably some of them had touched Hendy—and again, yet again, I was being stupid.

I found myself unable to look at her, unwilling to let my eyes intrude on her shame. So I turned so that I was lying with my face upward, looking into the moonlit sky, as she was.

"I was ten years old," she said softly. "I was in a strange village and I was frightened. They gave me wine, very strong wine. Then I wasn't so frightened. And they began to touch me. They told me what I had to do, and when I balked, they gave me more wine. After a time I didn't know where I was or who I was or what I was doing."

"No," I said. It was monstrous. "No one would treat even an animal like that!" Out of embarrassment for her I was still looking upward instead of at her, and as she had done I spoke to the sky, so that we were like two disembodied spirits holding a conversation.

She said, "I was in a strange village. They felt no ties of kinship to me. I had no House. To them all I *was* was an animal. A female animal, something to be used." Abruptly there was a frightening edge on her voice. "So they used me. After a time they didn't bother with the wine. I fought them, I bit them, I kicked them, but it didn't do any good."

"This happened more than once?"

"I was in Tipkeyn for four years."

"Gods! No!"

"Then I escaped. I walked off into the forest, one day when there was a storm and the whole sky was full of lightning and they were all so terrified that they ran and hid. But one of them saw me anyway, and came after me and said he'd kill me if I didn't come back with him. He had a knife. I smiled at him in the way that they had taught me to do. Put down your knife, I said, and let us make the Changes right here and now, for the storm is ending and I desire you very greatly. So he did. And I took the knife and cut his throat with it. Three women of our village found me wandering in the outer fields, some time later—a few days, a week, a month, I don't know. I was half crazy from hunger and exhaustion. They brought me home. No one recognized me in my family, because I was a grown woman now and I had been a child when I was stolen. No one wanted me, because of what had happened to me in Tipkeyn. That was the first thing they asked me—did they force you?— and I said yes, yes, they did, many times. Perhaps I should have lied, but how could I hide a thing like that? So they would have cast me out again. But the heads of the Houses came to see me, and your kinsman Meribail was there and he said, 'What shall we do with her?' and then the head of my own House said—"

"Which House is that?" I asked. I realized that I had never known.

"Holies," she said.

"Holies? But—"

"Yes. The Pilgrimage is forbidden to us. But the head of my House said, 'We should ask the girl what she wants,' and I said, 'To be a Pilgrim.' Because I didn't belong in our village any more, and I'd kill myself before I went back to Tipkeyn, and where else was there to go but the Wall? My Pilgrimage had already begun, the day the men of Tipkeyn stole me, and everyone knew it. And so it was arranged. My name was stricken from the list of the House of Holies and it was agreed with the Masters of the House of the Wall that

I would be among the Pilgrims of my year-group. I would be allowed to go up on Kosa Saag and lose myself there. So when they held the Winnowings, I was always passed over, because the Masters knew that I had been chosen in advance to be a Pilgrim. And so here I am."

"Gods," I muttered, over and over again. "Gods, gods, gods!"

In a curious remote voice, thin and light as the sound of an air-flute, she said, "Why am I telling you all this?"

"I don't know."

"I don't either. I had to tell someone, I suppose." I was aware of movement beside me, and I looked around to see that she had turned toward me and that the space between us was now no more than a finger's breadth. She said in that same distant voice, "What I want is to go to the gods at the Summit and be purified by them. I want them to transform me. I want them to turn me into someone else. Or even *something* else, I don't care. I don't want to be who I am any longer. The memories that I carry around are too heavy for me, Poilar. I want to be rid of them."

"You will have your wish. The gods are waiting for us up there, Hendy, that much I know. And I know also that they'll make everything right for you when we reach them."

"You think so? You really do?" She was so eager.

"No," I said. Like a cracked bell is how I sounded as I uttered the word. But my glib lie had turned sour in my mouth. What did I know of what was waiting for us at the Summit? And Hendy was no child; how could I let myself console her with some sort of sweet fable? I shook my head. "No, in truth I *don't* think so, not really, Hendy. I have no idea at all what's in store for us up there on top. But I hope the gods are there, and that they are gentle gods, and that they'll take your pain from you. I pray that they will, Hendy."

"You are very kind. And honest."

Again there was silence for a time.

She said then, "I often wonder what it is like to *choose*

a lover for the Changes, as others do. To turn to someone and say, 'You, I like you, come down here beside me, let us make pleasure for each other.' It seems so simple. But I've never been able to bring myself to do it."

"Because of Tipkeyn."

"Because of Tipkeyn, yes."

I looked at her. The flap of the bedroll was turned partway back and by the light of the five moons I could see that she had begun to slide into the female form, that her breasts had appeared and that her skin was glistening with the fine coating of perspiration that meant the Change was going on lower down. That was ordinarily all the invitation any man would need. But if I took it that way and embraced her now, unasked, would she be *choosing*? Perhaps she was unable to help herself, and was drifting automatically into Changes simply because the two of us were lying close together like this. Perhaps she was desperately fighting it within, frantically trying to force herself back to the neuter state.

My own maleness had emerged and it was all I could do to control myself. But I compelled myself to wait.

The timeless moment of my hesitation went on and on, and nothing happened. We remained as we were, side by side, close but not touching.

At last she broke the tense silence. "You don't want me," she said. "Because of Tipkeyn."

"Why would that matter?"

"They soiled me. They covered me with their filth. They made me into something dirty."

"They used only your body, Hendy. Your body, not you. You were still *you*, when they were done with your body. The body can be soiled but not the spirit within."

She was unconvinced. "If you wanted me, you'd reach toward me. But you haven't done it."

"I haven't been asked. I won't, without being asked."

"Is that true?"

"You told me that you had never chosen. I'm trying to let you do it."

"My body is choosing," she said. "My body and me both." She put her hands under her breasts and pushed them upward, toward me. "What do you think these are? Where do you think they came from, and why? Oh, Poilar—Poilar—"

It was enough. I put my hands over hers, and we both cupped her breasts for a moment, and then her hands drew away. My lips grazed against the side of her cheek, and down into the hollow along her throat.

"I'm afraid," she said in a very small voice.

"Don't be."

"But I don't know how to do it the right way. All I know is how to lie here and be used."

"You only think you don't know. Do what feels good, and whatever it is will be right."

My hand slid down her belly to the warm place between her thighs. She was ready.

"I'm afraid, Poilar," she said again.

"Do you want me to leave?"

"No—no—"

"What are you afraid of, then?"

"That it won't—go well—for you—"

"Forget about me. Let it go well for you."

Then she did a very strange thing, which was to slide down in the bedroll and put her hand to my crooked leg, timidly at first, then more boldly, stroking the ankle with the gentlest of touches. No one had ever done that before, and it amazed me. I nearly pulled away from her. But then I realized what she was telling me with that touch, which was, I think, that she accepted my deformity as I was accepting hers, mine being one of the body and hers being something within, something of the spirit. It was a way of declaring love. So I let her stroke my ankle for another moment or two more, and then, gently, I drew her up toward me again so that we were face to face, and I smiled at her and nodded in the darkness. Her eyes were bright. I saw fear in them and eagerness also.

"Poilar?"

"Yes?"

"Poi—lar—"

"Yes. Yes."

For a moment I thought of the men of Tipkeyn standing in a circle around her, filling her with wine and laughing as she got drunk. Angrily I shoved them from my mind. They must not be in my mind if they were ever to be expelled from hers.

I covered her with my body.

"Poilar," she said softly.

"Yes."

"Poilar. Poilar. Poilar."

WE BATHED AFTERWARD IN the stream. She was quiet, calm, apparently happy. When you make the Changes, it lifts you up out of the prison of your solitary flesh, and carries you toward the gods; and for a little while you feel that you are one with them, though you must all too soon return. I hoped it had been that way with Hendy. I asked her nothing about what she had experienced or how she might feel now, though, not so much because I was afraid of getting a displeasing answer as that I wanted simply to let the moment exist for itself, without examination, without analysis and introspectiveness. She knew what she had felt. I knew what I had. Let that be sufficient to each of us, I told myself.

Everyone seemed to know, the next day, what had taken place between Hendy and me. It was as if they had all been standing lined up along the stream in the night, watching us. There were little smiles, quizzical glances, knowing looks. Certainly Hendy and I had given them no clue by our daytime behavior: she said barely a thing to me all day, marching along in the back of the group as she customarily did, scarcely even looking at me when we halted and the whole group was together. She knew and I knew and to us that was enough. But the others knew also. Well, there are very few secrets in a band of Pilgrims. I doubted very much that we had been spied upon; I suspected rather that there was an aura around Hendy and me, a glow of the kind that people give off when they have deliberately kept their distance from each other for a long while and then have allowed themselves to come together. Such a thing shows. It always shows. There is an intensity in the air that can't be hidden, a radiance, and all attempts at hiding it only make it glow all the more brightly.

I wondered what some of the other women with whom I had made the Changes during our journey might be thinking. There must always be those who tell themselves that there is something special about making the Changes with a leader. They cherish it as a mark of his favor, for whatever that may be worth. Would there be resentment at my beginning a new mating, one which promised to be other than casual? I hoped not; but if there was, then so be it. I owed none of them anything. There had been no sealing with any of them; there never could be. On the Pilgrimage you meet, you are attracted, you do the Changes, you drift apart. Perhaps you come together again for a while and do it all again. That was how it had been for me with Galli, with Stum, with Marsiel, with Min, with Thissa. There are no sealings there. There are no obligations. If I had mated with Galli once, and with Thissa afterward, and with this one and with that one, and now I was with Hendy, so be it. It is how things are. I might seal with Hendy some day, when we were no longer on the Wall. I might not. Who could say? Who knew if we would ever leave the Wall? We were on the Wall now, and that was the essential thing. Our lives were suspended while we climbed. And we might climb forever.

I said to Muurmut that day, as I had promised myself to do, "My plan is to seek a way up between those two peaks. It seems to me that that line of trees in the cleft between them indicates a watercourse, and we might be able to follow along it. What do you think?" And I pointed at random toward a distant pair of the jagged red cliffs that surrounded us, two which happened to have a dense streak of green running down the steep slope that was their meeting-place. Wild grezbors could not have climbed that slope. Nor could we, not without wings to lift us to its top.

"Well," Muurmut said, and I knew at once from his hesitation that he had no more idea of the proper way to go than I did. "You may be right, Poilar. But I tell you, I know a little sky-magic, and I've cast a spell that gives me an entirely different slant on things."

The thought of stolid beefy-faced Muurmut the Vintner practicing sky-magic, or any other sort of magic, almost made me laugh out loud. Casting spells is the prerogative of the House of Witches, of course, and no one else. But I was making an effort to be conciliatory, as was he in his way also, I suppose. So instead of snorting derisively I simply said, "Ah, and which route would you suggest, then?"

He was taken aback. I don't think he had expected me to ask him point blank that way, right there and then.

"That one," he said after a moment, nodding toward the east, halfway around the bowl of peaks from the direction I had just proposed. He was plainly stabbing in the dark, just as I had done. "Do you see that short-shouldered mountain over there, with the look of a saddle to it, and the trail of cloud above it like a spear? If we mount that saddle we can ride right up into the sky."

"You think?"

"So the spell that I cast said, very definitely."

"Then that is the way we'll go," I told him, and he looked at me thunderstruck. But what did I have to lose? If Muurmut's way proved to be the right one, then we were free of this grassy valley at last and would be able to continue our ascent, which in truth was the only thing that really mattered. And if his sky-magic proved to be the nonsense that I suspected it to be, well, at least no one could say thereafter that I was willfully depriving us of the benefits of Muurmut's sage advice for the sake of enhancing my own glory.

So I called the whole group together and proclaimed the word. "We are changing our route," I said. "Muurmut's sky-magic tells us that the saddle-shaped mountain is the one we must climb. So we will attempt it; and all credit be to Muurmut if it turns out that his spells have opened the way for us." And I gestured to him as though he was the very fount of wisdom; and he smiled and nodded and waved like one who has just been chosen to be the head of his House. But his face grew even more red than usual, and I knew that he had seen through my cleverness, and hated me all the more for it. Well, so be it. He had wanted to lead. Now I was giving him his chance.

THAT NIGHT WE CAMPED in a meadow of saw-
edged red grass just below the mountain of Muurmut's choice, and as I lay half-dreaming beside Hendy
a vision came to me of the gods in their great palace at the
Summit.

What I saw was this:

I had climbed the last stretch to the top of the mountain alone, through a bitter landscape of ice and whirling
snow sharp as knives, and hard winds that bit into my flesh
like whips of fire. But now I came stumbling half dead, or
more than half, into a wondrous realm of golden light
where soft breezes blew and the air was sweet as young
wine; and I saw the crystal columns of the palace of the
gods, and the gods themselves walking about within it, clad
in scarlet robes and wearing high, narrow crowns of gold.
There stood Kreshe the Creator, a shining being who was
neither male nor female, though I had always thought of
him as a man until this moment: from the hands of this
great god, which were long and tapering and so beautiful
that I wept at the sight, came streams of bright light that

rose into the air and arched out to encircle all the World, so that they were like strands of the finest gold that held all things in communion with all other things through their linkage with Kreshe. Nearby, with a beaker of foaming drink in his hand, was a cheerful sunny-faced one, Thig the Shaper, he who had taken the formless world that Kreshe had made and given it its form. Thig was radiant as the sun; but beside him, pouring wine into Thig's beaker, was dour Sandu Sando the Avenger, darker than a moonless night, with a face like a cluster of swords and hands like daggers, and when he laughed at some joke of Thig's his voice fell upon the air like a hatchet.

I saw two beautiful young lovers making the Changes, and I knew without needing to be told that they were Selemoy who rules the Suns and Nir-i-Sellin the goddess of the Moons, embracing each other so that his light fell upon her, and hers upon him; and not far from them were the Three Babes, fat and naked and happy, with green star-stones in their navels; and also I saw Veega who brings the rain and Lasht who sees that the fruit ripens on the branch and Sept who gives the stars their brightness, and they were all laughing and joking together, like happy members of a House who have come together for a Naming-day, or old friends celebrating some great occasion. There were other gods besides, ones I could not recognize, unknown gods not yet revealed to mankind, but all of them had the bright auras of god-beauty and god-radiance, and there was such perfection in every aspect of them that I wept for sheer joy at the sight of it. For what this vision of mine was telling me was that the World indeed had meaning and purpose, that there really were gods and the gods were good, that all things however dark and terrible converged at that golden Summit above us on Kosa Saag, where wonderful beings lived lives of daily wonder and allowed some reflection of that wonder to descend to the lowest levels of the world and enter into the humble creatures that we are. At one time and another I had doubted all that. But now I felt the presence of the grace of the gods within me and all my doubts dissolved: how could I do anything else but weep in gratitude and delight?

"Poilar?" Hendy said. "Poilar, what's the matter? Why are you sobbing?"

I blinked and gaped and for a moment I was unable to speak. Then I said I had been having a vision of the gods, and was weeping out of happiness. At this hour of the night there were no moons in the sky, and I could barely see her face; but I heard her catch her breath as if I had said something wrong, something that had injured her. Which troubled me a little; but my vision was still with me a little, though it was ebbing fast, and I was too full of its splendors to think much of other things. I told her some of the things I had seen, though I could barely begin to describe the magnificence of it. Hendy listened without a word. And then when I had nothing left to tell her she said, "How I envy you, Poilar!"

"Envy me? Why?"

"For having dreams that are so beautiful."

"Not all of them are."

"But one like that—I've never had one like that, Poilar." She was trembling, though the night was warm. I slipped my arm about her shoulders. "Often I'm afraid of going to sleep, because my dreams will be so frightening."

"No, Hendy. No. No."

I held her. Her pain became my pain; and the joy that my dream had brought me washed away entirely, and I felt only guilt for having brought her to this sorrow by trying to share my joy with her. But I said none of that to her, knowing it would only make her feel worse. Gradually she calmed, and pressed herself close against me, and said very softly, "I'm sorry, Poilar. Tell me more of what you saw."

"I can't remember any more of that."

"But all of it was beautiful and wonderful?"

"Yes." I would not lie to her.

"Even the Avenger?"

"Even him, yes. Though he had a frightful look, nothing like the look we give him in the images we make. But I knew that even he was beautiful, frightening though he was. For they are all gods together: they all make up one harmony."

I could have said more about what I had seen, for although the vision had faded, the feelings that it had engendered in my spirit were still bubbling within me. But I was afraid of hurting her again.

After a while she said, aiming her voice not so much at me but into the air, as she often did, "Shall I tell you a dream I once had?"

"If you want to, yes, of course."

"Yes. Yes." Hendy paused as though she were summoning her thoughts. Then she said, "This was long ago, while I was still in Tipkeyn. I dreamed that I was dead. And do you know what death was like, Poilar? It was like being in a box exactly the size of my body. And my mind was still aware: I perceived everything, I could think, I could feel, I seemed to be breathing, I was still Hendy. Exactly as though I was alive. But I was in that box and there was no way to get out. And I knew that I would be in it for all time to come, because death never ends. Lying there forever, thinking, thinking, unable to move, unable to scratch myself if I itched, the air always stale and foul, the darkness always pressing down on me like a tight band across my chest. Trapped in that box. Forever. And ever. Thinking. Unable to stop thinking. Remembering, reliving the same things over and over, never anything new, for what new thing can there be when you're locked up in a box in the dark? Telling myself that I'll smother when all the air is gone, and then realizing that the air would go and I would still be there, fighting for breath and feeling that I was about to die, but I wouldn't be able to die, because I was already dead. Screaming, but no one would hear."

The words were pouring out and her voice was thick with emotion. She was beginning to tremble.

I put my hand on hers. "Wait, Hendy—slow down, catch your breath—"

But there was no stopping her. "Gagging on my own smell. Choking on it. A prickling in my toes, a numbness in my back. But the box was exactly the size I was, so there was no way to move. Not even a finger. I just had to lie there and lie there and lie there. Forever and ever, no escape, not ever, all of eternity to come, nothing ever changing, always Hendy in the box, fighting for every breath. I knew in my dream that is how it would be for me when I died, that it is that way for everybody. That's what being dead is like. Each of us lying there alone, aware, *knowing what has happened to us*, the body imprisoned but the mind still aware, and hating it, and having no escape, never, no end to it. Your time in the box is a thousand times as long as your time alive, a million times, it never ends, never—never—never—"

"Hendy!" And I gripped her and held her, and put my mouth over hers to halt the terrible torrent of words, and she shook in my arms like a twig caught at one end between two rocks in a swift-flowing stream. Only when she had stopped shaking did I take my lips from hers.

"I'm sorry," she murmured. Her eyes were not meeting mine. "You must think I'm crazy, saying things like that."

"No. No. It was only a dream."

"I've had it many times. Dozens. Hundreds of times. It keeps coming back. I'm always afraid to go to sleep because I think I'm going to have it again."

"Have you had it on Kosa Saag?"

"Twice."

I looked into the starry darkness of the sky. To have such a dream up here—in the very abode of the gods—what could it mean? I had dreamed of splendors; she dreamed of death that was no death at all, but an infinite torture.

Her dream appalled me. I had never heard anything so

frightening, so bleak. Death is nothing I spend much time thinking about; but I had always thought, as most of us do, that death is simply the end of life, a darkness, a silence, the return of our substance to the earth from which it came. Traiben and I had sometimes talked of it when we were young, and we both thought alike on the subject: there is no further awareness, any more than there is further light after a candle has been snuffed. It is an obliteration. One lives one's four tens of years, or a few tens more if the gods have given one the privilege of double life, and then one is gone, and that is that. But this terrible vision of Hendy's—this catastrophic fantasy of torment everlasting—it shook me as I have rarely been shaken. I lay awake for hours afterward, fearing that if I slept I would dream Hendy's dream, and dreading it. In time sleep took me anyway, and I dreamed nothing that I particularly remembered the next day. But when I woke it was not the glory of my own divine vision that remained with me, but rather the nightmare desolation of the thing that Hendy had described.

I climbed like a madman that day, going almost at a sprint up the sloping side of the meadow where it gave way to the barrenness of the red mountain, and then along the face of the rock into the saddle. The others were hard pressed to match my pace and quickly fell behind me. And when I came up into the saddle I saw that on the far side of it it turned upward, so that it provided us with access to the next level of Kosa Saag, which began just beyond us. Muurmut's sky-magic might have been a fraud and a bluff but it had brought us to the right place. I waited for them to catch up with me, and we halted and broke out the last of the wine that we had brought with us from home, and passed it around, hardly more than a few drops apiece. I called out a toast to Muurmut. Let him bask in his glory. What did that matter to me? We were on our way up again.

"Muurmut!" they all cried. "Muurmut, Muurmut, Muurmut!"

He grinned and smirked like the fool that he was. But we were on our way up. The gods in their crystal-columned palace awaited us at the Summit. Or so I told myself, in the hope that I could drive from my mind that other vision of darkness and terror and eternity spent in a box no bigger than my body.

WE EMERGED INTO A new realm entirely, a bare craggy land of broken red rock carved into a myriad fantastic forms, with caves and fluted spires and turrets everywhere. The sky was cloudless and a deep intense blue, a strange blue that was bluer than we had ever seen it. Little streams ran in rocky beds. After the sharp and frosty weather we had had below, the air was surprisingly warm and mellow here, but we had long since given up trying to understand the rhythms and climates of Kosa Saag. We knew that we were in another world up here.

The mountain rose before us as if in a series of wide flat steps. It looked as though we need do nothing more than put our feet to the first of those steps, and merely go up and up and up until we were at the top. But I sensed that when we actually reached the first of those great stone shelves we would discover that we were no bigger than so many grains of sand against it, and the climb would be no easy thing.

I ordered a pause for gathering food and water, for it looked like dry hard country ahead. While this was going on I went forward a little distance to reconnoiter, taking Traiben with me for company. But I said little as we walked, and when Traiben spoke to me I answered in the shortest way.

"Your mood is very somber," he said after a while, "for one who has just taken himself a new lover."

"Yes," I said. "So it is."

"It can be that way sometimes, I suppose. When you attain a long-held desire, and find that the reality can never be equal to the—"

"No," I said, snapping the word at him. "What do you know about these things? It's nothing like that!"

"Well," said Traiben, then. "I am mistaken. I beg your pardon, Poilar."

And now he was silent, and we walked on that way through a long morning, like two strangers trudging side by side on the same path. Both suns were in the sky. In the thin air of this high country, where there was not a single cloud to shelter us, white Ekmelios burned with great fury and even the distant red sphere of Marilemma seemed to be throwing forth heat upon us. The land began to rise steeply, and as I had suspected the terrain grew more parched the farther we went. And yet I felt a curious emanation coming from the first level of the stepped mountain ahead of us, an odd kind of beckoning, as though a deep sleepy voice were saying, *Yes, this is the way, come to me, come to me, come, come.*

I said finally, growing troubled by Traiben's silence and feeling abashed at having spoken to him so harshly, "My mood is dark, I think, because of a dream of Hendy's, that she told me a few nights back while we were in the valley. The shadow of that dream lies over me even now."

And I told it to him, just as Hendy had told it to me. When I was done I was shaking with the horror of it all over again; but Traiben only shrugged and said, without much feeling, "The poor woman. What a dark and fantastic notion that is to carry around in one's head."

"What if it isn't just a fantastic notion, though? What if something like that really happens to us when we die?"

He laughed. "After death there is nothing, Poilar. *Nothing.*"

"How can you be so sure of that?"

"We talked of this when we were boys, do you remember? Does a candle burn when you put out the flame?"

"We are not candles, Traiben."

"It's the same thing. Out we go and that's the end."

"And if not?"

He shrugged again. I could see that Hendy's dream was having no impact on him at all. Or else he was taking great pains to conceal it. Perhaps Hendy was a sore subject with him. It had happened before that he saw some new woman of mine as an impediment to our friendship.

The mountain still seemed to be calling. *Come ... come ... come ...* What could that be?

But I hesitated to ask Traiben if he felt the same call, for fear that he would think I was suffering from hallucinations. We seemed to be on uneasy terms with each other this day. Our souls were farther apart than I could remember their ever having been.

To lighten things a little I started telling him of my own dream, the happy one of the golden and glittering gods in their wondrous sun-lit palace atop the Wall. But Traiben scarcely seemed to be listening. He glanced this way and that, he picked up stones and skipped them into the air, he shaded his eyes and peered off into the distance.

"Am I boring you?" I asked, when I was no more than halfway through.

"It's a lovely dream, Poilar. Very pretty indeed."

"But a little on the simple-minded side."

"No. No. A beautiful vision."

"Just a vision, yes. And Hendy's dream is just a nasty fantasy. There's no reality at all to either of them, is that right?"

"Who can say? We won't know what death is really like until we die. Nor will we know what the gods are like until we reach the Summit."

"I prefer to think that the gods are as I saw them in my dream. That perhaps the dream itself was a sending from them, urging us to be steadfast, to stay on the upward trail."

Traiben gave me a strange look at that. "A sending, you think? Well, maybe so." After a moment he said, "I would rather believe in your dream than in Hendy's. But we won't know until we know. I once had a dream that was just the opposite of yours: did I ever tell you that,

Poilar? A blasphemous dream, a really awful dream, a true nightmare. I dreamed that I reached the Summit—and there were the gods, all right, and they were loathsome twisted ghastly things, the most depraved of creatures, such bestial driveling monsters that they would make the Melted Ones look beautiful beside them. And that's why no Pilgrims who have reached the Summit and returned will ever speak of what they have seen, because they can't bear to reveal the frightful truth about the gods we worship." He laughed again, the dry little Traiben-laugh that I knew so well, which was meant to be a casual dismissal of something that in fact was not at all casual to him. Then he said, "Speaking of sendings, have you been feeling anything of that sort while we've been walking along just now?"

"A message from the mountain? A pulling—a calling?"

"So you do feel it!"

"And you also."

"For some time now," he said. "A voice in my mind, urging me onward."

"Yes. Exactly so. A voice from the gods, do you think, telling us that we're on the right path?"

"You have gods on the brain today, Poilar. Who knows what that calling means? Gods—demons—more Melted Ones—another Kingdom ahead—?"

"We should turn back, I think. See whether the others have felt it too. And call a council, and discuss what action we ought to take."

"Yes," he said. "A good idea."

So we hurried along the rocky trail, returning the way we had come. The voice in my mind grew less distinct with every step we took. It was the same for Traiben. By the time we reached the camp we were unable to perceive it at all.

IN MY ABSENCE A stranger had come into the camp, and he was a very strange stranger indeed.

He stood in the midst of the group, and they were all

crowding tight around him, as though vying with one another for the closest look. Only Thissa stood to one side, in that brooding way of hers, watching somberly from afar. The stranger rose head and shoulders above nearly everyone: he was taller even than Muurmut and Kilarion. It appeared that he was laughing and joking with them, and that they were hanging on his every word. At first glance it seemed that he had no hair, but then he moved a little and I saw that he had hair only on one side of his head, hair of a very odd sort, white as mountain mist and thick as rope, hanging down in long strands almost to his waist. He was gaunt and hard—virtually fleshless, so you could almost see the outlines of his bones beneath the tight-drawn skin, which was mottled and piebald, black as night in some places and a glaring shiny white in others. His shoulders, though very broad, were oddly wrenched and skewed, as if he had been midway through some change of shape and had become stuck in it; and when I drew near I became aware that he was a crookleg like me, but to a horrifying extreme, for his left leg was far longer than the other one, reaching out at an angle and curving back in like a sickle's blade. His whole body was gnarled and distorted down its long axis, one hip higher than the other and turned at an odd angle to its mate, which was what caused that leg to jut out the way it did.

When he saw me approaching he turned to me and grinned. It was meant as a grin, at any rate, but it was cold and cheerless and more like a demon's grimace than a grin, a two-faced smirk, showing me a mouth of blackened snags, smiling on the one side and scowling on the other. The color of his left eye was different from that of the right, and both his eyes were small and glittering, but glittering in a dull way as though the fire that burned behind them had almost gone out; and the left side of his face was drawn up in a puckered twisted way that reminded me of Min's, but the thing that had happened to Min seemed like nothing in comparison with this man's mutilation. Here was surely another who had come in contact somewhere on the Wall with change-fire; but if Min had had a melted look when she came forth from the cave of the Source, this strange lopsided creature looked baked: baked dry, a parched man, baked down to some irreducible minimum.

I could find no words, for a moment.

Then Kath came forward out of the group and said, with something sly in his look, "Do you remember this man, Poilar?"

"Remember? From where?"

"From the village, long ago," Kath said.

"No." I peered close, and shook my head. "Not at all."

The stranger stepped toward me and offered me a hand that was as gnarled and twisted as the rest of him.

"My name is Thrance," he said.

I gasped as though I had been struck a blow in the belly. Thrance? *Thrance?*

Into my mind at once, with the mention of that name, leaped a dazzling unforgettable image out of my boyhood. I was twelve, and it was the Day of Procession and Departure, and Traiben and I were in the main viewing stand, waiting for the new Pilgrims to emerge from the Lodge. And the great wickerwork doors swung open and the Pilgrims came forth, and there was Thrance, Thrance the magnificent, Thrance the flawless, the athlete of athletes, famous for his feats of strength and valor, that man of shining beauty and perfect body, erupting from the Lodge like a force of nature, pausing only a moment to smile and wave before running off in that famous high bounding stride of his toward the Wall. How splendid he had looked that day, how fine! How like a god! And this was Thrance, now? This? This?

16

THEY WERE ALL STARING—at me, at him, at him again. They wanted to see how I would handle him. And I knew from the brightness of their eyes and the eager look of expectation on their faces that in some magical way this repellent stranger had charmed them, had won them to him in the short while I had been gone. There was something dark and frightening and fierce about him that drew them to him. The fascination of darkness can be irresistible.

My skin crept, as though it sensed a storm heavy with lightning rushing toward us. If this in truth was Thrance, and not some demon wearing his name, then he had been deeply damaged indeed. But despite that damage I could see that there was great strength in him even now, though perhaps it was strength of some kind other than the strength he had had before. It might even be that he was strong *because* of the damage he had suffered. Which made him unpredictable, and therefore dangerous.

For a moment we eyed each other like two wrestlers

preparing to begin a match. Looking into those lightless mismatched eyes of his was like peering into an abyss.

I knew that unless I acted without hesitation, he would move somehow to seek the advantage. So I took his dry scaly hand in mine and gripped it firmly, and said very formally, "Poilar is my name, son of Gabrian, son of Drok. I am the leader of this Forty, which comes from Jespodar bound on Pilgrimage. What is it that you want among us?"

"Why," he replied, speaking in a drawl as though he had found something humorous in what I had said or in the way I had said it, "I think I remember you. Poilar, yes. A little skinny crookleg child, forever scuttling around doing as much mischief as he possibly could, am I right? And now you lead a band of Pilgrims! What changes time will bring, eh?"

I heard the nervous laughter of my companions. They weren't accustomed to hearing me mocked. But I kept myself in check and held my eyes on his.

"I am that Poilar, yes. And are you really Thrance?"

"I said that was my name. Why would you doubt me?"

"I remember Thrance. I saw him come out of the Pilgrim Lodge and go running up the street. He gave off light, like a sun. He was as beautiful as a god."

"Whereas I'm not?"

"You look nothing like him. Not in the slightest regard."

"Well, then, if that's the case I must be very ugly now. Apparently I've undergone some disagreeable changes since coming to this mountain country. If I'm no longer as good to look upon as I once was, I beg you to forgive me for offending your eyes, my friend. Forgive me, all of you." And in a courtly way he made a little ironic bow to the others, which brought uneasy smiles to their faces. "But I am Thrance, son of Timar, former Pilgrim of Jespodar, all the same."

"Perhaps. Perhaps not."

"If I'm not Thrance, then who am I, pray tell?"

"How would I know? You could be anyone. Or anything. A demon. A ghost. A god in disguise."

He gave me that death's-head grin of his. "Yes," he said. "I could be. Sandu Sando, perhaps, or Selemoy of the suns. But in fact I am Thrance. The son of Timar the Carpenter, who was the son of Diunedis."

"Any demon could spout Thrance's lineage at me," I told him. "But that wouldn't make the demon Thrance."

The stranger looked amused, or perhaps he was merely growing bored with my obstinacy. "Against arguments of that kind no one could ever convince anyone of anything, isn't that so? I could name my forefathers for ten generations, or all the twenty Houses of the Village, or the other members of my Forty, or anything else you might ask, and you would still say that the demon has picked it out of Thrance's mind for the sake of deceiving you. Very well, then. Believe what you want. It makes no difference to me. But I tell you I am Thrance."

I looked toward Kath and said, "Where did this man come from?"

"He simply appeared among us," Kath said. "As if he had risen right out of the ground."

"A demon would do that," I said, with a glance toward the stranger.

"Be that as it may," said Kath. "One minute we were here by ourselves waiting for you to return and the next he was with us. 'I am Thrance of Jespodar,' he said. 'Have any of you heard of Jespodar, here?' And when we told him that we were Pilgrims from that very village he began to laugh like a wild man, and to leap up and down and dance about. Then suddenly he grew very stern and somber, and he caught me by the wrist with one hand and Galli by the other, and he said, 'Who remembers Thrance, then? If you are truly of Jespodar, you would remember Thrance.' And Galli said, 'We were only children when you left, if you are Thrance. So we wouldn't remember you clearly.' He laughed at that and pulled her close to him and kissed her, and bit her cheek so that it stung, and said, 'You'll remember me now.' Then she asked him about her older brother, who had been in the same Forty as Thrance, and he knew the brother's name, all right, though he said he had no idea what had become of him, which made Galli start to cry; and then he asked for wine. I said we had none to give him. He got very angry at that, and said again that he was Thrance of Jespodar. To which Muurmut replied, 'Thrance or no Thrance, we have no wine to give you.' And then—"

"Enough," I said. The stranger had wandered off during Kath's recitation and was standing with Tenilda and Grycindil and a few of the other women. "He is much altered from the Thrance I remember, if in fact this is Thrance. Did he speak at all of what had happened to him?"

"No."

I was unable to get from my mind that recollected image of the heroic Thrance in all his godlike beauty, nor could I easily reconcile it with the sight of that gaunt and hideously altered creature over there. But for his great height and the breadth of his shoulders there was scarcely anything about this ruined wreck of a man that might sustain his claim of being Thrance. And, although I have never been one to frighten easily, I felt a twinge of something close to fear now as I watched him among the women. There seemed to be madness in him, and some strange fury barely held in check. If he was Thrance, and had spent all these years on the Wall, he might be of some use as a guide to us in this new territory we had entered, or he might not; but almost certainly he was going to be troublesome. I found myself wishing most profoundly he had never appeared in our midst.

He was coming toward me again now, with his arm thrust through Tenilda's. That sweet Musician looked as though she would gladly have been back on the plateau again rather than so close to this malformed creature that called itself Thrance.

He leaned close to me and said, "They claim you have no wine, Poilar. Is this so?"

"The wine is long since gone, yes."

"But you must have some." He winked. It was a cold dead-eyed wink, with little charm or playfulness to it. "Hidden away, for your own use, eh? Come, my friend. Share your wine with me, before we set out from this place to begin our climb together. For old Thrance's sake. A toast to our success."

"We have no wine," I said.

"Of course you do. I know that you have. Do you realize how long it's been since I've had anything decent to drink? Or how I've suffered, all alone here on this mountain, Poilar? So get out the wine, and let's drink." There was a flat tone in his voice that robbed his words of urgency. I knew he was simply testing me, trying to see how much power he could exert over me. Very likely he had no desire for wine at all. He winked again, a false one as before, and nudged me in what was meant to be a sly conspiratorial way, but lacked conviction. "Just the two of us, you and I. We are brothers of the crooked leg, aren't we? Look—look—mine's even worse than yours!"

"The Thrance I remember had straight legs," I said. "And there is no wine."

"You still won't believe that I am who I say I am."

"I have nothing to go by except your word."

"I have nothing to go by except *your* word, when you tell me you have no wine."

"There is no wine."

"And I am Thrance."

"Then you are a Thrance transformed beyond all recognition," I said.

"Well, so I am. But Kosa Saag is a place where transformations happen. You must always keep that in mind, my friend. And now, about that wine—"

"I'll say it once more," I told him, "and then not again. There is no wine."

He gave me a skeptical look, as though he believed that if he only pressed me hard enough I would bring forth a flask from some secret cache. But there was no secret cache, and I looked at him in such a stony way that he saw that I either would not or, more likely, could not give him any wine.

"Well, then," he said. "If you say so, it must be true. There is no wine. We are agreed on that. And I am Thrance. We are agreed on that, also. Eh? Good. Good. What shall we talk about next?"

BUT I HAD HAD enough of dueling with this man before all the others. I pointed toward an open place across the way, where we could be alone, and suggested we continue our conversation in private. He thought about that a moment and nodded, and we went limping off together, two crooklegs side by side, to sit by ourselves and talk. As he had said, that leg of his was far more of a deformity than mine. His limp was so bad that he walked in a twisted, lurching way, stepping halfway around himself to move forward, and I had to take something off my pace to accommodate him.

We found a fallen spire of rock nearby that we could use as a bench and sat down facing each other. I hesitated a little, arranging my thoughts, but he waited for me to begin. Perhaps he was developing some measure of respect for me.

"All right," I said at last. "Why have you come here? What is it you want with us?"

His eyes brightened. For the first time there was true life in them, and not mere willed force. "I want to join your Forty. I want to climb with you to the Summit."

"How would that be possible?"

"Why, what difficulty is there? You take me in; I march with you and share your toil; we go to the top together."

"But a Forty is a Forty. We are pledged to one another

by special vows, as you must surely know. There's no way we can admit a stranger to our group."

"Of course there is. You simply do it. 'Here, Thrance, come join us,' is what you say. 'Be one of us,' is what you say. That's all there is to it. We are beyond the point where vows have meaning. Vows are for children; in this place your lives are at stake. I can be very useful to you. I know a great deal about the Kingdoms that lie ahead. Whereas you know nothing at all."

"Perhaps so. But nevertheless—"

"Listen, Poilar, I'll be your guide. You can have the benefit of my knowledge. It wasn't won easily, but it's yours for the asking. I'll take you around the obstacles. I'll keep you off false trails. I'll steer you clear of the dangers. Why should you have to suffer as I did?"

There was some logic to that. But nothing in our training suggested any precedent for recruiting new members to our group during the climb. It seemed almost a blasphemy. And the thought of having this dark turbulent stranger marching amongst us from this moment onward was far from pleasing to me.

"You have your own Forty," I said to him. "Why are you still here, after so many years on the Wall? Why aren't you climbing with them, far beyond this level?"

"Oh, no," he replied. "I have no one at all." There was nothing left of his group, the Forty that I had seen set out so bravely the year when I was twelve.

Thrance told me that at the outset of their climb they had chosen him by unanimous acclamation to be their leader; but—so I gathered from certain things he said—he had been a difficult leader, erratic and violent and rash, and soon some of them had begun to creep away from him, one by one, two by two, disappearing in the night. Others, though taking no issue with Thrance's leadership, had succumbed to the byways of the Wall, vanishing into this Kingdom or that and failing to come back. In the end he was left by himself. All these years he had wandered this level of the Wall and those adjacent to it, neither ascending nor descending any great distance, but mainly staying here, drifting in circles, aimlessly roaming this unforgiving land of broken red rock. A kind of madness had come to veil his mind. For long spells of time he forgot who he had been, or what he had hoped to be. Sometimes he caught sight of other bands of Pilgrims passing by, later ones along the path, but he shrank away from them like the wild animal he had become. He lived on roots and nuts, and whatever small beasts he was able to trap. He slept in the open, at all seasons of the year. The great strength that had made him such a master athlete had stood him in good stead. His endurance was enormous; but he passed his days in a long hazy dream. Occasionally the thought of resuming his Pilgrimage would occur to him, or else of going down into our village again and taking up lodging in the roundhouse of the Returned Ones. But he did neither. This dry barren zone of the Wall had become his home. It had become his world. He had virtually forgotten why he was on the mountain at all. But now, he said, seeing us coming up the saddle from the meadowlands below, it had come back to him: the purpose was to climb, to get to the top. That was all it was for him, apparently: just to get to the top. He said nothing of gods or the acquisition of wisdom or the fulfillment of ancient oaths. The urge to reach the Summit was reborn in him simply for its own sake. He had had enough of this level of the Wall, and it was time for him to move onward. But he realized that it was impossible for him to get very far on his own. And so now he was offering himself to us—a new member of our Forty, tempered by experience, familiar with many of the perils that awaited us. If we wanted him, he would earn his keep by helping us to avoid the pitfalls ahead. But if we chose otherwise, he wished us well, and would wait for the next year's band of Pilgrims to arrive.

He fell silent, and waited almost indifferently for me to speak.

I remarked after a moment, "In all this lengthy narrative you've told me nothing of how these changes in your appearance came about. Or where, or why."

"Is it such a mystery? You must surely know that Kosa Saag is a place where the unwary are at great risk of undergoing transformation. And the wary as well, sometimes."

"Yes," I said. "I know that. Below us, in the First Kingdom, the Kingdom of the Melted Ones, I saw how it can happen. Is that where—"

"No, not there," he said scornfully. A shadow crossed his twisted face. "It was higher up. I passed the First Kingdom without any difficulty. Who would want to live in that miserable land, and worship blood-drinking demons? I'm no Melted One, Poilar. They're hardly better than beasts, as you must already have observed. No, no, I am of the Transformed. And of my own free will, for the advantage I thought it would bring me."

It seemed a very subtle difference to me: Melted, Transformed, what did it matter which word you used? Either way, it was a horror, a mutilation, when you gave yourself up to the change-fire. But I let the question pass.

"Will you speak of it?" I asked.

"It was in the Kingdom of the Kavnalla that this transformation happened to me. This partial transformation, I should say. For the job went unfinished, which is why I look the way I do."

"The Kavnalla?" That name meant nothing to me.

"The Kavnalla, yes. You'll be finding out about the Kavnalla soon enough, my friend. You'll have your chance to greet the Kavnalla in person, and listen to its song. And unless you take great care, you'll find yourself tempted to offer yourself up to it as I did, and so to join the legions of the Transformed."

I thought of the silent voice that Traiben and I had heard on the trail that morning, that seductive murmuring in our minds, urging us forward. Had that been Thrance's

Kavnalla? Very likely it was. But we had turned away from that coaxing voice without difficulty.

"I doubt that very much," I told him. "I'm not so easily seduced."

"Ah, is that the case, Poilar? Is it really?" He smiled. He had a way of making me feel like a child with that condescending smile of his. "Well, perhaps. You do seem a little unusual. But many are lured by the Kavnalla, make no mistake of that. I was one of them."

"Tell me about it."

"All in good time, when we stand at the gate of its Kingdom. What I'll tell you now is what you already suspect, which was that my transformation was the greatest error of my life. I thought I could play the Kavnalla's game and win. Indeed I believed that I could make myself a King on this mountain. When I realized that I was wrong, I managed to get away—not many succeed at that, boy, not many at all—but not before I had been turned into what you see before you, which is a shapechanging from which there is no return." His eyes drilled into mine. I had not failed to notice that patronizing "boy" of his, but I chose to let that pass also. "The Kavnalla sings a very tempting song," he said. "I learned too late how to close my ears to it."

"Is it far from here, this Kavnalla?" I asked.

"Its domain is the very next Kingdom. You could be there in no time at all." Then that had been the Kavnalla's voice we had heard. "And before you know what's happening," Thrance said, "your people will be lining up and offering themselves up for transformation, if you don't take care. That was where I lost the greater part of my Forty, in the Kingdom of the Kavnalla. And as you see, I came close to losing myself as well. Many's the Pilgrimage that has come to grief in the Kingdom where the Kavnalla reigns. The change-fire is very strong there: it boils from the ground, it rises up and conquers everything that will not fight back."

"In that case, we'll go some other way," I replied at once. "There are more routes than one to the top."

"No. No, you have no choice but to go this way. Believe me. I know. I've traveled all these roads again and again, boy. If what you want is to reach the Summit, this is the only path, and it passes through the Kingdom of the Kavnalla. And the Sembitol beyond it, and then the Kingdom of the Kvuz."

Sembitol—Kvuz—those names were only noises to me. And I realized once more that they had taught us nothing, in the village. Nothing.

"How can I be sure that there's no safer route?" I asked him.

"Because I've been everywhere and seen everything, and I know which way you must go."

"And what if you're lying? What if you've come to us as an agent of the Kavnalla, who has sent you to win our trust and lead us right into its hands?"

At that he blazed up in anger; and for the first time he seemed to drop all masks and reveal the true man beneath, anguished, furious, tormented. He spat and threw up his arms and got to his feet, and went stomping away in that lurching crooklegged walk of his, which made my own seem like a dance-step, and when he swung around to face me again his eyes were glinting with rage. "What a fool you are, boy! What folly all your niggling little suspicions are! Well, if you think I'm a spy, then go up there without me! Stroll into the Kavnalla's cave, kiss it on the cheek, whisper to it that Thrance sends his love! See what becomes of you then! See what wondrous transformations overwhelm you when the change-fire rises up! Or—no, no, take some other route entirely, if you'd rather avoid the land of the Kavnalla. Go up that slope to the east, where the boiling lake is waiting for you. Go up to the west, into the land of the darkness-drinkers. Do whatever you want, boy. Do whatever you want!" He laughed bitterly. "An agent of the Kavnalla? Yes! Yes, of course that's what I am! How shrewd of you to find me out! Do you see how beautiful the Kavnalla has made me? And out of gratitude, I mean to deliver all of your people to it, so that you can be made beautiful too!" With a contemptuous wave of his mis-shapen hand he said, "Do whatever you want, boy," and turned his back on me.

After a long while I said, very quietly, "What do you want with us, Thrance?"

"You've already asked me that. And had your answer."

"To climb the mountain with us? That's all?"

"Nothing more than that. I've been wandering here at this level more years than I can remember. I've lived in my own company so long that the sound of my own breathing is disgusting to my ears. I want to move on. I can't tell you why, but I do. Take me with you and I'll share with you what I know about the Kingdoms that lie ahead. Or leave me behind and make it on your own, if you can, and I will take my own route, and so be it. I don't care. Do you understand that? I'm beyond all caring, boy!" And he shook his head. "An agent of the Kavnalla, he says!"

"It will have to be put to a vote," I told him.

THE DEBATE WAS A hard and heated one. Thrance lurked at the edge of the cliff, out of earshot and scarcely even glancing toward us, while we fought it out. At first we were nearly equally divided. Naxa and Muurmut and Seppil and Kath spoke out most vigorously against letting Thrance join us, and Marsiel and Traiben and Tull and Bress the Carpenter were for him, and the rest seemed to swing back and forth according to the arguments of whichever among us had been the most recent speaker. Muurmut, the strongest voice of the opposition, said that Thrance was a madman and a demon who would create turmoil among us and distract us from our task. Traiben, who in his quiet way led the other side, conceded the possibility that Thrance was mad, but pointed out that unlike any of us he had seen the country beyond this level of the Wall and it behooved us to make use of any information he might provide about those regions that were unknown to us.

During all this I played the role of a mere moderator, calling on the others but voicing no view of my own. This was in part because my mind was uncertain: to a considerable extent I inclined toward Muurmut's point of view, though I saw some wisdom in Traiben's, and it was so odd for me to be favoring any argument of Muurmut's over one of Traiben's that I did not know what to say. Also I had consulted Thissa before the outset of the meeting, and she had said, perplexed, that her witchcraft was of no use here: she found Thrance so strange and frightening that she had great difficulty reading his soul. That in itself was an argument for banning him from our midst, but Thissa didn't raise it in the debate.

I called for a preliminary vote, not binding but just an indication of feelings, and it was eight to eight, with more than half the group abstaining.

Then Grycindil, who had been silent, spoke up and said, "We'd be fools not to take him with us. As Traiben says, he knows things that we need to learn. And how much harm can one man do against so many of us?"

"Yes," said Galli, another who had taken no part up till now. "If he makes trouble, we can always kill him, can't we?"

There was general laughter. But I saw that the voices of these two strong and strong-minded women had done much to shift the balance. Muurmut saw it too; he scowled and paced, and glared at Grycindil, who after all was Muurmut's lover now and nonetheless had spoken out for Thrance.

Then Hendy looked toward me and said, "What do you think, Poilar? You've said nothing. Shouldn't you be sharing your ideas with us?"

A few people gasped. It was bold of her to have challenged me that way, especially since they all knew that Hendy and I had lately become lovers. I was annoyed that she had forced my hand, and glanced at her in irritation; but I saw her eyes shining with love for me. She had meant me no harm. She was simply looking to me as our leader, urging me to fulfill my responsibilities to the group.

Every eye was on me. Slowly I said, groping my way through the confusion of my thoughts, "I agree with Muurmut that he may be troublesome. I agree with Traiben that he may be useful. Balancing one against the other, I take into account what Galli says, that if he creates problems for us, we always have the option of getting rid of him. Therefore I vote for taking him in."

"And I," said Grycindil. "And I," said Galli and Malti and some others who had abstained before. I had swayed them all. Hands were going up all around the group. Muurmut growled and went stalking dourly away, taking his followers Seppil and Talbol with him; but of the others every vote went for Thrance, except that of Thissa, who held both her hands palm outward as if to say that she could not decide. So it was done. I went across to Thrance, who sat looking out the other way, across the great dark gulf of the lands that lay below us.

"The vote ran for you," I told him. "You are one of us now."

He seemed not to be greatly moved by that news.

"Am I?" he said. "Well, then. So I am."

17

WE CLIMBED, AND THE world itself altered as we ascended, flattening and broadening behind us, drawing itself together into a needle's point before us, while strange new lands rose about us and flowed past as though we were a rock sitting motionless in a river. And all the while two potent new forces exerted themselves upon us. One was the call of the Kavnalla, which was not long in making itself known to us, and the other was the presence of Thrance among us.

We had entered a new and darker phase of our Pilgrimage with his coming, and even the least thoughtful among us knew that. Perhaps Thrance was no demon—I quickly ceased thinking, even in jest, that he was—but his transformation in the land of the Kavnalla had turned him into some kind of elemental being, black and fierce of soul, who walked in our midst like a creature out of nightmare. His towering twisted form, so strange and monstrous in hue and shape, rose above us like the Wall itself.

There was a rough magnetism about him that drew us to him whether we wanted to be drawn or not. I felt it

keenly. He seemed to take nothing seriously, to turn anything into some occasion for harsh laughter, to offer biting
quips when a kinder word would have been more appropriate; and we expected it and even were entertained by his
manner. That he was heroic, a man of enormous strength
and endurance, we could not doubt. But he was also perplexing and difficult, a malcontent, a disturber of the peace,
every bit as troublesome as Muurmut had predicted.

He was forever taking favorites among us, but the
favorites kept changing. One day it was my company that he
sought, and one day Kilarion's, and then he would only
march with Galli on one side of him and Tull the Clown on
the other; and so it went. If he had no interest in you, he
would tell you straight out: "Keep away from me, you bore
me," he would say. He said that to Muurmut. He said it to
Naxa. But he said it also once to Jaif, that good-hearted
clear-souled Singer, and Jaif could never understand why.

The women in particular were fascinated by him,
hideous as he was: all but Thissa, who would not go near
him. Grycindil seemed especially drawn to him, which
didn't improve Muurmut's frame of mind. Often I saw her
jostling to be at Thrance's side, while Muurmut rumbled
and grumbled from afar. But at night Thrance always slept
alone, at least in the early days of our march. For a time it
seemed to me that he must have no interest at all in making
the Changes in the usual sense of that term; a Change had
been made upon him, certainly, a very great one, and it had
put him into a mode of existence that was not in any way
like ours. But I was wrong about that.

He never spoke of his life in the village, or of the fate of
the Forty with whom he had set out upon the Wall so many
years before, or indeed of any aspect of himself or of his
past. The majestic Thrance of my childhood, whom I had
watched so often racing in the winter games or casting
javelins or winning the high leap, was dead and buried
somewhere within his altered and deformed body. His
conversation was all banter and gibe and wild mockery, or

sarcasm and riddle. Perhaps the most mysterious thing about him was the volatility of his moods; for he was often fiery and outgoing, capering along the trail despite his limp and calling jubilantly to us to keep up with him, and then abruptly he would become sullen and ashen-souled and distant. It was as if a god sometimes would possess him, or some evil spirit; and when the god was gone from him, or the spirit, nothing remained but a husk. The change could happen three times in five minutes: you never knew which Thrance it was that you would be dealing with a moment from now.

When we had been on the trail with him for a week or so, he dismissed Muurmut from our midst.

I never knew precisely what happened. Grycindil was at the heart of the matter, that much was sure. Evidently she had gone to Thrance's sleeping-place in the night, and he had taken her in; so much for my theory that he was beyond the need or desire for making the Changes. And then—so Kath believed, for he had been sleeping nearby and heard a little of the dispute—Muurmut had gone to them to bring her back.

That was a childish thing to do, for although Muurmut and Grycindil had become lovers, they weren't sealed to each other—sealings are unthinkable on Kosa Saag—and Grycindil was free to sleep wherever she chose. But Muurmut would not have it. And so in the night there were words between Muurmut and Thrance. I heard them myself, angry sounds far away, but I was too tired from that day's march to give them much thought, and Hendy drew me down into her arms, sleepily telling me that it was nothing, that I should pay no attention. And in the morning Muurmut was gone.

"Where is he?" I asked, because his bulky presence was always conspicuous and so was his absence. "Who has seen him?"

Thrance gestured toward the steep slope behind us. "He has resigned from our company."

"What?"

"He fears the high country. He told me so. He thinks his soul will be devoured there. And I said, 'So it will be, Muurmut. You should go home. Slink down the hill to the village, Muurmut, and tell them to take you in.' He saw the wisdom in what I was saying to him. And so he is gone. He will be a Returned One, and he will be very good at it."

Thrance's words bewildered me. I had never known Muurmut to take orders from anyone, nor could any threat I was capable of imagining have frightened him into such a capitulation. "What nonsense is this?" I said, looking around. "Where's Muurmut? Who has seen Muurmut?" But no one had. We searched for his tracks, and Ment the Sweeper, who was skillful at such things, thought he saw a trail leading downward from our camp. I told Gazin and Talbol and Naxa to follow it and search for him. Thrance laughed and stood with folded arms, saying that Muurmut was gone and no one would find him. Some hours went by, and the searchers returned. We waited there all day, but Muurmut did not return. There was nothing to do but to go on. I took Grycindil aside and asked her to tell me what had happened, but all she could say was that Muurmut had come to her where she was sleeping with Thrance, and that Thrance and Muurmut had spoken in the night, and then Thrance had returned to her side. It had been a night of no moons. She had no idea which way Muurmut had gone, or why. Nor did we ever learn those things. What Thrance had said to Muurmut, or what enchantment he had worked on him, is something I do not know. I never will.

Strangely, I felt a great empty place in my spirit at Muurmut's disappearance. I hadn't ever liked him; he had been nothing but trouble for me; I should have rejoiced that he was no longer with us. But I am not like that. He had been a nuisance but he was of our Forty, and I mourned his going for that reason, and also because he was strong and sometimes valuable to the group. In a curious way I would miss him. It occurred to me that in trading Muurmut for

Thrance I had not improved my situation. Muurmut, negative force though he had been in the group, had been easy enough for me to outflank and control. Thrance was a different matter: older, shrewder, with that strange burned-out quality that made him indifferent to ambition but highly dangerous all the same, since by his own admission he no longer cared about anything at all. When most of us act, it is usually with some thought for the consequences of what we are doing. Not so with Thrance. For him every moment was an independent thing, born with neither antecedent nor successor. In Thrance, I realized, I had acquired a much more complicated and deadlier rival than Muurmut ever had been. I would need to keep close watch on him.

DURING THESE DAYS, ALSO, we were drawing nearer and nearer to the Kingdom of the Kavnalla.

We had all begun feeling its pull almost as soon as we left our camp in the place of the red spires. Dorn was the first to come to me complaining of it: he spoke of a strangeness in his head, like an itching or a tickling within his skull, and on his heels came two of the women, Scardil and Pren, and then Ghibbilau, to tell me the same. They were relieved to find that they weren't the only ones afflicted that way, that in fact we all were. I called the group together and told them that what we were experiencing was a phenomenon particular to this sector of the Wall and that there was nothing to fear from it, at least not yet.

"Is that the Kavnalla that we feel?" I asked Thrance. And he nodded and pointed up the slope, grinning almost as though he were looking forward to a rendezvous with an old friend.

The force of it grew stronger hour by hour. At first it was as Dorn had said, no more than a kind of tickling inside our skulls, a barely perceptible feather-stroke, odd and a little disturbing, but light, very light. Then it grew more powerful and it became as Traiben and I had experienced it on our preliminary reconnoitering march: a clear voice within our heads, articulate and unmistakable, saying to us, *Come, come, this is the way, come to me, come.* There was a definite pull, but not an unpleasant one, nothing troublesome or alarming: something was beckoning to us like a mother opening her arms to her children.

And if something was beckoning, we were responding. We were in a steep land now, heavily wooded, where the hills were of a grayish-white stone deeply pockmarked by caves, and though the path was difficult, we made our way up the ever more rugged incline with such frantic zeal that we outstripped our own strength, and from time to time had to halt and drop to the ground, laughing and gasping, until we could catch our breath. And then we were onward again, furiously slashing through brambles, scrambling over boulders, clawing our way upward, upward, upward, moving faster than we would have thought possible. The higher we went, the more urgent became the call. *Come to me! Come! Come!*

Traiben spoke to me and expressed his concern. I shared it. "We're starting to lose control of ourselves," I said uneasily to Thrance. "You said that you would guard us against the Kavnalla's song."

"And so I will."

"Shouldn't we be taking some precautions by this time, then?"

"Soon. Soon. There's no need at this point." Nor would he say more than that, however hard I pressed him.

And upward we sped, willy-nilly. We were all but running up the slope now. The thought came to me once again that despite his protestations Thrance might indeed be the creature of the Kavnalla, and was merrily leading us toward our doom.

Others now were beginning to wonder, not just Traiben. Our ever swifter pace was taking its toll on their bodies and stirring troublesome questions in their minds. Where were we going in such a hurry? they asked. What is this thing that speaks in our heads? Is there danger? Tell us, tell us, tell us, Poilar!

But there was nothing I could say. I knew no more than they did.

I felt that it was my responsibility to take some action. But what? Thrance was elusive. Often he walked ahead, moving with remarkable swiftness for one whose body was so transformed into twistedness and deformity. Watching him striding so swiftly, I was reminded again of the shining young Thrance of years ago, bursting from Pilgrim Lodge and running ahead of all his Forty up the road that led to Kosa Saag. So there is still some of Thrance within that ruined body, I thought. I pushed myself to catch up with him. He moved serenely, his breathing utterly normal, as though this pace were nothing for him.

I said, "We can't go on like this. The voice grows louder and louder, and people are speaking out. We have to know what we're getting into, Thrance."

"Wait. There's time yet for you to learn."

"No. Now."

"No, not now. The time will come." And with a new burst of speed he streaked ahead. I followed him, but it was hard for me to match his pace, and my bad leg began to ache. How did he do it? There *had* to be a demon in him. Again I caught up with him, and again I pressed him, and again he eluded me with grinning evasions, putting me off, telling me the time was not yet.

I felt a burst of rage. I should kill him, I thought. And take us all away from this place. Unless he is killed he will never let us alone, and ultimately he will destroy us. For he is a demon, or else he has one in him.

But the thought of killing Thrance appalled me. I tried to sweep it from my mind. Another day, I told myself, or two or three, and then I would confront him once again, and this time I wouldn't let him wriggle from my grasp. It was a weak decision, and I had no illusions about that. But

Thrance baffled me. I had never had to deal with anyone like him before.

My companions were growing even more restless now. After dark one night a delegation came to me, troubled and angry, when we had halted after a day of wild climbing that left us all exhausted: Galli, and Naxa, and Talbol, and Jaif. The pull was so strong now that we were climbing virtually from dawn to dusk; but finally we had stopped from sheer weariness, despite the insistent booming in our minds, and were camped in a place of little shallow caverns against the pitted and eroded Wall.

Hendy was with me in the small dank cavern I had chosen. Galli said, very brusquely, "Send her out."

"What is this?" I asked. "Am I to be murdered?"

"We want to speak with you. What we have to say is between you and the four of us, and no one else."

"Hendy shares my sleeping-place, and much else of mine besides. Whatever you have to say you can say in front of her."

"It makes no difference to me," said Hendy softly, and began to get up to go.

"Stay," I said, catching her by the wrist.

"No," Galli said. She seemed gigantic, standing there in the mouth of my shallow little cave. Her face was fierce. I had never seen her with such a look as she had now. "Send her outside, Poilar."

I was eager for sleep, and I suppose I had the doing of the Changes on my mind also, and the voice of the Kavnalla was louder than ever, like the beating of a drum in my brain, *Come, come, come,* making me short-tempered and impatient. I turned my back and said, "Let me be, will you? I'm in no mood for discussing anything with any of you now. Talk to me about it in the morning, Galli."

"We'll talk now," Galli replied.

Then Talbol said to her, "What difference does it make if Hendy hears this or not? Let her stay while we speak."

Galli grunted and shrugged, but offered no objection.

"Will you hear us?" Talbol asked.

"Go ahead," I said grudgingly.

Talbol swung around toward me. I remembered that he had been Muurmut's man. Just as well Muurmut was gone, I thought: I could imagine how much difficulty Muurmut would be making for me if he had been a member of this delegation too. I studied Talbol's broad flat face, brown as the leather that is the trade of his House. This was a strange alliance, I thought, my friends Galli and Jaif with Talbol and Naxa, who never had had much love for me.

He said, "What we want to know is simply this, Poilar: Why are we rushing forward in this lunatic way, when we don't know where we're going or what we're heading toward?"

"We're going into the Kingdom of the Kavnalla," I replied. "And through it, and beyond."

"Into it, yes," said Naxa, stepping forward to stand at Talbol's side. "But beyond it? How do you know? What if Thrance means only to deliver us up to this unknown thing that we hear speaking in our minds?"

"Not so," I said, looking away from Naxa in discomfort, for the fear that Naxa had voiced was of course one that I shared. But I couldn't say that to him. "He has a way of protecting us against it."

"Ah, and what may that be?" Galli asked.

"I don't know."

"But he intends to teach it to us, sooner or later?"

"When the time comes, is what he told me."

"And when is that?" she asked me. "What is he waiting for? It seems to us that the time is very close. He protected his own Forty so well that of them all he's the only one who still survives. My brother was a member of his Forty, Poilar. And now we fly toward your Kavnalla day by day, and its voice grows stronger and stronger within us, and Thrance tells us nothing."

"He will. I know he will."

"You know? You think? You believe? You hope? Which

is it, Poilar?" Great heavy-set Galli rose up before me like a tower, her eyes ablaze in the dimness of the little cave. "Why don't you demand that he tell you right now? Are you our leader, or is he? When will he teach us what we need to know in order to defend ourselves?"

"He will," I said again, with less conviction than before. "In the proper time."

"Why do you trust him, Poilar?" Galli asked.

I had no answer for that.

"What I think is that we should throw him over the cliff," said Talbol abruptly. "And make our way down from this place and take some other route upward, before we discover that there's no longer any turning back for us. There is change-fire here, somewhere nearby. We are in great danger. And he brings us ever closer to it."

"Just so," said Jaif, who had hung back until this moment, saying nothing. "Kill him now, while we still can."

"Kill him?" I said, astounded. This from Jaif, the kindest of men?

"Kill him, yes," Jaif said again. He looked a little stunned at his own audacity. But then Galli nodded vehemently and said, "There's something to the idea, Poilar. I took Thrance's side when he first came to us, but also I said then that we should kill him if he made problems for us. I didn't really mean it then, but now I do. He's rotten through and through. He's nothing but trouble, don't you see?" Naxa too spoke up in favor of our ridding ourselves of Thrance, and Talbol also, and suddenly they were all talking at once, crying out for an end to him and an immediate descent from this hill of voices, while beneath all their hubbub I heard the Kavnalla's urging louder than ever, pounding like the beating of a drum in my brain, *Come, come, come.*

My head was whirling. There was a great roaring in my ears.

"Quiet, all of you!" I cried out over the turmoil, and there must have been such madness in my tone that it awed them all into silence. They stood in the opening of the cave, gaping at me. Then in a quieter voice I said, "There'll be no talk of killing Thrance, or anyone else, unless it comes from me. I'll speak again with him tomorrow, and tell him that the time has arrived for him to teach us how to ward off the song of the Kavnalla. And he will give me the answer we need to have him give, or he'll regret it, I promise you that. And now good night to you all. Go. *Go.*"

They looked at me and went, without another word.

My skull throbbed as though someone had been drumming on it. My thoughts raced in circles.

Hendy said, after a long while, "What if they're right, Poilar? What if Thrance is really our enemy?"

"If that is so, then I'll deal with him as he needs to be dealt with."

"But if we're already caught in the snare of the Kav—"

"You too?" I asked. "Gods! I see there's to be no peace for me tonight." I lay stiff and trembling. Her fingers crept along my shoulders, trying to give me some ease. But my every muscle was tight and my forehead ached dismally. The voice behind it seemed louder and louder. *Come to me. Come to me. Come to me.* The Kavnalla wasn't merely beckoning any longer, but commanding. Despair engulfed me. How could we ever resist that urgent pull? I have led us all into the serpent's jaws, I told myself. We will be swept up in the change-fire that blazes in its lair, and our forms will be lost and we will become as monsters. And why have I brought us to this dire place? Because Thrance had once been a glorious hero whom I revered; because I had allowed myself to be deceived for the sake of the Thrance that once had been, when I was a boy. I should have thrust him away when he first approached us in the land of the red spires. Instead I had taken him into our Forty, and this was how he had repaid us. In that moment I could have killed Thrance with my own hands.

Hendy rubbed against me and I felt the soft swelling of a breast. She had begun to enter the Changes. But pleasure now was far from my mind, or even the higher unity that the Changes give us. I murmured an apology to her and got up, and went out into the night.

A light rain was falling, more of a mist. The blurred light of several moons glimmered faintly through it. I saw a figure moving about not far away, and thought at first it was one of the sentries of the watch, Gazin or Jekka; but a moment later, when my eyes were better adjusted to the darkness, I recognized the grotesque elongated form of Thrance, outlined like a bizarre nightmare wraith against the darkness.

He waved to me. "You want to kill me?" he said. He sounded almost cheerful. "Well, then, here I am. How do you want to do it? A knife? A cudgel? Or with your bare hands, Poilar? Do it and be done with it, if you like."

"What are you talking about?" I asked him. My voice was like a rasp in my own ears. Thrance made no immediate reply, but sauntered toward me in his lopsided way, his head bobbing and weaving and lurching about with every awkward step he took.

I squared myself away, in case he had some thought of striking first. But when he came closer I saw that he was unarmed, and his stance was not that of a man who was expecting combat.

He said, "I have many enemies in this camp, I see. Well, all right. What do you want to do?"

"You were listening?"

"I was out and about. Voices carry." He seemed utterly indifferent to anything that had been said. "That Galli—I remember her. Her brother was my friend, once. A lively girl, Galli, but a great deal too fat for my taste, is what I thought back then. And of course still too young for the Changes when I left Jespodar. I had my pick of them, back then. But that was when I was beautiful." He bent himself over into a sort of crooked arch, so that his eyes were on a level with mine. "What do you say, Poilar? Am I really as despicable as they say, your Galli and her friends? Kill me, then. And then deal with the Kavnalla whatever way you can."

"There'll be no killing. But this thing called the Kavnalla frightens us."

"You need only sing to it," Thrance said coolly. "That's the whole secret. I was going to tell you tomorrow. But now you know it. Sing. Sing. Open your mouths and sing. There, the secret's out. You can kill me, if you like. But why bother?" And he laughed in my face.

IT WAS AS HE said, nothing more. The way to counteract the lure of the Kavnalla was simply to sing. Anything, the more discordant the better.

Who would believe such a thing? But that was all we needed to shield ourselves against this dread monster.

In the morning Thrance told me to summon the entire group; and as we gathered round him, he explained what we must do. The Kavnalla waited for us just on the far side of these white hills. From the moment we broke camp, he said, we must raise our voices in song, loudly, lustily, bellowing any tune that came into our heads, or no tune at all. It was the noise that was important. More than a moment or two of silence could be fatal. And if anyone should lose their voice through overuse, those nearby must seize them and hold them tight, pulling them forward through the Kavnalla's territory until they had recovered.

"And what is the Kavnalla itself, then?" Traiben asked.

"A dire creature of the Wall," said Thrance. "A thing that is placed here to lure the weak from their proper path. More than that, what can I tell you? A gigantic thing: a parasite: an enemy of our kind. Sing, and pass it by. Why do you need to know what it is? Sing, boy. Sing and run past, and save yourself."

Of true Singers we had only two, Jaif and Dahain. We placed them at the head of our column next to Thrance, for by virtue of their House they knew the secret of making a very great sound with relatively little effort. The rest of us, but for a few, had no ear for melody at all, and when we sang it was more of a croaking or a screeching or a wailing than any kind of a music. But Thrance said our lives depended on our singing, and so we sang. I moved up and down the ranks, listening to the others while I sang myself, making certain they were doing as Thrance said. Thissa, always shy, was giving forth only a tiny silver thread of sound, and I took her by the shoulder and shook her, crying, "Sing, woman! For Kreshe's sake, sing!" Little Bilair the Scholar likewise could produce no more than a pitiful breathy wheeze, out of fear, I suppose, and I stood beside her, roaring a crude drinking-song to which I knew hardly half the words, and made encouraging gestures at her with my hands until she managed to bring some volume of sound up from her lungs. I went by Naxa, who was droning away on a single terrible wearisome note, but very loudly, and Tull, who sang a rollicking clownish tune in a high, stabbing voice, and Galli, booming some bit of bawdiness in a voice fit to bring down the mountain upon us, and Grycindil almost as loud, and Kath babbling a hymn of his House in quick tumbling phrases, and Kilarion red-faced and grinning as he yelled tremendous raucous whoops into the air. Thrance's own song was a raw tuneless rasping thing, like metal against metal, very painful to hear. And so we all went. If Thrance were playing a joke on us by this, he was getting his full measure of amusement. Surely no such noise had ever been heard in the world's whole history as we made upon that morning on Kosa Saag.

Thrance was playing no joke, though. Beneath all our horrendous noise I still could hear the Kavnalla's own song, trying to lure us on. *This is the way, yes . . . come . . . come. . . .* But it was buried beneath the force of our outcries. It was down there in the depths of our mind, but it was small and scratchy and tinny now. You know what they say, that a sound is so great that one can scarcely hear oneself think? That was what we achieved with our singing. And if we could not think we could not succumb to the pull that we felt in our minds. We were hiding the Kavnalla's urgings from ourselves with all our crazy clamor.

Roistering and braying and howling like a pack of madmen, then, we came over the crest of the white hills and found ourselves in a broad basin rimmed by soft low yellow slopes half covered in sand. New peaks rolled upward as always beyond the basin's far border: jagged fierce black ones, sharp as awls, forbidding, dismaying, stabbing deep into the ice-blue sky. Dark birds that must have been of great size, but seemed to us no bigger than specks, circled above those remote daggers of stone.

Closer at hand, at the edge of the rounded yellow slopes just to our left, I saw a long shallow-vaulted cave, broad-mouthed and dark within, with a deep track beaten in the sand leading up to it. I knew without needing to be told that within that cave lay the source of the secret voice that we had been hearing all during this part of our climb. Thrance saw me staring at it, and sang into my ear in his croaking tuneless way, "The Kavnalla is there, the Kavnalla is there!"

"Yes," I sang. "I feel the pull pulling." I stared into the darkness, frightened and fascinated. "Tell me," I sang, "will it come out, will it come out?" And Thrance sang in reply to me, "No, no, the Kavnalla goes nowhere, nowhere, nowhere, it lies in wait and we go to it."

And just at that moment the Scholar Bilair bolted from the group, no longer singing but merely whimpering and murmuring to herself, and began to run up the sandy slope toward the mouth of the cave. Instantly I saw what she was doing and ran in pursuit. Thrance also came. We caught up with her midway up the slope. I seized her by one shoulder, spun her around, stared into a wild-eyed face, frozen in a strange grimace.

"Please—" she muttered. "Let—me—go—"

Without pausing in my singing I struck her across the face, not really hard, but stunning her for a moment. Bilair looked at me in bewilderment. She blinked and shook her head; and then the light of understanding returned to her features. She nodded to me and muttered a few indistinct words of thanks and I heard her take up the piping song she had sung before. I released her and she ran like a frightened animal back to the others, singing as loudly as she could.

I turned to Thrance. He laughed and a strange diabolical sparkle came into his eyes and in the same hateful rasping singsong he had been using before he sang, "Let me show you the Kavnalla, let me show you the Kavnalla!"

"What are you saying, what are you saying?" I asked him, singing at the top of my lungs in a rhythm very much like Thrance's own. It was absurd for us to be singing to each other like this. Behind me the whole group had halted and were staring at the dark cave-mouth also, and it seemed to me that some of them had stopped singing. "Sing!" I yelled at them. "Don't stop, not for a moment! *Sing!*"

Thrance gripped my shoulder and bent his head toward mine and sang, "We can go in, you and I. Just for a look! Just for a look!"

Why was the demon tempting me this way?

"How can we risk it?" I sang back. "We should just keep moving!"

"Just for a look, just for a look." Thrance beckoned. His eyes were like fiery coals. "Keep singing and nothing will happen. Sing, Poilar, sing, sing, sing, sing!"

It was like a madness. Thrance began to trudge toward the cave-mouth and I followed him, helpless as a slave, along that tight-packed beaten path. The others pointed and gaped but they did nothing to stop us; I think they were too dazed and bemuddled by the proximity of the Kavnalla's powerful mind. Only Traiben left the group and trotted toward us, but it wasn't to prevent me from going in. He ran up to us still singing, and what he sang was, "Take me too, take me too!" Of course. His hunger to know was ever insatiable.

So despite all reason we three went into the cave, right into the mouth of the enemy.

Never once did we cease to sing. Perhaps we had lost our minds but at least that much common sense remained to us. My throat was ragged and inflamed now from this misuse, but still I barked and shrieked and bellowed for all I was worth, and so did Thrance, and Traiben also, the three of us making such a terrible din that I thought the walls of the cave must surely bend outward beneath its force.

Within the cave an eerie gray light prevailed. It came from dark glossy mottled mats of some living, growing thing that clung to the surfaces of the rock; and when our eyes adapted to it, as they did after a moment or two, we saw that the cave was a huge one, deep and extremely wide, and that this light-yielding plant illuminated it even in its farthermost depths. We went in. Occasional clouds of dark spores rose from the mats on the rocks and a thick black juice ebbed constantly from their rough, pebbly surfaces, as if they were bleeding.

"Look, look, look, look!" Thrance sang, on rising pitches.

In the middle sector of the cave were waxy-skinned black creatures crawling about over the mottled mats. They were long and low, with elongated limbs with which they pulled themselves slowly around, and they kept their heads down, feeding in slurping bites on the sticky substance that the mats exuded. Narrow tails of enormous length extended far behind them, tails that were more like long ropes, sprouting from their rumps and snaking off for impossible distances into the rear of the cave.

Thrance, capering about, went to one of these creatures and lifted its head.

"Look, look, look, look!"

I was so astounded I almost forgot for a moment to keep singing. The thing's face was almost like a man's! I saw a mouth, a nose, a chin, eyes. It made a grunting sound and tried to pull away, but Thrance held it up for a moment, long enough for me to realize that the face was not simply *like* a man's, it *was* a man's: I knew that I must be looking at a Transformed One, that what was groveling and nuzzling here before me in the slimy muck of the floor of the cave had to be one who had yielded to the call of the Kavnalla. I trembled at the thought that so many of our kin from the village had been lost this way on the Wall.

"Sing!" Traiben reminded me. "Sing, Poilar! Or you are lost!"

I was numb with amazement and horror. "What are these? Who are they? Do you know them?"

Thrance's laughter traveled up and down the notes of the scale. "This was Bradgar, this was Stit, this was Halimir," he sang. He pointed to one who wallowed not far from me. "That one there was Gortain."

I remembered that name.

"Gortain who was Lilim's lover?"

"Gortain who was Lilim's lover, yes."

And I trembled and came close to weeping, for into my mind flooded the memory of sweet Lilim who had been the first to make the Changes with me, and who had told me of her lover Gortain who had gone up the Wall. Lilim who had said to me, "If you see him there when you go up, carry my love to him, for I have never forgotten him." Lilim's Gortain crawled at my feet now, a black waxy-skinned thing with a tail, transformed beyond any recognition and linked by that long ropy appendage to the unknown monstrosity at the rear of the cave. I could not help myself. I knelt beside him and sang Lilim's name to him, for I had promised her that I would. I hoped that he would be beyond understanding; but I was wrong, for his eyes went wide, and I saw such terrible pain in them that I would gladly have ripped my heart from my breast if it could have given him peace. He wept without shedding tears. It was an awful sight. But I had promised Lilim long ago that I would look for her Gortain and give him her greeting, though I was sorry now that ever I had, or that I had found him.

"Sing!" Traiben cried. "Don't stop, Poilar!"

Sing? How could I sing? I wanted to die of shame. I was

silent for a moment with my head bowed, and in that moment I heard the Kavnalla's voice thundering like ten rockslides in my mind, ordering me to come to it and yield myself up to it, and I took a faltering step inward; but Thrance caught hold of me with a strength beyond all comprehension, holding me back, and Traiben struck me between the shoulders to bring me to my senses, and I nodded and opened my mouth and a shriek came out that someone might shriek while being flayed alive, and another shriek after that one, and another, and that was the song I sang.

"Lilim—" murmured the thing at my feet, in a voice like a groan, which for all its faintness cut through my shrieking like the blaring of a brass bindanay. "Bring me to Lilim—Lilim—I want to go home—home—home—"

I knelt to him. His face was smeared with the juice of the thing he had been eating. Black tears rolled from his tormented eyes.

"Poilar, no, keep back, keep back—"

Thrance. But I paid no heed. I looked into those desperate eyes with pity and love; and Gortain reached to me and wrapped his arms about me like a drowning man. I thought it was a hug of companionship, but then I felt him pulling at me, tugging me, trying to drag me across the floor of the cave toward the Kavnalla. Of course he could not do it. He was just a crawling squirming thing on the ground and his limbs had lost whatever strength they once had had. But I felt the pull all the same, not in my mind this time but on my body, and fear took hold of me. With a sharp twist of my body I broke free of him and rolled to my side, and then, without even thinking, I drew my knife from its sheath and severed the interminable cord that linked him to the thing in the depths of the cave. Gortain howled and rolled himself into a ball, and quivered and jerked for a moment, and then went into wild leaping convulsions, arching up and falling back, arching up and falling back. "Sing!" Traiben ordered me again, as I stood there stupidly.

I opened my mouth and a croaking rusty noise came out. And Thrance, snatching the knife from my dangling hand, plunged it swiftly into Gortain's chest as the pitiful creature rose and fell.

Gortain was still. But all about us the other slaves of the Kavnalla were roiling and writhing and wriggling up close to us, as though they meant to surround us and drag us somehow toward the back of the cave.

"Out!" Thrance sang. "Out, out, out, out!" And we fled.

18

ON THE FAR SIDE of the basin of the sandy hills, when the Kavnalla's voice was only a tinny echo in my brain, I said to Thrance, "Why did you take me in there?"

"How do I know? I wanted to go in again. I knew I could withstand it. I thought you could."

"You were drawn."

"Maybe I was."

We had crossed a district of crumbling tawny rock that seemed to be a boundary. Now we were entering the country of the dagger-sharp black pinnacles, which rose high before us, gleaming like mirrors by the light of bright Ekmelios. Some of my earlier pessimism returned. The Wall exhausts the resources of even the most determined; it tests you constantly, draining you of your vitality and waiting to see if you will find some new reserve of strength. For the moment I could not. We will climb this Wall forever, I told myself dully, and there will always be some new level, some continued unfolding of the endless challenge, and there is no Summit anywhere, only Wall upon Wall upon

Wall. My head ached; my throat was as sore from all my singing as if I had been swallowing fire.

To Thrance I said, "The Kavnalla did its Changes on you, and still you escaped? How?"

"The transformation was only partial. I never was attached by the tail. First it puts its blood in you, which makes you very vulnerable to the change-fire that glows in every rock of this place, and you begin to shift shape, and become what those in that cave became; and then after a time you grow the tail, which is the last of the change; and finally you fasten it to the Kavnalla, and then you are lost forever. It's like that all over the Wall, whenever there are transformations."

"There are more Kavnallas?"

"That's the only one, I think. But there are other Kingdoms, and other kinds of transformations. Those who have a mind to surrender to the forces of the Wall are ever at risk on its slopes." Thrance spoke calmly, as though from an immense distance. I looked at him in wonder, understanding now something of why he was the way he was. He had slept with demons and had awakened to tell the tale; but he was no longer anything like the rest of us. He said, as we walked along, "I thought I could overpower the Kavnalla and take command of it, once I was connected to it. It's only a great helpless slug, a thing that lies there in the darkness at the back of the cave and depends on others to feed it. I would defeat it by the strength of my will, and then we would rule together, the Kavnalla and I, lying side by side in the darkness, and I would be the King of the Kingdom of the Kavnalla and the Kavnalla would be my Queen."

I couldn't take my eyes from him. I had never heard such strangeness, such insanity, from anyone's lips before.

He said, "But no, no, of course there was no way to achieve that. I realized that after a little while: the creature was stronger than I thought, there could be no overpowering it. Another day or two, and I'd have had a tail like all the rest, and I'd be a slave forever inside that cave, foraging like a beast in the muck. So I wrenched myself free before I was fully joined. I had that much strength. I sang my way out when I was only half transformed. And so you see me."

"There can be no changing back to what you once were?"

"No," he said. "I am what I am."

A NARROW GRAVEL-STREWN PATH bordered by little twisted shrubs with dusty gray leaves took us upward into the land of the narrow black pinnacles, which was the Kingdom of the Sembitol. What the Sembitol was, whether it was some parasitic denizen of the caves like the Kavnalla, is something I never learned. But I suppose that it must have been a thing of a similar sort, for it seemed to hold its people in some kind of spell of the mind, as did the Kavnalla. While we were still in the outskirts of their land Thrance pointed out to us the creatures who were in thrall to the Sembitol, moving about on steep winding trails high above us. Though at such a distance they seemed hardly bigger than little flecks, we could see that there was a strangeness about their movements, a curiously stiff and jerky way of carrying themselves, like dancers in the double-lifer dance, who pretend to be very old. And they never seemed to go one by one but only in chains of fifteen or twenty or more. Each member of the chain held a long wooden staff in one hand, with the tip pointed backward, and with his other hand grasped the staff of the one just before him as they traversed the narrow trails, which coiled around and around the outer edges of the black pinnacles the way the sacred inscriptions on a holy baton follow a coiling track along the length of the baton.

"Do they cling to each other like that because the trails are so dangerous?" I asked Thrance.

He gave me his remote, indifferent smile, no warmer than the light of far-off red Marilemma. "The trails are dangerous, yes. But they do it because they do it, and for no other reason. It is the way they are."

"And what way is that?"

"Wait. See." It was as if answering my questions was too much effort for him. He withdrew into himself and would say no more.

Soon a party of these strangers came into view, visible two or three turns above us on the spiral path, descending the same precipitous trail that we were climbing. They were altogether silent, moving in tight formation, separated only by the length of their staffs. At close range I saw the reason why they walked in such a stiff-jointed fashion; for their limbs were greatly lengthened and distorted, looking almost as if they had two sets of knees and elbows, though that was not in fact the case. Within this framework of long bony limbs their bodies, small and slender, hung like afterthoughts. They wore no clothing, and their skins were of a grayish hue with a faint glossy gleam, as though their flesh had hardened into a kind of rigid translucent shell.

Every one of them was like this: every one. Their faces were the same too, with tiny pinched features close together and large staring eyes that had little sign of intelligence in them. Nor did they vary at all in height. In truth they were all of them identical, as though they had all been stamped from a single mold, so that I could not have told one from another if my life depended on it.

They were an odd, disagreeable-looking bunch.

"What are they?" I asked Thrance; and he told me that these were the people of the Kingdom of the Sembitol.

I had no idea what to make of them, though I had a theory, and not a pleasant one. To Thrance I said, "They seem almost like insects; but can there possibly be any kind of insect the size of a man?"

"They were men once, just like us," he said. "Or women: there's no way of telling now. But they've all undergone transformation here, and turned into insects. Or something of that sort, at any rate."

It was as I had feared. Change-fire had been at work here as well.

"Will they make trouble for us, do you think?"

"Usually they're quite peaceful," he told me. "There's only the risk that they may want to offer you the chance to become as they are. Which can be easily enough arranged, I suspect; but I wouldn't recommend it."

I replied with a sour grin. But we had a more immediate problem to consider. The trail seemed barely wide enough for one person to pass at a time, and I wondered what would happen as the two groups came face to face. When we were still some fifty paces below the other group, though, they performed a rare and extraordinary act: for upon seeing us approaching them they wordlessly broke their tight file and each at the same instant wedged the tip of his staff deep into the soil at the edge of the trail. Then they knelt and lowered their long legs over the edge, and dangled there into the abyss, gripping their staffs with both hands, making room for us to go by.

It was a wondrous sight, those twenty solemn mountaineers hanging above the nothingness like that. As we passed I looked down at them and saw no fear in their eyes, indeed saw no expression at all. They waited, as impassive as boulders, looking beyond us as though we were invisible while we filed past them. Then they scrambled to their feet and freed their staffs, and resumed their formation, and continued along their journey, having said nothing to us throughout the entire encounter. It had been like a meeting in a dream.

Perhaps an hour later we met another party of these people on the same trail; and once again, just as before, they drove their staffs into the ground with one accord and swung themselves out over the nothingness to allow us to pass. But this time there was a mishap: for just as the last of our party—Kilarion and Jaif, who were at the end of our file—went by, the rim of the trail suddenly crumbled and fell away in one place, taking two of the insect-men with it. They plummeted into the void without a sound, and when they struck the cliff face far below there was an odd quick cracking noise, like the breaking of a clay vessel, and then silence.

That was horrifying enough; but what was worse was that the remaining insect-men seemed totally unmoved by their comrades' deaths, almost as though they were unaware of them. It was impossible that they could be, for they had been dangling one next to another in the usual close formation, and the neighbors of the two who had been lost must surely have seen them drop. But in no way did they react. After it had happened they simply hopped up onto the trail and freed their staffs and moved along without a syllable of comment, not one of them troubling to look down into the great open space that had claimed the lives of their two fellow-marchers.

"Life means nothing to them," said Thrance. "Neither their own nor yours. They are only vacant-souled things." He spat into the emptiness below.

I glanced back and saw the insect-men already two turns beyond us on the downward path, hurrying along toward whatever mysterious destination it was that summoned them.

THE HIGHEST REACHES OF the dagger-peak afforded us flat ledges where we could make camp, and we halted for the night. Our goal still lay a little way beyond us, a place where a natural bridge of stone connected the uppermost spear of this tapered peak to yet another realm beyond. But darkness was coming on quickly and it seemed unwise to try to go farther until morning.

There was no wood here, so we had to do without a fire. I could see lights blazing here and there on the nearby peaks, though: each one an encampment of the insect-folk, I supposed. Thrance told me that that was so. They dwelled in hive-like warrens all around these sharp-tipped black mountains. Every one of them was a former Pilgrim; they were villagers like ourselves who had freely chosen to undergo this transformation into something lower even than a beast. I was unable to understand it. To come this far, and then to give up all individuality, all the essence of one's unique self, in order to become a gray-shelled thing— vacant-souled, as Thrance had said—endlessly marching to and fro on these steep paths! It was incomprehensible to me. Just as the willingness of the victims of the Kavnalla to let themselves be turned into idle cave-dwelling worms feeding on muck had been incomprehensible to me. Those who had yielded to the Kavnalla had allowed themselves to become as infants again; those who had joined the soulless swarms of the Kingdom of the Sembitol in this higher level had descended to an even lower status, and had given up humanity itself.

But then I thought: What are we all, if not some sort of endlessly marching creatures, moving up and down along the trails of our lives? And toward what end? For what purpose is it that we have climbed this far, and will drive ourselves to climb even farther? Isn't everything ultimately only a deception designed merely to carry us through from one day to the next? And if the rim crumbles and our staff comes loose, what does it matter that we fall crashing into the abyss?

Dark thoughts on a dark night. Hendy, who was beside me as she was every evening now, sensed my turmoil and pressed herself closer against me. Gradually my spirits lifted, and I held her, and we entered into Changes, and then we slept.

But in the morning two of our number were missing.

I must have known, somehow, during that hour when my soul was succumbing to such bleak thoughts, that some terrible thing was happening to our group. For when we gathered by first light to make ready for our day's march I sensed at once that we were not all present, and a count showed that I was right. Of our original Forty we had already lost five along the way: but now I could count only thirty-three this morning, apart from Thrance. I looked up and down the ranks, trying to see who was missing.

"Ment?" I said finally. "Where is Ment? And someone else isn't here. Tenilda? No, there you are. Bilair? Malti?"

Bilair and Malti were still with us, toward the rear of the group. But Ment the Sweeper was gone, yes. And among the women, Tull the Clown. I sent searchers in all directions, in groups of three and four. Though we had camped a fair distance from the edge, I walked to it and peered over, thinking that they might have wandered in their sleep and fallen to their deaths; but I saw no bodies on the crags below. And the searchers returned without any news to report.

Ment had been a quiet, hard-working, uncomplaining man. High-spirited Tull had diverted us in many a somber moment. I was hard pressed to reconcile myself to their disappearance. I called Dorn over, for he was of Tull's House and knew her well. His eyes were red with weeping. "Did she say anything to you about leaving us?" I asked him. He shook his head. He knew nothing; he was dazed and distraught. As for Ment, he had never been one to open his soul to others. There was no one else of his House among us that I could question, nor even anyone who could be considered his friend.

"Forget them," Thrance advised. "You'll never see them again. Pack up and move along."

"Not so soon," I told him. I put Thissa to work casting a spell of finding. That was sky-magic, not as arduous for her as the other kind; we gave her some garment that Ment had left behind and a Clown-toy out of Tull's pack, and she sent forth her soul into the air to see if she could locate their owners. Meanwhile I ordered more search-parties out, and they roved the trail behind us and a little way ahead, but with no more luck than before. Then Thissa looked up from her spell-casting and said that she could feel the presence of the missing two somewhere nearby, but the message was confused: they were still alive, she believed, and yet she was unable to tell us anything more useful than that.

"Give it up," Thrance said again. "There's no hope. Trust me: this is how a Forty comes apart, when the transformations begin."

I shook my head. "Your Forty, maybe. Not mine. We'll look for them a little longer."

"As you wish," he said. "I don't think I'll wait." He rose and gave me a mocking courtly bow, and turned and started up the trail. I stared after him, gaping like a fish. Even with his limping gait he was moving at a phenomenal pace; already he was a turn and a half above us on the spiral path.

"Thrance," I called, shaking with fury. *"Thrance!"*

Galli came up beside me. She slipped her arm through mine. "Let him go," she said. "He's hateful and dangerous."

"But he knows the way."

"Let him go. We found our own way well enough before he was ever with us."

Hendy came to me on the other side. "Galli's right," she said quietly. "We're better off without him."

I knew that it was true: dark-souled Thrance was useful but at any moment had the capacity to turn disruptive and menacing. From the beginning my alliance with him had been a grudging one, a mingling of uneasy respect and practical need. But his transformation, partial though it had been, had taken him over into a world that was not my own. He might be our fellow villager, but he was no longer entirely one of us. He was capable of anything, now. Anything. Let him go, I told myself.

We searched for Ment and Tull another two hours. A long chain of the mountain-men came through our camp, thirty of them at least, while we combed the nearby caves and crevices for our companions. I put myself in their path and said, "We have lost two of our number. Do you know where they are?" But they looked right through me without responding and did not so much as break their pace. I cried out to Naxa to speak to them in Gotarza, hoping that they might at least understand the old language; he called out some harsh babble to them, but that drew no reaction either, and they went around us and vanished down the trail. In the end I had to abandon the search. And so we went on, having lost Ment and Tull and Thrance also, or so it seemed to me at the time. I fell into deep brooding, once again thinking myself a failure as leader; for it pained me deeply to have members of my Forty fall away from the group.

By midday we were at the natural bridge that would carry us on into the next Kingdom. It was a terrifying place, an airy vaulting span across the steepest of gorges: a curved sliver of shining black stone so narrow that we would have to go single file on it, with a gulf beyond all measuring dropping off on either side of us. Talbol and Thuiman were the first to reach the bridge approach, and hung back, wide-eyed, unwilling to go across; for the bridge seemed so fragile that it would shatter at the first pressure of a man's weight. They were no heroes, those two, but still I couldn't blame them for hesitating. I would have hesitated a moment myself, staring into that brink. But what choice did we have, except to go on? And others must have gone this way often before us.

Galli said, laughing robustly, "Will it break? Let me test it out! If it'll carry me, it'll hold anyone!" Without waiting for confirmation from me she set out across the bridge, head held high, shoulders pulled back, arms stretched far to her sides to give her balance. Quickly she went, taking step after step after step with supreme confidence. When she had crossed it she looked back and laughed. "Come on over! It's solid as can be!"

And so we crossed the bridge, though some had a harder time of it than others. We opened the sucker-pads on our toes to give us the best purchase, but still it was a frightening business. The bridge would bear us, yes; but this was not a place where one might stumble more than once. Chaliza was so green of face that I feared she would lose consciousness and topple to her death midway, though somehow she made it. Naxa did it on hands and knees. Bilair crossed it trembling and shaking. But Kilarion bestrode the bridge as if it were a broad meadow, and Jaif went across singing, and Gazin with a Juggler's easy stride. Thissa seemed to float across. Traiben moved like one who has no natural skill at these things yet was determined to manage it deftly, and he did. Hendy's crossing was an agony to me, but she betrayed no fear or uncertainty. And at last it was my turn, having held myself for last as if by staring at my companions from the rear I could help them keep their balance by sheer prayer alone. As I made my way over I had reason to curse my twisted leg, for it made gripping the bridge difficult on that side, but I knew how to compensate for the awkwardness of my deformity and I was skilled enough in mountaineering by this time to understand the art of narrowing my concentration to a single point just ahead of my nose. So I paid no heed to the chill currents of swift air rising out of the abyss and I ignored the flickering movements of the sunlight on the bare walls of stone to my right and to my left and I dismissed from my mind any thought of the huge shadow into which I would fall if I put one foot down awry; I took one step and the next and the one after that, keeping my mind empty of all distractions; and then Kilarion had me by one hand and Traiben by the other and they were pulling me the last step of the way and we were done with the bridge-crossing.

Except then Thissa said, "I feel a presence behind us. Below us." And she pointed back across the bridge.

"A presence? What presence?"

She shook her head. "Ment? Tull? It could be."

We had attained a wind-raked knob of rock, barren and stark and wholly exposed to the ferocity of the noon sun, which in the thin air of these heights was unrelenting. I saw the crackling flash of blue lightning above us, and that was strange, for the air here was cloudless and parched; and there were the usual dark sinister birds wheeling high overhead. So this was no place of placid repose where I cared to have us linger. But it would be folly not to trust Thissa's intuitions. I divided the group; most went ahead under Galli's leadership to find a campsite where we could rest while scouting out our next challenge, while I waited by the bridge with Thissa and Kilarion and a few others to see who or what might be coming toward us from the rear.

For a long while we saw and heard nothing, and even Thissa began to think she had been mistaken. Then Kilarion let out a whoop. We sprang up and stared into the glare of sunlight reflecting from the walls of the gorge: and there was a solitary figure laboring up the spiral path that led to the bridge.

I struggled to make it out against the searing brightness. I thought I saw long spidery limbs, a tiny body, a flash of grayish glossy skin. "One of the mountain-men," I said in disgust.

"No," said Traiben. "Tull, I think."

"Tull? But how—"

"Do the mountain-men ever travel by ones?" he asked me. "Look! Look close!"

"Tull, yes," said Kilarion. "I see her face. But her face—on that body—"

The creature came up the path on the far side, moving in mountain-man fashion but far more clumsily, as though well gone in drunkenness. It appeared to have little control over its elongated limbs, and its every step was a staggering slide. Then it halted, just before the approach to the bridge proper. It stood as though baffled, swaying, fitfully weaving its long narrow arms through the air. It took a tentative step forward and managed somehow to get its legs tangled, so that it had to drop to its knees and crouch there clinging to the ground, befuddled and helpless. I could see its face now: Tull's, Tull's, unmistakably Tull's, the familiar sharp features, the familiar wide grinning clown-mouth. But she wasn't grinning now. Her lips were pulled down into a terrible knotted grimace of terror and confusion.

"We have to get her," Kilarion said.

And so we crossed the bridge again, he and I, not for an instant pausing to consider the risks we faced. I have no memory of doing it; but then I was on the far side once more, and Kilarion and I took the altered Tull by the arms and legs, and we brought her across. One convulsion of fear from her would have hurled the three of us into the abyss. But she hung like old rope between us, and he and I moved as though we were a single four-legged entity, and not until we were safe on the other side did we drop down, shaking and shivering like men at the edge of their final illness. Then Kilarion began to laugh, and so did I; and we turned our backs on that terrible bridge for good and all.

The others had settled down a thousand paces ahead in a wooded bowl beneath a dusk-colored mountain so folded and gnarled that it had a look of unthinkable age. We brought Tull to them and our three Healers began their work on her, in the hope of bringing her back to her true form. The rest of us looked away, out of respect for her suffering; but I glanced over, once, and saw Jekka lying with her in his arms, doing the Changes, while Malti and Kreod held her hands in theirs, and Tull was half like herself again and half the other way. It was so awful a sight that I shut my eyes and tried to blot the image from my mind, but I could not.

It took two hours to return her to herself, and even then she carried a hint of strangeness with her, a slight elongation of the limbs, a faint gray tint in her skin, that I knew she would never lose. Nor did the gaiety that a Clown must have, or at least be able to feign at will, ever come back to her. But I was glad she was back. It did not seem proper to me to ask her why she had chosen to slip away, nor what had made her decide midway through her transformation to return to us; those were Tull's secrets, no business of ours.

As for Ment, she said, we would never see him again. He was of the Kingdom of the Sembitol now. And I suspected that that was true, so we spent no further time waiting for him.

We rested a little while longer from our bridge crossing

and then we went on our way into this new land of tilted and upturned layers of ancient gray rock. We had not traveled more than half an hour along the rough, lizard-infested trail when we came upon Thrance, sitting calmly against a huge boulder beside the road. He nodded to us very pleasantly, and got to his feet and fell in with us without saying a word.

19

WE HAD ENTERED THE Kingdom of the Kvuz, Thrance told us. This was the limit of his previous explorations; and it was, he said, by far the most dismal of the Kingdoms of the Wall. "In what way?" I asked him, thinking of the squalid snuffling of the long-tailed prisoners within the Kavnalla's cave, and the apparent soul-lessness of those spidery-limbed gray creatures of the high trails who had given themselves to the Sembitol. Thrance only shrugged and said, "Every man is at war against all other men here. It is the worst of places. See if I'm not right, boy."

Certainly there was no beauty in this Kingdom. It was a parched and crumpled land, somewhat like that grim plateau we had crossed so long ago, but even more brutal to the eye. We went past a place where small conical moun-tains belched fire and smoke and foul stinking gases, and had to cross a dark plain that was like a sea of ashes which crunched and clinked with every step we took. Dry lakes and withered streams that were no more than streams of gravel lay everywhere. Every gust of wind lifted clouds of fine dust. Now and then some bleak bubbling seepage came out of the ground, with grim little clumps of doleful shrubbery with knotted trunks and dull black leaves springing up around it. Such living creatures as we saw were pallid scuttering legless things like worms, but long as a man's arm and covered everywhere with short bristly spines. They would wriggle with surprising swiftness across the sandy soil whenever we came upon them and vanish hastily into underground nests.

It was hard for me to see how any sort of settlement could flourish in this cheerless desert. Indeed I had decided it was a Kingdom without a population and said so to Thrance, who said to me, pointing toward a run of low eroded hummocks just to our left, "Look there, there in those stumpy hills. There is the Kingdom."

"What Kingdom? Where?"

"Do you see holes, down near the ground? In there, that's where you'll find it."

I narrowed my eyes against the sun-glare and was able to make out some small openings hardly big enough for a man to crawl through, sparsely arrayed along the face of the little hills. They were like the burrows of some reclusive animal. Thrance beckoned, and we went a little closer, so that I saw little groupings of sharp stakes set in the earth in front of each one, a sort of defensive palisade. Eyes shining with suspicion looked out at me from opening after opening.

"Those are their homes," Thrance said. His voice was edged with contempt. "They huddle in the darkness, one by one, each one crouching in there by himself all day long. No man trusts another. Everyone's hand is lifted against all others. Each has his own time to come forth and search for food; and if by chance two come out at once, and they happen to cross each other's path, one will kill the other. For they all believe that the population of the Kingdom is too great to provide everyone with enough to eat, and only by murdering the rest does any of them have a hope of surviving."

"What are they?" I asked in wonder.

Thrance laughed his harsh laugh. "Transformed Ones. Pilgrims who have lost their way. Thus far they came, and no farther, and here they let the change-fire work its way with them, and they clambered into these holes." Then his eyes glittered with sudden savage fury. "Do you know what I'd do, boy, if we had time enough? I'd build fires and smoke them out, one at a time, and club them to death as they emerged. It would be the kindest thing. Their lives are a living death."

All this while we kept up a steady pace. The others of the Forty had noticed the holes now, and the mysterious suspicious eyes peering from them. I saw Galli making pious signs as quickly as she could, and Traiben staring with the deepest curiosity, and Kilarion grinning stupidly and nudging little Kath to look.

Hendy came up to me and clutched my forearm. "Do you see them, Poilar? The eyes?"

I nodded. "They are the people of this Kingdom."

"In those little holes?"

"Their homes," I said. "Their palaces."

"People?" she said. "Living in *there*?" And her fingers tightened on my arm so hard that I winced.

We turned a sudden corner in the trail just then, and came upon a citizen of this Kingdom out of his hole. He— or it—was even more surprised than we were. This must have been its feeding-time, for it had emerged some ten or fifteen paces from its burrow and was making its way toward a moist sump-hole in a declivity some fifty paces farther on. As it saw us it halted, frozen in utter horror, and stared with bulging eyes; and then it bared long yellow fangs and began to make a repetitive chattering sound at us so sharp and piercing that if noises were daggers we would all have been flayed to bits by it.

This inhabitant of the Kingdom of the Kvuz was a loathsome thing, with no trace of humanity about it that I could detect. It sprawled low against the ground like a serpent, but a serpent that had limbs: its legs were tiny shrunken things, but its arms, though short, were thick and obviously muscular, terminating in evil curving talons. Naked and hairless it was, with colorless skin that hung in folds around a gaunt, baggy body, and its face, swollen and contorted with fear and hatred, was all eyes and mouth, with the merest slits for nostrils and no sign of ears.

I could have wept for its ugliness, and its misery, and its terrible transformation: for if Thrance had told us true, this was someone of our own kind, or had been once.

"Vermin! Monster!" Thrance yelled, and snatched up a flat rock to hurl it. But I knocked it from his hand. The creature looked up at me in such amazement that for a moment it ceased its wild chattering cry. Then it grabbed up a rock itself, and flung it my way with a seemingly casual backhand flip. I ducked just in time. The rock flew past me with enough force to have smashed my skull.

"Do you see?" Thrance asked. "How well it rewards your charity?" He reached for another rock; and this time I think I would have let him throw it. But the creature had pivoted around and was scampering for its burrow with tremendous speed, moving on its belly like one of those legless spiny wrigglers we had seen a little while before. In a moment it was safely out of our reach. We saw it watching us with smoldering eyes from the darkness of its hole, and now and then it uttered a burst of its baleful chattering noise until the last of us had gone by.

At the seepage-place we saw the fresh corpse of another of the same sort, lying to one side and already decomposing. So there had been an encounter here not long before, and a slaying. Nor had it been the only one: little heaps of whitening bones were scattered here and there, turning slowly into powder under the merciless sky. I poked at one of these skeletons. It showed how the transformation had reached down even to the bone; for the legs, though crumpled into mere tiny appendages, had all the proper bony parts.

We helped ourselves to water—brackish stuff, but it was all there was—and moved ourselves along our way.

That was the Kingdom of the Kvuz. We crossed it as quickly as we could, for Thrance had spoken the truth: it was indeed the most dismal of places. Each of the Kingdoms we had passed through, I realized, brought a different kind of transformation to those Pilgrims incapable of fending off its pull. The Kavnalla brought pitiful helplessness and the Sembitol brought barren selflessness and the Kvuz brought bleak and utter isolation of the spirit. I wondered what allure it could have had for those who chose to dwell in it; or what flaw of character it was, rather, that had driven certain Pilgrims to make it their home. I saw, not for the first time, of course, that the Wall was a testing place; but the nature of the test and the essence of the Pilgrim's response to it was still a mystery to me. I knew only that the Wall offered mysterious temptations amidst all its dread ordeals, and that the weakest links in each Forty thus were stripped away by the differing force of the secret, invisible change-fire that prevailed in this place or that as the ascent went on.

Now and again as we proceeded we saw beady eyes gleaming in a hillside hole, and there were other bodies and crumbling skeletons at every watering-place. Once we caught sight of a battle under way at a great distance, two struggling serpent-men writhing desperately in each other's grip.

We were so frightened of this Kingdom that we kept close by one another, going elbow to elbow as we marched. I asked Traiben what possible temptation there might be to cause a Pilgrim to defect and take up living in this place; but he only shrugged and answered that these must be ones who had parted with the power of reasoning under the adversities of the climb, and had turned themselves into these rock-dwelling things because they could not bear facing whatever hardships lay ahead. Which did not strike me as a satisfying answer, but it was all that he offered.

I watched my people carefully after that, in case any of them should feel such an urge. But none was so inclined.

IT WAS AN UNKIND country in every way. We heard thundercracks and saw the flashes of blue lightning again, which were so strange to have when there was no hint of rain. But it was a bird that caused them, a lightning-bird that flew low above us, hurling fiery bolts from its rump. They left scorching tracks in the land, and Ijo the Scholar had his arm singed by one, though he was not badly hurt. We pelted these pests with rocks and drove them off, though sometimes one made a quick foray past us even so, stitching the ground with its blazing emissions. Then one day a thing that looked like a huge upright stone wheel came rolling toward us; but it was an animal of some sort, sharp-edged, and this was its manner of hunting. It passed so close to Malti the Healer that I thought she would lose her leg, but she jumped aside just in time. Talbol and Thuiman knocked it over with their cudgels: once it had fallen it had no way of rising again, and we beat it to death.

There were other such creatures, just as unappealing. But we were able to fend them off and we suffered no harm.

As we marched Thrance amused us with tales of things he had seen in his years of wandering in these heights. He spoke of other crests that were inhabited, this strange Kingdom and that one, and of the false Summit that ended nowhere and had claimed the lives of so many Pilgrims who had wasted months or even years on its futile slopes. He talked of the Drinkers of Stars, who lived on some high headland and drew energy from the sky that allowed them to rove freely through the night like gods, though they had to return to their bodies by dawn or they would perish. He told us of places where mirages became real and where reality turned into mirage, and of the swirling tempests of the highest levels, where the clouds were of fifty colors and gigantic rainbow-hued wind-whales grazed placidly in the sky. And also he told us, as Naxa once had done, of the Land of the Doubles, which hangs inverted above the Summit and is populated by our other selves, who live in a life beyond life and watch us with kindly amusement, chuckling when we make mistakes and suffer harm, for they are perfect beings. "When we get higher," Thrance said, "we'll see the tip of the Land of the Doubles pointing downward, almost touching the Summit. And I hear that there are Witches up there who are in touch with the Double World, and who can put us into dreams that allow us to consult our other selves and receive advice from them."

I asked Thissa about that. But she only shrugged and said that Thrance was speaking of matters about which he knew nothing, that he was spinning fables out of air.

That seemed very likely to me. By Thrance's own admission he had never gone beyond the Kingdom of the Kvuz; and though he had lived a long while on these high slopes, no doubt hearing many a traveler's tale, how could we be sure that anything they might have told him, or anything he was telling us, had any basis in reality? I was reminded of the solemn teachings that had been offered us in Jespodar village during our years of training, the stories of the dancing rocks, the demons who pulled their limbs loose and flung them at Pilgrims, the walking dead people with eyes in the backs of their heads. These tales of Thrance's had to be like those stories which are told credulous young Pilgrims-to-be by the instructors in the village, who speak in ignorance of the very subject that they claim to teach. We had seen many a strange thing on Kosa Saag, but nothing such as we had been warned to expect, at least not yet. For the teachers know nothing; the Wall is a world unto itself and the truth of its nature is made known only to those who go and look for themselves.

The things that Thrance told us may not have been real but they were at least diverting. And diversion was what we badly needed as we made this dreary crossing. We scarcely dared to sleep at night, for fear we would wake to find some crawling denizen of the Kvuz among us, lifting its yellow fangs to strike. Or perhaps the lightning-birds would come in the darkness; or the whirling wheel would roll through our camp. None of these things happened, but they preyed on our minds.

Then at last we began to come to the end of the Kingdom of the Kvuz. But there was little comfort in that, for over the past several days a dark shadow had begun to appear ahead of us, and as we drew near to it we recognized it for what it was: a wide cliff that rose in a single great vertical sweep, a lofty barrier that cruelly terminated these somber plains, confronting us once more with a wall within the Wall. We would surely have to climb it if we meant to continue our Pilgrimage; but it seemed so steep that climbing it was unimaginable.

Well, we had faced such things before; and we were hardened now to the difficulties of our Pilgrimage. Beyond any question we were bound for the top of the Wall and, having come this far, we meant to let nothing stand in our way. But when I asked Thrance if he knew a route that would carry us up this formidable obstacle, he shrugged his familiar shrug, and said with his familiar indifference, "This is as far as I ever managed to go. For all I know there's no way to climb it at all."

"But the Summit—"

"Yes," he said, as though I had uttered some meaningless sound. "The Summit, the Summit, the Summit." And he walked away from me, laughing to himself.

WHEN WE WERE DIRECTLY under this challenging cliff we saw to our great relief that as was often the case it had cracks and furrows and crevices and chimneys in it that would probably allow us some way of scaling it. But it was bound to be a fierce struggle for us; and also we had lost most of our ropes and other climbing gear very early on, in the rockslide that nearly had buried us on the slopes above the Kingdom of the Melted Ones.

As I stood with Kilarion and Traiben and Galli and

Jaif, staring upward and contemplating the task that faced us, Jaif touched my elbow and told me quietly to turn and look. I swung quickly about.

A curious figure in a hooded robe had emerged from the shadows like some sort of apparition and was coming toward us, moving in a slow, laborious way.

When he came close he pushed back his hood, revealing a face that was like no face I had ever seen. In bodily form too he was very strange, stranger even than Thrance. He was thin and long and stiff-framed, and carried himself oddly, as though his frame were strung on a set of bones that were very little like ours. His legs were too short for his torso, and his shoulders were wrong and his eyes were set too far back in his head, and his nose and ears and lips, though I could recognize them for what they were, were nothing much like ours. Something was wrong about his hands too. From where I stood I wasn't sure what it was, but I suspected that if I were to count the fingers the number would be unusual, four on each hand or at best only five. They had no sucker-pads on them that I could see. He had pale skin that looked like something that had been dead a long time and his hair was rank and soft, like dark string. His breath came in heavy wheezing gusts. So this must be another of the Transformed, I thought: yet one more of the grotesques with which these Kingdoms of the Wall are so abundantly populated. Automatically I drew back a little in surprise and alarm; but then I checked myself, for I saw how weak and weary the newcomer seemed, as though he had wandered in these parts a long while and was nearing the end of his strength.

In his hand he held some small device, a box with the bright sheen of metal. He lifted it and at once words came to us out of the box. But the accent was thick and odd and all but impossible to understand. At first I failed to realize even that the stranger was speaking in our language. But then he touched something on the top of his little box and repeated his words, and this time, curiously, they were somewhat easier to comprehend.

What he said to us, quietly, almost feebly, was: "Please—friends—I mean you no harm, friends—"

I stared and said nothing. There was a strangeness beyond strangeness about this being. And the voice of the box was like a voice that spoke from the tomb.

"Can you understand me?" he asked.

I nodded.

"Good," he said. "And are you planning to climb this cliff?"

"Yes," I told him. I saw no harm in that.

"Well, then. If you do, I ask you to take me up it with you. Can you do that? There are friends waiting for me at the top and I'm not able to manage the climb by myself."

I looked at my companions, and they looked back at me. We were all at a loss to know what kind of creature this strange travelworn being might be; for though he was something like us in superficial form, having two arms and two legs and a head and an upright stance, the differences seemed almost as great as the similarities, or perhaps even greater.

This was a very strange one, I thought, even for a Transformed. Unless he was not a Transformed at all but something else, a god or a demon or something that has come forth out of someone's dream and made itself real. But in that case, why did he look so tired? Was it possible for a supernatural being to get tired? Or was his appearance of great weariness and frailty only some form of deception that he was playing on us?

He held one hand toward me. As if imploring me—begging me. "If you would be so kind," he said. And again he said, "My friends are waiting for me. But I can't—I'm not able—"

"What are you?" I asked, and made some of the sacred signs at him. "If you are a demon or a god, I conjure you in the name of everything holy to speak the truth. Tell me: Are you a demon? A god?"

"No," he said, and his face curled to one side in an

expression that might have been a smile. "No demon. Not a god, either. I'm an Earthman."

That word was meaningless to me. I glanced puzzledly at Traiben, but he shook his head.

"An Irtiman?" I said.

"An Irtiman, yes."

"Is that some kind of Transformed One?"

"No."

"Nor any sort of demon, nor a god? You swear?"

"Not a demon, absolutely not. I swear it. And if I were a god, I wouldn't need any help getting back up the mountain, would I?"

"True," I said, though of course gods can always lie, if they so choose. But I preferred not to think that. "And these friends of yours that are waiting for you above?" I asked him. "They are Irtimen also?"

"Yes. People like me. Of my kind. There are four of us altogether."

"All Irtimen."

"Yes."

"And what may Irtimen be?" I asked.

"We came here from—well, from a place very far away."

Indeed it must be, I thought: very far away and very different. I tried to imagine a whole village full of people who looked like this. Wondered about their Houses, their rites, their customs.

"How far away?" I asked.

"Very far," he said. "We come here as visitors. As explorers."

"Ah. Explorers. From a place very far away." I nodded as though I understood. I thought I did, almost. These Irtimen must be one of the unknown peoples who are said to live on the other side of the Wall, beyond even the lands subject to the King, in the remote regions where no one of our village has ever gone. That was why this being looked so strange, I thought. But I was wrong about that. He came from much farther away even than the far side of the Wall: farther than any of us could conceive.

He said, "The highlands were all that we really intended to explore, just the uppermost zone of the mountain. But then I decided to go part way down, in order to find out a little of what conditions were like down below, and now I can't get back up to the top, because this cliff here is too much for me. And my friends tell me that they're not able to come down and help me. Having problems of their own, they say. Not possible just now for them to offer assistance." He paused a little, as though the effort of so much talking was a great strain for him and he needed to catch his breath. "You're Pilgrims, aren't you? Coming up from the lowlands?"

"Yes. That is what we are." Then I hesitated, for I was almost afraid to ask the next question that had come into my mind. "You say that you've been to the top?" I said, after a moment. "The Summit, you mean?"

"Yes."

"And have you seen the gods, then? With your own eyes?"

Now it was the stranger's turn to hesitate, which made me wonder. For a time I heard no sound other than that of his hoarse wheezing breath. But then he said very quietly, "Yes. Yes, I've seen the gods."

"Truly?"

"Truly."

"At the Summit, in their palace?"

"At the Summit, yes," the Irtiman said.

"He's lying," said Thrance sharply, a harsh voice out of nowhere. He had come hobbling up alongside us while we spoke and I had not seen him arrive.

I signaled to him angrily to be silent.

"What are they like, the gods at the Summit?" I asked the Irtiman. I leaned forward eagerly to him. "Tell me. Tell me what they're like."

The Irtiman grew restless and uneasy. He paced about

to and fro, he scratched with the toe of his boot in the sand, he shifted his little speaking-box from one hand to the other. Then he looked at me with those strange deep-set eyes of his and said, "You'll need to go and discover that for yourselves."

"You see?" Thrance cried. "He knows nothing! Nothing!"

But the Irtiman said, calmly speaking over Thrance's outburst, "If you are Pilgrims, then you have to experience the great truths yourselves, or your Pilgrimage will be without meaning. You must already know that, having come this far. What good is it to you if I tell you what the gods are like? You might just as well have stayed in your village and read a book."

I nodded slowly. "This is so."

"Good. Then let's not talk of the gods down here. Do you agree? Finish your Pilgrimage, my friends. Go onward to the Summit. You'll find out what the gods are when you get to the top and stand in their presence at last."

"Yes," I said, for I knew that what he was telling me was right. "We must finish our Pilgrimage. To the Summit—to the home of the gods—"

"And you'll take me with you, then?" the Irtiman asked.

Once more I was slow to reply. His unexpected request baffled me. Take him with us? Why should I? What was this Irtiman to me? He had no place in our Forty. He wasn't even of our kind. We have an obligation to help our own kind, yes, but it does not extend to those of other villages and surely not to those of an alien race. And this Irtiman looked half dead, or more than half; he would be so much helpless baggage on the way up. It would be challenge enough just getting our own weakest Pilgrims up this cliff, Bilair and Ijo and Chaliza and ones like that.

And there was Thrance pressing up against my side like a dark angel, hissing at me the very things that were already in my own mind: "Leave him! Leave him! He has no strength; he'll only be a burden. And he means nothing to us, nothing at all!"

I think it was that poisonous hiss of Thrance's and the hateful glare in his eyes that turned me in the Irtiman's favor. That and a sense that if I left this weary creature here he would not be likely to survive for long, for he was almost at the end of his strength. His death would be on my conscience, then. And who was Thrance to tell me what I should do, he who was not even a member of our Forty himself? He too had asked us to take him in, and we had; how could he now deny the same kindness to another? I looked quickly about the group, at Traiben, at Galli, at Jaif: people of good will, whose souls were clean, whose spirits were free of the venom that had corrupted Thrance. And I saw nothing on their faces but assent.

"Yes," I told the Irtiman. "We'll take you. Yes." Sometimes you must make a gesture of this sort out of pure charity's sake, with no regard to whether there is wisdom in it. Thrance, who had small understanding of such things, grunted and turned away, muttering. I glowered at his broad twisted back in contempt and anger. But then it seemed to me that I felt some pity for him mingled with my contempt.

BEFORE WE BEGAN TO climb I took out the tiny image of Sandu Sando the Avenger which I had had unwillingly from the madwoman Streltsa at Denbail milepost, and which I had carried with me all this way in my pack. It seemed like a thousand tens of years ago that she had given it to me as we were leaving the uppermost precincts of the village, and I had rarely thought of it since. But I wanted the special protection of the gods now in the ordeal that lay just ahead, and although the Avenger is perhaps not the appropriate one to invoke for such a reason, the little idol was the only thing of that sort that I had with me. So I looped a bit of cord between its legs and anchored it over its little erect penis and fastened it around my neck. Also I asked Thissa to cast a climbing-spell for us, and ordered everyone down to kneel and pray. Even Thrance knelt, though I would not want to guess what sort of prayer went through his mind, or to whom. Only the Irtiman stood to one side, not kneeling; but I thought I saw his lips moving silently. And then we commenced our ascent.

It was a long time since we had faced any such climb of this kind, on a bare rock face, and though our long march through tier after tier of Kosa Saag had hardened us beyond all measure it had also taken some measure of resilience from our muscles. And as I have said we were without most of our ropes and climbing-hooks and other such gear.

So we would have to rely on shrewdness as we climbed, and of course agility, and luck, and beyond all else the kindness of the gods. We would need to calculate every move we made on this unforgiving rock with unusual care: the angle at which we leaned to meet the tilted stone slabs, the way we balanced the backward push of one foot against the forward stride of the other as we climbed, the shifting of our weight in every step, the placement of our fingers in the little crevices on which our lives depended. To deal with the Irtiman required special measures that we had to devise on the spot: with some of our remaining rope we fashioned a kind of sling, and I took one end of it around my waist and sturdy uncomplaining Kilarion took the other, with the Irtiman lashed to its center. This meant that Kilarion and I would have to climb in close parallel tracks, however different the rock formations we each might encounter; but I saw no other way. Kilarion would have carried the Irtiman on his back if I had asked him, but I would not do that. The presence of the Irtiman among us was my doing, and therefore I must share in the risk and effort involved in transporting him to the top.

We gave what remaining rope we had to the least proficient climbers among us, who were mainly women, though Naxa was a poor climber also and so was Traiben. Naxa was glad of the help, but Traiben refused to let himself be roped, I suppose because he was weary of all the favors of this kind I had done for him along the way, or abashed by them; and in fact he was one of the first to spring up onto the rock wall, setting out with such defiant haste that I feared more than usually for him.

Yet once we were climbing we all moved with wondrous precision and excellence, so that we might almost have been so many ants, walking untroubledly straight up the stone face as though we were on a horizontal surface. Of course it was not as simple as that. But in many places the grade, though steep, was nevertheless well within the range of our abilities, and we could go forward quickly at only a slight lean, steadying ourselves with our hands on the ledge above. Where the rock was slick we found ways of holding on. And when I came to a place where the only way ahead for me was through a narrow chimney where I would have to brace myself against one side with my feet and against the other with my back, Kilarion was able to wait for me and even to ease me upward with the rope that linked us, which took some of the pressure off my crooked foot.

So we all steadily made our way. From time to time I risked a quick glance toward the others, and saw them advancing strongly, Galli here with Bilair roped to her, and Traiben there well beyond me, and Jekka and Malti climbing side by side, and Grycindil, and Fesild, and Naxa, and Dorn. We were scattered all across the face of the cliff. Far off to my left was Thrance by himself, pivoting and twisting and wriggling up the rock like some crawling thing of the forest floor that must double itself up into a loop with every movement it makes; and when our eyes met he grinned at me fiercely, as if to say, *You hope I'll fall, don't you, but there's no chance of it, boy, no chance whatever!* But he was wrong about what I felt. I wished him no harm.

Then I turned my gaze away from the others and lost myself totally in the effort of my own ascent. I paid no heed to anything except the need to find the next handhold, and the next, and the next.

But as I continued to climb a terrible thought came over me, which was that the ascent had been easier than expected only because we were being beguiled to our destruction by some treachery of the governing spirits of the Wall once we were high up above the drylands; and I had a sudden vision of the mountain angrily shaking as soon as we were a little higher, throwing us off like fleas, all my bondfellows falling to their deaths, those I most loved, Traiben, Galli, Hendy, Jaif. All of them, one by one flung out into the void and tumbling into oblivion.

For an instant or two I trembled with fear and nearly lost my own grip. It was only the brooding fantasy of a bad moment, though. The Wall has no reason to want to slay us so casually; it wants only to test us, and eliminate those who are weak or unworthy, and send the best of us onward to the end of our Pilgrimage. So we would not perish here. And indeed I looked and my companions were still all about me clinging to the face of the cliff, working their way steadily upward.

So I grew calm again, for a little while. But my soul must have been disturbed in some fashion that day. Perhaps it was Streltsa's Avenger amulet working some dark magic in me. For now a different strangeness came over me and it began to seem to me that I had done all this before: not just that I had climbed other rock faces much like this, but that I had climbed *this* one, that I had climbed it many times before, that I would climb it many times again, that I was doomed to spend the rest of eternity climbing this same rock again and again. When I reached the top of it I would find myself at the bottom, and have to begin again. And I felt hot bitter tears running down my face, realizing as I did that for me there was no way back and no way forward, but only this endless rock unrolling beneath me like a scroll that extends itself farther at one end even as it is rolled up at the other. I would live on this rock and I would die on it, and I would be born again, and still I would be climbing, and there would be no end to the climb.

Thus in despair and anguish and, I suppose, a kind of madness, I clambered up and up, with hot dry crosswinds raking me as I went. Then suddenly there was nothing more above me. I had fallen into such a mechanical rhythm of climbing that I could not at first understand where I was and what was happening; I groped for the next handhold, and found none, and brought my right foot a little higher on the rock and reached again, and again there was nothing. It was like falling into a dream within a dream. There was a roaring in my ears and my brain was spinning in my skull. I heard Kilarion's voice from very far away, and it seemed that he was laughing as he spoke, but the words were indistinct, like sounds heard under water.

I realized then that I must be at the top of the cliff, that there was no place further to go except up and over; and I pulled myself across the edge of the rock face. As I did I scraped the side of my neck against some sharp place and the string that held my little amulet broke, and the amulet fell away quickly, bouncing from rock to rock and vanishing below. I felt a quick pang at the loss of it after having brought it this far; but I was already in the midst of the final levering gesture that brought me to the flat place on top, and I had to think only of what was before me, not behind.

I scrambled up and over. Kilarion, just to my right, came up at the same moment and we brought the Irtiman in his rope sling over with us.

I took a couple of steps forward, shaky-legged, as one often is after such a climb, and it was an instant or two before my eyes cleared and I could focus on my new surroundings. Then what came into view stunned me and astounded me to the roof of my soul; for there were mountains on all sides, a tremendous host of them, a ring of peaks of every shape and size stretching off as far as I could see. Often before I had felt as if this thing that was Kosa Saag was one chain of mountains piled on another on another, world without end, rising infinitely into the sky, and that we must proceed eternally from level to level, coming always into some new realm when we had left the last behind; and once again that was how it seemed to me now, at least at first glance.

But then I saw that this time one mountain stood clearly above the others in the center of the ring, a great jagged king of a mountain. Its upper reaches were streaked with rivers of white snow that glittered brilliantly in the sunlight and its very tip was shrouded in dense clouds so that it could not be seen at all, and I began to tremble as I looked toward those dazzling heights; for I knew beyond doubt that this was the final peak, the mountain of mountains, the true and only Summit of Kosa Saag.

20

WHEN WE CAME UP over the rim of the cliff into this sublime and ultimate realm the one thing that we all wanted was only to rest awhile, every one of us. We could look up and see the abode of the gods almost within reach, yes, or so it seemed to us then; but there was not one of us who had the strength or the determination to venture onward immediately, not even Traiben, whose boundless curiosity seemed at last to be overmeasured by fatigue. We had spent ourselves freely, too freely, perhaps, in the crossing of the land of the Kvuz and the conquest of that bare rock face, and now we had to recollect our energies and renew our will before pushing onward toward whatever the next challenge was that might lie ahead.

On this innermost plateau that was the pedestal for the highest of the peaks of Kosa Saag we had entered into a vast enclosed place of forests and rivers and streams and valleys. It was like a secret world atop the Wall. The air was even thinner here, but we knew well by now how to adjust our bodies to cope with that, and for all its thinness it was sweet and cool and fresh; and there was thick blue grass everywhere underfoot, and the great cloud-tipped mountain rose above us in stupendous majesty and beauty. We found ourselves a pleasant site beside a swift stream and made our camp there, thinking to stay a day or two, or perhaps three, before pushing onward. But we stayed longer than that: how much longer, I could not say, for one day flowed serenely into the next and time slipped past without our realizing it. A great deal of time, I suspect.

This was an easy place, though, and we had not had many of those during our journey up the Wall. Here was a place where we could strip and bathe and cleanse ourselves, and drink cool water, and pluck succulent fruits from trees whose names we would never know. And so we did, for day after day after day. It was as if we were enchanted. Perhaps we were. No one spoke of moving onward: as I have said, not even Traiben. Indeed Traiben and I avoided each other's eyes much of the time, for neither of us had forgotten that as boys we had vowed to rise through Kingdom after Kingdom until we had attained the Summit, and if that was what we had sworn to do, why were we still here? Many a time I saw one of the others looking at me worriedly, as if fearing that at any moment I would pick up cudgels and flails and drive everyone back to the upward task with all my old zeal. But the inner fire that had carried me this far was banked for the moment. I was in as much need of rest as any of the others, and they had no reason to fear any renewal of discipline just yet from me. I had loosened my grasp on them; I let the idle days go by.

Only the Irtiman showed any eagerness to resume the climb. He came to me and said, "Poilar, I owe you my life," and I nodded uneasily at that, for he was pale and even thinner than before and it seemed to me that he had hardly any life left in him. Then he said, with a touch of anxiety in his tone, "Will we be staying in this valley much longer, do you think?"

I indicated the long shadow of the great mountain, falling far across the land. "We'll stay here until we're fresh again," I told him. "We're going to need all the strength we can muster for what lies ahead."

"No doubt we will. But as the time passes, you see—"

The voice out of the speaking-box trailed off. He stared at me sadly.

I knew what was troubling him. He had suffered greatly in his solitary wanderings and such little strength as he still had left was fading: he saw the end coming and wanted to die at the Summit among his friends. Our long delay here must have been maddening to him. Well, I understood his need; but we had needs of our own. The long unrelenting skyward march had drained us deeply. We were none of us young; we were in our third ten of years and even the strongest of us felt the burden of this climb. And the most daunting ascent of all still stood before us. We were not yet ready to attempt it.

The Irtiman was aware of that; and he knew also that he had no claim on us. So he put his impatience aside. For my part I promised him that I would bring him to his fellow Irtimen at the Summit, no matter what: and that was a promise which I was to keep, although in a strange way indeed.

We talked for a while afterwards. I asked him about his village, where it was situated in relation to the Wall and whether it had the same sort of Houses that ours did, Musicians and Advocates and Carpenters and all the rest, and if they acknowledged themselves to be subjects to the King. He was silent a long time when I had asked these things, and drew so deep into himself that I feared for him. Then he said, "I told you that I came from a very distant place."

"Yes."

"And so it is. I was born on a world beyond the sky."

I didn't know what to make of that. "A world beyond the sky," I said in wonder, dully repeating his words like a simpleton because I had so much difficulty comprehending them. "Then you *are* a god?"

"Not at all. Mortal, Poilar, very much so."

"Yet you say you come from one of the worlds of Heaven?"

"A world called Earth, yes."

I thought of my star-dream of long ago, when I had danced at the Summit and looked upward toward those worlds from the Summit, and saw the cold fire of them, and felt the potent god-life of them pouring down upon me.

"Those who live in Heaven are gods," I said. "Their homes are the stars, and the stars are fire. Who can live in fire except a god?"

He smiled patiently and said, in that sad, sad, weary voice that came slowly out of his little speaking-box, "Yes, the stars are fire, Poilar. But many of them have worlds much like this world close by them, the way your world is close by its star Ekmelios. And those worlds are solid and cool like your world, with oceans and mountains and plains, and people can live upon them. Or upon some of them, anyhow."

"Ekmelios is a sun, not a star. It's much bigger than any star, and brighter, and hotter. And there's Marilemma, also: we have two suns, you know."

"And both are stars. Suns *are* stars. Ekmelios is close at hand, and Marilemma is a little further away; and still further, far out in the heavens, are other stars, millions of them, more than you could ever count. Each one is a sun, bright and hot. They seem to you to be little points of light only because they're so far away. But if you were closer to one of them you'd realize that it's a ball of fire very much like Ekmelios and Marilemma. And most of them have worlds moving around them the way your world moves around Ekmelios and Marilemma."

All this was difficult for me to follow, but he let it sink in for a moment or two, and as I revolved it in my mind it began to make a kind of sense to me. Still, I wished that Traiben were beside me now to hear this, for I knew he would understand it much more completely.

The Irtiman said, "My world has a yellow sun. I could try to show it to you in the night sky, but it's not very big and so it's very hard to find. It's so far away that the light that comes from my world's sun takes an entire lifetime, and even more, to reach your world."

"Then you must be a god!" I cried, feeling proud of myself for so quickly seeing the flaw in the logic. "For if it takes more than a lifetime to get from your world to mine, then how could any mortal hope to live long enough to make the journey?"

"He couldn't," said the Irtiman. "Not me, not you, not any of us. But we have a special way of traveling, which takes us from *here* to *here* without having to pass through every point between. And so the trip from Earth to here requires only a year or two instead of a lifetime and a half. But for that I could never have hoped to come here."

I was lost. What did he mean, a special way of traveling? Magic of some sort, I supposed. A spell that brought them flashing across the sky in a twinkling. Well, then, what else could they be but gods? No one other than a god could work such a miraculous magic. But if they were gods the question arose again: How was it possible for a god to become weary unto death, as this Irtiman surely was? And I realized that I did not understand at all.

He told me more, much more, things which I understood even less.

For he said, as we sat together on a moist bank of blue grass beside a cool swift-flowing stream under the mighty fortress that was the last and highest pinnacle of Kosa Saag, that he and his three friends were not the first Irtimen to have traveled from his world to ours, that others had come long ago, many of them, traveling in a great ship—had come here, in fact, to found a village of their own on our world; and they had settled on the high slopes of Kosa Saag, because the air of the lowlands was too hot and dense for their lungs and it would choke them to breathe it.

He said they were still up there at the Summit, those

long-ago voyagers who came from the world called Earth; or rather their descendants were, to be more accurate. They had a village there, a settlement of some sort. It puzzled me to hear this, because it was hard for me to see why the gods would tolerate having travelers from another world living amongst them at the Summit, that holiest of places—and why did we ourselves know nothing about the continued presence of these strangers atop the Wall? Nothing I had ever heard had hinted at such a thing.

So I could comprehend little or none of this. I said, "And the gods, then? The Creator, the Shaper, the Avenger? Do they still dwell at the Summit too? And did you see them there?"

The Irtiman was silent a long while. His eyes closed, and his breathing became very slow, and then I could hardly detect it at all, so that once more I began to wonder whether he might have died. But at last he said, "I was there only a little while, you understand."

"You didn't see them, then?"

"No. I didn't see them. Not the Creator, not the Shaper. Not the Avenger."

"But they must be there!"

"Perhaps that's so," he said, in a very remote voice.

"Perhaps?" His tone of doubt made me so angry that I could easily have struck him. But of course I did not. This stranger was weak from exhaustion, he was gravely ill, he had already entered into the sickness unto death. His mind might be deranged by fever. He was speaking madness. It would be a sin to lift my hand against anyone in his condition.

So I put aside my wrath. "But surely the gods are to be found at the Summit!"

He shrugged. "For your sake I hope so, Poilar. All I can say is that I saw no gods while I was there. If there are gods at all, it may be that they live in a place beyond the range of our vision."

"If there are gods?" I cried. "If?"

Once more I saw a red haze before my eyes. I had to fight back my anger all over again. It was a killing anger; but this Irtiman was doomed already. I could not allow myself to do him harm, no matter what.

He saw me struggling with myself and said to me mildly, "I meant no sacrilege. I can only tell you that so far as the gods of Heaven are concerned, I have no more knowledge of their whereabouts than you do. On my world as on yours, men have searched for them since the beginning of time, and some, I think, have found them, but most have not." The voice from the machine came to me now as if across an immense distance. "I wish you well, Poilar. I hope you find what you are seeking." And then he said that he was too tired to speak of these things with me any longer. I could see that that was so. Simply to draw breath was becoming a great chore for him. His lips were quivering with fatigue and his eyes had a deathly glassy sheen.

I went to Traiben afterward and told him everything that the Irtiman had said, as well as I could, praying that I wasn't garbling any of it. Traiben listened in silence, nodding to himself and now and then sketching a little diagram in the soft earth. From time to time he would ask me to repeat something. But he didn't sound particularly confused or troubled or upset. That strange mind of his, that was so much like a sponge, seemed to be taking it all in easily and happily. "Very interesting," was all he said, when I was done. "Very, very, very interesting."

"But what does it mean?" I asked him.

"It means what it means," he said, and grinned a mischievous Traiben-grin at me.

"That a settlement of Irtimen lives among our gods?"

"That the gods may *be* Irtimen, for all we know," said Traiben.

I shook my head at that in bewilderment and amazement.

"How can you say such a thing, Traiben? Even to admit the possibility of it is blasphemy!"

"He's been to the Summit. We haven't. He saw no gods, only Irtimen."

"But that doesn't mean—"

"We need to go up there and see for ourselves, don't we?" he said. "Don't we, Poilar?"

THE THINGS THE IRTIMAN had said had reawakened my desire to attain the Summit, so that I might show him the gods he had failed to find: that and Traiben's renewed eagerness to finish the climb, for he was aflame now with all his old curiosity. So I gave the order to break camp and resume the climb within the hour.

Malti the Healer came to me as we were filling our water-jars and said, "Poilar, your Irtiman is very weak."

"I know that," I told her.

"We can't possibly bring him with us. He's not strong enough to walk. He has difficulty taking food. It's obvious that he can't last much longer."

"What are you saying, Malti? Is he going to die today?"

"Not today, no. But soon. A few days, a week at most, perhaps. There's no way we can heal him. He's too feeble; and in any case we don't understand the way his body is put together. If you really want to set out up the mountain this afternoon, Poilar, we should leave some food with him and go on without him. Or else stay here another few days to see him out, and give him a decent burial before we move on."

"No," I said. "We've stayed here too long already. We leave today. And I've promised him that I'll take him up to the Summit and deliver him to his Irtimen friends. If we have to carry him all the way, we will."

She shrugged and went away. A little later I visited him. He was in a bad way, looking even worse than he had before, much worse. His skin was like paper now and fine beads of sweat were standing out on his brow. He seemed to be trembling from head to toe. His eyes would not focus and he kept looking past me, as though I were standing behind myself. But he told me how glad he was that we were going onward at last, and thanked me again very warmly for all I had done for him. He hoped that he would last long enough, he said, to be reunited with his companions at the Summit. That was the only thing he wanted now, to see them again before he died.

We adapted the sling with which we had hauled him up the cliff face into a hammock-like litter that two strong people could carry between them. Thissa cast a spell of sky-magic that might let him hold his spirit in his body a little longer, and Jekka and Malti, after a long conference, offered him a potion of certain herbs they had gathered nearby, which they said could perhaps do some good and in any event were unlikely to make matters any worse for him. It must have been bitter stuff, for he made ghastly grimaces as he drank it down; but he said he felt better afterward, and possibly that was so.

A path of gentle slope that seemed as if it would lead us onto the flank of the mountain lay before us; and once more we took up our climb. It reminded us of the very beginning of our Pilgrimage, for this was like leaving the village all over again; quickly the pleasant wooded valley where we had camped in ease for these days or weeks, and which had begun to seem almost as familiar as home to us, dropped away behind us, and we began to wind up and up a mountain trail into a cool, rocky country of which we knew nothing at all. And above us once again rose a colossal mass of stone that came close to filling the sky, just as in the first days of our climb. Back then, though, in our innocence, we had had no way of knowing that what we called the Wall was only the merest foothill of Kosa Saag; and now we understood that this tremendous overhanging peak on whose lowest outcroppings we trod was in truth the last of our challenges and the goal of all our striving.

What lay ahead for us on the flanks of this mountain, we soon would discover, was a richly populated land. For in the new realm which we were entering we were to find that one Kingdom tumbled upon the next in enormous profusion; and I can scarcely tell you of them all, so many and various were they. On this innermost and loftiest peak, all those whose Pilgrimages had carried them this far had stayed and settled and bred and multiplied. We soon were seeing their Kingdoms on every side, here just below the abode of those whom we took to be our gods. Each of the many Kingdoms of the Wall, it seemed to me, embodies some lesson for the Pilgrims who pass through them: certainly that was true of the Kingdoms of the Kavnalla, the Sembitol, and the Kvuz. But in the higher reaches of the Wall the Kingdoms are so numerous that one could spend ten lifetimes seeking to learn such lessons as they offer, and still not have encompassed a fraction of the whole.

Many a strange fate waited for us in those Kingdoms before those few of us who survived would stumble up the last few paces to the Summit.

But our Irtiman was not one of those who did.

The end arrived for him just as we were crossing into one of the populated territories of the mountain; for I was ahead of the column of marchers, studying the smoke of settlements not far ahead of us on the path, when Kath the Advocate jogged up alongside me and said, "You had better come."

He was lying against Galli's bosom, shivering convulsively. Jekka and Malti crouched beside him, and Thissa was murmuring spells not far away, with Traiben watching dourly from a distance. But it was obvious that neither Galli's comforting presence nor the potions of the Healers nor Thissa's witchcraft would be of any use now. Life was leaving the Irtiman so swiftly that you could almost see his soul issuing forth above him like rising steam. And as I went to his side his eyes rolled up in his head and he made a little whimpering sound.

I bent forward over him.

"Irtiman? Irtiman, can you hear me?"

I wanted to ask him this final time, as he stood on the threshold of eternity, whether he had been telling me the truth about the dwellers on the Summit when he had said that he had seen only Irtimen there and had not found the gods. But there was no possibility of asking him any such thing now. The little box through which he spoke to us had rolled from his hand and lay uselessly in the grass. He could not have understood me, nor I him, even if he had still been conscious.

"Irtiman!"

He jerked back in one last quiver and was still, with his arm upraised and his fingers spread out toward the sky, toward the Summit, where his companions were. I looked at that outspread hand, those upthrust fingers. There were five of them, as I had thought: a thumb at one side but none at the other, nor any sign that there ever had been one there, and four others that were arranged in the usual way of fingers. I took that strange alien hand in mine and held it a moment, and then I lowered it to his breast and folded the other one across it, and closed his eyes.

Traiben said to me, as I turned away, "I tried to talk to him a little while ago about the gods and the Irtimen, to find out more of what he had seen and what he knew. I saw that it was our only chance. But he was already far gone, and unable to speak."

I had to smile at that. Traiben was ever my other and cleverer self, thinking of the same things I did, but always sooner. This time, though, even Traiben had been too slow.

Kilarion came up to me and said, "I'll dig a grave for him. The ground here shouldn't be too hard. And there are plenty of rocks for a cairn."

"No," I told him. "No grave, no cairn." An idea had come to me in that moment: a mad one, perhaps, engendered by the thin air of that lofty place. I looked around. "Where's Talbol? Get me the Leathermaker. And Narril the Butcher. And Grycindil too—a Weaver, yes."

They came to me and I told them what I wanted done. They stared at me as if I had taken leave of my senses, and maybe I had; but I said that I had promised to deliver the

Irtiman to his friends who dwelled above, and I would keep that pledge regardless. So they drew the Irtiman's body aside and went to work on it. Narril emptied it of its organs—I saw Traiben peering at them in wonder—and Talbol did whatever it is that Leathermakers do to cure a skin, using such herbs as he could find by the roadside, and finally Grycindil filled the empty body with aromatic preserving herbs that Talbol found for her, and strips of cloth and such light filling things, and sewed up the incisions that Narril had made. The whole thing took three or four days, during which time we camped where we were, keeping out of sight of the habitants of the Kingdom just above us. When it was done, the Irtiman lay as though sleeping in the hammock we had made for him; but he weighed practically nothing when we lifted him, and we carried him along without difficulty. Since he had been an Irtiman and it was plain even to the slowest among us that an Irtiman was a kind of being entirely different from ourselves, I heard no objections to what I had done; for who could say what the burial customs of Irtimen might be? Certainly we were under no obligation to bury one in the same way as we would one of our own, with a cairn and all. So we took him along with us on our march toward the Summit, and in time we grew quite accustomed to having him still with us, even though he was dead.

THE ROAD—AND A road was what it was, as distinct and well maintained as the one on which we had begun our journey up from Jespodar village—spiraled up and up around the outside of the mountain, and every few days there was a different Kingdom. The people of some of these Kingdoms came out to stare at us, and others took scarcely any notice of us as we went by; but in no instance were we interfered with. In these high realms of Kosa Saag Pilgrims evidently were allowed to go onward as they pleased.

The inhabitants of the high Kingdoms had once been Pilgrims themselves, of course; or at least their ancestors had. But you would not know it from the look of them. All these multitudes of people who had created a new world for themselves far above the world that was our world were failed climbers, who had given up the holy quest, just as the creatures writhing in the Kavnalla's cave had been, or the insect-beings of the Sembitol—all of them members of the legion of the Transformed, as varied and strange in form as the beings that populate our dreams.

But there was a difference up here. The folk of the high Kingdoms had pushed the limits of our ability to change our shapes beyond anything we had ever imagined, and they had done it willingly and knowingly. These were no victims of change-fire, I think. They were of another kind from the Melted Ones, those pitiful things that had been deformed and made hideous by the heat of an irresistible force outside themselves, nor were they like the hapless slithering servants of the Kavnalla, or the insect-like creatures who stalked the narrow trails of the Sembitol, or the hateful ground-crawling people of the Kvuz, all of whom had lost themselves to the potent rays that come from the mountain's core. No, it seemed to me that these folk must have altered themselves from within, apparently of their own free choice, here in these high Kingdoms. And in this shimmering mountain air they had drawn on inner resources to unleash the whole range of possibilities that the shapechanging power affords, and then had extended that range.

So we saw great airy beings twice as tall as the tallest of us, who wrapped themselves in wings of vast spread but never attempted to use them. We saw others that walked in sheets of white flame, and some that moved in globes of darkness, and those that seemed like flowing cascades of water. We saw men who looked like trees and women who looked like swords. We saw frail filmy things that drifted like wisps on the wind. We saw giant boulders with eyes, and mouths that smiled knowingly as we went by. And I remembered now the Secret Book of Maylat Gakkerel,

which we had had to read when we were youngsters training for our Pilgrimage, and which I had thought was all
fable and fairy-tale; but no, that was wrong, I saw now.
Maylat Gakkerel, whoever he might have been, had seen
these Kingdoms and had returned from them with enough
of his sanity intact to set down an account of them, and
however fevered and impenetrable and unreal that difficult
book may have seemed to us, it was no work of fancy but a
sober chronicle of the upper reaches of Kosa Saag.

It was here that I began to lose the members of my
Forty.

There was no way I could prevent it. Those who had
resisted the horrors below did not have the strength to turn
their backs on the beauties and strangenesses up here. They
slipped away as though they were fading into the mist. Even
if I had chained us all together wrist to wrist, they would
have found some way to go; for the temptation of these
Kingdoms was immense.

Tull the Clown was the first to depart. That was no real
surprise, for she had defected once already before; and
although she had come back that time she still bore the
taint of the Sembitol about her, and a permanent melan-
choly where once she had been all life and buoyancy. She
went in the night, soon after the Irtiman's death, and Thissa
said later that she could feel her dancing on the wind. Poor
Tull, I certainly prayed that she was.

But then Seppil the Carpenter disappeared, and Ijo the
Scholar, and our other Scholar too, little Bilair. They went
on different days and in different Kingdoms. I caused
searches to be made for each of them, though only in a
perfunctory way, for I suppose I was beginning to undergo
a transformation of sorts myself, and I no longer was as
concerned to lose my companions as I once had been. Let
them go, something within me whispered. Let them find
their own destinies up here, if the Summit is not what they
truly seek. Most who attempt the quest are fated to fail it,
and so be it. So be it.

Thrance sidled up to me and grinned his diabolical grin, and said, "So that's what it's like, when you reach the top of the Wall? You simply float away and join the Kingdoms? If that's the case, why did we bother to climb so high? We could have saved ourself the effort and stayed down below, and let ourselves be transformed by the Kavnalla."

"I wish you had," I told him.

"Ah, so unkind, Poilar, so very unkind! What harm have I ever done you? Didn't I guide you through some difficult places?"

I made a shooing gesture at him, as though he were a stinging palibozo hovering about my head.

"Go, Thrance. Turn yourself into air, or water, or a pillar of fire. Let me be."

He grinned again, twice as fierce as before. "Ah, no, no, no, Poilar! I'll stay by your side to the top! We are allies in this, you and I. We are colleagues of the trail." Then he laughed and said, "But it'll be only the two of us by the time we reach the Summit. The others will all long be gone."

"Let me be, Thrance," I told him a second time. "Or by all the gods I'll hurl you down the mountainside."

"See if it isn't so," he said. "You'll lose them all as we go up."

And that night Ais the Musician went from us, and Dorn the Clown; and two days afterward, in a Kingdom whose ruler lived in a glistening limestone mansion cut deep into the mountain, a place of great colonnades and porticos and torch-lit chambers and passages and halls and an immense throne-room fit for a god, we lost Jekka the Healer, which was a grievous loss indeed. When I counted up in the morning, there were only twenty-seven of us left, out of our Forty, and Thrance the twenty-eighth. This time I made no attempt at sending out searchers. It seemed a hopeless thing to do. I wondered whether Thrance might not have been right, that all the others would go, leaving only him and me at the end. Indeed I wondered whether I myself would be among the Transformed before this was over. For my resolve had weakened more than once along the way up; and if it weakened again here, it would be the end of my quest. I knew I must fight that; but would I be able to win? And so in perplexity I led the remainder of my people onward, along an ever narrowing trail, toward the cloud-shrouded realm above.

21

THOUGH WE WERE DWINDLING swiftly now, yet the core of my Forty still remained to me—the ones I loved best, Traiben and Galli and Thissa and Jaif and of course Hendy. Kilarion stayed with us, and Kath, and Naxa; the Healers Malti and Kreod did not leave, nor Grycindil, nor Marsiel.

We went higher. The air grew colder and colder, and it was so thin we had to make our chests expand like balloons to draw any sustenance from it. When we glanced back we found ourselves looking down at the tips of the surrounding peaks, far below us. It was like making our way up the side of a needle that pierced the sky. The roof of cloud that hid the Summit from our sight seemed almost to be pressing against my shoulders now, though in fact it was still far ahead.

Scardil left us, and Pren, and Ghibbilau. I regretted those losses but I did nothing to reclaim them. Then Ijo the Scholar came back, looking somewhat changed from what he had been; but he would not say where he had been or what had befallen him. On the day of his return we lost

Chaliza and Thuiman, and in a Kingdom where gusts of pale flame spurted from the ground we lost two more: Noomai the Metalworker and then Jaif the Singer, whom I had not expected to leave. That was hard, losing Jaif. We had never been close friends but we had been good allies. In the days just afterward Hendy said that she felt his presence still with us, hovering in the air: she could hear his song, she said. Perhaps so. But I could not.

Then one night the sky throbbed with bands of pink light from dusk to dawn, as happens sometimes rarely when Marilemma rises at twilight and remains overhead all during the hours of darkness. That is usually an omen. And the next day we went on into a place where I found myself confronted with a great and wonderful strangeness, which went beyond anything I had experienced thus far in my entire ascent.

This was a small Kingdom set into a stony ridge that was like a bowl with a high sharp rim, on an outlying breast of the mountain. Gray wisps of old snow surrounded its rock-girt border, for at these heights we were in cold territory indeed, with hard winds and frequent gales of sleet. I suppose we could have gone past this Kingdom without entering it, since it lay a little distance off the main road; but we were weary from the day's bleak oppressive march through this chilly country, and now I saw dark storm-clouds gathering. It seemed a good idea to seek shelter for the night, though it was still only a little past midday.

Kath and Kilarion were the first two to go over the rim, and I heard whistles of surprise from them. When I came up over it myself I saw why. We were looking down into a lush peaceful garden where the air was soft and warm and heavy, as though we had been returned in a moment's twinkling to our village at the base of the Wall. We heard the singing of birds and we smelled the fragrance of a thousand kinds of flowers, and in the distance rose a giant grove of thick-trunked gollacundra trees heavy with purple fruit amidst their brilliant sheaves of dangling golden foliage. This, in the cold and snowy upper reaches of Kosa Saag! And moving about in it were graceful and elegant people with strands of gold about their breasts and garments of woven scarlet at their loins, who seemed without exception to be in the finest flush of youth and beauty. Truly it was as if we had come stumbling into the home of the gods.

I stood dazed and awed atop the rocky ridge, with ice and chill behind me and this dazzling paradise glowing before me. Thissa said softly to me, "Careful, Poilar. Everything you see here is illusion and magic." And Hendy, at my other side, nodded and added her own words of caution.

"Yes," I said. "Yes, I will take care."

But Kath and Kilarion were already moving down the inner slope of the bordering rim into this Kingdom of ease and plenitude, and Marsiel also, and Malti, and Grycindil, and Thrance. They walked like those who walk in sleep. So the decision was taken from my hands, and I followed them on down, passing from a realm of snow to one of flowers and birdsong. The people of this Kingdom turned and looked up at us gravely as we approached, but showed neither alarm nor displeasure, as though it was the most usual thing in the world for some band of ragged frostbitten wanderers to come straggling down into their land.

"Come," they said to us. "You must go before our King."

They were all perfect, every one: sleek and beautiful and glistening with strength and vitality, and no one, seemingly, more than eighteen or twenty years old. There was no flaw to be seen on them, no sign of blemish or defect or disfigurement. They seemed all to have come from a single mold, for only their faces differentiated them one from another, and otherwise they all had the same long-limbed slender-bodied perfection of form. I had never seen such people as these; and as I looked at them I felt bitter shame for my own lack of perfection, the angry chilblains on my skin and the dust and dirt of the journey in my hair and on my clothing and the scars of the long climb everywhere on my body, and above all my leg, my leg, my twisted loathsome crippled leg, for which I had never felt a moment's embarrassment before but which now seemed to me a blazing mark of dishonor and sin.

They conveyed us to their King, whose royal seat was a crystal dome at the very center of this Kingdom. He stood on its portico, arms folded, awaiting us calmly: as flawless as any of his subjects, and as young, a boy-king, a magnificent youthful prince, serene and potent, wonderfully arrayed in gold and scarlet, with a high tiara of bright metal set with glittering gems.

As we drew near him Hendy suddenly gasped, and she dug her fingers deep into the flesh of my arm as though in fear.

"What is it?" I said.

"His face, Poilar."

I looked. There seemed something familiar about it. But what?

"He could be your brother!" Hendy cried.

Was it so? I looked again in growing confusion. Yes, yes, there was something about the shape of his nose, the set of his eyes, the way he drew his lips back in a smile of welcome. A certain resemblance, yes, an odd superficial similarity of expression and even of appearance—

A coincidence, only. That was what I told myself.

"I have no brother," I said to her. "I've never had one."

Thissa, behind me, was whispering Witch-words.

The young King of this magical land regarded us placidly, benevolently. "Welcome, Pilgrims. Who is your leader?"

"I am," I said. My voice was thick and husky. I came limping forward, inordinately conscious of my crooked leg in this place of perfection. "We are from Jespodar village, and my name is Poilar, son of Gabrian, son of Drok, of Wallclan of the House of the Wall."

"Ah," he said, and gave me one of the strangest smiles I

have ever seen. "Then you are surely welcome here." He took a step or two toward me, holding out his hand for me to take it. "I am Drok of Jespodar," he said. "Of Wallclan of the House of the Wall."

OF COURSE I REFUSED to believe it at first. It was too much to accept, that I should meet my father's father here beneath the shadow of the Summit of Kosa Saag in this transformed guise. Thissa had said it rightly: all was illusion and magic here, and this must surely be some deception, the King of this place slyly borrowing my own features so that he could pretend that he and I were kin, as a kind of mocking game.

But he took us within his royal home, where the floors were soft with thick rugs and the crystal walls were hung with crimson draperies and the air was heavy with sweet perfume, and his people bathed us and fed us and gave us sharp new wine to drink. If all of that was illusion and magic, well, it was skillful magic and pleasing illusion, and afterward we felt rested and comforted, illusion or not. Indeed we had not known such comfort since the day we left our village. It was almost enough to make one weep.

Then the King came to me and sat with me and spoke with me of Jespodar, while I stared intently at his face, clearly seeing mine now in his. He mentioned many names, few of which I knew; but when he uttered those of Thispar and Gamilalar I told him that they were still alive, that the gods had granted them double life, and he seemed genuinely astonished and delighted at that, for he said that he had known them when he was young. That was an odd phrase for him to use—*when he was young*—for he seemed much younger than me at this moment, a youth, a stripling. But I sensed the great age of him all the same, behind that unlined face. I told him that in our company was the son of the son of the son of Thispar Double-Lifer, Traiben by name; and he nodded and a far-away look came into his eyes, as if he was thinking of the passage of so many years.

He spoke then of our clan and family, and he knew the names. He asked of his brother Ragin, and I said he was dead, but that Ragin's son Meribail was the head of our House. He seemed pleased at that. "Meribail, yes. I remember him. A good boy, Meribail. I saw the promise in him even then." He asked me of his sister, next, and of his sister's children, and of his own two daughters and their children, and again he knew all the names, so that I became more and more certain I was in the presence of my father's father. There was always the possibility, I realized, that this was all some enchantment and he a demon, and that he was drawing these names from my own mind and passing them back to me by way of laying claim falsely to kinship with me. But once you begin believing such things, there's no end to what you are free to doubt: it was easier for me to think that this was indeed my father's father, alive on Kosa Saag after so many years, wearing this youthful body by virtue of the transformations he had undergone.

He had said nothing about my father Gabrian in all this time. So finally I introduced his name myself, and said, "I never knew him, not really, for he went to the Wall when I was just a small child." He offered no response to that, which left me a moment for thinking, and I added, "But you wouldn't have known him well either, I suppose; for you yourself began your Pilgrimage when *he* was still a little boy, is that not so?"

Still he was silent, and his eerily youthful face became furrowed, as if the thought of the three generations of interrupted families, of fathers who had gone to the Wall and left young sons behind, must sadden him immeasurably. But that was not it. For after a little while he said, in a somber voice he had not used before, "Gabrian, yes. A handsome child, he was. And he became a handsome man. We encountered each other once, here on the Wall."

"What?" And I leaned forward, tensely, like a hungry animal about to pounce. My heart was leaping in my breast. "You and my father met each other on Kosa Saag?"

He nodded. He seemed lost in dark reverie.

"Where?" I asked. "When? Is he still alive? By all the gods, *is my father in this very Kingdom right now?*"

"Not here, no, not now." He closed his eyes and sat rocking gently, but I felt that he was still seeing me all the same through his closed lids. As though speaking to me through a dense mist he said, "It was a long time ago, when I had been here only a few years, perhaps five or six. And his Forty arrived, looking much as you and yours, all tattered and shabby and worn, for they had been a long while on the Wall. Of course there weren't forty of them any longer, but only seven. Seven, exactly, and no more. The others had died along the way, or gone off to live among the Transformed Ones, as I suppose some of your people have done as well. There's never been a Forty to make it to these heights intact, you know, or even anything close to intact, although I've heard it said that some Pilgrimages have nearly—"

"My father," I said. "I want to hear about my father." It was hard for me to be patient with him. I was sure beyond any doubt now that there must be an old man behind this youthful facade, from the wandering way in which he was telling the tale.

"Your father, yes. I'm coming to him. He and his Forty of seven drifted in, just as you did, and we put them up and let them have baths and something to eat, for they were in a terrible way. I knew right away who he was: I saw his face and I said to myself, in much amazement, This is my own son who has come to me here, this is Gabrian, this really is Gabrian. I hadn't seen him since he was three years old, of course, but there are certain things you know no matter what, and with him I knew. Just as I knew with you. But Gabrian didn't tell me his name at first, as you did. Nor did he seem to recognize a family resemblance in us. So I kept my name from him as well. There we were, father and son, and he not knowing. I asked him things about the village, and he told me that, and then he spoke of his Pilgrimage, and the places he had been and what had happened to him along the way—a hard Pilgrimage, far worse than mine, traveling along false trails, years of delay on the way up, endless suffering, deaths, some murders, even—terrible, terrible, terrible. But at last the threshold of the Summit had come into view. He had endured everything anyone could imagine and now, he told me, now he was going to see the gods at last. There was a look of utter determination on his face. I could see it clearly: nothing would stop him. Nothing."

My eyes widened. "And did he get to the Summit, then?"

"I don't know. I think he did. But who can say?"

"He must have reached it. If he swore that nothing would stop him, and the Summit is very close to here—"

"Not as close as all that. It's close, at least, in comparison with what lies behind us on Kosa Saag. But not very close. And there are great difficulties along the way. I do think he got to it, though. And then, on the way back—"

He halted, and frowned, and stared off beyond me as though I were not there.

"Tell me," I said.

"Yes. Yes, I will, since you want to know. Your father and his six companions left here without his ever having learned who I was, and set out for the Summit. He went on to the next Kingdom, and the next, and the next: this I know, for I asked after him later, and they said he had been there, passing through. Then he went up higher and vanished into the land of fogs, and no one ever saw him again or any of those who went with him. He was bound for the Summit, and it is my belief that he reached it and saw what there was to see there, and then began to make his descent."

Again there was a painful silence, which went on and on, like a scream.

"And what happened then?" I prompted finally.

My father's father looked at me as if seeing me for the first time, and moistened his lips and said quietly, "It was during the course of his descent, I think, that he visited the Well of Life and underwent a transformation there, and perished there in the process of being changed."

I caught my breath. "He's dead?"

"Oh, yes. Yes."

"You know this to be so?"

"I saw his body at the rim of the Well. I buried it with my own hands."

For a moment I was unable to speak. The gift that had been offered me had been snatched away almost in the moment of giving. After a time I said, "What is this Well of Life, which is so badly named, since it seems rather to be a Well of Death?"

"It is the place where we are made young again," my father's father said. "We go to it every five years, or more often if we wish, and we enter it and come forth as you see us. But we enter and leave very quickly. To remain in it more than an instant or two is deadly. Do you understand?"

"And my father? He stayed in it too long?"

"We can only guess what he did, or why. Or whether it happened on the way up to the Summit, or on the way down. But I think I know. The Well lies in the last zone before the very top—in a place of perpetual storm, of wind and rain and fog. Whoever would go to the Summit must pass that way. What I think is that he passed the Well by and went quickly onward, to the top, and looked upon the gods in the place where they dwell; and then he came down again, and for the second time he and his people arrived at the vicinity of the Well—and this time—this time—"

AS HE SPOKE I could see it all in the eye of my mind, and I was sure that it was almost as it must have happened: the fog and mist, the whirling crescents of wind-blown snow, the black jagged peaks, the narrow path so difficult to follow, the dark abyss just beyond the edge. The seven weary, gaunt marchers struggling down from the Summit, exalted by what they had beheld there, but now at the last limits of their endurance. And the Well of Life lying shrouded in the darkness before them, a secret menace, a foaming pit of transformation. One by one they stumble unknowingly into it, blinded by the snow, which the wind hurls in their faces with diabolical force. A moment's immersion is enough to bring immense change; beyond that point the Well offers death, not life. Shouts in the mist: sounds of terror: figures thrashing in the darkness, sliding, falling, arising and falling again. My father groping for his companions' hands, finding them, losing them, grasping one now, seeking desperately to pull someone from the Well and being pulled in himself—or perhaps it was my father who had blundered in first, and the others had tried to rescue him and been lost with him—

So I imagined it, from what my father's father said and what I wanted to have heard. But the truth of what had taken place was somewhat different.

"Some days later," my father's father went on, "two people of my Kingdom who lately had been to the Well came to me, and said they had seen something strange and terrible along its margin. I knew at once what it must be, and set out right away. We found the seven heaps of discarded clothing first, and the packs they had been carrying, half covered by the snow. And then there they were, on the rim of the Well, hand in hand: fleshless now, and tiny, the pliant and delicate bones of seven newborn infants, linked in a dreadful chain in the hot mud. We scooped them out with long poles and buried them nearby. You'll see the seven tiny cairns as you go past. *If* you go past."

"If?" I said. "You told me it was the only way to the Summit."

"Forget the Summit. Stay here."

His words startled me. "I am pledged to it by oath," I said with a touch of heat in my tone.

"So were we all," he said. "Your father was. So was I. He kept that oath, I think. It cost him his life. I also went to the Summit. It brought me no benefit. Forget the Summit, child."

"You've seen it, you say?"

"Yes. And returned. And will never go there again. It is a loathsome place. Forget the Summit."

He closed in upon himself as though he did not want to speak of these things any more. Confusion swept over me in hot waves. The grim tale of the manner of my father's dying oppressed me and numbed me. And now this coyness on my father's father's part about the Summit itself. The Irtiman too had been elusive and vague when we spoke of the Summit. Why? Why? What were they hiding from me? I felt my anger beginning to rise, and I reached toward him as though to pull the answers from him with my hands. "Loathsome? What are you saying? Why loathsome? Tell me what the Summit is like. Tell me!"

"Never," he said. The calmly spoken word fell around me like an iron band.

I protested again, to no effect.

With a kind of sublime patience that I found maddening he raised his hand to silence me, and said, as calmly as before, "I'll offer you this, and no more: Whatever it is you hope to find, you won't find it there. There's nothing there but horror. Forget the Summit, child. Stay here with me."

I was shaking with fury. "How can I do that? You know that I've sworn—"

"Stay," he said, unmoved. "And live forever."

I stared at him, speechless, trembling. And he told me once more how he and all his people went periodically to the Well of Life, and immersed themselves in it for a fraction of a moment, and became smooth and young again as the Well turned back time for them. I could do that also, he said. And be eternally young, here in this enchanted Kingdom on the highest slopes of the Wall, where the air was ever sweet and mild and the snows were held at bay by magic. Why climb any higher? Why seek mysteries not worth finding? Stay, he said. Stay. Stay.

It was as if he had turned a key in my mind. To my astonishment my rage fell away from me and I found myself yielding to his will.

He spoke, and all my bold resolve melted in a moment. He spoke, and everything toward which I had worked for so long seemed to be without meaning. Stay, he said. Stay and live forever. Why not? Yes, I thought, amazed. *Why not?* It seemed so simple. Give up this bitter Pilgrimage, which had taken the life of your father and so many others; step away from the upward path and let your weary body rest. Stay here. Stay. *Yes,* I thought. *Why not?* Suddenly I was open to the sort of temptation that seems to be a quality of these uppermost lands of the Wall. Stay, he said. Stay. Stay. Stay. And as he said it, it was like a spell being cast on me, or so I thought in that moment: for to my surprise and bewilderment I felt everything changing within me, felt the rigidities of my spirit loosening their hold in this easy place, heard myself thinking, *Yes, Poilar, why not? Stay. Stay.*

STAY? HOW COULD I stay? We were bound by oath.

But my oath had not prevented me from idling for weeks or perhaps months in the valley of the blue grass at the base of this final peak, though there had been no reason to stay so long. It is the nature of those heights, I suppose, to weaken the resolve even of the strongest; for the air is thin and gives only poor nourishment, and where we may be vulnerable, that vulnerability will be made manifest. And now we were higher still and once again I began to drift away, for a time, from my own inner nature, from the ceaseless striving toward the goal to which Traiben and I had dedicated ourselves when we were twelve years old.

That night there were hot baths for us, and sherbet, and rich wines and fine meats. We slept under soft robes on comfortable piles of furs. And I thought: I could have this forever. Forever, Poilar, *forever.*

It was like a sickness that had come over my mind

between one moment and the next. Why go to the Summit? There was only great hardship to endure throughout the remainder of the way, and grief at journey's end. The Summit? What use was the Summit? It is a loathsome place, my father's father had said. You will find only horror there. He had seen it; he knew. Again and again I felt the dark tale of my father's death coursing through me like a river, leaving me shaken and weakened. What struck me with great force was not so much the image of those tiny bones, though that was terrible enough, but rather the question of what it was that had driven those seven Pilgrims to choose so frightful a death. I could not bring myself to face that question squarely, for it opened abysses in my mind. Therefore I told myself that all this questing was folly. Give it over, I told myself. You've struggled long enough, toward something not worth attaining. Settle here in your father's father's realm, and surrender to ease. Or move on a little way upward, maybe, and found a Kingdom of your own, and live there happily forever, and let the gods go about their business undisturbed. I do confess it: those were my thoughts. There is no one so strong that he does not falter again and again on the path that leads to the Summit of the Wall.

And so we stayed in the Kingdom of my father's father for a day or two, three, four, another day beyond that. From time to time I would step outside and see the path rising above me, and the snowy crags, and the roof of cloud that marked the Summit off from the lands just below it, and I knew that we should be on our way. There was our goal; and it was almost within reach. But I gave no order to make ready for departure.

Condemn me as you will. The fact is that some demon within me was encouraging me to remain in this soft place of everlasting life, and I found it difficult to resist. It was a kind of paralysis. I had not formally accepted my father's father's offer; but I was remaining, all the same. I will pause here another few days, I told myself each day. I have to gather my strength for the final assault.

What hurry is there? I asked myself. The Summit will wait. The gods can do without me a little longer.

And so the time passed.

"We need to move along," Hendy said to me, after a few days more of idleness.

"Yes. Yes."

"We swore an oath, Poilar," said Traiben some days later.

"Yes," I said. "So we did."

They were all looking at me, watching me, wondering. Some were eager to continue the ascent, some were not, but no one could understand why I held back from issuing the order to resume our march. Even Thrance, skulking crooklegged through the splendors of this Kingdom as though they were nothing but ashes and mud, turned his mocking grinning gaze at me and asked me coolly, "Are you afraid to go on to the Summit, Poilar? Is that it? Or is it just a sudden attack of laziness that keeps you here so long?"

I scowled at him and said nothing.

He said, "It's on account of a woman, perhaps. Eh? One of these sleek little girls with nice golden skin comes crawling into your bed at night, is that it? And you can't bear to leave her." Thrance pushed his piebald face close up against mine and laughed, with great gusts of stinking breath. "She's six tens old, Poilar! She's old enough to be Hendy's mother's mother's mother, and you think she's just a girl!"

"Get away from me," I told him.

"Six tens of years!"

"Away," I said. "Or I'll break you in two."

He laughed again. But he went limping away.

Indeed there was a little truth to this notion of Thrance's, but only a little; for I had in fact had some sport with the glittering women of this Kingdom here and there during this time. I know that I was not the only one who did that. The citizens of my father's father's realm swarmed over us as though we were new toys brought for their amusement, and they were not easy to resist. Very likely all the members of my Forty had lovers while we were in this land, the men and women both. In particular I took a fancy to one called Alamir, who was lithe and quick and had the sparkling sheen of a girl half my age. How old she might be in reality was something I didn't care to consider, though the question did cross my mind unbidden now and again, to my dismay. It was she who had put the notion of founding a Kingdom of my own into my head, with herself as Queen. And I played with the idea for a few days; but all it was was play.

It was not Alamir, though, who kept me tied to this place, nor laziness. But Thrance had hit upon the truth with his first hypothesis.

It was fear.

I knew now that my father's father had not cast any spells upon me. He had merely made a tempting offer, which the Poilar of an earlier time would have quickly refused out of hand with a shrug and a shake of the head. Even now, weary of the long climb as I was, I still was capable of refusing it.

But my mind would not let go of the tale of my father's strange death upon the heights of the Wall. It brimmed in my memory, and cascaded and overflowed; and the more I considered it, the more powerful was its impact. A thousand times I asked myself: What was it that my father had seen at the Summit, so horrible that he could purge himself of the knowledge of it only by casting himself into the Well of Life?

It was dread of that revelation that held me back, not anything so simple as the fear of dying. Death itself held no terrors for me: it never has. But that I might discover something in the abode of the gods that could drive me to take my own life, as my father and his six companions had done before me—that was what I feared. It paralyzed me utterly; and I found myself unable to share that fear with any of my friends. For a long while I concealed it even from myself, and believed that it was some newfound love of comfort that held me here, or some magic that my father's father had wantonly cast upon my mind. That was not it. That was not it at all.

I N THE END IT was Hendy who forced my hand and
brought about my departure from this Kingdom of
comfort and idleness. She was sworn to the Summit as
much as any of us, and it was she who drew me to my senses
and restored me to my pledge.

What she did, simply, was to disappear. We had had
no defections during all our time in this Kingdom, for
why, short of taking up our Pilgrimage again, would any
of us have wanted to leave this gentle place? But one
morning Hendy was not among us. I asked a few people if
they had seen her—Fesild, Kath—but they had nothing
to tell me.

Then Traiben said, "She's gone off to be transformed,
Poilar."

"What? How do you know?"

"I saw a woman on the far rim of the Kingdom late last
night, walking up the path to the outside. The moons were
bright, and she looked back once, and even though the
distance was so great I could see it was Hendy. I called to her
and she said something, but she was too far away for me to

hear it; and then she turned and went on her way and I lost sight of her."

"You just let her go like that?"

"What else could I do? She was high up on the trail, at least an hour's march above me. There was no way I could have overtaken her."

I grabbed him by the shoulders and shook him savagely, so that his head lolled back and forth and his eyes went very wide and his shape began to flicker.

"So you watched and you let her go? You watched and you let her go?"

"Please—Poilar—Poilar—"

I flung him from me. He struck the ground and sprawled out, and lay there, looking up at me more in astonishment than in anger or pain.

"Oh, Poilar," he said ruefully. "Poilar, Poilar, Poilar!"

He got up—I helped him—and he dusted himself off and checked himself here and there for bruises and cuts. I felt like a fool. After a moment I said, very quietly, "Will you forgive me, Traiben?"

"You've become very odd since we came here, do you know?"

"Yes. Yes, I know." I shut my eyes a moment and took a few deep breaths. In the same quiet tone I said, "You might at least have come to me and told me what was happening."

"It was very late at night. And weren't you with Alamir?"

"What does that have to do with—" I stopped. I was becoming angry again, but I had no one to be angry with except myself. "How can you be sure that she went off to be transformed?"

"Where else would she be going, Poilar?"

"Why, she could have—she might have been—"

"Yes?"

I scowled. What was he trying to suggest?

A thought came to me. It was so inane that I pushed it aside; but it came stubbornly back, and I said, to be rid of it,

"Do you think that she might have gone to the Well to make herself look younger?"

"That possibility has crossed my mind," he said.

I hadn't expected him to agree with me so readily. "Why would she? She doesn't look old, Traiben. She looks young and slender and beautiful!"

"Yes," said Traiben. "Yes, I think she does. But does she think so?"

"She should."

"But does she?"

I turned away, frowning. The more I considered it, the harder it was for me to bring myself to accept this notion I had put forth that Alamir was the cause of Hendy's disappearance. Hendy and I had never discussed it, but she was utterly untroubled, I was sure, by that dalliance; she must certainly have known that it meant nothing, and very likely she had been playing games of a similar sort with some narrow-waisted boy who might have been a hundred years old, though he looked no more than seventeen. Which would have mattered to me not at all.

"No," I said. "The whole idea's ridiculous. She couldn't have felt any need to run off to the Well to make herself look younger. Hendy can't possibly believe that Alamir means a thing to me—that she's anything more than a passing diversion, an amusement of the moment—"

"Ah," he said, "I have no idea what Hendy believes, about Alamir or any other subject." He reached out and took my hands in his. "Poor Poilar. Poor sad Poilar. How sorry I am for you, old friend." But it was hard to hear much sympathy in his voice.

I was lost in bewilderment. Why had she vanished? Where to? I had no answers.

Yet she was gone. That much was clear.

"What will I do?" I asked him.

"Pray that she comes back," Traiben said.

·   ·   ·

I WAS BESIDE MYSELF with chagrin, and frightened besides. What if I had totally misjudged Hendy's feelings toward what had been taking place? What if my involvement with Alamir had not seemed mere trifling sport to her, but a betrayal of our love? And so her jealousy and her sorrow had led her to the Well, perhaps, not to make herself seem more beautiful in my eyes—that seemed needless to me and surely would to her also, mere folly, a shallow unworthy thing to do—but to destroy herself. I had told her the story of how my father had met his death. Had it tempted her? The thought that even now Hendy lay shriveling in the dread waters of the Well of Life sickened me to my core.

No. That was just as unlikely an idea, I told myself, and brought forth all the reassuring arguments. Hendy understood how meaningless Alamir was to me. And she was aware of the depth of my love for her. She had to be. And her own fear of death—that monstrous dream, Hendy in a Hendy-sized box for all eternity—would surely keep her from rushing toward it. In any case no one kills herself for jealousy: no one. That was a contemptible thing to do, and very foolish. Even those who are sealed will sometimes take another lover for a short while, and nothing is said of it; and Hendy and I, of course, had never been sealed.

But why—where—

And then I remembered something. I heard Hendy's voice of long ago, speaking out of the depths of my mind, telling me:

What I want is to go to the gods at the Summit and be purified by them. I want them to transform me. I don't want to be who I am any longer. The memories that I carry around are too heavy for me, Poilar. I want to be rid of them.

Yes, that was it. The motive I had ascribed to her for running away was too trivial. Not out of a simple thing like jealousy had she gone, no, but out of the wish at long last to cast away the burden of her past, to step into the fire of the gods and come forth clean, new, purified—

I saw no chance that Hendy would be able to reach the Summit by herself, though. She must be lost in the fog and snow, desperately wandering through forbidding wastelands, searching hopelessly for the one trail that led to the top.

My first impulse was to give the order for us to leave this place and set out at once toward the Summit, so that we could find her. But I saw how impossible that was. For me to have delayed our departure for so long, and then suddenly to reverse myself and return to the upward road simply because my lover had run away? They would all laugh. It would be the end of my leadership of the group.

No. What I had to do was go after her by myself, up toward the Well or beyond it, find her wherever she was, even to the edge of the zone of the Summit itself, and bring her back. That too presented difficulties, though. The road was a mystery to me as much as it was to Hendy. I might survive my solitary upward journey, or I might not. I would be risking my life for purely personal reasons— jeopardizing the entire Pilgrimage—

And they would point out that I had let Ais go, and Jekka and Jaif, and a whole host of others, with no attempt at searching for them. How, then, could I show any sort of special concern for Hendy? I should be as casual about her departure as I had been about the others, instead of running in panic to find her.

I was stymied. I did nothing at all, except to stare hour upon hour toward the upward path, and search hopelessly for some workable plan.

Then Hendy came back of her own accord, while I was still hesitating and stumbling and leading myself down blind trails.

It was on the third day of her absence. I had not slept all the while, nor had I allowed Alamir to come near me. I scarcely ate or spoke with others. As I stood looking toward the road that ran up the rim of the Kingdom I saw a pale figure appear high on the trail, like a dream-ghost, bathed in Ekmelios's harsh white light. Slowly it descended; and I realized after a time that it was Hendy.

But it was a Hendy very much altered.

I went to her. Her hair was white and her skin was the color of death. She was very much taller now, tremendously elongated and thin as a skeleton, and her flesh, such as it was, was almost transparent: I was able to see the pulsing of her blood. So frail was this new Hendy that I could have put my finger through her with an easy thrust. There was no depth to her—no substance, virtually. She seemed terribly vulnerable, a woman without defenses.

"Hendy?" I said, suddenly uncertain.

"I am Hendy, yes," she said. And I saw Hendy's dark unmistakable eyes shining out of the gaunt pallid transformed face of this skeletal stranger.

"Where have you been? What have you done to yourself?"

She pointed toward the Summit.

I looked at her with narrowed eyes. "All the way up?"

"Only to the next Kingdom," she said. I could barely hear her words.

"Ah. And what sort of Kingdom is that?"

"A place where no one speaks."

"Ah," I said, nodding. "Transformed Ones, all of them?"

"Yes."

"Who have lost the power of speech?"

"Who have renounced it," she said. "They have been to the Summit and returned, and there they live, in a realm of total silence. They showed me the route that leads the rest of the way to the top, pointing with their fingers and not saying a word. I think they showed me the way to the Well, also."

"And they showed you how to turn yourself into this."

"No one showed me. It happened, that was all."

"Ah," I said, as though I understood. But I understood nothing. "Ah. Yes. It happened."

"I felt myself changing. I let it happen."

She seemed to be speaking to me from a land beyond death.

"Hendy," I said. "Hendy, Hendy—"

I wanted to reach for her and take her into my arms. But I was afraid.

We stood face to face for a while, saying nothing, as though we both were citizens of that Kingdom that has taken a vow of silence. Her eyes were steady on mine.

I said finally, "Why did you go, Hendy?"

She hesitated a moment. Then she replied, "Because we were staying here to no purpose, and the Summit is what we came here for."

"Did Alamir have anything to do with—"

"No," she said, in a way that left no doubt. "Not a thing."

"Ah," I said yet again. "It was the Summit, then. But yet you didn't go to it, when you had the chance."

"I discovered the road that goes there."

"And turned back? Why?"

"I came back for you, Poilar."

Her words went to my heart. I might have fallen down before her, but she held out her hands. I took them. They were cold as snow, brittle as sticks.

She had undergone a purification of a sort, yes. That was what this new form of hers meant. But some wounded part of the old Hendy still had not been burned away. Her Pilgrimage had farther to go yet.

"We must finish this," she said.

"Yes. We have to."

"But can you leave here?"

"Yes. Yes."

"Will you, though? This Kingdom is like a trap."

"I had to stay here for a time, Hendy. I wasn't ready to move on beyond this place."

"And are you now?"

"Yes," I said.

.   .   .

I ISSUED THE ORDER and we assembled our things—our few remaining supplies, our scanty supply of food, our patched and tattered packs—and took our leave. My father's father emerged onto the portico of his palace and watched us gravely in silence as we went. Some of his people came out also to watch us go. I saw no sign of Alamir.

Galli and I carried the body of the Irtiman. In this high country it was showing no sign of decay. His eyes were closed and his face was calm: he seemed only to be asleep.

Hendy walked beside me at the head of the column.

Her movements were steady and deliberate, with great strength and forcefulness about them. That frailty I had imagined in her at first was only an illusion. There was a kind of supremacy in her bearing that everyone accepted. Her changed appearance set her apart from the rest of us just as completely as Thrance's did; but whereas Thrance's grotesque, contorted form made him appear repellent and dark, Hendy now seemed ennobled and austere and majestic. I was beginning to see a sort of beauty in her strange new form, even.

She said, "There is the upward road."

It was a narrow white track rising into a steep gorge with high walls of black stone. Almost at once it took us beyond the soft air and lazy warmth of my father's father's Kingdom. How they achieved that enchantment there is something that I never learned, and I suppose I never will. We were outside its sphere of potency now, back amidst the ice and bitter wind of these extreme uplands. But we adjusted our bodies, as we had done so many times before, and were able, after a fashion, to cope with the steadily increasing adversities of our surroundings.

I looked back once. Behind me I saw only a formless jumble wrapped in azure haze. We had come so far that I had lost all sense of the terrain we had covered. Somewhere back there was the meadow of the blue grass, and below it the rocky face of the cliff that set a boundary to the Kingdom of the Kvuz, and still further back were the precipitous crags of the Sembitol and the squalid cave of the Kavnalla; and then, far, far below the plateau of the Melted Ones and all the rest, down and down and down, the rock that Kilarion and I had climbed, and the place where the Wall-hawks had attacked us, and Varhad, the domain of the ghosts who went about sheathed in fungus. With Hithiat milepost beyond that, and Denbail and Sennt and Hespen, Glay and Ashten and Roshten, and our own village of Jespodar at the very bottom, so far away that it might just as well be on some other star. My life there now seemed only a dream. It was almost impossible for me to believe that for two full tens of years I had dwelled in a flat busy crowded place down there where the trees glistened with moisture and the air was like a steaming bath. The Wall was my only life now, and had been for so long that all that had gone before it had become unreal. Everything we had passed along the way to this place was fading now into that same unreality. Nothing had any solid existence now except the white path beneath my feet and the gorge of glossy black stone that surrounded me, and the roof of thick dark clouds overhead, as dense and forbidding as a slab of iron.

We came to the Kingdom where they had forsworn the use of words. It was only a small place, a nest of delicate stone spires off the main road. I would have passed it by without seeing it, but Hendy pointed it out, and told me that its people lived in crannies and crevices of the stone. We did not pause to visit them. I had a single glimpse of a few thin, angular people of great height moving about near one of the spires, and then the wind wrapped them in gusts of mist and I saw nothing more.

There was another small Kingdom nearby, where the King was a slave and was carried around constantly in a litter, forbidden to touch his feet to the ground or to do anything to help himself, and another just beyond it that had three kings at once who enjoyed every pleasure, but if one of the three should die the other two would be buried alive in the grave with him. There were other Kingdoms too, but we kept clear of them, for I was weary of these strangenesses. I would not have believed that the Wall had undone so many of our people; but of course we have been sending our Forty onto the mountain for thousands of years, and so have other villages, and few of those who were sent have returned; death took many, and these Kingdoms the rest.

My father had come this way once. As had my father's father, and many others of my fathers before them.

"This is the way to the Well of Life," said Hendy.

She indicated a break in the gorge, where a subsidiary trail went spiraling upward around a dark fang of rock that disappeared into the ceiling of impenetrable clouds. I shivered, and not only from the cold which now was biting at me, at us all, with no mercy whatever.

"Must we go that way?" I said, knowing the answer.

"It's the only path," said Hendy simply.

The mountain narrowed and narrowed until it seemed to me we must be climbing the very tip of the needle. Icy descending winds tumbling out of the cloud mass above us struck us like fists. We clung together on the trail. I wondered if the buffeting would sweep us to our deaths. Lightning flashed, bleaching all color from this precarious craggy place; but we heard no following rumbles of thunder. We were trespassing on a place which only the hardiest could endure, and the mountain was asking us whether we were equal to the test.

Night came. But there was little difference between night and day for us under a cloud cover so heavy. Marilemma once again remained aglow and lit our way after a fashion, illuminating the far side of the clouds so that a dim tinge of scarlet came through. By that faint red gleam we forced ourselves onward through the hours of darkness. We had passed into some realm beyond sleep, it seemed.

When at last we halted and gathered into a group to catch our breaths and exchange a few words of good cheer, our number seemed wrong. There had been twenty-one of us setting out from my father's father's Kingdom, ten men and eleven women, and Thrance the twenty-second; but we seemed less than that now. A quick tally gave me only eighteen.

"Where are the rest?" I asked. "Who's missing?"

In this sparse air our minds worked but dully. I had to run through our roster several times before we determined the absentees: Dahain the Singer, Fesild the Vintner, Bress the Carpenter. Had they fallen from the trail? Turned back of their own accords under the force of the gale? Been quietly snatched from our midst by silent tentacles reaching out of rocky caverns? No one could say. No one knew. We were nine men and nine women, and Thrance. I had succeeded in bringing less than half my Forty to the verge of the Summit, and I felt shamed by losses so great. And yet, and yet, how many leaders had brought even that many this far?

Going back to look for the three missing ones was out of the question. We waited two hours for them, but there was no sign that they were following us. We went on.

Dawn was coming, now. We could not see Ekmelios's hot hard white globe through the ceiling of fog but we felt a change in the quality of the dimness. And then we saw a second glow, an unfamiliar orange one, rising on the horizon not far in front of us. A narrow subordinate path branched from our trail, leading off toward the place of the glow.

Hendy said, "We are at the Well, I think."

23

I HAD IMAGINED A seething pit of hot effervescent
waters, bubbling and churning and spuming and giving
forth a hiss of fervent power. But no: this was an unexpectedly tranquil place. All that lay before us was a quiet
gray oval surrounded by a narrow rim of pale mud. The
single indication of anything unusual was the soft orange
radiance that rose like a mist from its surface.

Seven small mounds, like little blisters, lay in a straight
line along the shore of the Well.

At the sight of them I was overtaken by such fear as I
have rarely felt in my life. It was like an earthquake in my
soul. I saw in my mind's eye the one image of my father that
I possessed, that tall strong man with bright eyes, gaily
flinging me aloft and catching me in his arms. Then I
looked toward those tiny cairns and wondered which one
of them covered his grave, and I shivered with dread. I
could hardly bear to look upon this place of his terrible
transformation. A chill ran along my legs as though they
had been plunged into ice. Behind me I heard whisperings,
and I knew what they must be saying.

But I went quickly forward. That is the only way with fear: attack it before it can vanquish you. I knelt beside the seven cairns, and let my hand rest lightly on the one closest to the Well, thinking that it was the first of the group and therefore must be my father's. What did it matter if I was wrong? The moment I touched it a great calmness came over me. He was here somewhere. I knew that I must be near him.

A faint warmth was coming from the cairn. It seemed harmless. I closed my eyes and said a few words without speaking aloud. Then I scooped a few pebbles and some bits of sandy soil from the ground nearby and scattered it over the cairn I took to be my father's, and over the others as well, as an offering. I prayed for his continued peaceful repose. I prayed for peace for myself too as I faced the ordeal ahead.

Rising then, I walked across the muddy rim to the edge of the Well and looked down into it. It was just a pool of gray water, dull-looking, unreflective. This close, the orange radiance that came from it was wispy and indistinct, a mere thin veil.

Involuntarily I made the signs that guard one against magic; and yet I knew that there was no magic here, any more than the change-fire that throbs in the lower reaches of the Wall is a force of magic. No, this was a natural place, I was sure, where some power in the fabric of the region existed that could strip away the passage of the years from one's body. In our snug village we are safe from such powers; but here on the Wall the mighty forces of the universe have full play, and our mutable bodies are subject to their impact in a hundred ways.

I was eerily calm. Here is life, I thought. Here is death. You take your choice: a second or two returns you to youth, a minute kills. That seemed strange to me, and yet I felt little awe or wonder. I wanted neither youthfulness nor death from this place; I wanted only to have done the thing that I had done here at my father's cairn, and move on.

Perhaps I had been too long on Pilgrimage. Awe and wonder, I suspected, were things that I had left behind me somewhere along the trail, I suspected.

"So?" a rough voice said. "Shall we jump in and make ourselves prettier?"

Thrance. I turned to him, glaring. I could have killed him then. My little moment of serenity was shattered and it angered me that he had broken it. But I forced my anger back.

"Aren't you pretty enough already?" I asked him.

He laughed and made no reply.

"Go on," Galli called to him. "Have a nice little swim, Thrance! Show us what the Well can do!"

Thrance bowed to her. "Let's swim in it together, lovely lady."

There was nervous laughter and some that seemed downright hearty, and even some applause. That astounded me. Each word of this banter was cutting ragged tracks through my soul; and yet my companions seemed amused.

Tension and dread came flowing back into me. I could not believe that I had managed to be so tranquil here, even for a moment or two. This was a hateful perilous place.

"Enough," I said. "I find this comedy distasteful. We need to move on." I pointed up toward the place where the cloud layer cut across the sky like an iron band and said, "There's the Summit, just beyond. Let's be on our way."

But no one moved. There was more whispering and a little uneasy giggling. Kilarion pretended to be dragging Naxa toward the edge of the Well, and Naxa pounded his fists on Kilarion's chest in mock outrage, and Kath made some cheerful silly quip about taking some of the water back to peddle when we returned to Jespodar. I glanced around in astonishment. Had they all lost their minds? Never have I felt so alone as in that moment when I saw how my companions were looking toward the Well. I saw fascination on some faces, a kind of eagerness on others, a playful excitement on still others. The seven little cairns appeared to signify nothing to any of them. Traiben's eyes were bulging with fierce curiosity. Gazin and Marsiel and two or three others were pondering the Well frowningly, as though in another moment or two they intended to dip themselves in it. Even Hendy seemed tempted. Only Thissa showed any awareness of the dangers that the Well posed, but she too had an odd glitter of speculation in her look.

Pushing and yelling and shoving, I got them all out of there. We went back up the narrow path toward the main trail. Once we were away from the Well its spell seemed to dissipate: there was no more foolish laughter, no more clumsy joking.

Yet we had lost two more of our number to it.

I thought at first that we had lost three; for when I halted to count up, there were just fifteen of us left, and Thrance. One woman was missing—Hilth the Carpenter, I realized—and two men. Which? I called off names. "Kath? Naxa? Ijo?" They were accounted for. Someone said that Gazin the Juggler was not with us. And then it struck me that Traiben was nowhere in sight either.

Gods! Traiben! That was hard to bear. Not caring what the others might say, I turned and ran in frenzy back toward the Well, hoping it might not be too late to pull him free of its deadly waters.

But there he was, trudging cheerfully up the path.

"Poilar?" he said, as I rushed toward him.

I came close to colliding with him and managed to keep from bowling him over only by swerving at the last instant and stumbling up against a boulder that rose beside the trail like a great jagged tooth. The impact knocked the wind out of me and I clung to the rock, wrapping my arms tight around it, until I could breathe again.

Traiben said, "Did you think I had gone in, Poilar?"

"What did you suppose I was thinking?" I asked him furiously.

He smiled. I had never seen him look so disingenuous.

"You know I would never have done that. But Gazin did, and Hilth."

I had half expected that, but the news shook me nevertheless. "What?" I cried. "Where are they?" I saw from Traiben's face that they had not come out of the Well, that they had used it not for rejuvenation but for obliteration. And then I realized that Traiben must have stood there watching it happen, studying it in that cold-blooded thoughtful way of his, looking on with aloof scholarly interest while a man and a woman to whom he had been bonded by oath were letting their bodies dissolve before his eyes. In that moment a gulf opened between Traiben and me that had not been there before and I was flooded with an immense sadness; and yet I knew that he had always been this way, that there was no reason for me to be surprised.

Together he and I went back to the Well. I envisioned us pulling the diminished bodies out and building two new little cairns over them to go with the other seven; but there was no trace of Gazin and Hilth at all. From the shore we poked in the water with poles that we found nearby, in all likelihood the same ones that my father's father had used to draw the skeletons of my father and his six companions from the Well. But we found nothing.

I realized then that my father and his friends, though dwindled back to the size of infants, must have changed their minds at the end in some twisting of their tormented souls and tried to come forth from the Well, and had perished on its rim, each one holding another's hand. But Gazin and Hilth had yielded themselves up completely. I did not even try to understand why. We built cairns in their memory, and then Traiben and I returned to the rest. I told them what had occurred. Later in the day, as we marched along a tongue of rock that seemed to be carrying us straight into empty air, Traiben offered to describe for me the scene he had witnessed. I gave him so terrible a look that he shrank away from me, and it was hours before he would come near me again.

·   ·   ·

WE WERE INTO THE fog zone now. It lay all about us like a thick woolen cloak, and we walked as though we were traveling ever deeper into a dream.

This was the end of all our striving, the last stage of our long journey. We all knew it; and no one spoke, no one violated the sanctity of the moment. Indeed we were as calm as dead men as we made our way up the final fang of the great mountain.

Behind us everything was white. Nothing could be seen. We were at the roof of the World and perhaps part of the way into the vault of the Heavens, and all that we had traveled through had vanished as though it no longer existed.

We could see nothing ahead, either. Nor was there any visibility to right or left. For all we knew we were moving along an upthrust strip of rock no wider than our two feet, with fathomless abysses on either side. We might even have been walking on nothing but air, following a path that traveled in the midst of utter nothingness. It did not matter. Nothing did. This was journey's end. In single file we went steadily forward. Thissa led the way, now, for in this ultimate realm, where we were all of us as good as blind, her santha-nilla powers were our only guidance. I walked behind her and Hendy behind me, and then Traiben. In what order the others followed I could not say, for they were invisible to me; but I think that Thrance must have been the last in line, capering along well behind the rest, since that was often his style when he did not choose to run far ahead of everyone.

Strangely, there was no wind. But the air was bitterly cold, so cold I could not possibly make you imagine it. It stung our nostrils and bit our throats and fell into our lungs like molten metal. We had done all the adapting to the conditions of these heights that we could, and now we had no choice but to endure in silence whatever hardship descended on us. I imagined that my skin was turning hard and flaking away, my eyeballs becoming rock, my fingers and toes breaking off when I flexed them.

I gave myself up to the cold as though it were a warm blanket. I embraced it as though it were a lover. I strode on ever deeper into it as though it were the one thing I had come here to find. There was no gradation to it: it was *absolute* cold, *complete* cold, the perfect achievement of coldness. That was comforting, in its way. No matter how much higher we went it would not get any colder for us, for here at the top of the World we had found the utter bottom of coldness. And so we went on, calmly, almost unfeelingly, up the invisible stone ramp that was taking us to the final point of our Pilgrimage.

HOW LONG THAT LAST stage of the climb lasted, I could not tell you. A minute, a year, a hundred tens of years—it would all have been the same. You are in a time outside of time as you approach the top of Kosa Saag.

The whiteness thickened. I could see nothing now, not even Thissa just in front of me. And I halted, not out of fear—we were in a realm beyond the possibility of fear now—but simply because it seemed wise to halt. I stood motionless, and it was a time out of time, so that I might have been standing there a thousand tens of years.

But then I felt a pressure against my right hand, as though the air had closed itself around it. Gradually I realized that Thissa had reached back and taken my hand in hers; and because it somehow seemed the right thing to do I put my other hand behind my back, and groped through the woolly air until I found Hendy's. So it went down the line until we must all have been linked like a chain of the spider-men of the Sembitol. Thissa tugged gently, and I took a step forward; and she tugged again and I took another; and again, and yet again.

All this while I saw only whiteness.

One more step and everything changed. The whiteness

broke open around me. Bright sunlight came smashing in, as if the gods had dropped Ekmelios at my feet. Thissa pulled me forward, and I pulled Hendy, and Hendy pulled Traiben, and so on and so on, and one by one we came out of the fog into a flat open place that was surrounded on all sides by narrow gray spears of rock.

Thissa released my hand and swung about so that she was facing me, and we stared face to face; and I saw her eyes wide as moons, and saw gleaming tear-tracks running down her cheeks, and she was smiling in a fashion that I had never seen before. She said something which the wind carried away before it reached my ears, for there was wind again here that ripped across us in savage battering gusts. I nodded as if I understood and felt the tears go coursing down my own face like water breaking through a dam, and I said to Hendy what Thissa had said to me, though I had not heard Thissa and could not even hear my own voice as it spoke the words. "Yes," Hendy said. She nodded too; she understood. We all understood. We needed no words. We had passed through every Kingdom of the Wall and now we were on the roof of the World; we were in the abode of the gods; we were at the Summit of Kosa Saag.

IN THOSE FIRST FEW dazzled moments we shuffled about like dreamers who had awakened into yet another dream. The light was so bright that it beat against our eyes with the force of a flail, and the air, dry and sharp and clear and unthinkably cold, was almost like no air at all.

Gradually I became able to see more clearly.

It was a smaller place than I had expected, the Summit. I suppose one could cross it from one side to the other in a couple of hours. I had imagined a single tapered point of rock here at the tip of the Wall, like an auger or an awl, and from below it might indeed seem that way; but to us who stood upon it it was more like a plateau than a needle-point. It was more or less circular in shape, and all around its rim was a rocky palisade of rough sharp-edged crags. The sky was more black than blue: the stars were shining at midday, and even two of the moons. Below us lay the vast blank cloud-barrier, sealing off the World from us so that we were left in a solitary realm of barrenness and chill.

But we were not alone up here.

To our right, close by, stood a strange gleaming house—more like a machine than a house, I should say, for it was all of metal and rose on curious jointed struts, as though it were some giant insect making ready to walk away. There were windows of a sort in this house and we saw faces peering through. Far to the left, virtually at the opposite side of the plain, was a second such house; or the ruins of one, rather, for it was corroded and decayed, an ancient twisted shattered thing with great openings torn in its metal sides. This one was much larger than the newer one that lay close beside us.

Could these be the palaces of the gods?

And if they were, where were the gods themselves? I saw no gods here.

That puzzled me greatly. For surely this was the Summit: there could be no other. And at the Summit was the home of the gods. So we all had been taught our whole lives; so we believed with passionate force. But I saw no gods here.

What I did see, moving about in the open space between these two houses, was a roaming band of a dozen or so wild uncouth creatures, strange howling beasts who had the semblance, but only the semblance, of men. They seemed more like apes, and ugly, shambling, clumsy apes at that. They had arrayed themselves in a wide loose ring around the newer metal house, the shining one, and appeared to be laying siege to it. With tremendous vehemence and ferocity they capered about it, screaming madly and grimacing and pelting it with stones, while whoever was within looked on in apparent dismay but took no action to defend themselves.

They were frightful degenerate bestial things, these creatures of the Summit. Their arms were too long and their legs were too short and they were ugly in all their other proportions as well. Their bodies were covered with hair, thick and coarse and shaggy, but not so thick that it succeeded in concealing the myriad blisters and ulcerations and scars that sprouted everywhere on their skin. Their eyes were dull and blank and their teeth were mere broken snags and their shoulders were slumped and rounded. Despite the cold they were naked, or nearly so. And they all seemed to be in a state of Change, for I could see breasts on some, and the dangling complexity of male organs on others. The thought came to me that these strange savage beings must be some primitive creatures ancestral to us, perpetually in a state of sexual readiness, incapable of assuming the neuter form.

I had no time just then, though, for further speculations. For these apish Summit-dwellers, having noticed finally that a group of strangers had come over the horizon of their little domain, were turning their attention to us. Suddenly we were under attack. Shrieking shrilly, prancing and cavorting, they shook their fists at us, spat into the wind, scooped up handfuls of pebbles and flung them at us. Nor did they throw only pebbles. A fair-sized rock struck Malti in the shoulder and knocked her down. Another hit Narril in the cheek, and he dropped into a crouch, covering his face with his hands. I spun around quickly as a sharp three-sided chunk of stone went whizzing past my ear, but as I did a second one caught me in the flat of the back and made me gasp for breath.

For a moment I was too stunned to think. Then I heard outcries from my left—Thrance's voice, shouting something above the wind—and an answering whoop from Kilarion—and when I looked up I saw the two of them charging fiercely forward, waving their cudgels as though they were flaming swords. Behind them came Galli, Grycindil, Talbol, shouting and brandishing their cudgels also; and then most of the others, all but Thissa and Traiben and Hendy.

The Summit-dwellers appeared amazed to see this unexpected phalanx rushing toward them. They were thrown into confusion. Halting their onslaught at once, they stood still, looking toward one another and uttering high-pitched chattering cries of alarm; and then they turned and ran, scampering like rock-apes across the flat open space. In no time at all they vanished on the far side of the ruined structure, disappearing into invisible lairs set in crevices of the bordering rocks.

We stared at each other in surprise and relief, and then we began to laugh. It had been so easy, driving them off! Who would have thought they would turn and flee at the first sign of resistance? I called out my thanks to Thrance for his quick wit and my congratulations to all for their courage.

Traiben stood silent beside me, his face stricken with horror.

"What is it?" I asked him. "Are you hurt?"

He shook his head. Then he pointed off into the distance, toward the rocks where the Summit-dwellers had taken refuge. His hand was trembling.

"Kreshe and Thig, man! What *is* it?"

"The gods," Traiben said, in a voice that sounded more dead than alive. "There they are, Poilar. Kreshe and Thig, Sandu Sando and Selemoy. There. There. We've just seen them. Those are our gods, Poilar! The creatures of the Summit!"

My head ran in circles. What monstrous madness was this that Traiben was spouting? I felt an abyss opening beneath my feet. Those beasts the gods? What was he saying? What was he saying? I was bewildered at first and then I was furious, and I came close to striking Traiben for his blasphemy. Even at this moment, here on the bleak and rocky Summit of Kosa Saag, I still felt an abiding certainty that Kreshe and Thig and Selemoy and the rest, Sandu Sando and Nir-i-Sellin and the others of that golden band, must be waiting for us somewhere nearby in their gleaming palace, the one I had seen in my vision that night as I lay under the stars beside Hendy. But I held my hand, out of love for him, and struggled to understand what he was trying to say.

"Do you remember," he asked me, "what the dead Irtiman said? About the ship that came from the world called Earth, and landed here at the top of Kosa Saag, and the settlement that was founded here?"

"Yes," I said. "Of course I do."

"What can these animals be," Traiben said, "if not the fallen remnants of that Irtiman settlement of long ago?"

I considered that. And realized that something of what Traiben had said must be true. These debased creatures looked nothing much like Irtimen, and yet in form they were much more like the Irtiman we had found than they were like us. There was a similarity of outline, at least. The Irtiman had been nowhere near as disagreeable in appearance as these creatures, but his proportions indeed had been very much like theirs, the long arms, the short legs, the odd set of the head against the shoulders. And there was one other thing in common, for he had never entered a neuter form that I had ever noticed, but had always remained male, as the males of this tribe seemed also to do.

So these capering animals were more likely the Irtiman's kin than ours, the pitiful hideous descendants, I supposed, of those Irtimen who had come to the Summit to found a village long ago. Yes, I thought: they must surely be Irtimen of some sort. But that did not make them gods. Wild decadent Irtimen, that was all they were, who had slipped into barbarism during the thousands of years of their settlement here.

I said as much to Traiben.

"And where are the gods, then?" he asked me, in a hard sharp-edged tone that seemed not like his voice at all. "Where, Poilar? Where are they? We are at the Summit—is there any doubt of that? But I don't see the shining palaces. I don't see the golden courtyards. I don't see the feasting-hall of Kreshe. The First Climber said He found gods here when He finally reached this place. Well, where are they?" He waved his hand once again toward the rockbound lairs of the savage Irtimen. "Where are they, Poilar?"

24

To Traiben's questions I had no answers. His words struck at me like hammers, and I stood there and accepted the blows, but my heart cried out from the pain and there was a moment when I thought I would rather hurl myself from the mountain than have to listen to any more of what he was saying. For something perverse within me said to me that Traiben was right, as he so often was, that there were no gods atop this mountain or else that these creatures were our gods, or the children of our gods, and some terrible mistake had been made and perpetuated across the thousands of years of the Pilgrimage.

I could not face the possibility that that was so. Not only was it blasphemy: it was an absurdity besides, the negation of everything I believed. To have come this far, and suffered so much, for *nothing*? It could not be. The mere thought of it sent a black wind roaring through my soul.

But I could not refute Traiben's arguments, either. For where were the palaces I had dreamed of beholding up here? Where, indeed, were the gods? We could see virtually from one side of the Summit to the other. And all that we had found here were two metal houses—one house small and gleaming with a few frightened faces peering out from it, faces that did not seem to be the faces of gods, and the other one large and old and rotting— and a band of strange naked creatures capering and shrieking and hurling missiles with wild uncertain aim.

It was an awful moment. Everyone was looking at me, waiting for me to tell them what to do. They had not heard what Traiben had said, nor did any of them know a thing of what the dead Irtiman had told me in his final hours about the Summit and the gods. But here we were at the Summit, and what was to happen now? What could I say, how could I explain? This was the culmination of our Pilgrimage. Was this all there was, these two metal houses, these strange shrieking creatures? Were we now supposed to turn around and slink back down through all the myriad Kingdoms to the half-forgotten village at the bottom of the Wall that we had set out from so long ago, and take up life in the roundhouse of the Returned Ones, and maintain a silence about all that we had seen at the Summit, as those who had returned before us had done?

The taste of ashes was in my mouth. I had never known such despair. I could not hide, I could not flee, I could not offer any explanations. But perhaps this shining metal house held the answers I wanted, or some part of them.

On legs that felt like slabs of wood I stumbled forward, with no plan in my mind, until I found myself standing beneath the little gleaming house on metal struts. The faces still were peering from the small windows.

This close, I recognized them plainly for what they were. Not the faces of gods, whatever the faces of gods might be like—no, almost certainly not gods.

They were the faces of Irtimen. The three friends of our Irtiman, to whom he had been so eager to return before he died.

Well, I had promised to bring him to them. And I had.

"Irtimen!" I cupped my hands to my mouth and shouted with all my strength. It seemed to me that the wind was blowing away my words; I could scarcely hear my voice myself. But I persevered. "Irtimen! Irtimen! Listen to me! I am Poilar Crookleg of Jespodar village, and I have something for you!"

Silence. A terrible stillness on the plateau.

"Irtimen, do you hear me? Use those little boxes of yours that let you speak our language!"

But how could they hear me, locked up inside that metal house of theirs?

I turned and looked back. Kilarion and Talbol had carried the preserved body of the Irtiman the last leg of the journey to the Summit. Now it lay like a child's discarded doll at the edge of the plateau, where we had come up into this place.

I gestured to Kilarion. "Bring it here!" I called.

He nodded and scooped the Irtiman's body up, perching it across his shoulder so that it dangled downward, and carried it toward me. I told him what to do and he set it down on the ground facing the little metal house of the Irtimen, propping its back against a rock in such a way that it was looking up at them.

"Irtimen!" I cried. "There is your friend! I found him wandering far down below, and we brought him with us for you, and we cared for him until he died! And kept him with us even after that! There he is! We have brought you your friend!"

I waited. What else could I do, but wait?

The faces disappeared from the windows of the metal house. But nothing else happened. It was a moment that seemed to stretch forever. I heard my people murmuring behind me. Perhaps they thought I had gone out of my mind. I was beginning to wonder myself whether I had.

But I waited. I waited.

Then a kind of door began sliding open on the metal

house. A hatch, rather, in its side. A ladder appeared. It occurred to me that this must not really be a house, but rather the ship in which the Irtimen had traveled between the worlds. And the other house, the ancient ruined one, must be the one in which the settlers had come from Earth to our world thousands of years ago.

I saw a foot on the topmost rung of the ladder. An Irtiman was coming down.

He was very slender, with long flowing hair that looked like gold, and he carried a speaking-box under his arm like the one that our Irtiman had carried. Or under *her* arm, I should say; for this Irtiman wore only a light simple garment despite the biting cold, and I saw what surely were the swellings of two breasts beneath it. So this Irtiman was a she, in the sexual form. Had I interrupted a mating? No, no, more probably she wore that form all the time. How strange that seemed to me, that these people's bodies should always be ready for mating like that! More than anything else it said to me that these Irtimen, who resembled us outwardly in so many trifling ways, were indeed alien creatures, creatures of some other creation.

The female Irtiman stepped forward until she was no more than a dozen paces from me. She glanced at the dead Irtiman on the ground, and although I had no real way of comprehending the meaning of an Irtiman's facial expressions it seemed clear to me that the look on her face was one of displeasure, distaste, even disgust. I think I saw some fear there also.

She said, "Did you kill him?"

Her voice, coming to me out of the language-box, was lighter than the other Irtiman's had been, a high clear tone.

"No," I said indignantly. "We are not murderers. I told you: we found him wandering on the mountainside, and we cared for him. But he was very weary and before long he died. And I decided to bring him to you, because he seemed so badly to want to return to you, and I thought you would want to have him back."

"You knew that we were here?"

"He said you were."

"Ah." She nodded, and I had no doubt of what that gesture meant. Then she turned and beckoned behind her, and another Irtiman came from the ship, and the third one after that. The second one looked male, with a heavy body and a broad dark face, and the third had breasts like the first and flowing hair that was amazingly long and of a startling scarlet color. Both of them had little tubes of metal in their hands. I noticed that the other one, the golden-haired one that had come out first, had a tube of the same sort fastened to her hip. I suppose they were weapons, these tubes. But the golden-haired one gestured to the other two and they put their tubes into little hip-cases like hers.

All three stood facing me. Insofar as I was able to read the meaning of their movements, it seemed to me that they were wary and uneasy. Well, they had good reason to be afraid of us. But they had come out of their ship; that was a sign of trust. One of them—it was the scarlet-haired one—went over to the dead one and knelt and stared into his face for a moment, and then she touched his cheek gently with her hand. She said something to the others, but she was not carrying a speaking-box, so of course I was unable to understand.

"Are you Pilgrims?" the male Irtiman said.

"Yes. There were forty of us when we left Jespodar, and these are all who remain." I moistened my lips and took a deep breath. "If you know what Pilgrims are, then you must know that we have come here seeking our gods."

"Yes. We know that."

"Well, then, is this the Summit? Are the gods to be found on it?"

He looked down at the speaking-box a moment, and ran his hands along its sides as though he needed something to do with them just then. At length he said, somewhat warily, "This is the Summit, yes."

"And the gods?" My throat was so dry I could barely get the question out.

"Yes, the gods." A quick tense nod. "This is the place where your gods live."

I could have wept at those words. My heart surged up in my breast with joy. The darkness of my despair dropped away from me. The gods! The gods, the gods, the gods at last! I looked toward Traiben in triumph, as if to say, *See? See?* As if to say, *I knew all along that the gods must be here; for the Summit is a holy place.*

"Where are they?" I asked, trembling.

And the Irtiman pointed, as Traiben had done, to the crevices of the far wall, where the savage Irtimen had run off to hide.

"There," he said.

IT WAS THE MOST difficult hour of my life. It was like that for us all.

We sat in a circle on the pebbly ground in front of the little metal ship of the Irtimen that had come to rest on that cold flat place at the top of the World, and they told us the bitter truth about our gods.

The dead Irtiman had tried to hint at it, but he could not bring himself to reveal it directly. My father's father had spoken of it too—the horror at the Summit—but would not tell me what it was. Traiben, of course, had understood it the moment we had attained the Summit. He had dreamed long ago that it was like this here: I remembered now his telling me that. And as for me, I had tried to reject it at every turn, obvious though it may have been. But this time there was no denying the validity of it even for me; for I was at the Summit and I could see with my own eyes what was here and what was not, and the things the Irtimen had to tell us now fell upon me with inexorable unanswerable force.

These were the things I learned from the Irtiman of the Summit at that dark hour. This is what I must share with you for the sake of your souls. Listen and believe; listen and remember.

They said—it was the golden-haired one who did most of the talking, the one who had come out first—that the race of Irtimen was a race that had journeyed everywhere in the Heavens, that traveled between the stars more easily than we went between one village and another. There were many worlds in the Heavens, some beautiful and pleasant, some not. And whatever world they found that had good air and water and things that Irtimen could eat, there they would plant a settlement of their own kind, unless that world was already peopled with its own people and had no room for them.

So it was that they had come to our world, which we call the World; and part of it was fit for Irtiman life and part was not, so they settled only in the part that suited them, here in the heights of Kosa Saag. That was long ago, hundreds of tens of years, more years than I could easily comprehend.

They could not comfortably go into the lowlands, because of the heat and the thick heavy air. And no one from the lowland villages ever came up here, because of the rigors of the journey and the increasing chill and thinness of the air in the higher levels, and because we had no need to venture into such remote difficult places when we had all the richness of the valleys to sustain us. We stayed in our own territory; and indeed we made it unlawful to climb to these heights, saying that Sandu Sando the Avenger had cast us down from them and we were never to return. And so all unknowing we shared the World with the people who had come across the Heavens from Earth; or if we knew anything of the beings who dwelled atop the Wall, we thought of them as gods, or demons, or some such awesome things.

Then the First Climber dared to ascend the Wall—breaking the prohibition against that which existed among our people—and reached the Summit, and encountered the Irtimen. And He was welcomed by them, and taken in, and they spoke with Him and showed Him the wonders of the village they had built up here. And—just as the Book of the First Climber relates—He learned from them the use of fire, and the way to make tools and raise crops and build sturdy buildings, and much else that was useful besides. Which He taught to us when He came down from the Wall, and that was the real beginning of our civilization.

It was the beginning also, the golden-haired Irtiman told us, of the annual Pilgrimage.

For we fell into the custom of sending our best people to the Summit to go before the Irtimen—whom we came to think of as gods, though in truth they were only mortal Irtimen—and pay homage to them, and learn such things from them as we still needed to know, and bring that knowledge back to the lowlands the way the First Climber had done. The journey was a long and difficult one, and only a few who attempted it survived to reach the Summit, for there were many perils along the way, and especially the thing called change-fire that the mountain gives off, which tempts us to alter our bodies beyond recognition; and of those who avoided the dangers of the Wall and did attain the Summit, just the merest handful ever returned. But to make a successful Pilgrimage was a great achievement, and those who managed it attained the highest honors we could bestow. So we contended amongst ourselves for the right to undertake the journey, and whenever any of us attained the Summit they were greeted warmly by the Irtimen, who taught them many valuable things as they had done for the First Climber.

That was a hard thing to swallow, that our beloved gods were mere mortals, strangers from some other world clinging to a precarious hold at the Summit because they were too feeble to go down into the lowlands. And that the First Climber whom we all revered had been so simple as to fall down before those strangers and offer them homage as if they were divine, and to perpetuate the obligation of that homage down through all the generations that followed

Him. It was like gulping down lumps of hot metal, to accept those things as fact.

But there was worse, much worse, to come.

Time passed, said the golden-haired Irtiman, and things changed in the village at the Summit. For now she spoke of the thing we call change-fire. There are forces at work on Kosa Saag, said the Irtiman, *natural* forces, which cause living flesh to ebb and flow into strange new forms, bringing about bodily transformations far more startling than anything we of the lowland villages can achieve. So she confirmed what we had already come to believe, that the transformations on the Wall were brought about by the nature of the Wall itself. It was not magic that had created the Kingdoms and their dwellers, nor any decree of the gods; it was done by the work of physical forces. The prime one, she said, confirming our own belief, was change-fire, that is, a kind of secret light that the rock itself gives off; but she said that that was only one of many factors that brought about bodily change on this mountain. There was also the thinness of the air, which allowed the harsh light of Ekmelios to penetrate the loins of the Irtimen settlers and alter their seed. And also it was the water they drank; and also it was something in the soil. All these qualities of the Wall brought about great change in the course of time for the Irtimen who dwelled at the Summit. They underwent a strong and terrible transformation, these visitors from the stars. "Their minds grew dim," she said. "Their bodies became deformed. They lost their knowledge. They turned into beasts."

And she gestured toward the rocky crevices of the far wall, where the snarling shrieking savages who threw the rocks had fled.

"Yes," Traiben murmured. "Of course."

I glanced at him. He sat transfixed, fascinated, his great saucer eyes wide and staring. He seemed scarcely to be breathing.

"Can it be so?" I asked him. "Can the gods have turned into—into—"

Traiben waved me irritably into silence, and pointed toward the golden-haired Irtiman, who was speaking again.

"The Pilgrimages continued," she said, "although now there was nothing for your people to learn from ours. It had become the custom to ascend the mountain, and the custom was so powerful that it could not be halted. But those who reached the Summit—and it was always only a few who made it all the way—were horrified at what they saw. Many of them chose not to return to their villages in the lowlands, because they were unwilling or afraid to reveal the truth. These settled along the slopes of Kosa Saag: this was the beginning of the Kingdoms of the Wall. The change-forces began to affect them as they had affected us. Other Pilgrims did go to their homes again, but they came back stunned into silence or madness by their experience."

I looked around at my companions. The truth had come rolling in upon them like a boulder. Hendy was weeping; Thissa, very pale, stared off into remote distances; Naxa the Scribe and Ijo the Scholar, sitting side by side, had their mouths gaping open loosely as though they had been struck on the head by clubs. Of the others, some were wide-eyed with indignation and disbelief, some were trembling, some looked numb. Even stolid Kilarion was frowning and muttering and peering into the palms of his outstretched hands as though he hoped to find some sort of consolation in them.

Only Thrance seemed unshaken by what he had heard. He was sprawled out comfortably on the ground as if we were simply gathered around to hear a performance by a Singer or a Musician; and he was grinning. *Grinning!*

The Irtiman said, "The ship that brought me here, and my friends, landed here not very long ago. We knew that an Earth colony had once been planted on this world, and it is our task to go around from star to star, and visit the colonies that were founded on all the different worlds, and send back reports to Earth on whether they still exist, and what they have achieved. We found the children of the settlers who had come here from Earth, and attempted to make contact with them: but they are as you see them, wild creatures, ignorant, barbaric. And dangerous, though we didn't realize that at first."

She told us how the Irtiman we had found below had volunteered to go as far down the mountain as he could, in order to meet with the peoples of the Kingdoms and discover from them what had taken place here since the founding of the Irtiman colony. The others had remained with their ship, hoping to establish relations of some sort with their degenerate and brutish kinsmen. But once the wild Irtimen of the Summit had realized that there were only three of them, they had begun an almost continuous siege, using sticks and stones and crude spears, keeping them penned up in their vessel so that they could not go to the aid of their companion below.

"But you have weapons," I said. "Why couldn't you have driven them off? We had no trouble with them at all and we have only cudgels."

She turned to face me. "Our weapons are lethal ones. If we used them we would have had to kill our own kin; and that was something we would not do."

Which was a problem I had never considered before: when you only have weapons that kill, and none that merely injure, then it may come to pass that your weapons are of no value at all. And so you must huddle within your ship for safety, though you are almost as powerful as gods and your attackers are little more than beasts.

"When we had arrived at the Summit," she went on, "we had frightened them away for the moment—perhaps because they thought we were the vanguard of a large army. But we were aware that very likely they would resume the attack before long, now that they saw how few we really were. And soon they will."

That seemed to be all that she had to say to us. She thanked us for bringing back the body of their colleague; and then she and her two companions went back inside their ship, leaving us bereft and empty on this cold pebbled plain where the palaces of our gods were not to be found.

"THERE YOU ARE," THRANCE said, in the harshest of voices. "There you have it. Gods! What gods? There are no gods up here. There are only these monsters! And we are fools!" And he spat into the air.

"Be quiet," Kilarion said to him.

Thrance turned to him and laughed, in that way of his that was like the scraping of metal against metal. "Are you upset, Kilarion? Yes, yes, I suppose you are. Who wouldn't be? To climb all this way and find that your gods are nothing but a pack of dirty debased beasts no better than a bunch of rock-apes?"

"Quiet, Thrance!" Kilarion said again, with real menace in his voice.

I thought that they would fight. But Thrance only meant to goad; there was not even enough honor in him to follow through on his goading. Kilarion rose halfway and seemed about to spring upon him, and Thrance grinned and made a placating bow, practically touching his head to the ground, and said in a high, piping, infuriating voice, mockingly pathetic, "No offense meant, Kilarion! No offense! Don't hit me! Please don't hit me, Kilarion!"

"Let him be, Kilarion," Galli muttered. "He isn't worth wasting your effort on."

Kilarion subsided, grumbling and murmuring to himself.

Thrance wasn't finished, though. He said, "Do you know, once upon a time I was told that it was like this up here? That was when I was in a Kingdom called Mallasillima, on the border of the Lake of Fire. Some people of this Kingdom had been to the top and had seen the gods, so they said, and they told me what they were like. I thought they were lying to me, that they were inventing it all; but then the notion came to me that it might just be the truth, and I decided then and there that I would find some way of coming up here and seeing it myself. And now I have. Now I have seen with my own eyes that the tales that they told me in Mallasillima were true after all. Imagine! No gods! All a myth, all a lie! Nothing here but a bunch of degenerate—"

"Enough, Thrance," I said.

"What's the matter, Poilar? Can't you face a little reality?"

But my despair had returned blacker and deeper even than before, and it had numbed me in my heart and in my mind so that I could make no answer to him.

Kilarion, seeing I was silent, rose again and went to Thrance and stood above him. "If you weren't such a coward," he said. "I'd teach you a little about reality. But Galli's right. I shouldn't soil my hands on you."

"No, you shouldn't," Thrance said. "If you touch me, I might just change you into something that looks exactly like me. I can do that, you know. But you wouldn't like to look like me, eh, Kilarion? Or would you? Would you?"

I went over to Thrance and moved between him and Kilarion, pushing Kilarion back a little way, and said to Thrance, "Listen to me. If you speak another word now, it'll be your last. Is that clear?" Thrance bowed again, almost as deeply and just as contemptuously as he had bowed to Kilarion, and looked up into my face and said with his lips alone, not his voice, *No offense, Poilar! No offense!*

I turned my back on him.

To the others I said, "Let's start setting up our camp."

"Camp?" Naxa asked. "Are we staying here?"

"At least for tonight," I replied.

"Why? What for?"

I gave him no answer. I had no answer. I was utterly bewildered, a leader without a plan. My mind was empty; my soul was empty. The whole purpose of my life had collapsed away from me. If what the Irtimen had said were true—and how could I deny it?—there were no gods; the Summit was inhabited by monsters; the Pilgrimage to which I had devoted half my life had been a hollow meaningless endeavor. I would have wept, but they were all watching me; and I think in any case this air that was hardly air at all had taken the capacity to weep away from me. I did not know what to do. I did not know what to think. Thrance, jeering mocker that he was, had spoken the truth: we were face to face with reality now—not a reality that we had expected to find, and it was a hard one to confront.

But I was still leader. I could continue to lead, even if I had no idea why, or toward what end. And possibly I would yet come to find—as even within the depths of my despair some small part of me still fiercely believed—that there are gods here somewhere, that the Summit was indeed the holy place we had thought it to be.

"We'll sleep over here," I said, indicating a little declivity that was sheltered somewhat from the raking Summit winds by a low outcropping of crumbled rock. I set Thissa to work casting a spell of protection. I sent Galli and Grycindil off to search for such firewood as this forlorn place might yield, and Naxa and Malti to hunt out a spring or pond of fresh water. Kilarion, Narril, and Talbol I appointed as the first patrol, to march up and down in a wide circle along the open zone beyond the Irtiman starship and keep watch for any stirrings among the "gods." For so I thought of them still, those beast-like things—the degenerate children of the gods, perhaps, but gods of a sort all the same.

Traiben said, "Do you have any work for me just now? Because if you don't, I'd like to do a little scouting on my own."

"What kind of scouting? Where?"

He nodded toward the ruined ship of the ancient Irtimen.

"I want to see what's inside it," he said. "Whether there are Irtiman things there—holy things remaining from the old days, things the Irtimen might have fashioned back in the time when they still really were gods—" And I saw a gleam in Traiben's eyes that I knew only too well: the gleam that was the outward manifestation of that hunger of his to learn, to know, to poke his nose into every mystery the World had to offer.

It occurred to me that if ever we returned to the village—though whether we ultimately would or not, I could not say; I still had no plan, no sense of anything beyond the needs of the moment—we might indeed want to bring with us some tangible sacred object, something that had felt the touch of the gods, the true gods who had lived on this mountaintop in the days before their decline had begun. But it dismayed me to think of Traiben going into that tumbled mass of rusting girders and twisted metal sheeting by himself as night was beginning to descend. Who knew what skulking "gods" he might encounter in the darkness? I would not let him have permission to go. He begged and pleaded, but I refused to yield. It was madness, I said, for him to risk his life over there. Tomorrow, I told him, a larger group of us might investigate it, if it seemed safe then to make the attempt.

Dusk was coming on. The dark sky grew darker. The stars came forth, and a single icy moon. The Irtiman starship cast a long sharp shadow that reached almost to my feet. I stood by myself, staring somberly across the plain at the place where the miserable creatures whom we had hoped would be our gods were hidden.

Hendy came up to me. Transformed as she was, she towered over me by a head and a half, though she seemed as filmy as a ghost. Fleshless as she was now, she must be freezing in this bitter cold; but she showed no sign of discomfort. She put her hand lightly on my arm.

"So now we know everything," she said.

"Yes. Yes, I suppose we do. Or enough, at any rate."

"Will you kill yourself, Poilar?"

I looked at her, amazed. "Why would I do that?"

"Because we have the answer now, and the answer is a very dark one. Either there are no gods and never were, or the gods are here and have undergone a terrible fall, which is even a sadder thing. So either way there is no hope."

"Is that what you think?" I asked her, and I remembered her vision of eternal death imprisoned in a box precisely large enough to contain her body, and not a bit larger. She had spent much of her life dwelling in some cheerless frostbound realm of the soul very different from the one I had inhabited. "Why do you say that? There's always hope, Hendy, so long as we're alive and breathing."

"Hope of what? That Kreshe and Thig and Sandu Sando will appear, despite everything, and lift us up to their bosoms? That we will see the Land of Doubles in the sky? That life will be good and kind and comforting?"

"Life is what we make it," I said. "The Land of Doubles is somebody's fine fable, I suppose. And Kreshe and Thig and Sandu Sando and all the rest certainly exist, somewhere else, perhaps, far beyond our range of vision. It was only a story, that they lived at the Summit, invented by those who had no idea of the truth. A fable and nothing more. Why should gods who are capable of building worlds live in a disagreeable rocky place like this when they have all of Heaven to choose from?"

"The First Climber said they were here. The First Climber whom we revere."

"He lived a long time ago. Stories become distorted over a long span of time. What He found up here were wise beings from another world, who offered useful knowledge. Was it His fault that we decided that they were gods?"

"No," she said. "I suppose not. They *were* gods, in a way, I suppose. At least we can think of them that way. But as you say, it was all a long time ago." She seemed to disappear into her own bleak thoughts for a moment. Then she gave me a close look. "Well, what will we do now, Poilar?"

"I don't know. Go back to the village, I suppose."

"Do you want to?"

"I'm not sure. Do you?"

She shook her head. She seemed more wraith-like than ever, as remote from me as the stars and just as unreachable, though she was standing right beside me. I felt as though I could almost see through her.

"I have no place in the village," Hendy said. "When I was stolen away from it, I lost my place in it forever. After I came back I always felt like a stranger there."

"So you would settle in one of the Kingdoms, then?"

"Perhaps. Would you?"

"I don't know. I'm not sure of anything anymore, Hendy."

"The Kingdom where your father's father rules, for instance? You liked it there. You could return to it. We both could."

I shrugged. "Maybe. Maybe not."

"Or some Kingdom lower down, one that we didn't pass through on the way up. Some pretty place, not too strange. Nothing like the Kavnalla, or the Kvuz."

"Or we could found one of our own," I said, more to hear the sound of my voice than for any other reason, for I still had nothing like a plan, no plan at all. "There's plenty of room on Kosa Saag for new Kingdoms."

"Would you?" she asked me, and there was almost a note of eagerness in her tone.

"I don't know," I said. "I don't know anything, Hendy."

I felt utterly drained, a hollow husk. This day's revelations had cut the heart from me. No wonder Hendy had wondered if I was going to kill myself. I would not do that, no. But so far as what I *was* going to do now, I had no idea of that whatever.

25

O F C O U R S E T R A I B E N W E N T to the ancient ship that
night anyway, once it was too dark for anyone to see
him slipping away. I might have expected that of him.
Kilarion was on sentry duty in that part of the plain, and
somehow Traiben got past him unnoticed, and went sprint-
ing off into the darkness.

The first I knew of it came when I heard voices somewhere nearby me, a muffled cry, the sound of a scuffle, a
yelp of pain. "Let *go* of me, you idiot!" someone said.
Traiben's voice.

I opened an eye. I was lying by myself, neither sound
asleep nor fully awake, near the outer edge of our group,
huddled down miserably in my bedroll trying to fend off
the cold. There was no woman with me. Since Hendy's
transformation she and I had neither slept in the same
place nor made Changes together, nor had I been with
anyone else.

Focusing my awareness as quickly as I could, I looked
up and saw, outlined by moonlight against the dark,
Traiben wriggling in the grasp of someone much larger

who had caught him around the neck in the crook of his arm. Talbol, I realized. He was the sentry on duty in this section of the sleeping-area.

In a sharp whisper I said, "What's going on? What are you two doing?"

"Make him let go of me," Traiben cried, in a strangled voice.

"Quiet! You'll wake the whole camp!"

I trotted over to them and slapped Talbol's forearm to get him to let go. Traiben backed away a few steps, glaring sullenly.

Talbol looked just as sullen. "He comes creeping into camp in the middle of the night without saying a word. How am I supposed to know he isn't one of those apes coming to attack us?"

"Do I look like an ape?" Traiben demanded.

"I wouldn't want to say what you—" Talbol began.

I waved him into silence and sent him off to resume his patrol of the perimeter. Traiben rubbed his throat with his hand. I was angry and amused all at once, but more angry than amused.

"Well?" I asked, after a moment.

"I went there."

"Yes. Against my direct order. How absolutely amazing, Traiben."

"I had to see it."

"Yes. Of course. Well?"

Instead of answering he thrust something toward me, a dark shapeless thing that he had been holding in his left hand. "Here. Look. It's a god-thing. The ship is full of stuff like this, Poilar!"

I took it from him. It was a corroded metal plaque, maybe three fingers long and four fingers wide. I held it up into the faint moonlight cast by Tibios and was able to make out, just barely, some sort of inscription on it in lettering unlike anything I had ever seen.

"It's Irtiman writing," Traiben said. "I found it lying half buried on the floor of the ship."

"Do you know what it says?"

"How would I know that? I can't read Irtiman writing. But look, look, Poilar, there's a whole treasure-house of god-things in there. Of course everything's broken and rusted and useless, but you just have to glance inside to know how ancient they are. The original Irtimen must have used those things! The ones whom we worship as Kreshe and Thig and—"

"Stop saying that," I told him irritably. "The Irtimen were teachers, not gods. The gods are beings of a higher plane than Irtimen *or* us."

"Whatever you like," said Traiben, with a shrug. "Will you come with me in the morning, so we can explore the ship together, Poilar?"

"Perhaps."

"We'd all better go. The Irtimen might make a little trouble. The ones from the caves, I mean. I saw a couple of them lurking around the ship while I was there. It's a kind of shrine for them, I think. They've got a sort of altar on the far side, with twigs and painted stones piled up around it, and when I went around to look at it I saw that they were burning little wisps of dead grass and chanting something."

I stared at him in astonishment. "You walked right into their midst? They could have killed you!"

"I don't think so. They're more afraid of us right now than we are of them, I suspect. They must have had some bad experiences with Pilgrims in the past. When they saw me they sprang up and ran off right away. So I went into the ship, and when I came out there weren't any of them in sight. But eventually they're going to figure out that we aren't much of a threat to them, and then—"

"Poilar?" a new voice said.

I looked around. It was Thissa. Even by the dim

moonlight I saw fear glistening in her eyes. Her nostrils were quivering as though she could smell danger on the air.

"What is it?" I asked her.

She looked uncertainly at Traiben. "I need to tell you something," she said to me.

"Go on."

"But he—"

"You can speak in front of Traiben. You know that I trust him, Thissa. —This isn't some matter concerning him, is it?"

"No. No." She came closer and held out something in her hand, a small gleaming amulet. "Touch it," Thissa said. Traiben murmured with interest and bent low to examine it. In annoyance I pushed him aside and put the tip of my finger to the little carved jewel. Its surface felt warm.

"What is this thing?" I asked.

"It is a santha-nilla thing," she said. "It belonged to my mother, and her mother before her. When there is treachery nearby it begins to glow."

Traiben said, "You mean it's actually some sort of thought-sensitive device, which is able to detect—"

"Not now, Traiben," I told him impatiently. To Thissa I said, "What sort of treachery? By whom?" I had learned long ago to take Thissa's premonitions seriously. Pointing toward the starship of the Irtimen, I said, "Them?"

"I don't think so. One of us, I think. But I'm not sure. I feel betrayal in the air, Poilar. That's all I know."

"Is there a spell you could cast that would tell you more, do you think?"

"I could try."

"Go, then. See what you can learn."

She went away. I sat perplexed beside my bedroll, unable to sleep, beleaguered by complexities far beyond my powers of understanding. Traiben stayed with me for a while, trying to offer comfort, companionship, explanation. He meant well, but he was full of contradictory incomprehensible ideas that made my head ache, and I drew little comfort from his companionship just now; so after a time I sent him away.

Hendy came to me, then. She too was finding sleep impossible this night.

She knelt beside me and put her hand—her strange altered hand, fleshless and dry and cool, a skeleton's hand—into mine. I held it, though I was afraid to squeeze it too tightly. I was glad to have her near me, but my mind was awhirl with the revelations of the Summit and there was nothing I could say to her. I was lost in confusions.

"We should leave here when the sun comes up," she said. "There's nothing but grief for us in this place, Poilar."

"Perhaps so," I answered. I was barely aware of what she had said.

"And I feel even more grief coming toward us."

Without looking at her I said, in a toneless incurious voice, "Do you? Thissa said the same thing. Have you transformed yourself into a santha-nilla, Hendy?"

"I've always had a little of the power," she said. "Just a little."

"Have you?" I said, still with no great show of interest.

"And it's become stronger since my transforming."

"Thissa says there'll be treachery."

"Yes. I think so too."

"From which direction?"

"I feel it everywhere around us," Hendy said.

This was leading nowhere. I dropped into a dark silence and wished I could sleep. But this was not a place where sleep was easy. We sat without speaking, side by side in the dimness of the one-moon night, and the hours slipped by. Perhaps I slept a little while without knowing that it was happening: certainly I had no sharp sense of the passage of time, but I became aware eventually that it was much later in the night, close indeed to morning. The stars had shifted position and a second moon had risen— Malibos, I think, bright as new metal against the eastern horizon and sending shafts of cold light across the Summit.

Suddenly Hendy grabbed my wrist. "Poilar! Poilar, are you awake?"

"Of course I am."

"Look there, then!"

"What? Where?" I blinked and shook my head. My mind seemed wrapped in cobwebs, and half dead of frost.

Hendy pointed. I followed the line of her pointing arm.

A figure stood sharply outlined in the icy light of Malibos high atop a rock midway out in the plain. It was Thissa. Her left arm was upraised and both her thumbs were outstretched in the stabbing gesture of accusation.

"I see the traitor!" she cried, in a high ringing voice that must have carried from one side of the Summit to the other. "Do you see him? Do you all see him?" And she stabbed her hand into the air three times, very fiercely, aiming it in the direction of the ancient ruined starship. "Do you see him? Do you see him? Do you see him?"

I saw no one, nothing.

Then out of the grayness of the distance came a twisted distorted form that limped toward her at a furious pace: a man with a monstrous elongated crooked leg, who nonetheless was running so quickly that he seemed almost to be flying. Thrance, of course. He leaped up on the rock beside Thissa with the kind of agility that I remembered from the Thrance of old, the master athlete of my childhood. Three swift bounds and he was beside her. I heard her cry his name in a ringing tone of denunciation. Thrance said something in return, low and muffled and threatening. Once again Thissa cried out his name. And he raised his cudgel to her and struck her such a blow as would have broken a tree in half. I heard the sound of it, and saw her crumple and fall.

I stood rigid for a moment, frozen in my place, unable to move. There was a dead hush on the Summit, with only the rushing sound of the wind sweeping against my ears.

Then I was on my feet and running.

Thrance fled before me like a hawk through the sky; but I followed him like lightning itself. Across the plain I sped, around the rock where Thissa's bloodied fallen body lay, past the slender starship of the three Irtimen. Thrance was racing toward the older starship, the gaunt dark ruin at the far side of the Summit. I thought I saw shaggy figures lurking about it, the skulking forms of the bestial "gods" of this place. Was he going toward them? What alliance had Thrance concocted with them in the night?

There was a terrible roaring sound all around me. I realized, after a time, that it was coming from my own throat.

Thrance was nearly at the ruined starship now, and the "gods" seemed to be welcoming him to it. It struck me that he must have been to them earlier that evening, and had secretly arranged with them to lead them down upon us and kill us as we slept.

But I was closing the gap quickly between him and me; for, swift as Thrance was, I was running with the fury of the Avenger in my soul and my feet scarcely troubled to touch the ground. Unexpectedly Thrance turned to the left just as he was approaching the wrecked ship, and sprinted around the vessel to its far side. I followed him there, and saw more of the "gods" gathered there, by a place of stacked twigs and painted stones that must have been the altar that the debased Irtimen had constructed. Thrance ran right through the midst of it, scattering "gods" on every side, and up a craggy staircase of rock just beyond.

That was a great mistake on his part, for there was nothing on the other side of that rocky pile but the abyss. He had trapped himself.

He ran up right to the top, where he must surely have been able to look down into the realm of fog and realize that there was only a great emptiness below him. There he halted; and turned; and looked toward me, waiting for me to come to him.

"Thrance," I muttered. "Thrance, you bastard!"

He was smiling.

To the end, nothing mattered to him. Or maybe one thing did: perhaps he had come up here with us because he had wanted his death to find him in this most sacred of places. Well, I would give it to him. I jumped up alongside him and he was ready for me, balanced and braced like the wrestler he was, and he grinned right into my face. Then we seized each other in a grip from which only one could emerge alive.

He was strong. He always had been, an athlete of athletes; and I felt the power of him still, the old Thrance within this twisted hideous thing, the Thrance who had excelled in every game, who had hurled the javelin farther than anyone in memory, who had vaulted the tall hurdles as though he had wings. And for a moment I was the wide-eyed boy of long ago who in such awe had watched the great hero at his games. That moment of remembering weakened me; and Thrance was able to twist me and turn me so that I was leaning outward and my face was turned into the abyss and I saw the white fog below me glistening in the moonlight. It seemed to me that I could almost make out the great clefts and spires of the distant slopes beneath the fog. Smiling still, he forced me backward—backward—

But I had not forgotten the sight of Thrance striking down the slender delicate Thissa atop that rock; and the thought of that vile crime brought back my strength. I planted myself firmly, wedging my good foot tightly into a crevice in the rock and pressing the crooked one against an upraised slab behind me, so that Thrance was unable to push me further toward the edge. We were stalemated for a time, gripping each other, neither capable of budging the other.

Then I began to turn him.

I swung him around and with both my arms around his hips lifted him so that his normal leg was off the ground and only the deformed, grotesquely extended one was still in contact with it. As I held him above me he looked down at me, grinning even now, defying me to do my worst. Shifting my grip so that my arms were around his chest, I pulled him up higher.

He still had his longer leg dug into a crack in the rock to anchor him. I kicked at it with my good foot, putting all the force I had into it, and knocked it free. Then, pivoting off my crooked leg, I threw him from the mountain. A single sound came from him as I lifted him and flung him, but whether he was laughing or crying out in rage or fear, I could not say. He seemed to hover in mid-air an instant or two, his eyes staring right into mine, and it seemed to me that he looked more amused than afraid, and then I saw him begin to fall. Down he dropped like a falling star, plummeting through the fog. A kind of brightness sprang up about him, so that I could see him descending the first journey of the way, striking the rock face here and there, two or three times or more, and rebounding from it. Then the layers of fog closed around him and I lost sight of him for good as he fell through the misty depths far below. I imagined him falling all day, from dawn to noon to eve, dropping down the entire height of the Wall, bursting into flames as he dropped, until at last the final cinder of him came to rest at its base, at Roshten milepost, at the boundary of our village itself. And I crouched there by the edge of the Wall's highest point, looking out over it as though I could see Thrance falling, falling, falling all the way.

At length I rose and looked around, breathless, half dazed, astounded by what I had done.

Three or four of the stumbling animal things that I still somehow thought of as "gods" were visible nearby in the rising light of dawn. They were coming slowly toward me, though it was impossible for me to make out their purpose, whether it was to do harm to me or simply to see what sort of creature I was.

And as I stood there looking at them, at those whom I had hoped were my gods, I knew that I had profaned the holiest of all places, that I had committed an act of murder at the Summit itself. No matter that Thrance had merited death for his crime against Thissa: it had not been my right to impose it on him.

A haze of shock and bewilderment swept across my mind as that thought came to me, and for a moment or two I lost all awareness of who I was or why I was here. I knew only that I was guilty of the most monstrous of crimes and must be fittingly punished; and the gods were coming toward me to accept my atonement and mete out my retribution.

I waited gladly for them. I readied myself to kneel before them. Despite everything I knew of them, I would kneel.

But then they were only a few paces from me, and I stared at their coarse faces and drooling lips and looked straight into their dull empty eyes and I knew beyond all question that what the she-Irtiman had told us was true, that these were no gods, but only the fallen children of gods, the dreadful hollow nightmare semblances of gods. I owed these creatures no obeisance and certainly not my death; and this place where they dwelled was far from holy, whatever I may have believed at the beginning of my Pilgrimage. It had been holy once, perhaps, but certainly holy no longer. So I had nothing for which to atone.

I saw what I had to do now. But I hesitated a moment. In that moment Hendy came up from somewhere and moved toward me.

I turned to her, and she saw in my face the thing that I was going to do. And she nodded.

"Yes, Poilar! Go on! Yes! Do it!"

Yes, she had said. *Do it*. It was all I needed.

I felt a moment's surge of pity for them, these sad shambling things that were the relics of the great ones who had taught us the ways of civilization. But the pity melted in an instant into loathing and contempt. They were abominations. They were monstrosities. They disgraced this place by their very presence here. I rushed forward then, and plunged furiously into their midst. And seized one and held him aloft as though he had no weight at all while he babbled and dribbled and snuffled, until after a moment I flung him away from me, out into the void. Then I took each of the others, one by one while they milled about me in consternation, and likewise I hurled them over the edge of the cliff, down into the abyss, down the side of the Wall to follow Thrance into death. And stood in silence by the edge, breathing hard, looking at nothing, thinking nothing, feeling nothing. Nothing. After a time Hendy touched me, very gently. I was grateful to her for that.

AND THAT WAS HOW my Pilgrimage ended, with the slaughter at my own hands of the gods that I had come here to worship.

By now the two suns had risen, both of them at once from opposite sides of the sky, and by the mingling pink light I saw my comrades running toward Hendy and me, Kilarion and Galli in the lead, and then Talbol and Kath, and behind them all the others, Grycindil and Narril and Naxa and the rest. They had seen me slay the "gods"; and as they gathered around me I told them what had occurred between me and Thrance.

Then we saw the rest of the "gods" emerging from their caves and coming toward us across the plain. They were fewer than we had imagined, no more than fifteen or twenty of them, and some females and children. Why they came to us at that moment I could not say: whether it was to slay us or to worship us, it was impossible to tell. Their dim eyes and slack faces told us nothing. We fell upon them as they neared us and carried them to the edge and pushed them over, every last one of them, just as once long ago we had killed the winged gods of the Melted Ones when we were on the lower plateau. Now we were killing our own. The Summit needed purification. It had once been a holy place and then it had been befouled; and until our coming, no one had had the courage or the wit or the strength to do what needed to be done. But we did. They screamed and whimpered and fluttered about in fright, helpless before our wrath.

We destroyed them all; and when we were done with it, we went into their caves to be certain that none were lurking in there. The squalor and sheer evil filth that we found in those caves is something that I will not even attempt to describe. Two more of them were hiding beneath the dirt, the last of all their kind, blubbering and trembling. Without hesitation we dragged them forth and hurried them to the brink. And so in the violence of bloodshed the reign of the gods atop Kosa Saag came to its end at last.

Now that it was done we could barely speak.

We stood close together, shivering in the bitter air, dazed by the events that had just taken place. We knew that what had happened here had been a necessary thing, that we had purged not only our own souls but those of all our race, and that we had freed the Irtimen settlers of the World also from the curse that had overtaken them. But nevertheless it was a heavy thing to have done so much killing, and we were stunned by the impact of it and hardly knew what to think or say.

It was at this moment that the three Irtimen emerged once again from their ship.

They stepped down the ladder and stood close together just before it, standing uneasily, with their little weapon-tubes in their hands as though they half expected us to attack them with the same berserk fury as we had the others. But we had no reason to do that, and in any case all fury was gone from us now.

I went forward, weary and dazed as I was, and knelt on the ground before them. By twos and threes my companions joined me, until we were all of us kneeling, with our heads bowed.

Then the Irtiman with the golden hair raised her

speaking-box and said, speaking simply and quietly as though she too had been drained of strength by what had taken place here, "We have no further business on this world, and we will be leaving it now. You must all move back, to the far side of the plateau, and stay there until we are gone. Do you understand what I say? Fire will come from our ship; and you will be harmed if you are close to it."

I told her that we understood.

She said then in a softer voice that she wished us well, and hoped that we would grow in understanding and wisdom all the rest of our days. And she told us that we need never fear the intrusion of Irtimen into our world ever again.

That was all. They went back into their ship, and we withdrew to the far side of the plateau.

For a long time nothing happened; and then we saw dust rising around the ship, and moments later a pillar of fire burst into life beneath it, and lifted it upward. The little gleaming ship stood as if motionless before us an instant or two on its fiery tail. Then it was gone. It vanished from our sight as though it had never been.

I said, "These were the true gods. And now they have left us."

With that, and with no other word being spoken, we began to make ready for our descent from the Summit.

BEFORE WE LEFT WE dug a grave for Thissa and built a cairn over it. She will always lie in honor at the roof of the World. We built a cairn in memory of Thrance also, since whatever his sins may have been he was nevertheless a Pilgrim and a man of our village and that was his due. Then we stood together in a tight circle for a long time, close against one another, needing each other's comfort; for this was the end of our Pilgrimage and the end of all Pilgrimages, and we knew that we had achieved something mighty, though we were not yet sure what it was. I heard weeping nearby me, from Malti first, then Grycindil, then

Naxa and Kath; and then I was weeping too, and Traiben, and Galli. We all wept, we survivors, we remaining ones. I had never felt such love for anyone as I felt for these people now, with whom I had gone through so much. We had formed something new on this long journey: we had become a House unto ourselves. Everyone understood that, and so no one spoke of it. We did not even dare look at one another, the moment was so solemn: we stared at the ground, we drew breath deep into our lungs, we held each other's hands tightly and let the weeping pour forth until there was no weeping left in us. At last we looked up, after that, and our eyes were shining and our faces were aflame with the new understanding, which we all felt even though we could not have put it into words.

We assembled then such belongings as remained with us after all this time and in silence we went down the way we came, putting the Summit behind us, descending into the chill depths of the fog zone and through the realm of wind and storms to the Kingdoms beyond, and so onward and downward, onward and downward, toward the place from which we began. Hendy walked beside me. She walks beside me now.

What befell us on the journey down is of no importance, and I will pass over it here. What matters only is that we ascended Kosa Saag, enduring all hardships to attain its Summit, and saw at that Summit the things that we saw, and learned what we learned there, and came home with the knowledge. Which I have set down in this book for you all to ponder and learn.

The gods are gone. We are alone.

And we know now that the changes that befall our people upon the Wall are not god-changes; for those whom we had thought were gods were changed just as so many Pilgrims have been. What causes the transformations on the Wall, so I now believe, is not the presence of the gods at the Summit sending down the radiance of their power, but rather the inherent nature of the air up there, and the powerful light of the sun, and also the force that wells up out of the rocks and plays across our flesh, the heat of change-fire that kindles and inflames our natural shape-changing faculties and makes them all the more potent. I know that this is heresy; but yet that is what the Irtiman told us and that is what I have come to believe, and so be it. At one time there were superior beings on the mountain, yes—gods indeed, perhaps, or close enough to it—but it was not they who worked the magics of the Wall upon the climbers.

And the Kingdoms? What are they?

They are the resting-places of those who have failed to learn the lesson of the Wall. Some who climb Kosa Saag die along the way in making the attempt, and some few succeed, but lose their minds in trying; most, though, simply fail. Those are the ones who have created the Kingdoms as halfway places for themselves, between the jungle and the clouds; for there is no going home for them, and no going upward either.

There is nothing to reproach in that. You have to be something of a madman to want to fight your way to the Summit—as is Traiben, as is Hendy, as was Thrance in his way. As am I. Most people are simpler and easier people than we are, and they fall away from the quest. The Kingdoms are for them. We who are meant to have the knowledge of the Summit are the only ones who will persevere that long and that far.

And now I have returned, and I have brought the knowledge of the Summit with me, and I share it with you now, as I go among you with the marks of the mountain on my flesh and you look upon me with wonder and fear.

What I have to tell you is this, and nothing but this:

The lesson of the Wall is that we cannot continue to hope for comfort and instruction from the dwellers atop it. It is time to lay that fable aside. Those whom we took to be our gods are no longer there to help us along the path of our lives. Without expectation of their aid, then, we ourselves must discover the new things that need to be discovered, and we must put those new things to work assisting us to discover even more. It was given to me, and those who returned with me, to bring this lesson home to you, where no one else had done so; but I have the blood of the First Climber in my veins, and perhaps His spirit guided me as I led my Forty to the Summit.

What we need to do is to break a path through to the fountain from which wisdom flows. It will be our task to build wagons to carry us between villages, and then sky-wagons, and then star-wagons that will take us into the Heavens; and then we will meet the gods again. But this time it will be as equals.

These things are not impossible. The Irtimen achieved them. They were little more than rock-apes, once, long ago, and they made themselves into gods. So can we.

So can we.

We can be as gods: that is the truth that Poilar Crook-leg offers you. For there are no other gods within our reach; and if we do not make ourselves gods, then we must live our lives in the absence of gods, which is a terrible thing. That is the wisdom that Poilar Crookleg has brought down for you from the Summit of Kosa Saag, out of all his sufferings. This is his book, which tells of all that happened to him and his comrades there, and what they saw, and what they discovered. These are the things I experienced, this is what I learned, this is what I must teach you for the sake of your souls. It is knowledge that was not easily won; but I offer it all freely to you, and, if only you will accept it, it will set you free. Listen, then. Listen and remember.

ABOUT THE AUTHOR

ROBERT SILVERBERG's many novels include the best-selling Lord Valentine Trilogy, the Nebula-winning *A Time of Changes,* and *Dying Inside.* He is also the co-author, with Isaac Asimov, of *Nightfall,* as well as the co-editor of the new Universe series of original short-fiction anthologies. He has won numerous awards for his fiction, including five Nebulas, which is more than any other writer, four Hugo Awards, a Jupiter Award, and the Prix Apollo. He lives near San Francisco with his wife, Karen Haber.

A dazzling collaboration by two of science fiction's
most gifted storytellers.

ISAAC ASIMOV &
ROBERT SILVERBERG

❏ THE UGLY LITTLE BOY
(56122-7 n* $5.99/$6.99 Canada)

To contemporary Earth, he is a beast, a Neanderthal ape-boy
torn from the primordial past. But to his nurse and protector,
Edith Fellowes, he is much more than a time travel experi-
ment; he is a lonely, terrified child whose every friend and
relative—his very race—is 40,000 years dead. When Edith
discovers Stasis Technologies' true intentions for the boy, she
forms a bizarre and daring plan, placing at stake not just her
charge's life, but her own as well.

❏ NIGHTFALL
(29099-1 * $5.99/$6.99 Canada)

When academics at Saro University determine that 12 hours
of darkness are coming to a world that has for over 2,000 years
known only the light cast by two suns, a group of religious
fanatics begin to prey on the fear of the populace by "saving"
converts and damning non-believers. The scientists and
zealots—who have been in conflict for centuries—both know
that the coming night will mean the end of their civilization,
for the people of Lagash have a proven fear of the dark, and
in the wake of unspeakable horrors, they must rally to save
the fragile remnants of their world.